MW01241131

Plant Daddy

COMPLETE BOOK 1 IN THE SUBMISSIVE DIARIES

A CLUB ALIAS SPINOFF SERIES

KD ROBICHAUX

Edited by Barb Hoover & Vanessa Morse

Cover Photographer *and* Model: Ashley Brooke–Boudoir By Brooke
(@boudoir_by_brooke on Instagram)

Contents

PLANT DADDY

USA *TODAY* BESTSELLING AUTHOR

KD ROBICHAUX

BLURRED LINES SERIES

Plant Daddy

PART ONE

Edited by Barb Hoover & Vanessa Morse

Cover Photographer: Ashley Brooke–Boudoir By Brooke (@boudoir_by_brooke on Instagram)

Cover Model: Billy Rubino (@billyrubino22.4 on TikTok and IG)

For Doc
Forever my favorite voice in my head.

And for the doormats.
The people pleasers.
The annoying ones who are "too much."
This one is for us.

Chapter One

SIENNA

The fact that I'm balls-deep in a full, smelly dumpster late on a Friday night, *alone*, does nothing to stop me from gasping aloud at what I discover at the bottom of it. Not that I don't immediately regret the deep inhale of God only knows what I'm standing in—but exasperation wins out as top emotion in this particular moment.

"You have got to be freaking *kidding* me!" I whisper-yell, propping one foot against a broken display for flashlights and the other atop a pile of cracked cedar fence posts.

I wrap one gloved hand around a splintery slat that's in the middle of a stack of five pallets, then carefully lean down and forward, reaching out with my other green gardening glove covered fingers to pinch just the very edge of the black plastic container I spotted.

"Ow! Fuck... shit!" I hiss as needles stab into my knuckles, but I dare not let go. This is one of the greatest finds I've made to date. Lord knows what I'll be infected with, allowing something at the bottom of a dumpster to pierce my skin, but it's freaking worth it.

At least that's what I'll continue to tell myself until I eventually end up in my bathroom, soaking in a tub of Lysol and peroxide.

My treasure is heavy as hell, and it's a circus-worthy balancing act to keep from toppling in any one direction as I lift the bounty high enough so I can then stand up straight and let go of the pallet. Wrapping my free arm around the container, careful to avoid any more puncture wounds, I grin when I look closely to find the prize within it completely flawless. It makes me both do a happy dance *and* pisses me off that something so precious and valuable to me and many others, was just tossed like it was completely worthless.

And as usual, it breaks my heart that I feel more connected to and identify with something deemed "trash" at the bottom of a dumpster than I do with 99.999% of the human population.

"Mama's got you now, big boy," I murmur, shaking off the pain in the center of my chest and gently pulling a shredded napkin out of the dangerous spikes. As a wad flutters to the cavernous opening below my spread, locked legs, my eye naturally follows its descent, and I have to catch my balance when my shock sends my head jerking backward enough to make the rest of me bobble in my precarious position. "And you have a twin brother?" I let out the whimper of a proud mother who just witnessed her child do something she believes is extraordinary but is probably just some milestone every kid reaches at some point in their life. "Well, can't leave him here all by his lonesome, now can we?"

I lift the heavy container high above my head, suddenly wishing I stuck to all the workout classes my friend Astrid made me take with her at our gym, as I prop the black plastic on the top edge of the dumpster and slide it slowly across the metal lip until it's safely perched. Looking down, I allow my eyes to adjust to the dimness after having looked up toward the streetlight a second ago, and then I spot the second buried chest of gold—doubling down on my best night of dumpster diving yet.

In the past several months, I've lost countless hours on the TikTok app, falling down all sorts of rabbit holes during this… early midlife crisis I find myself in at the ripe old age of thirty-four. As an author of filthy BDSM romance novels, this crisis of mine includes, but is definitely not limited to, a going-on-nine-months bout of writer's block.

So in the last year and a half, not only did I suddenly find myself single after being mostly happily married for eleven years, which meant I was no longer living in a dual, huge income household, but I also haven't written a single word since my last book release nine months ago.

But hey, the divorce was amicable, so at least there's

that. We don't have kids, and we basically just divided everything right down the middle and went our separate ways.

My lifestyle itself completely altered, and I've been watching my savings account shrink at an alarming rate. Yet the most shocking part of this period in my life, though, is that as my wealth dwindled, so did my list of "friends." Women who I thought of as my ride-or-die besties, who would be at my fucking funeral after we were old and gray, suddenly wanted nothing to do with me. They befriended each other after I introduced them a long time ago, and at the time, it was amazing, finally having this group of girlfriends to do damn near everything with. I was an auntie to their children, attended every birthday party and weekend get-together, right down to being the emergency contact on school forms and doctor visits.

But then Art and I divorced, and my writer's block hit. Then depression snuck in not long after, due to not having words in my head that could form a complete sentence, much less compile a whole book, which to an author feels like the purpose for their very existence has been taken away. And since I was down in the dumps—ha! Not the fun kind I discovered later—sleeping a ton, not answering their every beck and call the moment they messaged, and since I no longer owned a bottomless bank account, the women— all but one in our group of eight—I believed would be by my side to my dying day, decided I was no longer needed in their lives.

They had each other, after all. So there was no use for me anymore.

That left me with just that one very special human outside of my blood relatives who was steadily in my pitiful corner. The one person who gave a big middle finger to all those bitches and chose me over all the rest of them. The one friend I had since *before* I ever thought about writing my very first book.

Vivian Lowe.

Completely ironic in itself, really. Authors always seem to talk about how they *lose* all the friends they had before their career took off, because they don't have anything in common any longer or because their ex-friends just don't "get" them anymore.

My experience was the complete opposite.

I lost all the "friends" I made *after* becoming an author.

Vi pointed out that probably meant they were only my friends because of my "status" and what they thought they might gain from me as my "star" rose.

Which was just extra depressing to think about, all those years believing they loved me like family the way I loved them.

And if I'm being totally honest, it hurt more when they deserted me than it did when Art and I decided a divorce was the best next stepping stone in our life's path. At least he had a damn good reason to separate his journey from my own. A reason I fully support him in. I'm so very happy he's truly found himself along the way.

But by going our own ways, that was one less person in my everyday life for me to worry about. And yes, I'm fully aware that when people say "that's one less thing to worry about," that's usually a good thing. Like a weight lifting off one's shoulders. But not for me.

For me, I literally *live* to worry about other people. I have "the disease to please," as a former therapist once told me— a people pleaser "to a fault" and "most likely to the detriment of my own self." Taking care of and nurturing others is my lifeblood. In the past, if I went a full day without helping someone with at least one task, my mind and body reacted like I didn't take my daily dose of Prozac.

With so many people to socialize with—my husband, my big group of friends, their kids, acquaintances, and even strangers at the gym—those days were few and far between. Yet then Art moved out, and I didn't feel much like staying digitally connected 24/7 while I tried to keep myself busy, finding it irritating to stop what I was forcing myself to focus on to be drawn into a group message about which shoes one of them should wear with a certain dress and having seven fucking people who threw in their input and then went off on countless other tangents.

To me, that wasn't really helping anyone. Telling you to go with the black pumps instead of the knee-high boots along with other people, does not add a single drop of happy hormones to fill my nurturing cup. But when I stopped giving my input for something six other women voiced their two cents for, suddenly that made me a bad friend. And add to that a girl can only stand seeing "check your DMs" on her public social media posts so many times before she finally psychologically snaps.

Posts, I could handle all right in my downward spiral. I could just like someone's comment in acknowledgement. If someone's response sparked any sort of life into my existence, then I could muster up a quick reply—a GIF if I couldn't come up with words or something more than just a like. I didn't want my amazing readers to think I was one of those snobby bitches who thought they were too important to mingle with their fans.

But messages... FML, if you open one, then the sender could see you read it. If you read it but didn't respond, that opened up the exhausting dialogue that went along with being "left on read." If you *did* respond, then that wouldn't be the end of the conversation. Oh, no. That was just the *opener* for being sucked into a back-and-forth conversation that could go on for hours. And when you're diagnosed as severely ADHD and with God only knows how many anxiety disorders, and top that off with a hefty helping of "the disease to please," it sends a person into a downfall that lands them in the fetal position on the floor of whatever room they were trying to pretend they were okay in.

Hello, burnout. My name is Sienna. Not so nice to meet you.

But there was one—juuust one—person who never once gave me shit about my message-answering infrequency. Just one, single, solitary human who didn't guilt me, or make me feel like I was lacking or not good enough, who didn't complain one time about *anything* that has to do with me.

Vivian Lowe.

Where the hell would I be without Vi in my life?

God, it's scary to even think about. She's been "my person" for nearly a decade now, and after every other person in the universe dropped out of my world, it made me realize I don't need anyone else. She's proven time and time again that she'll be there whenever and wherever I truly need her. Even though she's married and has kids who take up most of the time she doesn't spend writing her own books—she was already published when I first met her—I know if I have a body to hide, she'll tell her husband Corbin to watch the littles, drop her headphones and glasses on her laptop, and be there beside me with a shovel in tow.

I miss all the time we usually spend together, writing our books—complete silence between the two of us, but just the other's presence soothes our artists' souls. I think I miss that part of my career more than I do the income. If anything could get me out from behind my writer's block, it should've been that—getting to spend all those hours with Vi, typing away. But instead, trying to force words out of my fingers while sitting across from her in our favorite coffee shop made my depression worse. It added comparison to the mix of shit a person shouldn't do if they want good mental health. Her fingers would fly across her keyboard while I just plucked at my delete button.

So our writing dates dried up, because I didn't want to

bring her down, and without her acting as my writing accountability partner, I didn't feel any type of urge to put fingers to laptop keys.

The only thing my fingers seemed to have the strength and function to do was swipe up. To scroll through pages and pages of shopping sites.

And it was while I was scrolling—on TikTok this time, fighting my addict-like urges to scour Amazon instead for some retail therapy, hence the reason my savings account was super depleted, because this conductor of the Hot Mess Express needs an obscene amount of therapy—that I discovered this lady who makes a living off dumpster diving. She found all sorts of brand-new stuff just tossed out for no other reason than to make room on the store's shelf for new inventory.

Yet while she created a website to sell the items she salvaged, I have no interest in all that. The idea of having to deal with packaging and shipping stuff gives me hives on the best of days. But just seeing what I could possibly find in dumpsters in my area seemed exciting, the most excitement I felt in the past year and a half, actually. So much, in fact, that when I checked the time—2:24 a.m.— I rolled off my couch, then threw on my tennis shoes.

Because if I had no extra funds to shop my misery away, then maybe I could find some cool shit for free! At the very least, it would pass some time and get me out of the house. Even if it was in the middle of the night.

Out the door I went, and before I knew it, I was hiking

my leg over the top lip of a giant green dumpster behind a sporting goods store.

It was the first store I found with an actual dumpster, because all the other ones I passed before it had these metal containers that attached to the back of the business—which I came to learn later in this journey were trash compactors.

I was a little disappointed there weren't huge trash bags filled with cute workout clothes, shoes, or even… sporty shit I could give to my friend's kid, but what I *did* find set off the creative side of my brain that hadn't been activated in nine months of writer's block.

At the time I unearthed it from beneath enough cardboard to ship every book I'd ever sold thrice over, I thought of it as a "big, wooden spindle thingy," but googling my DIY gem the moment I got in my SUV after wrestling it out of the dumpster and into my trunk, I learned it was a cable spool. The dumpster was, in fact, right between the sporting goods store and what will eventually become a new franchise gym that was under construction. The cable spool was apparently what all the electrical wiring and stuff came on for the new business, and they just tossed this huge, wood, could-be-turned-into-a-masterpiece, blank canvas into the trash.

I also discovered during my Google search that other people were bitten by the creativity bug when they saw a cable spool, and they made tables and different pieces out of them, that they then sold on Etsy for hundreds and even thousands of dollars.

But no way was I going to sell my very first cherry-poppin' dumpster treasure find.

Within a day, I had it sanded, stained, and sprayed in weather-proofing stuff—all found in the shit Art left in the garage when he moved out. Which was exciting in itself, seeing what I already owned that I could use on my little project—no diving or spending required.

When it was finished, I stood back, my hands on my hips, the biggest smile on my face in over a year, as I took in what I had created out of literal trash. It now sits dead-center of my adorable potting shed I built with my own two hands, and it acts as my potting bench when I want to sit in the dirt for some much-needed grounding—something else that's 100 percent new to my life.

Right along with the *need* for a potting bench inside a potting shed, seeing as nine months ago, I couldn't even keep a cactus alive—one of the reasons I never had kids.

Because not long after my first great discovery and the DIY masterpiece I created out of it, I dove into the very dumpster inside which I now squat. And that's when I learned that the orange-aproned big-box home improvement store just... tosses out perfectly healthy plants.

That first night inside this dumpster, I truly couldn't believe what I was seeing. Stacks upon stacks of flats of slightly-wilted petunias. I didn't know what the hell they were at the time, but there were enough of the little flower labels to fill an entire novel. I was so confused by finding the pretty, colorful, little flowers at the bottom of the trash that my mind just couldn't wrap around what I was seeing. I tugged a flat upward until I could hold it in the light, turning it this way and that, checking for... I didn't even know. Bugs? Maybe some spots that could be a weird plant disease?

Could plants get diseases?

I didn't know at that point. All I knew was if you watered a cactus too much, it would melt. Literally. It would just turn into this slimy goo substance practically overnight that would never return to its former solidified state.

But this was not a cactus. And it had definitely not been overwatered. They were beautiful flowers that were just a little sad-looking, and after reading the label, and after googling once I brought all fourteen flats of petunias and two flats of daisies home, it seemed the little fellas just needed a good soaking and some sunshine. So as soon as the sun came up—I hadn't even gone to sleep yet, researching the two species of plants I'd found as that night's bounty—I planted them in the ever-empty space around a tree in my front yard. The tree was in the center of a circle of bricks that at one point held some red mulch back from spilling into the grass.

I did my best, remembering from some point in my childhood when my dad taught me you're supposed to loosen the dirt a little when you pull the plant out of its bucket so the roots could... I don't know, move around more easily once they were in the ground? I just recall thinking the roots could wiggle and dig like worms once you couldn't see them beneath the dirt.

I watered them with the garden hose I had to actually search the perimeter of my house for, since I never used it in all the years I've lived here, once I got all sixteen flats planted around the tree. The poor little wilted things looked even unhappier as the water hit them, seeming to buckle under the weight of the droplets, so I turned the nozzle to Mist instead of Shower, which seemed to at least keep the leaves and petals from breaking off.

I wound the hose back up and trudged inside, finally passing out on my couch at about 8:00 a.m., feeling a little extra depressed that all my dive-and-rescue efforts the past eight hours had most likely been for nothing. Because those petunias and daisies looked like mud-covered sadness by the time I finished forcing my "love" on them.

Yet when I woke up after six hours of uninterrupted sleep for the first time in ages and I walked outside to clean up the rest of the mess in my front yard—having just tossed all the little black pots and plastic flats all around the tree as I got in the rhythm of freeing each flower, then sticking it in the ground—I stopped dead in my tracks halfway between my front porch and my new flowerbed.

My new flowerbed.

My new bed *full* of flowers.

Full of flowers that were blooming their little *asses* off as the sun shined on their now perky stems, unfurled leaves, and wide-open petals.

Just about as wide-open as my eyes must've been, standing there and staring at the very first of what I now lovingly call my dumpster babies.

In just a matter of hours, they'd gone from the bottom of the trash, on their way to a landfill, looking like someone had peed in their Cheerios—if plants ate Cheerios—to making my front yard look like someone actually gave two shits about my curb appeal. So bright and colorful and smile-inducing...

That it pissed me right the fuck off.

Why the hell had I found... $1.98 per plant, at eighteen plants per flat, and a total of sixteen flats...?

I don't fucking math.

But that seems like a lot of freaking money thrown in the goddamn dumpster.

Why just throw perfectly good plants away?

So with indignation-filled movements, I gathered up all the pots and flats, stacked them all neatly together—something tells me to keep them instead of throwing them away —set them in my garage, and went inside to... you guessed it... Google why the fuck live plants got chucked.

I quickly learned I was not the only one concerned by this flabbergasting waste. Articles, forums, Facebook Groups, you name it, tons of people aware and pissed off over the fact that *that* particular home improvement store just throws away perfectly good plants.

Actually, to be perfectly clear, it's not the store itself that does the tossing of the plant babies. From what I can discern, they rent space to plant vendors—basically the brand selling the plants in bulk—and those vendors go into each store once a week, look for anything that doesn't look quite perfect, and stack them all up in a shopping cart to get rid of.

Because they have to make room for their new incoming inventory.

Yeah.

They pluck the ones that aren't exactly "right" off the tables to just throw in the dumpster so some fresh, new "perfect" ones can take their place.

That was the first time I ever felt totally connected with the plants I started rescuing like my life depended on it. With the mind I was born with, I deep-dove into this connection I felt, and the deeper I went, the more indignant I became.

Yes, those new perfect flowers would replace the ones that didn't make the cut, but soon, those once perfect babies would *become* the ones being tossed if someone didn't buy them in time.

Right now, they felt like they ruled the world. They were full of hope and trust, thinking surely someone would take them home and love them, keep them forever through their entire lifecycle. Because after all, they were beautiful, and sparked joy, and brought happiness to the ones who saw them.

But with one dreary, overcast day, or one move of the sprinkler that didn't quite reach their pot, leaving them unwatered, or even one super-sunny day after a taller plant had been moved, taking away its shade and exposing it directly to the burning rays...

And there they'd go, becoming the ones taken off the table and put into the cart to be tossed in the dumpster and replaced by something that was literally *them* not that long ago.

Fucking depressing.

But not as depressing as the Reddit I found with people talking about how some orange-apron stores had even started resorting to pouring paint all over the plants to deter people from dumpster diving to rescue them.

When I pulled myself out of that sickening rabbit hole, I read a lot of plant enthusiasts boycott stores that practice that particular atrocity and instead only purchase from to the "blue" home improvement store, because at least they put their imperfect babies on a clearance rack. And people brave enough to try bringing them back from the brink of death are rewarded by only having to pay half-price.

Fucking noted.

But that was the day I discovered I don't have the "black thumb" I always thought I had. Because since that first rescue mission, I've managed to bring back and keep alive almost every single plant I've found.

I say almost, because some were either too far gone, or I accidentally killed them by giving them too much love. Some plant babies literally thrive on neglect, and I'm really, really bad at neglecting people and things I love.

One of those neglect-thriving plants being the one I'm presently lifting with just the tippy-tips of my thumb and pointer finger by the very edge of its black plastic pot, trying my damnedest not to get stabbed once again by the golden barrel cactus's thorns. Which is quite a feat, because this big boy is heavy as shit. But I'll be damned if I leave him and his twin brother to be hauled off to a landfill. Not on my watch!

And it has nothing to do with the fact that each one of these babies has a sticker on the side of their pot that says they're sold for a whopping $59.00 a piece.

Truly.

Even though I rescue a surplus of plants that I couldn't possibly take care of by myself, and even though a bitch be broke, I refuse to sell any of them. I either give them away to people in my local plant-lovers groups on Facebook who can't afford new ones, or I use them to trade for cuttings of other gardeners' plants that I've been dying to collect. I had no idea this whole plant-obsessed world existed just months ago, and now I can't imagine living anywhere else. A world where someone will happily snip off a stem from one of their babies just so another plant-lover can propagate it— grow it into a whole new full-sized beauty.

But *these* guys will not be part of my giveaway stash. No way. They'll live long and prosper in my cactus corner, a super-bright, full-sun area of my yard that gets zero shade, so nothing else can survive in that spot. At least nothing *I've* attempted to keep alive.

I've got the second golden barrel just high enough I can finally wrap my other arm around the bucket, when suddenly a loud clang—something hard hitting the side of the metal dumpster—reverberates around me, making me scream it startles me so badly.

"What the fuck!" I shout, losing my balance and falling forward, but thankfully I catch myself with my free hand, gripping the black pot in a football hold between my bicep and my side.

"Ma'am, this is private property. You're currently trespassing, and I'm gonna have to ask you to leave," comes a deep male voice.

My body trembles, but I don't know if it's with rage or from my precarious position. I manage to force out, "Dumpster diving isn't illegal in our state." And it's not. I did a ton of research after I found that lady on TikTok.

There's a sound... a slight chuckle? But then he reiterates, "You are correct, ma'am. But the dumpster is on private property, on which you are trespassing at the moment, seeing as it is past business hours."

My legs start to shake in their locked position, and my arm holding my body up from tumbling ass-over-head is screaming, but I'll be damned if I'm letting go of my prize. Through gritted teeth, I state, "There isn't a No Trespassing sign on the dumpster," remembering that's what my research told me to verify before diving in.

"While that may be true, there are No Trespassing signs posted along the back of the building, stating this is private property. And the dumpster is on that property. So again, I'm asking you to leave, or I'll have to call the police." There is an unmistakable smile in the voice, letting me know the sound before most likely *was* a chuckle, which makes me frown.

What the fuck is so funny?

What kind of sadistic bastard laughs at the idea of sending an innocent plant rescuer to jail? Has he no humanity? Has he no soul?

Of course not. He works for the company that allows perfectly healthy plants to be just tossed in the trash, then threatens to call the cops on someone just trying to save the poor things.

But I make nice, because the last thing I need is to be locked up in some jail cell, when I have dumpster babies to repot and water before they're too far gone.

"Fine. I'm getting out. It's just going to take a sec, because you startled me, and I've gotta figure out how to get not only myself but this golden barrel out of—" The rest of my words are cut off by my own scream…

Of fright.

Of shock.

Of dread.

And then of unmatched pain.

Chapter Two

SIENNA

So much pain. And in so many places.

But mostly, my poor hand.

Just as I was explaining to the tattletale that I needed to figure out how to get out of the dumpster with the cactus in tow, I had gathered enough waning strength to attempt to push myself off the pallet with my bracing hand. But the movement upset not only the stuff I was standing on, but also the apparently super-dry root system of the cactus. So dry the soil had pulled away from the sides of its plastic bucket, allowing the whole thing to slip right out of the pot. And being the person—nay, idiot—I am, with the instincts to try to catch whatever I drop—even things with three-inch-long sharp-as-fuck needles covering its entire exterior —I may manage to make it upright, but not for long, as the golden barrel lands spikes-down in the open palm of my garden-glove-covered hand. And anyone who knows anything about gardening gloves knows they don't do anything to protect one's hands against cactus thorns.

"Mother of fuck!" I holler, but I refuse, fucking *refuse*, to drop my treasure. With God as my witness, this dumpster baby is making it to my cactus corner if it's the last fucking thing I do on this earth!

"Ma'am? Are you all right?" the deep voice asks, but the humor that was there only moments ago is now gone.

"Jesus H. Jefferson Christ! Ow, ow, ow, ow! I... I can't move or I'll—"

The voice comes from above me now, instead of right on the other side of the metal wall. "Ma'am, drop the cactus and reach up so I can help you out of there."

Something in the man's tone makes me tilt my hand to do just as he ordered before I realize what I'm about to let go of, and I right my palm currently holding the desert plant like some fucked-up bowling ball. But instead of my fingers being sunk into holes to keep a grip, this spiky fucker sank its needles into my flesh to keep a hold of *me*.

"Not happening," I try to say firmly, but it comes out more like a whimper.

I hear a growl that somehow gets past all the pain I currently feel and awakens my lady garden like I'm not at the bottom of a dumpster at the moment, and I glance up to try to see the man leaning over the top and looking down at me. But because he's backlit by the streetlights, I can't make out a single one of his features. I can, however, tell he's wearing a baseball cap, and his shoulders are... wide. Jesus are they wide. Either he's a big ole boy who has a beer gut the size of Texas, or he has one hell of a six-pack. Nothing else could accompany shoulders that look like *those*.

It doesn't take long to figure out he does not have the former, because no one with a belly that would match those boulder shoulders could move the way this guy does. One second, he's peering down at me from above; the next, he does some crazy ninja move that reminds me of those guys who can do the trick pull-ups. Not regular pull-ups, but the ones where they go way above the bar and then seemingly levitate as they switch from one side to the other and even "walk" their legs up straight out behind them and just... stay there. Yeah, one of those guys.

And then he lands like a freaking cat, right on his feet and crouched to the left of me, perfectly centered on a piece of plywood a couple of feet higher than where I've landed on my ass on something hard but thankfully flat. My best guess is a piece of countertop, or maybe a wide paver. Definitely stone, according to my crying Sitz bones.

There's just enough illumination to make out his orange apron and a teensy glimpse of light—either platinum-blond or silvery-white—facial hair before he rights his face mask, looping the one side that came loose back over his ear just beneath the dark backward baseball cap.

An ear that has three tiny silver hoops in the lobe, making me instantly think of a hot pirate.

I can't tell a thing about him other than that, because

he's quite literally covered from head to toe. Not a bit of his skin is showing besides the space between the adjustable strap of his hat and the top of the black mask, and a tiny sliver between the bottom of the mask and the crewneck of his black long-sleeved tee. Even his hands are covered in brown leather work gloves.

In my stupor, I almost ask him why he's wearing a face mask if he's outside, but then I remember where we are and figure it must be because he didn't want to smell whatever could've been decomposing inside the dumpster. Smart man. I'm pretty sure someone drove by and tossed their food-related garbage, because that scent wouldn't be coming from anything sold inside the store.

"Drop the cactus and give me your hand," he orders again, even more sternly this time, holding his leather-covered one out toward me. And even though I get that same urge to do exactly what he said, I grit my teeth and shake my head. I see his head drop and hear his sigh of annoyance before he asks, "Is this really the hill you're choosing to die on, sweetheart?"

The endearment along with the calmness of his tone instead of hearing anger in his voice and words makes my goddamn vagina clench.

Ignoring the weirdo betwixt my thighs, I give him a firm nod. "Yes, sir," I reply, because if he's being kind enough to not only rescue me out of this situation—even though he's the reason I'm in this position in the first place—but also being nice about it instead of a total dick, then I can most certainly show him respect. Especially when he looks upward… at the sky, the light, or maybe to the heavens to give him the patience to deal with my ass—he wouldn't be the first and definitely won't be the last—and the lighting catches just right to where I can see the facial hair along the bottom edge of the mask *is* silvery-white and not platinum-blond. Meaning he's most likely much older than me, and I was taught to always respect my elders.

Although by the shape of this man's body, time has not aged the rest of him at the rate it did the color of his hair.

He blows out one long, deep breath before angling his face back toward me, and I see his slight nod.

"All right, little one. Can you reach the bucket to the right of your leg there?" he asks, and my lady garden seems to illuminate with fairy lights at the nickname that's always had that effect on me. I use it occasionally in my books, saving it for only my very favorite characters.

What the hell is wrong with me?

Maybe I'm more masochistic than I thought.

Because how else could I be getting this aroused while I'm in this much pain?

I force myself to concentrate on what he asked me though, and I glance down and to the side, seeing the bucket I dropped when I suddenly turned into Humpty Dumpty.

"Speaking of which, do you realize that nothing in the nursery rhyme states that he's actually an egg?" I ask, easily picking up the empty black pot and lifting it toward the man. My eyes follow to where his should be, even though I still can't exactly see them, and I realize I spoke that out loud but not the thought that preceded it.

Before I can correct myself and explain that my mouth sometimes blurts shit less quickly than my brain switches subjects, I see his head tilt to one side, almost like a curious puppy, before he takes the plastic container out of my hand. And then, shocking the shit out of me, he replies as if he heard the entire conversation I was holding inside my mind. "I believe I read somewhere it's because it was originally posed as a riddle, asking the reader who or what Humpty Dumpty could've been."

A smile pulls at the corners of my lips, first at what he said and then because he holds the pot in both his hands and tilts it toward the upside down cactus stuck to mine. I lift the heavy plant and align it with the bucket so that as I finally do tip my hand enough to let gravity do its thing, it lands squarely back inside its black plastic home.

Which in turn wipes the smile clean off my face as the cactus pulls free of my flesh wrapped in the green gardening glove. Before I can even begin to use my sudden sharp inhale of air to curse up a storm, the man stands with the same ease and balance of the feline he landed like moments ago, places the dangerous dumpster baby next to its twin brother on the metal ledge, and then bends to grab my wrist, my injured hand still in midair where I tilted it above the bucket. And then he lifts me off my ass and onto the plywood as if I weigh no more than the damn cactus did, his other arm wrapping like a steel band around my back to hold me to his much larger, much harder body.

I'm so surprised by what happens in those seven seconds that all the bad words I wanted to let loose just dissipate into the ether, as all I feel is every bulge and plain of his body fitting exactly to every dip and curve of my own. Everywhere he's hard, I'm soft, and it causes us to mold together like I've never felt before.

My breath hitches in my throat as I look up, finally getting a better view of his eyes. It's still impossible to make out the exact color, but they're definitely light, not brown, and I'm able to confirm once again, up close this time, that it's most definitely *white* salting his eyebrows and the hair at the edges of his black mask.

Which I'm extra thankful for—the mask, I mean—because I know I have to smell god-awful, a mix of mosquito spray and garbage. *Mm, delightful.*

Yet there's something about the strength of this man's body in conjunction with the age the visible part of his beard implies—it's too wide-spread to just be one of those birth marks that shows up as unpigmented hair—that does spectacular things to my long-dormant libido. Add in the fact that *both* his ears are pierced with all those little silver hoops, and I'm damn near ready to tell the pirate-ish stranger he can plunder my booty right here in the dumpster.

I feel myself melt against him, relaxing my entire body-weight along his ridges, when he tightens his grip on me even more and leans down to speak directly in my ear, the only thing separating his lips from my lobe the cloth of that damn mask—which I'm suddenly less grateful for.

"Let's get you out of here so I can take a look at that hand, little one."

I nod, feeling almost hypnotized by his voice and his words. And it's what I later come to blame for the shit that leaves my mouth in this moment as he carries me out of the metal container. "You keep calling me that and using that tone and I'm going to be forced to show you just how *little* I am."

Which made complete sense in my brain as I spoke the words, knowing I meant my pussy that had been in hibernation for almost a year now. Meaning: I'm probably cat-lady tight after this long.

But I'm so embarrassed it came out of me at all—as in with my outside voice and not just one of my many, *many* in-my-head voices—that I don't absorb any reaction my rescuer might've outwardly shown. God only knows if he's able to read my mind to catch my meaning like he did with the Humpty Dumpty thing. If so, FML for verbally and sexually harassing some poor guy just trying to do his job and kick the dumpster-diving crazy plant lady off the property. If not, at the very least, he'll think I'm even more psycho than he already did after I chose to go down with my cactus ship.

Before I can figure out any type of logistics of how exactly he'll be getting me—us—out of here, the next thing

I know, I'm on the outside of the dumpster, his hands are no longer hidden inside leather work gloves, and I'm watching in awe at how such masculine fingers can be so gentle as they peel off my gardening glove. I flinch just a little as the palm and fingers of the fabric come loose from my skin, definitely feeling some thorns pulling free along with it. It's not until his warm *paw* is holding my tiny-looking hand up to the light that I finally realize where my body actually is.

Perched upon this stranger's lap.

On the rolling metal staircase that was parked over next to building when I first climbed into the dumpster almost an hour ago.

Which explains how he was able to "parkour!" his way inside a few minutes ago.

And for some reason, I just don't care why my mind is more fixated on the fact that he somehow rolled the stair-case over without me ever hearing him—*oooh, that was probably the loud clang that scared the shit out of me as it hit the side of the dumpster*—than it is on my ass being snuggled right up against so much hardness it really should *not* be this comfortable.

He sighs behind his mask, drawing my eyes back to his instead of where his giant hand is making mine look like a child's, and I watch as he uses his other one to yank his apron out from beneath my thigh before reaching into one of the pockets. My brows furrow as he pulls out a penlight, clicking it on, then aiming it at my sore palm. It seems like such a random thing for someone to have so handy, but I guess he'd need it more often as an evening-shift employee than one who works during the daytime, and it'd be much lighter in his pocket than some big flashlight.

Not that this guy has to ever worry about the "piddly" weight of a Maglite that would have me breathing heavily.

With all these muscles.

Even hidden beneath a solid layer of clothing, there's no way to hide the width and massiveness of his shoulders, the bulging biceps, the sinewy forearms....

Jesus, Sienna. The "sinewy forearms"? You've fallen into full-on romance author description mode. Take a breath, woman!

I bite my lip as his eyes narrow, making the slight angle of them—higher at the outer corners than the inner—more apparent as he shines the penlight on my abused flesh. I'm so zoned in to trying to figure out just what color they really are that I actually jump a little when his growl—even as quiet as it is—fills the space between us.

"Just what I thought," he murmurs, but it's more to himself than to me, and he doesn't even bother making eye contact with me or speaking as he stands up, taking me right along with him as if he's just standing from a table with his cup of coffee in hand.

He spins and gently sets me on the top step, the metal as hard as his thighs but not nearly as pleasant, and he backs down the stairs while holding the railing.

"Don't move. I'll be right back," he orders, and somehow it doesn't come off as bossy and annoying. Something about him makes me *want* to listen to him, to follow his lead. Like, if I just do as he says without question, every-thing will be okay.

I nod, my arm stretched out in front of me, my elbow resting on my knee, palm up so he can do whatever it is he's going to do when he returns.

And never once do I worry that this stranger could possibly hurt me.

Chapter Three

FELIX

I knew who she was the second I saw her little green SUV parked beside the dumpster. The hatch was open, the lights off, and I could clearly envision her turning them off in order to stay incognito, stealthy in her mind, as if the street-lights shining down on her vehicle weren't as bright as a damn spotlight.

Well, no, that's not exactly the truth. I don't know *who* she is, but I do recognize her. Thankfully, I don't have to worry about her doing the same.

I've also seen her out *here* before, several times, even took on as many Tuesday and Friday night shifts as I could to make sure no one fucked with her while she climbs inside and digs for all the plants the vendors threw away on those scheduled days. How she figured out those were the best days to come, I could only guess. She must've done some serious recon, because she didn't come nearly as often the rest of the week like she used to. She probably discovered a pattern, that there weren't many plants to unearth on those other days.

Most of the time, I thwarted anyone going to bitch at her, saying I'd take care of it myself but instead secretly standing guard while she did her thing. She talks to herself a lot. Out loud. And I hear her murmuring and cussing like a sailor, the harsh words floating out of the dumpster in such a sweetly feminine voice it made me hard the first time I heard it. But through these adorable gripes, I learned she's careful while she's diving.

"You have to leave, *ma'am*. If you get hurt, you could sue us, *ma'am*," she had bitched in a mocking tone that first night, following it up with "As if I'd embarrass myself like that. Who do they think I am? Those crazy people who sued McDonald's for making them fat!"

I immediately liked her, the way she thought. It was refreshing after being around not-so-bright people every day.

Not being a dick—just speaking the truth. A symptom of my high-functioning autism that's gotten me called colorful names throughout my half-century of life.

But now, we have a new night manager who is entirely too gung-ho about "whipping this store into shape," and he made it clear that he would call the cops on her if he discovered her dumpster diving again. And while she's right, it's not illegal in our state, I was *also* speaking the truth when I told her she's technically trespassing on private property. Thankfully, she knew I wasn't just being an asshole making shit up, and she didn't try to argue.

But then chaos ensued.

As I stride toward my truck, pulling my keys out of my pocket, I fight the urge to adjust my cock, feeling her eyes on me from where I left her at the top of the rolling stairs. I ignore the erection, knowing it's at least not tenting my pants and she can't see it behind the apron tied at my neck and the back of my waist.

Almost fifty fucking years old, and just having her sit on my lap made me spring a boner like an adolescent with their mom's Victoria's Secret catalog.

I pull open the back hatch, keeping my back angled toward her so she can't see much around my width, especially from across the parking lot, and I grab one of the black leather bags of tools and things I keep in the trunk.

Like I always say, keep a bag packed like you're never coming back.

I could literally survive out of my truck for years with everything I've got stored within its hidden depths.

I snag the small personal care kit and a couple of the medical supplies, then shut the trunk, clicking the remote to lock it back up. After sliding my key back into my pocket, I start my way toward the much younger woman with the personality I haven't been able to figure out just yet. She seems different each night I hear her talking to herself—and to her "dumpster babies," I've heard her call the plants—

her mood changing several times throughout the minutes or hours she spends searching for "buried treasure." And being who I am, even though I haven't quite nailed down the person she is, I had her diagnosed—at least a little—within that first encounter she was never made aware of.

I was unable to keep the smile off my lips as I listened to her bitch about the injustice of this big corporation throwing away perfectly good plants, then the next sentence out of her mouth was her cooing at how "murdery" a coleus looked and deciding to name him Edmond after her "favorite serial killer." I quietly leaned up against the back side of the dumpster, opposite of where she got in and out of it to take the plants and things she found to her car, more entertained than I felt in ages.

ADHD for sure. No doubt about that. Hell, that was easy enough to pick up on because I'm diagnosed and medicated for it myself. But she also had something going on much deeper than that, less common and harder to diagnose —although ADHD is way less frequently diagnosed in women than in men and has only just recently been taken more seriously. She has an anxiety disorder of some sort, but I couldn't even hypothesize without gaining more insight, without actually speaking with her and asking questions that would narrow down what was really going on in that fast-paced mind of hers.

I can't make an educated guess without at least a little information on the subject. I was only on the very first step of the scientific method, as fucked-up as it was: Observation—getting an overall impression of the woman herself. And after I did that for a couple of nights, never once making my presence known, I moved on to the second step: Formulating a question. And for me, there were many.

Who is this girl?

Why is she here, dumpster diving for plants? Dumpster diving at all?

And the one I was most interested to delve into: *What's making her thoughts so erratic?* My recognition of the simple answer to that question was immediate after I asked it: Adult Attention-Deficit/Hyperactivity Disorder. And she was definitely the combined type, not just ADD but full-on ADHD. The way she spoke out loud even when she believed no one was around to listen was evidence of that. Not to mention, she was inside a metal container of trash at almost one in the morning, digging for buried treasure.

But what about the less obvious thing going on with her? ADHD would explain her inattention, her impulsivity to jump into a huge garbage container and look around. But what made her keep coming back? Night after night, then taking the time and focus—something that would be very tough for people like us—to learn schedules, look for patterns, figuring out when the best days and times to come for the biggest payoff would be?

And now that I knew the *real* question I wanted an answer to, along with at least a limited amount of evidence to refer to, I could move on to step three of the scientific method—Form a Hypothesis, or an educated guess—before following it up with step four: Experimentation.

The mere thought of *that* was enough to make my cock swell to half-mast.

My hypothesis for the woman currently trying her best not to stare open-mouthed at me as I walk back toward her across the parking lot is that she most likely lives with the exhausting reality of an anxiety disorder. I could mark off agoraphobia, since she clearly had no problem leaving her house. She could have a specific phobia, but that didn't seem right, since again, she has no issues getting into a dumpster, where bugs and critters and all sorts of germs could be.

Generalized anxiety disorder? Maybe.

Social anxiety disorder? Very good possibility, seeing as she's always alone when she's here.

Panic disorder? She could, but even in the craziness that just happened that required her to be rescued like one of her plants, she didn't have a panic attack.

There's quite a few more on the list of anxiety disorders, but my best guess, my official hypothesis before actually speaking with her about... literally anything other than the legalities of trespassing on private property, would be—

"You had all that in your car?" Her curious voice cuts off my own rapid thoughts.

I glance down at the few items in my hands before looking back up at her, perched at the top of the steps, her arm stretched out and resting on her bent knees, palm up.

Just how I left her when I told her not to move. She didn't move a muscle except to keep her eyes on me.

Obedient little sweetheart.

"Earth to Mr. Poppins. You okay, there?" she prompts, and I narrow my eyes.

Although a bit mouthy.

"Mr. Poppins?" I ask, climbing up the steps and taking a seat on the one just below hers.

She gives a little snort of laughter. "Yeah, because you must have a Mary Poppins bag in that big truck of yours if you had a whole-ass manicure kit and first aid supplies."

I smile behind my mask, which I always keep on while working here part time a couple of evenings a week. I don't need this job—far from it, at least from a financial standpoint. But I enjoy having it to pass some of my time after I get off from my real job. If not, there would be entirely too much free time for these idle hands of mine. But it's also my quiet time in which I don't normally have to speak to anyone except for in the occasional meeting. I spend all day talking to so many people, and if I were to be recognized here, it would cease to be my oasis of mindless tasks.

So I keep the mask on, usually along with a beanie that covers my earrings but is currently sitting in my dryer at home after I washed it, and long sleeves to cover my tattoos. Gloves disguise my hands from anyone who might identify them from being on their body—whether at my day job, where they work tirelessly to heal people, or from my occasional nighttime activities, where they either inflict requested pain or dole out immeasurable pleasure. Either way, it would be easy for someone with my own level of observation skills to distinguish who I am if we've had close contact before.

I'm not exactly the type of guy who blends in with the crowd.

Not unless I'm doing it on purpose, like here at my little part-time job.

"I like to be prepared for anything," I tell her, pulling my glasses case out of my apron. I replace my penlight I had tucked between my ear and my cap with the black frames and shove the case back in my pocket, clicking on the little light that doesn't leave my body unless I'm fully naked— which is only to shower or sleep. I don't even fuck naked— an impossibility when I have to keep my true self hidden.

I clamp the penlight between my teeth and set to work using the tweezers from the kit to pluck the cactus needles out of her soft, warm flesh. They're hard to spot, and not just because it's after one in the morning in a mostly dark parking lot. No, it's not an easy task, because the needle tips actually broke off in her skin, and I'm only able to tell I've found another, and then another, when I gently run my fingertip over her palm and digits and cause her to flinch and suck in a breath when it snags.

And my body's response to those little winces and hisses is unlike anything I've felt before. I'm not an actual sadist—I don't derive *sexual* pleasure from providing a submissive her desired pain—but I *always* find it, at the very least, entertaining. Mostly, I find it just a pleasant experience, since I'm giving the sub what she needs from me. And it makes me feel good that she's getting it from me specifically, because I'm highly trained and experienced, and I know what the fuck I'm doing, as opposed to her seeking it out from a true sadist who doesn't. I've seen too many girls—and guys—not only physically hurt but psychologically damaged by trusting someone who told them they're an experienced Dominant, when that person doesn't know the first thing about what that really means in the lifestyle.

I once had a little fuckstick in my ER who brought in the sub he met online. Not only had her limbs turned purple from the way he tied her up from neck to ankles, but she had lost consciousness, from not only the ropes but the gag and hood he wrapped around her head. It scared the shit out of him—enough that he rushed her to the hospital. He was at least willing to do that, so I had to give it to him. When she gained her composure hours later, the poser sticking around—showing another bit of humanity I had to give him credit for—instead of ghosting her, I asked him in front of her what the three fundamental principles of BDSM are.

His confused "Uhhh… whips, chains, and handcuffs?" made my fist clench so hard my knuckles popped, echoing around the silent exam room.

She had obviously done at least some research, because she let out a disappointed sigh, although the look on her face wasn't one of surprise.

"No. The three principles, the three *fundamental*—meaning first and foremost, the most important—rules of the lifestyle you're fucking around with—" I lowered my chin but stared deep into his eyes, unblinking, my voice staying eerily calm. "—are Safe, Sane, and Consensual."

The asshole I had given the modicum of credit lost all my respect as he just shrugged. Although the gesture was likely out of intimidated nervousness, it didn't negate the fact that he was trying to blow off what I was attempting to teach him.

"So therefore, you broke the very first rule of BDSM. Which was what again?" I prompted, leaning closer and getting in his face.

This time, he didn't shrug. He sat up a little straighter, smartly paying attention this time. "Uh... sa-safe. Sir. You said safe as the first one."

I lifted one corner of my mouth, but the half smile didn't reach my eyes, as I continued to stare at him, knowing it made pricks like him sweat. "Good boy."

The recovering sub in the hospital bed let out quick giggle before slapping a hand over her mouth, an apology in her eyes directed only at me even though both men in the room looked at her.

I turned my head back toward the young man, dialing back my harsh stare just a couple clicks so he'd be more likely to absorb the information I was about to give him.

"It was incredibly decent of you to bring her here as quickly as you did. A lot of boys in your position would've panicked and ran, leaving her alone wherever you two were," I told him, feeding him a compliment to open him up to what I have to say. "And more so, you stayed with her here. Again, a lot of boys would've ditched her if they had the humanity to at least get her to the hospital."

He nodded, even though he winced slightly each time I said the word boy, his face eventually relaxing. Now I knew he'd remember the next words out of my mouth.

"It's called a *lifestyle* for a reason. If you want kinky sex, say that. But to convince a submissive that you are an experienced Dominant, when you are clearly so uneducated in the alternative lifestyle that you don't even know the first rule? It's as dangerous as someone posing as a cop... or a doctor." His brow furrowed, confused once again, so I spelled it out for him.

"How would you have felt if you brought her here, putting both your lives in my hands—because if she had gotten brain damage or died, you would've landed in jail— since you're supposed to be able to trust a doctor, right?" My brows lift to let him know the question isn't rhetorical, and at his frantic nod, I continue, "But then I was like, oh, sorry. I don't know how to help her. This is just a pair of scrubs I picked up next to the pajama section at Walmart and somehow got a job here." I shrug like he had earlier to really drive it home, and his face goes pale. "She wouldn't have gotten the immediate medical attention she needed, huh?"

He shakes his head. "N-No, sir."

"Good boy," I repeat, and his eyes look like they damn near tear up. "Seems to me you make a better submissive than Dominant, my guy. So if this lifestyle is something you're truly interested in and not just your schtick for picking up women who are so desperate to give up control that they ignore all the red flags I'm sure are all over your profile, then I suggest putting a little bit more effort into researching what a Dom truly is."

Now that I'd taken away his man card, I knew I should circle back to end the conversation on a brighter note so he wouldn't go on the defense after he left here. "But you have potential, son. You're a decent human being who cared enough about the girl to get her here, even when you knew you might get in deep shit. That's not only what defines a man but also a Dominant. So you've got that in you, at least." I glanced at the sub—who was staring at me like she'd drop to her knees and suck my cock right here in the exam room, forgetting all about her poser, if all I did was snap my fingers—before turning back to the guy for his answer.

He nods again, lowering his eyes to his clasped hands in his lap. "Thanks, sir."

The sub's look that night hadn't even made my dick twitch, because I see it so often. After decades of it aimed at me—even before I realized who and what I was—the sultry invitation in the eyes of both women and men rarely has any effect on me anymore. And in addition to the looks and verbal solicitations, I've also become desensitized to noises of pain and complaint after gaining the ability to easily distinguish between groans and screams that mean "it hurts so good; keep going" and "Jesus Christ and all the saints, stop, or I'm going to pass out" when it comes to sex. Just like I can between hisses of discomfort and "I should probably take the time to numb this up with some lidocaine."

No matter the case or situation, nor if I'm in or out of bed with the person making the noises, they don't set off the feeling I have inside my chest in this moment, plucking cactus needles out of this tiny plant vigilante's hand, who I literally pulled out of the dumpster. It actually pains me that I'm causing her even the slightest discomfort she didn't whole-heartedly beg for.

I must be going soft in my old age.

To her credit, she doesn't even try to pull away. She doesn't try to stop me and say she'll take care of it herself later. Like an obedient little thing, she attempts to relax into the pain, allowing me to help her as if I spoke the command aloud to a well-trained sub.

Finally, when I run my fingers over hers and across her palm several times without a reaction from her, I use the first aid supplies to clean her up, apply some antibiotic ointment, and then wrap her hand in gauze.

"Leave it on overnight, and in the morning—well, later this morning, that is—wash your hands with antibacterial soap and you should be all good," I tell her, immediately slipping into my doctor persona out of pure habit.

"Yes, sir," she says, watching as I tear the gauze tape off

and stick down the end, all while my eyes never leave her face, specifically her mouth, where she keeps nibbling on her plump bottom lip. I could bandage up pretty much any wound while blindfolded at this point in my career, so keeping my focus locked on those perfectly straight white teeth sinking into that dark pink flesh doesn't even slow me down. It only makes me want to drop all the supplies, reach around the back of her head, dig my fingers deep into her messy knot of thick, dark hair, and yank her to me to replace her bite with my own on that tempting mouth of hers.

Only I'd sink my teeth in hard enough to leave a mark but not break the skin, intense but not painful, one that would throb and live there just long enough for her to see as she checked in a mirror, maybe even snap me a photo to keep, after being delightfully exasperated I had the audacity to do that to her.

Evidence of my mark on her, my ownership.

What the fuck?

It's been years... *years*... since I even had the thought to actually keep a sub of my own. I play regularly, often enough to take the edge off, with trusted and experienced submissives. But I haven't found anyone who sparks the desire to take it further than that.

No one has even stacked the wood and found the kindling in order for there to be a *need* to get the match *ready* for a spark. That's how far removed that idea has been from my mind. It's been so long that the thought of being someone's Owner and Master, of training a sub to be my perfect partner, of a woman accepting and wearing my collar, is almost foreign. As if I had lost all hope and given up on being free to live my life the way I truly longed for.

I almost chuckle when I realize I let my fairy-tale thoughts that got me the nickname "Romantic Sadist" from one of my previous submissives fill my head, before remembering where I am and that I'm not alone.

Those are the types of thoughts I locked away in a deep, protected corner of my mind, so far down and around twists and turns that it had become hidden even from myself. Because like a childhood memory being unlocked by a vaguely familiar scent of perfume or flavor of a sweet treat, I'm suddenly flooded with the realization of just how lonely I've been, unable to allow myself to truly connect with someone in a way only felt between a Dominant and his devoted submissive, a Master and his more than willing slave.

I've been able to keep those desires at bay for almost four years.

Until now.

Chapter Four

SIENNA

It's not the fact that I'm washing my hands in order to get the tiny dots of dried blood and sweat off that makes me call the bestie for an emergency coffee date. It's the fact that the first thing that popped into my head as soon as I opened my eyes was *his command* to do it, and that I felt this compulsive need to do what he said without hesitation. And I did just that. I hopped out of bed, came into my attached bathroom, unwrapped his handiwork, and set to doing his bidding—washing my hands with antibacterial soap.

And when the thought occurred to me I was doing it because he said so, not because it's what one should do anyway, I told Alexa to call Vi right away, since my hands are still beneath the running water.

"It's been a while since we had a coffee date. Has inspiration struck?" she asks after agreeing to meet me in half an hour at our favorite little shop, and I finally turn off the faucet and grab a fresh hand towel from the drawer.

I snort. "God, I wish. No. This is even crazier than if my writer's block were to suddenly shove its ass out of the way and let me type words in an order that actually make sense."

"Good Lord. What the hell happened, woman? Did you find *actual* treasure in one of those dumpsters you dig in?" Vi questions, her voice full of shock, and I narrow my eyes at my Echo even though it's not the Show device and she can't see me.

"I *always* find *actual* treasure, bitch face," I tell her, and she laughs, since we call each other these things as endearments that most people would call someone they *really* don't like. "I didn't hear you complaining when Corbin was able to build you a whole-ass floor-to-ceiling, wall-to-wall bookcase out of the perfectly usable lumber I pulled out of there."

She sighs dreamily. "With a rolling ladder so I could glide like Belle."

I shake my head and roll my eyes as I hang the hand towel on the rack and open my walk-in closet door next to the shower. "Exactly. Sounds like actual treasure to me," I poke, and she laughs.

"All right, all right. You've made your point. So are you going to tell me what happened, or what? The suspense is killing me!"

I snort. "Well, at least I still have that going for me. I think I'll drag it out a little longer, make it a slow-burn, just so when I actually *do* tell you, the relief from finally knowing will overshadow if the plot is really any good or not."

She scoffs. "Woman, you do not write slow-burns. They are so not in your wheelhouse. Instalove or die, baby."

I grin and nod once toward the Echo Dot. "Instalove or die," I repeat our writing mantra.

"But!" she continues. "You also don't have to *trick* your readers into thinking the plot is good, because yours always are. Your twists and turns tie into a perfect little bow at the end of each book. You don't just fill chapters with a bunch of nonsense to throw people off, then slap on a crazy sex scene here and there as duct tape to hold it all together and hope for the best."

My eyes widen at the undertone of hostility in my friend's voice. "Are you speaking of a specific book-slash-author, or are you talking about the romantic suspense genre as a whole, dear BDSM erotica author bestie?" I tease, since her stories are heavy on the sex and very, very light on the plot. Her books center around shedding a better, more accurate light on the BDSM lifestyle and how loving and romantic it can be in a D/s relationship, as opposed to how mine are equal parts suspenseful thriller and super-kinky sexy times.

"I guess we both have something to hold over each other's head until one of us finally breaks then," she says, and I can hear the wicked smile she most certainly has on her pretty face.

"You're a dirty ho. See you in twenty," I tell her, and she laughs.

"I'm already out the door, ya whore." I shake my head as Vi snorts. "I'm a poet and didn't know it," she singsongs. "What you wanna drink? I'll go ahead and order it so it'll be ready when you get there."

"My usual," I reply, deciding on a pair of seersucker overalls and a navy cropped tee so I can get to work on my garden as soon as I get back home. I won't even have to come inside to change.

"Is your usual *still* your usual? It's been… a long time, babe. Seasons have changed and all."

I'm sure she adds the last bit to soften the blow of just how long it's been since we had one of our writing dates, and I tell her to grab my usual for cooler weather—which she knows is a pumpkin spice latte, because I'm 100 percent a basic bitch—before we hang up.

Hell, now that I think about it, it's nearly been as long since we had girl time just the two of us as it's been since we used to write the day away. There have been plenty of dinners and parties and running into each other with other people around—all hers, of course… kids, husband, extended family since she grew up here, and all sorts of close friends and their families she met through Corbin's work.

Which might be surprising to anyone who doesn't live an alternate lifestyle to learn people in the BDSM community can become like family. Corbin is one of the co-owners of our coveted local BDSM club. And while "local" gives it an air of amateurishness, a small-town vibe, Club Alias is anything but.

People from all over the globe vie for a membership at Club Alias, the elite lifestyle club just outside the city limits of Ft. Vanter, North Carolina. But even the richest of the rich have to go through the same vetting process as those who have to save for years upon years to pay the five-figure membership fee. No one gets past that unmarked entrance next door to the security business in one of the oldest buildings in town unless Doc—our Lord and savior, I always tease him—the renowned psychologist who specializes in sexual assault survivors and uses an alternate lifestyle as a form of therapy, deems them worthy.

If they make it through all his sessions deep-diving into their mind, their past and psyche, their motivation for being in the community, the reason for their very existence, it seems, only then can they become members. But before they even make it to that round of eliminations, they first have to have a sponsor to vouch for them. Otherwise, they wouldn't know about the club in the first place.

After all, it's called Club *Alias* for a reason. For those who desire to keep their identity under wraps have nothing to fear, because with a membership fee the same cost as an extremely nice vehicle, there's a certain class of people with highly respected jobs who make up the majority of the members. So besides the formalities of NDAs and other contracts signed as pinky promises not to tattle on each other, there's a mutual unspoken and cherished agreement between those in our community.

What happens in the club, stays in the club.

And then there's the agreement that *is* spoken and written.

If you recognize a fellow member outside the club, no, you don't.

Unless there has been a conversation in writing and signed by one of the four owners, stating they have permission to approach and converse outside the club's walls, your ass better pretend you've never seen them in your entire life.

Even if last night you had her hogtied and suspended while seeing just how many clothespins you could fit on each one of her tits in exchange for her stomping on your junk with her red pointed-toe stilettos once you cut her down.

"Nope. Never seen her before in my life."

"Who? The divorce lawyer on all the billboards in town who's known as a hard-ass and puts the fear of God in anyone who represents the spouse against him? Nooo, I definitely wasn't changing his diaper fifteen hours ago while he sucked his thumb and called me Mommy."

There are, however, the rare few like me, who just don't give a shit if everyone knows them in and out of the club. I literally make a living off highly explicit romance novels— no fade-to-black here. If people were going to look at me funny after learning I'm a submissive, then they probably already do for writing "pornography." So therefore, most of the time, I don't even bother wearing a mask at Club Alias unless I just want to feel pretty and dress up. People just call me by my real name, instead of my alias, which wouldn't be my nickname anymore anyway, since I'm divorced and unowned. That name was given to me by my former Dom, and when we split, he took the name with him.

And that may sound a little harsh or sad, but really, in my case at least, it's not at all. That nickname signified what and who I was to him and him alone. It wouldn't apply to me any longer, because I'm not that same person. I'm not even that same type of submissive. I would never be nor do the things I was and did for him with anyone else. It just wasn't for me, and I couldn't give him what he truly *needed*— not just wanted—in this life, so that name is *happily* not mine anymore. With no bitterness left in its wake.

"I wonder if people give themselves their own nick-name," I murmur to myself, something I do often when I'm alone to fill the silence. As overloaded as noises can make me feel with my serious case of auditory sensitivity, thanks to my ADHD—a symptom my meds don't seem to help with whatsoever—I also can't stand complete silence. Sometimes the absence of sounds seems to be just as loud as too many going on at once.

There's a fine line for me, one I don't realize I've been toeing until I've crossed over to either one of the sides. So most of the time, I wear my headphones, whether they're turned on or not. Sometimes, just having them as a barrier between my sensitive ears and the world provides enough comfort to keep the panic at bay. And since the invention of earbuds, it's so common now for people to wear them in public that I don't get funny looks anymore. Although I still prefer my noise-canceling, over-the-ear headphones. They're the only ones I can wear for hours at a time while I write, without them making my ears ache, like they do with the on-the-ear version and in-ear buds.

Speaking of, I grab my beige macrame bag that holds my headphones, laptop, glasses, spare chargers, notebook, and pens of different colors on my way out the door to meet Vi. I don't have the slightest bit of hope of writing, but for what I have to discuss with her, it could lead to lots of rabbit holes of research to fall down in. And I'd much rather do that comfortably on my computer with my notebook to jot down reminders than trying to do everything on my cell, relying on copying and pasting links and shit into the notes app. I'm old school, and Mercury Retrograde has fucked me too many times to trust technology whole-heartedly.

Planets on their period won't affect good ole paper and ink.

As I drive to the coffee shop, I chuckle remembering how adamant Vi was about not believing in astrology, alignment of the planets and moon, all my "weirdo hippy shit" she used to call it. But after years—*years!*—of pointing it out anytime something "weirdly hippyish" happened while Mercury was in Retrograde, things that never, ever, *ever* happened at any other time and had no other explanation, ruling out coincidence, she finally started giving in when I showed her that the "lovely" few times a year it happens is on the calendar in the Farmer's Almanac.

And we were also told by a fellow submissive at our club who is a flight attendant that they take a number of flights off the schedule during Mercury Retrograde, because there is documented evidence that shows more crazy shit happens during those times than any other during the year. For example, more issues with planes, like the service engine light coming on when nothing is actually wrong, or scheduling conflicts with layovers that should be impossible because of how the system is set up.

Anything that has to do with electronics and communication, good luck, bruh. It's why they say never to make big decisions or sign any contracts during Mercury Retrograde. And you shouldn't trust your conversation skills while it's going on either. Many a fight have broken out between the best of friends, just because that little cunt Mercury was wreaking havoc on that part of our brains.

Guess what was happening in the world of astrophysics when my good ole former-BFFs decided to take offence to the fact that an author interview that came out about me, written by a woman-owned coffee company, in which the article didn't show me gushing and thanking my friends profusely, crediting *them* for every good thing that's ever happened to me. Ya know, since it was them who did all the work. It had *nothing* to do with the years made up of countless hours and literal blood, sweat, and tears I put into writing and building my career.

Go ahead.

Guess.

Ding, ding, ding!

Mercury *fucking* Retrograde!

Even after my disease to please took full control of my mind and body, at which point I found myself emailing the coffee company and begging them for a copy of the two-hour Zoom interview. Instead of writing—or hell, anything remotely more important than that bullshit—I spent the next several hours scouring the interview, screen-recording every single time I *did* credit my girlfriends for their support while writing, during author signings, helping keep up with my social media, et cetera. And then I sent aaall those clips to them so they could see for themselves I did, in fact, give them all sorts of kudos during the interview that didn't make it into the article.

One—because I didn't write the damn article myself. The company who reached out to me—who wanted to feature me on their girl-power blog, my first *real* interview as an author that wasn't done by one of my book blogger friends—they were the ones who wrote it.

And two—and as Vi oh-so eloquently put it before she ripped them a new asshole when she found out they "had the audacity to be pissy little cunty fucking assholes" to me about it—"Nobody fucking cares about the personal assistant and the people who help produce the digital and paperback copies of a book when they open up an article to read about an author. So why would they waste time and words talking about someone who put your readers' auto-graphed copy orders together? Nobody gives a shit about monotonous behind-the-scenes crap like that. If they had put in the article every nice thing you had to say about all of us, I could almost guarantee the person reading the article would DNF that bitch in a heartbeat. Did. Not. Fucking. Finish. Because it's boooring."

Sweet little Vi had turned rabid on my behalf, continuing her rant. "You did your job as a good friend. You always, always make sure to thank them over and over again while you're signing the paperbacks live on Facebook. You always gush over them to the readers watching, and in posts in general, all the time! Not to mention, you put us in your acknowledgments in the back of every single one of your books, and you name your goddamn characters after them. Repeatedly. Using first, middle, last, and maiden names! Even their kids get put into the stories. That's how much you care about them and want them to know how much you appreciate them. Us. Me included. But I don't want to be fucking grouped with those bitches. Because you know what all this bullshit is telling me? Oh hell yeah, girl. My Spidey senses are going apeshit right now. You wanna know what their shitty-ass attitude is telling me?"

She had a wild look in her eyes that made me verbally agree out of self-preservation.

"It's telling me they've had ulterior motives this whole time. Why else would they get all pissy about not being mentioned in your first big, national interview? A real friend —hello, that's me! A real friend would be nothing but thrilled for you, sharing the link to that damn interview on every fucking social media they could think of. Shouting to the rooftops, proud of you, because they've seen how hard you've worked to finally get to this point of recognition. No... a real friend who cares about you wouldn't get butt-hurt that *their* name wasn't said in an article that was all about you. So that tells me maybe they've been riding your coattails this whole time, letting you do all the work, doing juuust enough to make you feel like you need them, because they knew eventually all your hard work would pay off. And there they'd be, soaking up all this glory they had no right to."

Vi had grumbled to herself for a moment before stopping, placing her hands on her hips, and looking heavenward before narrowing her eyes on me. "Didn't one of those assholes mention she sat down recently and wrote her very first chapter of a book ever?"

I tilted my head at her, immediately picking up on what she was throwing down. "Yeah. It was—"

She interrupted me with a squawk. "That dirty whore! God, I hate women! They sure are masters of the long-game, aren't they? Didn't I tell you? Didn't I say from the beginning I didn't like them? For the longest time, I thought two of those hussies were the same person, because I refused to give them much thought when you talked about them. I had a bad feeling about them, Sienna. Didn't I fucking tell you when these fangirls started moving in on you and making you feel like you were the greatest author who ever lived that you needed to be careful? Narcissistic little cunts. They love-bombed you."

"Us," I reminded her gently. "When they didn't go away after a while and you realized they'd be hanging around with us, you opened up to them too. They made you feel the same way, Vi, and it's all my fault for letting them get close."

She frowned with her whole damn body, if that's even possible, hissing out, "Bitches." She shook her head as she paced in front of my fireplace, the passion in her eyes burning hotter than the gas-fed fake logs behind her. "No, you are *not* allowed to feel guilty or in any way bad about this situation. You've been there for all of us even when you had your own chaos going on. You did your job as a good friend. More than your fair share, actually, since you went all crazy pants to prove to them you had talked about them in the interview, when you didn't have to even mention them at all."

This was the part where I opened my stupid mouth and compulsively confessed that not only had I sent them proof of all the things I said about them, but I also emailed the coffee company in a complete panic and begged them to add a few sentences to the article to include my girlfriends.

I knew I was on the wrong life path when even the founder of the company emailed me back after putting two and two together of what was going on, the only reason I would be asking for such a thing. She very nicely told me I needed to reconsider who I believed to be my closest friends in the whole world. Because she had a feeling taking a step back from the situation and viewing it without whatever emotional bond I felt toward these women would show me just how fucked up it was.

She also very nicely let me know I wasn't the first and definitely wouldn't be the last person to ever feel used "for clout," as the kids say these days. She too had to drop some dead weight along her road to creating the first ever woman-owned brand of coffee.

She added the sentences as I requested, but she made it known that the second I saw things more clearly, she'd revert the article back to its original form in a heartbeat.

The article stayed that way for a number of months, several of which I held out hope that one of them would apologize. One of them might possibly see things less self-ishly and put me out of my misery. Because surely I couldn't have been *that wrong* about the people I was closest to in life. Surely, I couldn't have been that blind to someone's true nature. Years of friendship, becoming part of each other's fucking family, couldn't possibly have been all a lie, a long-game as Vi put it.

My message letting them know the parts I had gushed all about them in the Zoom interview were added to the written article sat as the last thing ever exchanged between me and them. Left on read. Not even a thank you for all the effort I put into getting them the proof of my gratefulness for them. Not a single word after I gave them what they so desperately wanted, their name mentioned in an article that was supposed to be about me and my books.

Vi finally talked me into sending the email the coffee company owner had apparently been anxiously waiting for, and the article was immediately edited back to the way it was originally posted—without them in it. Just like my life now—without them in it—since at some point in the last year they had unfriended and unfollowed me on all social media.

Even though the handy-dandy analytics let me know they still quite often checked up on me.

And now, after I turn into a parking spot at the coffee shop and turn the car off, I grab my bag out of the passenger seat and hop out of my car. I grin as I spot my one and only true best friend as she waves excitedly at me through the window, seated on her side of our favorite booth. The only friend I'll ever need, who was there for me long before all the fangirls, and who I know will be by my side when we eventually get a shared unit in a retirement home for crazy people. Because surely by then, "bitches" will have driven us both mad.

Well... more than we already are now.

Chapter Five

SIENNA

"Okay, I'm done with your mind games, woman. Tell me right now what the heck is going on with you!" Vi orders as soon as I slide into the booth so that I'm facing her. Her closed laptop is on the table along with her reading glasses, and next to those are her coffee and a muffin with a bite taken out of it. On the table in my spot is my pumpkin spice latte, the lid pulled off so it could be cooling for me.

There's something to be said for being best friends with a fellow people-pleasing submissive. We remember damn near every detail and quirk the other has and make one another's life a little easier and a lot sweeter just by being thoughtful.

Just like how I reach across and snag her glasses case off her laptop, pull the cleaning cloth out of my bag, and start wiping the fingerprints and smudges off her lenses. She can never, ever, *ever* find her own wipes, constantly setting hers down in random places after using them, then forgetting where she left them. Then she just says fuck it and tries to squint and see through her dirty glasses, defeating their entire purpose. So a long time ago, my OCD—actual diagnosed Obsessive Compulsive Disorder, not some "omg, I'm so OCD because I like my closet to be sorted by color" exaggeration—took control of the situation and made it a ritual.

My version of the mental illness thankfully doesn't take the path of Contamination OCD, or what people like to call germaphobes. But my mind is completely saturated in intrusive thoughts, including the ones that make someone believe something bad will happen if they don't perform a certain task—also known as a ritual. In some people, this is way more obvious to others, because they'll have visible tics, repetitive behaviors, sounds they have to verbalize in order to make what I personally call "my voices" quiet down.

Mine shows up in the way I nurture people, so it doesn't stand out as much to an untrained eye. So no, cleaning my best friend's glasses has nothing to do with wanting to wipe the germs off. But it has everything to do with the fear of her not being able to see through the smudges and then some wild *Final Destination* type shit happening, like her coffee suddenly taking full effect, to the point she can't hold it, so she jumps up from the booth without taking her dirty glasses off to run to the bathroom at the very same time Austin—our favorite barista—is coming up behind her with a glass carafe of boiling-hot coffee that Vi collides with, not only causing the scalding liquid to pour all over her, but the glass breaks and—

Yeah.

My brain is a dumpster fire.

But hey, at least I'm not a germaphobe, right? Otherwise, dumpster *diving* would've never become my favorite pastime.

And then I would've never met—

"Dumpster Daddy," I finish my thought out loud, forgetting I was supposed to be answering Vi's question. But unlike the nameless, faceless, pretty much everything-less man who got me out of the trash safely, she doesn't seem to possess the ability to read my mind and know what the hell I'm referring to.

"Excuse me?" She tilts her head to the side, her eyebrows displaying her confusion.

"Let me rewind about—" I glance at my Apple watch. "—nine hours. No ten. Because I was in there digging for about an hour before…." I let my words trail off dramatically, pretending I can't feel Vi's dagger eyes aimed right in the middle of my forehead as I take a careful sip of my latte to make sure it's cooled enough before putting the lid back on.

"Befooore…?" she prompts, but I purse my lips and raise my eyebrows in a hoity-toity expression just to make her a little crazier while I keep her waiting, using my thumbs to press the lid down, circling the top five times before my voices stop taunting that the lid isn't on all the way and is going to cause a disaster to ensue if I don't.

Being the amazing friend she is, even though I was *just* teasing her seconds ago, she doesn't interrupt the ritual and waits until I take an extra-careful sip from the opening in the lid to make sure it's on tight. Too many times she's watched me have to repeat a process if I lost count, and she's also witnessed full-on panic attacks if I wasn't given the chance to.

I'm such a fucking joy, I tell you.

No wonder those "friends" gave up on me so easily. Even the chance to have someone "on the inside" of the book industry wasn't worth all the shit they had to put up with just being around me.

"Befooore?" Vi singsongs a little more aggressively, distracting me from my thoughts, and I lift my eyes to her glaring ones.

I sigh and say in a breathy British accent, "Before I was rescued by a handsome prince." I snort at that, shaking my head and continue in my own lightly Southern-accented voice. "Actually, I have no idea if he was handsome. But he had pretty eyes and cool earrings. That's about all I saw of him though. Oh! No... he also had great hands." I nod quickly. "Big. Very vascular."

She lifts an already arched dark brow at me. "Very vascular?"

I slouch and narrow my eyes at her now. "Come on, wordsmith. You know! Like... veiny. Masculine. Fucking manly *man* hands."

Her expression goes back to its former confused state. "How exactly did you only manage to see this man's eyes, earrings, and masculine manly man hands if he was rescuing you? And more importantly, why was he rescuing you? What happened?"

I take a sip of my latte, then sit back against the cushion of the booth, getting comfortable to set the scene for her. "Picture it, Sicily, 196—"

"I swear to God!" she finally yells, making me bust out laughing.

"Fine!" I give in, and I lean toward her instead before starting from the very beginning of the night, when I decided to hit my usual Friday-night spot, the orange-apron container of doom. When I get to the part where I found the golden barrel cactus and start to veer off on a highly detailed explanation of where that particular cactus hails from and its water and light-exposure needs, she gestures with her hand for me to hurry up and get back on track.

"Sorry. Right. Okay. And then there was this loud bang that scared the ever-loving shit out me, and I fell forward and almost dropped it. And that pissed me right the hell off, especially when this jerk starts telling me I had to leave. But I stood my ground. You'd be so proud of me, Vi. I didn't just tuck tail and run. I know the laws. So I argued. Me! You know I don't do confrontation. But come on. Golden. Barrel. Cactuses. They're like sixty bucks a pop!" My voice has risen with my excitement, and she's nodding with a small smile on her face. I know it's probably more for my benefit than what she's actually feeling, because I haven't gotten to what will be the entertaining part for her.

"That is a big deal for you, babe. Then what happened?" she encourages.

I make crazy eyes at her along with a grin that takes over my whole face before bringing my expression back to a serious neutral. "Then... he had a point I could no longer argue with. I technically was trespassing on private property and had to leave, so I decided my two new plant babies were more than enough treasure for one night and would call that a win. But just as I was maneuvering to get out, the goddamn pegboard I was standing on snapped—or something, I don't really know exactly what I was standing on. But it had a bunch of holes in it yet seemed sturdy enough. Anyway. I managed to catch myself and the cactus, but..."

Her eyes are wide with concern now, and I catch her looking me over to see if I have any visible injuries. "But?"

I hold my hand out to her so she can see the tiny dots all over my palm and fingers. "But I unconsciously reached out and caught it with my hand in midair instead of letting it hit the ground and then picking it back up. Damn reflexes."

She pulls my hand across the table to her side so she can look closely at my sore skin, tilting it this way and that to use the overhead light to see better. "I swear to God, Sienna, you belong in a damn episode of *Loony Toons* sometimes. That's straight up Wile E. Coyote shit right there."

I sigh and nod, because she's definitely not wrong. "Truth. So anyway, there I am, the cactus in my hand like a giant sandspur from hell, but I refuse to let it go. I've now shed blood and sweat for it, but no tears. There's no crying in dumpster diving."

She looks at me sternly, so I continue on.

"And the man I was arguing with pops his head over the edge and tells me to leave my prickly child behind while he helps me out of there. But fuck that. No plant left behind!" I call out dramatically, lifting my fist into the air, and Vi just shakes her head at me. "And this guy just… gives in. He doesn't call me stupid or any other mean name. He doesn't try to convince me otherwise by mansplaining anything. He's just like, 'all right, lady. Let's get you and your new hand piercings out of there.'"

"He said that?" she asks with a smile.

"Nah, but that's the vibe he was giving off. Like he was humoring me and just wanted me gone. The path of least resistance. So he didn't bother arguing with me anymore. Probably so he could finish his work and go home. It was super late." I shrug.

She narrows her eyes at me and purses her lips, like she's not quite convinced that's the reason he was so nice about the whole situation, but I'm too excited to tell her the next part to go off on a tangent with her to figure it out.

"So then he jumps in like some kind of Marvel character, doing the superhero landing and everything!"

Her narrowed eyes are no more. They are wide with wonder. "Down on one knee, the other leg stretched out a little, bracing with one hand on the ground?" Her voice is even a little breathy.

I nod slowly like Jack Nicholson with the crazy eyes in *Anger Management*. "Exactly! And he had body karate, girl. Seriously. He looked like he could be standing there right along with the Avengers."

"Holy shit, we need to tell Seth about this guy," she inserts, talking about one of the other co-owners of Club Alias. He's a goofball and is fluent in movie quotes and pop culture references, Marvel's *Deadpool* being his favorite. Such a cute, nerdy, and fun-loving guy, you'd never guess he's actually jacked as hell under those dark clothes and used to be quite the sadist before he fell in love with a virgin and no longer felt the urge to cause pain for his own pleasure.

Lucky Twyla.

The exact opposite of my marriage.

I shake myself out of my envy and keep going with my adventure, but only after I give her every single detail I can about the way this man looked. I paint a clear picture, and with her author's mind so similar to mine, I know she can see him inside her head as if he were standing right next to us. "So anyway, he does the landing, then he does what any superhero would do. He saves the baby first." I let out a dreamy sigh, then explain how he got the cactus up on the ledge of the dumpster before he helped me out of there. "The next thing I know, I'm sitting on his lap. His lap, Vi! I don't even know what happened. It's like he put his hands on me and I blacked out for a second, and when I came to, I was snuggled up to his big body while he was checking out my hand."

She just stares at me a second, then wiggles in her seat a little. "Yep, just checked. I've got lady-wood."

I snort. "Right? Like, holy hell! And then he went and got some first aid stuff out of his car and fixed me up."

Her head pulls back in surprise. "Like, right out of his car?"

I nod. "Tweezers and everything. Wrapped me right up and sent me home with doctor's orders to leave on the bandage until I woke up."

"Wow." She purses her lips and nods along with me. "Impressive. Who was this guy?"

I shrug and shake my head. "I have no clue. Just an employee. So that's why I've been calling him Dumpster Daddy in my head ever since."

"You didn't ask him his name?" Her tone is shocked, so I answer a little defensively.

"Of course I did. The guy not only rescued me but helped me carry the heavy-ass cactuses to my car, which I'm sure he could be fired for if someone found out. But I did that thing where I accidently rapid-fired off a bunch of questions at once, and I didn't realize he answered all of them except for giving me his name until I was already halfway home."

She smiles a little, her eyes curious. "What were the other questions?"

My brows furrow as I try to remember. "There were so

many things I wanted to ask him, and I kind of just word-vomited them all at the same time. I know I asked him why he had first aid supplies in his car, along with the little toiletry bag he got the tweezers out of, and he just said he likes to be prepared for anything. But that was earlier. I don't remember exactly how I worded the questions, but I remember his answers clearly. He was a boy scout and fireman when he was younger. Did I mention the salt-and-pepper beard?"

"You did. About thirteen times while you were naming off each and every detail about him. Which is also kind of impressive since you really couldn't tell much about him, because he was all covered up. But seeing as most of the Doms at our club dress similarly, we know good and well just how different each one can look, even when they're all dressed alike from head to toe. Aside from height and weight and muscle tone, just their own personal vibe, their aura, can make them seem so different from someone else, ya know?"

I nod frantically. "Yes! Totally get that. Like the first time I ever met Sarge and saaay, Knight?" I say her husband Corbin's Dom name, since that's how I was actually introduced to him the first time, and the fourth co-owner of the club, Knight, also known as Brian outside of Club Alias. His wife, Clarice, is the photographer for all our book covers. "Sarge is like half the size of Knight, but if I were to meet them in an alley, it's Sarge who would be the scarier of the two. Knight is like... a big ole gentle giant.

But Sarge...." I shake my head, not knowing how to explain it to her, since she's his wife, and I don't want to offend her in any way. While she's my best friend, I have a tendency to put my foot in my mouth no matter who I'm speaking to. It's why I like to stick to writing, where I can backtrack and delete things, unlike when words leave my mouth.

"I know exactly what you mean," she assures me, and I immediately relax. "The first time I met them, I was barely eighteen and they came into my rock climbing gym together. Brian was like seventy-three feet taller than me, but Corbin... he gave me chills. And while he probably gets that reaction from most people, I'm the weirdo who was turned on by his scary aura."

"I can only imagine being that young, a virgin, and suddenly feeling all those very adult feelings for the first time when you encountered... him. I mean, he's never been anything but nice to me. He's great, truly. But he's still kinda terrifying," I say with a nervous laugh.

Thankfully, she just giggles and shakes her head at me. "I mean, he's an award-winning marksman with two Purple Hearts. I'm sure a lots of people find my honey... intimidating." She lets out a dreamy sigh of her own. "So fucking hot."

I wave my hand between us. "Hey, none of that. This is supposed to be about the hotty I found. Not yours. You always get to talk about your hotty. This is brand new territory for us! A new hotty!"

She straightens with a firm nod. "You're right. Tell me more."

Now that I have the floor, I don't know how to proceed. "Well, that's the thing. I don't know what the hell is wrong with me, Vi. I don't even know this man's name, no idea what he even looks like. But one quietly spoken order from him and my mind went into full-on 'yes, Master' mode without me even being conscious of it until my body was doing his bidding on its own."

"When did he give you orders?" she asks, switching to mama-bear persona in an instant. "No one is allowed to give you orders without your consent, Sienna."

I pat the air down with both hands in the international sign for "calm thy tits." But I do admit, at least internally, that I fucking love that my best friend is this protective over me. "He didn't mean them as *orders*-orders. I unconsciously just... reacted to his instructions that way. Like he told me not to move when he ran to get the supplies to fix my hand. And then he told me how to take care of it once I woke up this morning."

She visibly relaxes, her shoulders dropping from where they had hiked up nearly to her ears. "What do you mean you reacted to them that way? Like... how did it stand out to you, feel different, than if maybe I told you to sit still?"

I tilt my head to the side and back, looking up toward the ceiling but not seeing it. Instead, I'm visualizing through my mind's eye, seeing and hearing the way he spoke the directions and then watching myself act on them.

"I… I guess because once I realized I was in the middle of doing what he said, I was conscious of the fact that I was doing it *just* because *he* told me to. Not because I would've anyway. It was almost like, even though he wouldn't know I did exactly as he told me to, I still wanted to do it just to… please him. Like… if he were to find out, it would make me happy that it made him happy I followed his orders." I blink and shake my head before meeting her eyes across the booth. "I know it sounds weird and like I just talked in circles. I don't know how else to put it."

She's waving off my regret before I even finish. "No, no. I get it. I totally know what you mean. Sarge will order me to write five thousand words within five hours and send them to him… 'or else,'" she adds, using her fingers to make quotation marks and making her voice all sultry on the last words. "And even though I need to do that anyway, and probably would without his order, I find myself… more excited, maybe even more willing, to do it, since it's 'for him.'" She makes finger quotes again, and I nod.

"Exactly! Yeah, I would've washed my hands with the antibacterial soap, but I probably would've been lazy about it. Procrastinated. Fucked off on my phone or played with my plants before moseying into the bathroom to unbandage it and wash it off. But since he specifically said to do it when I woke up, I was in the middle of scrubbing them clean before I even opened both eyes."

She grins. "You need to find out who this mystery man is. Shall we go on an adventure to the home improvement store to see if we can discover his identity?" She rubs her hands together mischievously, but I'm already shaking my head.

"No. No way. It's one thing to be caught balls-deep in garbage in the dark of night with nothing but a streetlight to reveal my hot-messness. It's entirely another to show up during the day with the sun shining or at night when the whole store is lit up."

She frowns at me. "You say that like you're some creature from the dark lagoon or something. You do realize that you're hot, even when you're balls-deep in garbage, and even if you were to be doing that particular activity in the light of day, right?"

I roll my eyes. "You have an obligation to say that as my bestie."

She scoffs. "Bitch, you know I'm always the first person to be like 'what the fuck are you wearing?' Don't give me that shit. I only speak the truth to you. I just do it in a way that doesn't cause emotional damage."

I smile. "And that's why I love you the most."

"Okay, enough of that gooey crap. I see you brought your laptop. What are we researching if we aren't going on a mission to find this guy?"

Reaching for said laptop, I pull it out of my bag and get everything situated in front of me while I tell her the devastating news. "Before I actually drove off last night, Dumpster Daddy told me there's a new manager who is cracking down on all the rules, policies, and codes at their store. He let me know that they're going to be tightening up on lots of things that had been lax, and one of those things is the store after hours. People have been coming and taking the empty pallets in the back of the building, the empty metal shelves, perhaps honestly thinking they were trash. But if they'd done their research like I did, they'd know some of those things are just rented. Like the vendors pick up the empties when they bring the new inventory."

"Okay, so we're researching the codes and policies so you can find loopholes and continue dumpster diving there?" she guesses.

"Nope. Dumpster Daddy informed me that the asshole store manager is going to set up drive-bys with the police to check the property—specifically the back of the store where the dumpster and pallets are kept—multiple times a night. And if I'm caught by the actual police, I might get a warning the first time, but after that, I will be charged with trespassing. And ya girl can't afford bail or a ticket or whatever monetary consequence that might entail," I reply.

"All right, so we're researching how to get out of a trespassing charge when that eventually happens?" she guesses again.

I snigger. "Nope. On my way home, after I came out of the weird hypnosis he put me in just by fucking speaking, it hit me I won't have my weekly hit of plant-induced oxytocin, and that will not be good for my already overworked Prozac prescription."

"Okay, I give up. Just tell me." She leans forward, her tone conspiratorial.

I laugh. "Oh my God, Vi. It's nothing crazy. I was just going to get on Reddit and see if anyone has some magical way of getting free plants that I haven't thought of. Like maybe nurseries that give away overstock. I know Lowe's puts their wilted babies on clearance, which is great, but I can't even afford those any longer."

She looks disappointed for a solid minute. Obviously, she was expecting something way more exciting.

"Woman, what could I have possibly been about to realistically research other than that? This is not one of my suspense novels. We do not live a life full of... I don't know, secret vigilante heroes who rid the streets of rapists and murderers and make it look like an accident. We are not the sweet and quirky heroines in our stories who land the super-hot gajillionaires," I remind her, and she makes a face I can't quite translate other than uncomfortable, and then I remember. "Oh wait... you *are* the sweet and quirky chick who landed the super-hot BDSM club owner, so let me rephrase. *I*... am not the endearing weirdo who's going to seduce the delicious, wealthy alpha male with her awkwardness. So I ask again, what did you think I was going to say?"

She puzzles over my question for a minute, and then her eyes light up as if the idea bulb inside her mind is a real thing. "What if...?" She lifts her hand to her face and taps her finger on her chin, pulling her pursed lips to one side. And then she looks at me with a challenge in her sparkling eyes. "Have you come across those girls on TikTok who are sugar babies?" she asks, lifting a brow.

Not thinking much about her question as I open my laptop and touch my finger to the unlock button for it to read my print, I reply, "Oh yeah. Those girls are geniuses. They join dating sites that hook up those ambitious, pretty young things with 'sugar daddies'—super-rich loners who have so much money they don't know what to do with it." I pull up the Reddit site and log in to my account.

"Exactly!"

After a moment of silence, Vi not saying anything else, I lift my eyes to glance over the top of the screen to see her staring at me expectantly. "What's wrong with your face?"

She frowns. "Nothing's wrong with my face, ho. Sienna! Think about it! You should totally join one of those sites."

My own face scrunches up to display the "what the fuck" that doesn't need to be said. "Woman, I am a thirty-four-year-old divorcee who looks like Swamp Thing's mother ninety-eight percent of the time. The girls on those sites are freaking Instagram models in their twenties. What rich bastard is going to pick *me* over one of *them*?"

She's straight-up glaring at me now. "I'm not going to dignify any of that with even a second of acknowledgement. I'm going to move forward in the conversation to the part where I remind you that, one, a lot of those women have completely fake profiles and never once meet up with the men they get into a relationship with. They just chat with them on the internet or on the phone, and maybe they send them a sexy photo or something. It doesn't even matter if it's really them or not. And two—and the more honest and likely side—there are men who go on there to find an intelligent and mature woman to spend time talking to. Some don't give a shit about twenty-year-old Barbies, especially if they'll never meet them in person anyway. They want to have a stimulating conversation—whether that means naughty or not depends on the man, I guess—with a female who has a brain."

When I don't blow her off, she takes that as her cue to deliver her final argument.

"And what would be more exciting for a dirty old man who wants a stimulating conversation than a best-selling filthy romance novelist?"

I sit back in my seat and cross my arms, keeping my eyes on my best friend but not really seeing her. Instead, I'm visualizing what her suggestion could look like.

My mind takes many routes, and the longer it travels, a feeling I'd almost forgotten starts to fill me from my head to my chest, making my heart start to pound. I'm vaguely aware my eyes are making rapid movements as my thoughts start to align into a meet-cute, then they skip ahead to a happily ever after with an epilogue that may or may not include babies, depending on my mood that day. A few of the thoughts sprinkle over the timeline, landing as plot bunnies that start hopping in place, excited to be expanded on until they each form a scene. And eventually those individual scenes will connect when I fill the gaps between them with character development, making the hero and heroine and side characters feel real by having them do mundane, everyday activities mixed in with picking and choosing different foods and music and movies and hobbies they each love or hate.

In the end, my mind has chosen a winner from the many possible routes it scouted, but the destination is the same as it was minutes ago, when Vi's words were the spell that avada kedavra'd my writer's block.

"Plant Daddy," I whisper.

She sighs but smiles. "What are you talking about now?"

"You, my love, just planted the seed that is currently growing into an entire plot with characters and everything inside my twisted little mind at this very moment. But you know I can't talk about it until I jot everything on a sticky, so hold up," I tell her, opening up the Stickies app on my laptop and quickly typing out some notes so I don't forget anything my brain conjured about the book I'm now anxious to start researching for.

Vi is squealing quietly as she bounces in her seat, clapping her hands. And when I give her the signal that I'm done putting my thoughts down so I don't forget them, she bursts forth with a question she's clearly dying to ask. "What is up with you lately? Have you suddenly developed a daddy kink I should worry about showing up in your next book?"

I laugh out loud at that. "No. Ew." I slap my hand over my mouth then slide it off, genuinely ashamed that came out of my mouth. "I'm sorry. That was rude. I will never,

ever, *ever* be someone who yucks another person's yum. But no, the daddy thing is not for me. I was entirely too close to my father before he passed away to ever call another man Daddy, and especially not as a sexy nickname."

"Then are the daddy names a new trend I just haven't come across in my algorithm yet?" she asks. "First, there was Gym Daddy you told me about a while back—"

"Mmm… Gym Daddy. I've missed getting to count his pull-ups from afar while I've been off the workout wagon. Hell, that might be incentive enough to get my ass back there," I insert, sighing wistfully.

"—and then came Dream Daddy, when you pointed out Sir Jeremy at the club." She ticks this one off on her finger, seemingly realizing there are enough names to make an entire list.

I moan and melt down into the bench until Vi has to close my laptop in order to see me. "My God, could you imagine being on the receiving end of his—"

"It's been *years*, but Dulce still holds the record for the most Os, with seventeen before she fainted. The man has no sympathy when subs volunteer for forced orgasms. If you don't use your safe word, he just keeps on going."

"And going. And going. And going," I say, my voice breathy. And then I blink and look at my friend. "You seriously don't know who he is in real life?"

She shakes her head. "No idea. And even if I did, I'm under just as many NDAs as you and every other member of the club is. And before you ask, no, I don't have access to Seth's crazy computer system. Again, even if I did, he was literally a child prodigy who graduated from an Ivy League college with his Master's in technology before most kids his age graduated high school. There's no way in hell I could get past even the first restricted page he put up, much less whatever fortress he's put everyone's identity inside."

"Well what good are you then?" I gripe, but my smile takes any meanness out of the words, and she rolls her eyes.

"Anyway. So that's Gym Daddy, Dream Daddy, and then Dumpster Daddy, and now Plant Daddy. You, my dear, have a closet daddy kink," she teases.

I sit up straight. "I don't have a daddy kink!" I hiss across the table. "It's just want I call older men, and... I maaay or may not have a thing for older men," I admit.

"Ya *think?*" Vi squawks, and my eyes widen as I look around the coffee shop to see if her volume drew attention our way.

"Why'd you say it like that?" I whisper-yell.

She gives me a bug-eyed look, her mouth dropping open before her expression turns flabbergasted. "Are you telling me you are just now becoming aware of your attraction to older guys, Sienna?"

I shrug. "What? It's a new development."

She shakes her head. "No! It most certainly is not a new development. Woman!"

I mimic her bug-eyed stare and repeat, "What?!"

She sits forward to speak quietly, but the words are

sharp. "Gym Daddy. How long has it been since you went to the gym?"

"Rude." I pout. "I don't like your tone. But it's been about five months now. I've been busy rescuing—"

"Five months since you've been, and you saw him the first time when?"

I have to think about that for a second. "Not too long after Art and I divorced, so a year and a half ago. You made a big deal about it because he was the first man outside the club I was even remotely attracted to."

She nods. "That's right. You and Art had to be legally separated a while before you were able to file for divorce, and in all that time, the only guys you had the hots for were Dream Daddy and Dr. Walker. But Doc doesn't count, because everyone and their brother has the hots for him. But still… much older than you."

"That man is sex on a stick," I insert.

"And just gets finer with age," she agrees.

"So unfair," we complain in unison, and we burst out into girly giggles.

When we catch our breath, she continues with her plight. "And how did you describe Gym Daddy again?"

I whimper as I picture that gorgeous man who always works out over in the "big boy" equipment, as Astrid got me calling it. Yes, Astrid, as in Doc's wife—the same Doc Vi and I were just talking about like schoolgirls. But Astrid is completely secure in her marriage and knows she has absolutely nothing to worry about, because Doc is completely obsessed with her. She finds it funny that we girls all have a crush on the handsome therapist and have no shame in making it known to him and everyone around that we think he's hot as hell. Always in a joking manner though. She knows none of us would ever try to tempt him away from her—not that anyone could. If someone didn't believe in soul mates, they'd just have to hear their story one time and they'd suddenly be a true believer.

I blow out a breath and close my eyes, visualizing the second man I nicknamed after finding myself calling him "the hotty at the gym" over and over every time I would mention him to Vi. "Muscles. So many muscles. And his giant arms are painted in tattoos. But he's just fucking... beautiful. He looks no older than us, but he's got a white close-cropped beard, so either it's premature graying, or he's just taken really good care of himself for a long time. Or maybe it's just because I see him mostly from a distance—I don't think I'd be able see any lines or small details that would identify his age. But what really gets me going when I see him, if I had to pick just one thing out of a whole grocery list of things about him that fill my lady garden with butterflies... he's like *Gaston's Song* in *Beauty and the Beast*." And then I sing, "Every last inch of him's covered with hair!"

She throws back her head and laughs, and I can't help but grin.

"Shut up. I know you're probably picturing some sasquatch-lookin' dude in your head right now, but that is *not* even remotely close to what his is like. He just looks… so manly. So masculine and virile." My eyes are at half-mast, and my shoulders shrug forward, making my boobs squeeze together, and I'm not at all surprised to clearly feel that my nipples are hard and sensitive against the soft cups of my bra. My body always has a physical reaction when I see or just think about Gym Daddy. "And it's not like… black, coarse… pubes all over him or something."

Vi makes a gagging sound I ignore.

"It's lighter. A little darker than blond, and it looks like it would be soft to the touch. He wears tank tops, so I can see it's literally all over, aaall the way down, because his shirt lifts enough for me to see below his belly button when he does pull-ups." I could go on and on about the way this man looks. I've memorized every single detail my eyes have been able to pick up on, when he's lifting weights and I'm over on the machines or the treadmill. "Could you imagine what all those hairy hard muscles would feel like against your naked skin? Jesus," I murmur.

"It's yummy, for sure," Vi says dreamily, and an image of Corbin pops into my head. I've never seen him shirtless, so I have no idea what his skin looks like beneath his ever-present black Henleys, but there's no hiding how ripped he is with the way those shirts fit him like a glove. So if he's got body hair, even if it's less than the amount Gym Daddy has, then Vi would definitely know how stimulating it would feel.

"I've never been with anyone who's hairy before. You've seen Art. He has a teensy bit between his pecs and a happy trail, but that's about it. And while he isn't fat, he isn't muscular either. He's always been really good-looking, but he's average in the body department, if not a little skinny. And before him, there were only teenaged boys against my teenaged girl body. So Gym Daddy is just... sexy as fuck to me," I finish.

Vi nods, as if I just gave her even more evidence for her argument. "And now Dumpster Daddy. Who you mentioned an over-the-top amount of times has a salt-and-pepper beard."

"And super muscly too," I add.

"And super muscly," she agrees. "So are you seeing a pattern here for what's been... setting off the butterflies in your garden for over a year?" She giggles and shakes her head.

"I have a thing for Hot Santa?" I lift a brow.

She snorts. "And I mean, even before you and Art separated, all your celebrity crushes were older men too. Johnny... Jared... Jeffrey...."

"Mmm, Jeffrey Dean Morgan. He's been the muse for many of the heroes in my books. Le sigh. But if you're trying to make a point about me having a thing for older guys, then we might as well go all in, throw in my ultimate old-man crush."

She looks at me with her brow furrowed, obviously trying to think of who I've mentioned is my tip-top favorite male actor over the age of fifty. Well, sixty now, but at the time this hardcore crush began, he was approaching a half-century's worth of years, while I was a mere nineteen. "I give up. Who's your ultimate?"

"Almost a thirty-year age gap and he still has a face good enough to sit on. None other than Dr. Gregory House," I say through a long sigh with hearts in my eyes, and I bat my lashes at her.

She tilts her head to the side. "Hugh Laurie? Really?" She doesn't make any sort of face, positive nor negative, just curious. I love my bestie. Never judgmental, no matter what kind of shit comes out of my mouth.

I shake my head. "Not Hugh himself, but him as his character, House. He's British in real life, and while that accent is sexy in its own way, his voice when he puts on the American accent while portraying the asshole doctor just does very exciting things to the muscles in my vagina. They get all clenchy. Like they're a hand making a 'gimme, gimme' gesture."

She bursts into laughter again, and my face splits into a huge grin. I love making her laugh. She's got such a dry sense of humor that when I can make her react this way, I feel super accomplished.

Still smiling from ear to ear, she makes her final argument. "So by all accounts, to me at least, it sounds like you would be the perfect candidate for signing up on one of the sugar daddy sites, bestie. Even if it's just to take a peek, look around one to see what it's like and what might be available. Surely, there's gotta be more possibilities there than what you'll find in a dumpster."

"But Dumpster Daddy was yummy," I grumble, and she narrows her eyes.

"You don't even know what Dumpster Daddy looks like."

I make a face at her. "So? Are looks so important that if he were to reveal his face and was an ogre, it would change the way my body instinctively reacted to his instructions?"

She makes a haughty expression and crosses her arms, sitting up extra straight. "Okay then, let's go find out who he is. Right now. Midday. When the sun is shining and neither of you can hide in the shadows."

I pout at that. "Hey, I said his looks wouldn't make a difference to me. That does not negate the fact that I don't want him to see *me*, the way I look most of the time. I can't even remember the last time I washed my hair, and I ran out of dry shampoo months ago."

"You perception of yourself is very skewed, my friend," she murmurs, and I wave off her words before they can make me teary-eyed.

"Either way, I'll give your suggestion some thought. It couldn't hurt just to get on one to snoop around. If anything, I need to get on to research it. Because a bitch is finally inspired!"

She claps excitedly and wiggles in her seat. "Yay! You better keep me informed if you find anything interesting."

I nod, even as I tell her, "You're a bossy little thing. Are you starting to lean toward the Domme side?"

She makes a freaked out face and shakes her head

adamantly. "Hell no, that's all Clarice," she says, mentioning our cover photographer again. She and her husband, Brian, are switches, which means they take turns being the Dominant and the submissive in their relationship. It's just amazing and super entertaining to get to watch when Clarice is in Domme mode, because she's like five-foot nothing, and he's damn near seven feet tall, but she's able to command him like he's her toy poodle.

A very large, muscular, slightly terrifying toy poodle who could snap someone's neck with his pinky finger.

I give Vi what she is clearly desperate to hear. "Fair enough. I promise to keep you updated while I look for a Plant Daddy... for research purposes, of course."

Chapter Six

SIENNA

Once every last wilted leaf is pruned and I've run out of potting soil to repot the new plant babies I rescued out of the grocery store florist's trashcan when I stopped to grab wine on the way home from the coffee shop, there's nothing left to do but go inside my house. It's only 10:00 p.m. I've still got at least five hours before my mind will finally shut off enough for me to pass out.

It's Saturday, so I *could* get dressed and go to the club, to see if there's anything entertaining to watch or participate in. But I just don't have it in me. Being around all those people, most of them matched up into couples, or throuples, or whatever comes after that—fouples? The thought of actively trying to find someone, someone new, and having to get to know them—small talk and all that shit—makes me feel like I'm going to pass out... or maybe just take a nap. Either way, it sounds daunting as fuck.

So as pathetic as it makes me feel, I grab the bottle of my sweet red wine and my wine glass that is stamped with pretty script that spells out the words **Crazy Plant Lady** surrounded in monstera leaves, and I take them to the couch. Since I am the ultimate wine connoisseur who only drinks the bougiest of wines, I *twist off* the cap and pour the dark red liquid all the way to the very top, to the point I have to lean down to my TV tray and sip from the glass instead of picking it up.

"Mmm," I moan when the sweetness overwhelms my tastebuds and makes my mouth water as I put the metal cap back on the glass bottle and set it on the table next to the couch. "Now, where to begin." I open my laptop and slip my glasses on, using my fingerprint to unlock the screen. I don't know why I've been procrastinating doing this all day, especially with how excited and motivated I was about it when the idea for the book hit me. It feels almost like I'm a debut author again, writing the very first page of my very first story. I felt like such a poser, like I was just playing pretend. There's no way I could write a whole book and then publish it, right?

Almost thirty books later... I need to pull on my fucking big girl panties.

I straighten the fuck up and put my fingers to the keyboard. "Okay, let me think. How about...?"

I type in the words **sugar daddy dating site**, and

immediately a whole slew of websites highlighted with the word **Ad** next to them pop up, taking up almost the entire first page of the search results. I don't know why, but for some reason, I've always scrolled past all the ads without looking at them to get to the websites that haven't been sponsored. The first one that pops up is a very infamous one, known for hooking up married people who want to cheat on their spouses.

Not to be confused with married people in ethical non-monogamous relationships, as in open marriages for example, but people actively and knowingly hooking up with married people who have spouses who aren't aware. Extra-marital affairs. There are very, *very* few reasons in my mind that could make this type of relationship morally acceptable.

Yes, there are *some* reasons that exist, like my old friend Winston, who was stuck in his marriage because of a fucked-up prenuptial agreement. He and his wife were separated for years, living completely apart in every way, but if he divorced her, he would lose everything he ever worked for, and she was bitchy enough to take it all. Thankfully, all that worked out in the end, albeit a bit dramatically.

I also read about someone getting trapped in a marriage with a person who completely played them, making them think they were everything they ever wanted, their perfect match. And it wasn't until they had kids their true colors came out. While I don't necessarily agree with staying married just for one's children, if they themselves had a bad experience being a child of divorced parents, then I can totally see their trauma making them want to give their own kids a different upbringing than they had.

My reasoning for this example of an affair being forgivable may be morally corrupt, but in my head, if you portrayed yourself one way and got the ring on your finger, then later on down the road, your reveal you were lying about who you were, then your spouse didn't marry *you*. They didn't say vows *to you*. They said them to the person you made them believe you were. So those vows are as null and void, as fake as the persona you were putting on.

But deciphering such intricate details of a man's marriage would take so much time and building of trust. I definitely don't have the mental capacity for dealing with a complication like that, when I could just stay away from a site that screams **Click Here for Extreme Anxiety and Other-Woman Drama**. Plus, I wouldn't get much information on sugar daddies there, I don't think, so I scroll to the next one.

This one looks a little more promising. It's like they're trying to word it discreetly, making it seem like an exclusive dating site specifically for wealthy people. It does not say it's for sugar daddy—or mama—situations, or that one person in the relationship would have lots of money to pay for the company of the other. And since the next few sites in the search results have sketchy words like **escort** and **champagne room** in their previews, I scroll back up to the discreetly worded one.

Clicking on it, I see it looks like any other social media or dating site, with its login or sign-up screen. I try to look around the site without creating a profile, but I'm blocked immediately by a pop-up that gives me the option for a free profile or a paid one with "perks." Sighing, and since I don't want a gazillion emails being sent to my already stuffed-full inbox, I open a separate tab and get on Google really quick to create a new email address.

I take a moment to think of something witty, just in case people on these sites will get access to my email address. Taking another large gulp of my wine, I giggle as the new name hits me.

"WillDive4Plants," I say aloud as I type in each letter. Hopefully, people will chuckle at the innuendo and make them want to message me to break the ice by asking to clarify my screenname. "Sorry, ladies. I will not *muff dive* for plants. I am strictly dickly."

I go back on the website and use my new email address to sign up for a profile, using the same WillDive4Plants as the screenname, instead of trying to think of something else. Coming to the first personal question, I'm reminded of what Vi said about some men wanting a woman more mature than a college co-ed.

I shrug, talking to myself as I always do, "Might as well be honest," and scroll through the calendar in the form to pick my birthday, including the real year. "Sex? Female." *Click.* "Sexual Orientation? Straight." *Click.* "Occupation? No-vel-ist," I sound out as I type it in the blank. "Marital

Status?" I snort. "If someone is married and on a dating site, are they really going to be honest here?"

I click on the arrow to open up the choices, and I let out a surprised "hm!" There are the usual Single, In a Relationship, Married, Divorced, and Widowed, but there are also a couple of choices I've never seen on any form before. Open Marriage and Poly-Relationship are there for the ethical non-monogamy crowd, and then there are some for... honest adulterers, I guess you would call them, although that sounds like a total oxymoron—In a Relationship, and Married, with **(Discretion Required)** next to each option.

I click on Divorced, since that's not as much of a dirty word as it used to be in the dating world. I can only think of a few people I know who are still married to the original person they wed. I chuckle, thinking about my best friend's real-life love story. Vi actually divorced and then remarried her one and only husband. I could never imagine remarrying Art, but in Vi and Corbin's case, those two went through some shit that tore them apart. Yet when fate gives you a soul mate, nothing will keep you away from them— even if it takes a decade to refind each other.

I move on. "Looking For? Hmm...."

I take a minute to think about this. I'm kind of nervous to just jump in and actually start looking to talk to someone, so instead, I take the chicken way out and choose: "Just looking for friendship." Then I use the About Me section to state that I'm an author researching dating sites for my next book. I give in and put a little more, saying aloud as I type, "I have not been on a dating site since before I was married, so I just need to make sure everything is still the same or see if sites look a whole lot different than 14 years ago."

Back when I met Art, the only sites for dating and meeting new people were Plenty of Fish and Adult Friend Finder. There was also Myspace, but that was used more for people you already knew, not for meeting anyone new.

The last step is to add a profile picture. Next to the Upload button is a statement in bold that says there's a 75% higher chance of having success on the site if you include a photo. I decide to upload my professional author picture that's on Amazon and everywhere else my name is mentioned on the Internet.

Yes, it'll reveal my identity, but that would take effort. If someone takes the time to dig and find out more about me, then in my "broken" brain, that doesn't say "stalker." That says to me they're really interested. I've read and heard way too many stories of assholes sending out a blanket, copy-and-paste generic message to every woman within driving distance they come across on a site.

"God, how horrible would *that* feel, to find out that, out of hundreds, you're just the lone loser who actually took the bait?" I mumble, swallowing more sweet wine.

Also, if they go searching to find out who I am, they'll be able to see I really am an author and being truthful in my profile, and not someone who's catfishing, just *pretending* to be an author doing research. Because just like Vi said, if a guy really were looking for someone interesting to hold an intelligent conversation with, having Novelist as one's occupation would definitely catch their attention, so I'm sure it's been faked before.

After all, just like at Club Alias, I have nothing to hide. Not only am I doing research for my book idea, but I am a single woman who's finally ready to get to know someone new, as long as it's not complicated. And from what I've heard, online dating isn't as taboo as it used to be. It seems like it's the first option any single person chooses when they decide they want to try dating. And I totally understand that.

You feel much safer behind your computer screen than you do putting yourself out there and approaching someone in person, like at a bar or at the club or even at the garden center. I know I personally speak pretty much effortlessly when typing my words rather than when I'm trying to speak them. When Art and I would get in our little tiffs, it wasn't uncommon for me to go silent vocally, then work things out with him over text messages, even if I was just in the next room.

Call it childish, immature, whatever. But there is just something in me that cuts off my ability to speak with my actual voice sometimes. Yet as soon as my fingers hit the keys, all the words in my head align, and I'm able to get everything I want to say across in an articulate and eloquent way. Some people would call me a keyboard warrior, but that's not true. Keyboard warriors are jerks who would never say the shit to someone's face that they're only brave enough to say with the knowledge they'll never meet them in person. I am not a troll. Anything I say with my fingers on keys, I wouldn't hesitate to print out and read aloud to the person's face.

When the circle on my screen finally closes, indicating the very second my picture is uploaded and my profile has been published to the site, the little envelope icon at the top of the page immediately dings with three messages. I click on it and see the first one is a welcome message from the site. The other two are from male members who couldn't have had the chance to do anything but see my photo.

"If they even saw that. They could have it set up to auto-send a message to any new profiles. Or maybe the ones that fit a specific browsing criteria," I murmur, my lip curled in disgust. I immediately click the Xs next to both of their names, getting the heebs at the idea of being just another random profile amidst thousands.

Call me old fashioned, but I at least want to feel a little bit special.

"Is it too much to ask for someone to at least read my About Me before they send me a message asking what I'm up to tonight?" I ask my cat, Kronk, as he comes out from where he was hiding and hops up on the couch next to me. He allows me three swipes of my hand from his head to the end of his tail before he bats me away and curls up on the pillow. "Already, I've got a sour taste in my mouth, and I haven't even been on the site for thirty seconds."

I know some women would be thrilled to have gotten results so quickly, but for me, I feel only bitterness. Which is strange, because I didn't even feel bitter toward my ex-husband when we decided to get a divorce. So to get the sour taste out of my mouth, I take another sip of my wine, discovering I must've been drinking it without consciously doing so, because I have to tilt it way back in order to get the last ounce from the bottom of the glass.

Without looking away from my screen as I start scrolling through the browsing options, I reach over and grab the wine bottle next to me. I have to stop scrolling in order to unscrew the cap and pour myself another glass, this one not as full as the last one, being careful since my laptop is open. With my glass in hand, I decide to start narrowing down my search just for fun. I choose that I am only interested in males, and I slide the scale for the person to be at least my age but don't pick a limit for how old.

Because certainly someone too old wouldn't know how to use one of these sites to begin with, right?

I narrow the radius to twenty-five miles, which will include a few of the surrounding small towns along with the one I live in, because I have a feeling if I were to choose the smallest radius, which is five miles, then the only people who would show up are my neighbors. And while I'm kind of curious to see if any of them are on a sugar daddy site, I could really go without any of them trying to pick me up when I plan on living here for the foreseeable future.

Surprisingly, in the twenty-five mile cluster of small

towns, there are 108 profiles within the confines of my filters. As I scroll, I'm relieved that I don't recognize anyone in the profile pictures. However, forty percent of the photos are dick pics, which means I would have a very small chance of recognizing them by their profile picture anyway, unless they happen to be members of Club Alias *and* have an astoundingly recognizable cock.

Like that one guy who has a Jacob's ladder piercing, barbells going all the way up his massive ten-inch schlong.

And if a penis is that recognizable, I would have to be very desperate in order to contact them for a date. Because if I can distinguish a penis from it being so highly recognizable, then that penis has been around the block. It has made its rounds. And while I don't mind a man having a very high number of past sexual partners—no slut shaming from this "porn" author—I would prefer any cock I'm interested in to not have been in a countless number of people I know.

"Why do men think that a woman would rather see a picture of their cock instead of their face?" I turn to ask my cat.

Sure, maybe down the road, after we've spoken for a while, I might be more open-minded if a guy were to send me a photo *that included his member with the rest of his body*. But I don't ever see myself wanting a photo just of someone's beans and wiener. To me, there is nothing attractive about a screen full of just cock and balls. If the image happens to be a full frontal, including a muscular torso and nice manly legs, I might be able to swallow it—snort—a little more easily. But again, not until I've gotten to know him at least for a little while.

Somebody's penis doesn't have nearly a high-enough percentage of importance to me when choosing a man to spend time with, for me to give a shit about your dick-pic-taking skills. How big or small you are won't interest me in the slightest if you can't even greet me with some level of intelligence. The design of your manscaping will have no effect on my lady garden if the second you open up a conversation with me, I want to shoot you with mosquito spray.

With my profile complete and no one really catching my eye after clicking through the pages that did not include a dick pic, I decide putting all my eggs in one basket isn't a good idea. After all, there are people on Instagram who refuse to create a TikTok account. There are TikTokkers who left Facebook. And there are people who still stick with Facebook as their one and only social media. So I might as well dive in to the deep end and see what a few of the other sites have to offer.

Making it easy on myself, I copy the About Me from my first profile and use it to make the process much faster while creating the new ones, using the same screenname on each one to keep it simple. If someone happens to see me on multiple dating sites, it's not like they can say anything bad about it, since they're obviously on them too.

While I'm at it, I also create a new profile on Fetlife separate from the one I've had for years. All the friends I've made on the social media site for fellow kinksters were found while I was married, and all the photos and posts and general information about me on that profile revolves around that relationship. I haven't been on it since the divorce. All the groups I'm a member of don't even pertain to me any longer. I'm not that person anymore. I shouldn't have even tried to be to begin with.

That's not true. I was doing my best to be a good wife and a good submissive, to give my husband, my Dom, what he needed. But instead of completely losing myself in order to be who Art needed, with Doc's guidance, we chose to go our separate ways. It was a mature decision that was best for everyone, and while it was sad our marriage came to an end, we got what we needed from each other.

Not everyone is meant to come into your life and stay to the end of it. Some people enter your world, perform their purpose—whatever they're meant to teach you about life—and then once they complete that task, they leave. I learned so much from Art, and we're still very good friends. But things were stagnant as far as our marriage goes, and not the kind that just needs a little spice added. There wasn't really anything to rekindle. We were more roommates than anything, especially at the end, when I let him play with a true masochist, a sub who *needed* the sadism Art could provide.

Seeing the relief and joy on her face, and seeing not only those same emotions on Art's but also the pure erotic pleasure he couldn't disguise—I knew I'd never be able to make him feel that way. And I didn't want to. If the only way to make him feel such bliss was to take the pain the other sub took that night, there was no way in hell I was ever going to be the one to do that. Ain't no fucking way.

He drew blood with the dragon tail whip. And the more he broke her skin, the more desperately she begged for more, tears streaming down her face as her eyes met mine at the edge of the scene, mouthing her thank-yous to me over and over.

Welts? Hickies? Scratches? Handprints? Bruises so deep they turn black and blue? Fine. In fact, totally hot. Even bitemarks make me wet. But the second you draw blood...

I'm out.

That girl? I have no idea how she could even sit for the next two weeks while her ass and thighs healed from what I would've found torturous.

But it was at the end of that scene I finally understood what a relationship between a true sadist and a true masochist could be like. She needed that pain the way that I need to please people.

Not giving her that pain would be the same as telling me I'm not allowed to comfort someone.

Not making her bleed equated to someone hatefully snapping at me that they don't want or need my help.

I don't know that sub's life story. Doc linked us up with her when we agreed to try his experiment, to allow Art to fully give in to his sadism and release it as much as he could, to see if it really was what he needed, since he'd never been able to before. Not that far—not with me. But whatever that young woman went through in life to make her crave such physical pain, it made my heart ache for her. And then the ache went away when I saw how far gone into subspace she floated. I could only hope those moments in heaven were worth whatever she'd experienced in her past.

I blink back to the present and decide I'll take my time and great pleasure in setting up my new Fetlife profile. With so many options to choose from as far as sex, sexual orientation, relationship, and D/s relationship statuses, it makes one deep-dive into their own mind and really think about who they are and who they *want* to be. And on this site, it makes it easy to just say "fuck it" and put it out there, be who and whatever you want. If I so desired, I have the option to say I'm an asexual unicorn in a relationship with The Universe as its pig boy.

Instead, I choose the ones that feel true to myself. Straight, unowned female. I pick submissive, although I'm surprised to discover there are other options that are quite… titillating as I think about applying them to me as I read down the list.

- Dominant
- Domme
- Switch
- Submissive
- Master
- Mistress

- Slave
- Kajira
- Kajiras
- Top
- Bottom
- Sadist
- Masochist
- Sadomasochist
- Disciplinarian
- Kinkster
- Fetishist
- Swinger
- Hedonist
- Sensualist
- Exhibitionist
- Voyeur
- Daddy
- Mommy
- Caregiver
- Babygirl
- Babyboy
- Ageplayer
- Little
- Middle
- Big
- Brat
- Princess
- Slut

- Doll
- Toy
- Cougar
- Bull
- Hotwife
- Stag
- Vixen
- Cuckoldress
- Cuckold
- Cuckquean
- Feminizer
- Sissy
- Furry
- Pet
- Kitten
- Pup
- Pony
- Handler
- Primal
- Primal Predator
- Primal Prey
- Spanko
- Spanker
- Spankee
- Rigger
- Rope Top
- Rope Bottom
- Rope Bunny

- Rubberist
- Leatherman
- Leatherwoman
- Leather Daddy
- Leather Mommy
- Leather Top
- Leather Bottom
- Leather Boy
- Leather Girl
- Leather Boi
- Bootblack
- Drag King
- Drag Queen
- Evolving
- Exploring
- Vanilla
- Undecided

Princess? I wonder what that means exactly. It makes me think she receives only pleasure with no punishments. While that seems amazing at the moment, it would get boring fast. I want to be appreciated, not babied. I want to be coddled by a big, strong alpha when I don't feel good or my feelings are hurt, giving me the sense I'm extra protected and cared for, but not all the time. I want to be the one doing most of the pampering.

Primal prey? That one makes me shiver excitedly. The thought of some... Gym-Daddy-looking man chasing after me, easily catching up to me and tackling me to the ground, tearing my clothes from my body and taking me right there, all growly and delicious above me? Fuck.

"That would give anyone a wetty," I tell Kronk, who sighs and rolls to his other side to face away from me. The cat is obviously over my shit.

Other things make me pause, wondering what the hell they could be. A spanko? A middle? A rubberist? What— like that person in the all-black Latex catsuit in the first season of *American Horror Story* who keeps showing up in the sex-addict husband's dreams?

Nope, so not me, but I definitely admit to using my vibrator a time or three while watching that show.

Evan Peters.

Nuff said.

I'm just about to Google what boi specifically spelled with an -i means when my computer makes a noise I've never heard before, making me jump. With wide eyes, I check my tabs across the top of the screen and see one of them is flashing with a notification. It's the one still open with the first site I signed up for, and since it's been about an hour now that I've been creating all these other profiles, I decide to check this message with a more open mind.

The photo is thankfully of a man's smiling face. He's not what I would call handsome, but he's not ugly by any means. He has one of those completely average faces that wouldn't stand out to you until you got to know him as a person, before it would fall into either the hot or not side of the equation. I click on the message, and right off, I can tell he actually took the time to read my information.

Good evening, if you find this soon after I send it. I just came across your profile, and I'd love to get to know more about you. I've never met an author before. What kind of books do you write? And I see you're only looking for friendship. Do you mean to meet people and start out as friends that could eventually grow into more, or are you here ONLY to do research?

Hope to hear from you.

I sigh, a little irked that the first question was the dreaded "what kind of books do you write?" that almost all romance authors hate answering. The response we get after people find out goes one of two ways: either the person is super excited, because they're a romance reader—highly unlikely when it's a male—or there's a sliding scale of negativity that ranges from a snide "what, like *Fifty Shades?*" to pure hostility, blaming our genre for women's "unrealistic expectations" in men. I always love shutting down that last one by letting them know that all my books are based in reality as far as the heroes and sex goes, and that the only fictional parts of my stories are the suspenseful thriller-like plots.

The second question doesn't bother me, since my profile doesn't make the answer clear. I kept it vague on purpose. I go to his page to check him out, because how hypocritical would it be if I don't take the time to read what he reveals about himself.

Single. 42. Spent his twenties and thirties building his business and focusing on his career and realized life is passing him by. Now looking for someone to spend time with to share everything he's worked so tirelessly for.

I guess instead of the classic "I want someone to honestly fall in love with me for me, not because I'm rich" thing, he took the opposite fork in the road and said "fuck it, I ain't got time for that." At least he knows whoever he picks is also being honest about why they're here, instead of always having to wonder.

I type a response that will leave the ball in his court. If he has a knee-jerk reaction to respond in any negative way toward my life's work and actually sends it, then the guy isn't very intelligent and has no game. An easy way to tell within the first correspondences if he's worth my time.

> **Hi there ☺ I write romantic suspense novels. For now, I'm just doing research, but if I happen to meet someone I really click with while I'm at it, then that would be a happy outcome for all my hard work lol!**

His reply is quick, and I'm pleasantly surprised by the positivity in his message.

Romantic suspense sounds interesting. Is that like… a mystery novel but with a love story? What kind of research are you needing to do for your next book?

I make a freaked-out face, feeling put on the spot about the research. But as I get my thoughts in order and let the wine loosen up the tension I've felt since writer's block set in nine months ago, the answers to his questions seem simple. Especially since I took the time to write all my ideas down on a digital sticky note.

Plant Daddy. My next book is called Plant Daddy, and it's about a woman who joins a sugar daddy dating site to find someone to fund her expensive plant addiction. And yes, that's exactly what my genre is. Good guess!

Ah, that sounds like a fun story. Is plant code for something? Like… 420-friendly?

I have no idea what the hell he's talking about, so I open another tab to google what that last phrase means.

"Oooh… duh. Well that makes sense," I say aloud, feeling a little dumb that I didn't make that correlation before my last message.

Ha! No. Not marijuana. Like... houseplants. There are variegated monsteras that go for over $400, and that's just for one rooted cutting!

I send before thinking about whether he's going to understand a word that just came out of my fingers. But if he does, that would be a good sign, right? If he speaks plant language?

I didn't realize regular old flowers and bushes could be so expensive. I have a couple of ZZs, and they never die as long as I remember to water them every couple of months. Lol!

I wilt a little that he doesn't speak my language like I hoped. But to be fair, I didn't understand any of it before a few months ago either, so I can't be too judgey.

Albos are so NOT regular flowers or bushes. You know those big green leaves with the slits in them that are printed on all sorts of shirts and pillows and such? That's a monstera. Very common. But the albos are variegated, a mutation that makes it not just solid green. They're green and white, and a lot of the little bastards like to revert to a solid green after a while. They're slow-growing, which means they take a long time to propagate. Which

also means demand for them is high and their availability is low.

"God, I'm such a nerd. Talk about not having any game." I roll my eyes at myself.

After a solid five minutes with no reply, I figure I lost him with my lesson in botany, so I click back to my Fetlife profile.

I go ahead and click the Save button, deciding I can always go in and add stuff to my page whenever I want. I'm curious to jump in to the search bar to see what my fellow kinksters have to say about these dating sites.

After falling down a couple of rabbit holes, I discover a few of the sites I joined earlier are not the kind of place I want to do research nor meet new people—marked only as hook-up sites, a place for people who want sexual encounters with no interest in getting to know the other person. Which also makes the sugar daddy aspect seem way too much like prostitution, so I jump back onto those sites and terminate my profiles. Then I go into my new email address's inbox and click the Unsubscribe button on those sites as well so I don't get confused.

Back on Fetlife, I find a couple sites that had not popped up in my Google searches, and also a few dating apps, including one that's specifically for people in the alternate lifestyle community. A lot of the members commenting about the app had great success and are still in relationships with the people they met on it. And although this particular app has nothing to do with the research I'm doing on sugar babies and daddies, I can't help but feel excitement over a safe place for my likeminded people to mingle openly.

After seeing there's no way to join it on my computer, I grumble as I grab my phone and go to the App Store to download Feeld. I go through the same process as before, filling out the form and making my profile. When I'm in, I go to the menu to start my exploration.

I've never been on Tinder, seeing as I've been married the last decade, and it came out after I was off the market. But everything I've heard about it reminds me of what I'm seeing on this app. It says it's going to show me profiles one by one, and either I can click the heart to indicate I'm interested in the person, or I click the minus sign to say I'm not. Or I can just swipe through all of them without choosing either button, just to see what's out there.

This app is also proximity-based. It shows people who are within whatever parameters you set, starting with the ones who are closest to you, and it actually tells you how many miles away they are. On all the other sites, you could narrow down your search by location, but the closest it would tell you was ten miles. This app seems to me like a good way to accidentally run into people you know. So surely people on here wouldn't be anyone who wants to keep their identity secret. Otherwise, they're running a big risk of someone they know easily coming across their profile with a simple swipe of a finger.

I glance up to see my inbox icon bouncing at the bottom

of the laptop screen. I set down the phone next to my magically empty wine glass and lean forward to open my mail. "What... the fuck?" I breathe, seeing there are at least a hundred new emails from users on all the different sites I joined. "What the hell did I sign up for?"

Chapter Seven

FELIX

My silenced phone lights up with a notification as it sits on my desk next to a stack of notebooks. While all of our charts and paperwork at the hospital have been consolidated to only electronic now, with patients filling out forms on an iPad handed to them instead of a clipboard of papers and a pen, I still prefer to make my own notes by hand.

It's not that I need them that way in order to refer back to them, but just the process of writing things down helps me remember them. Not a day goes by that I don't create a list or schedule out my time on paper. It's just how my brain works.

Seeing the orange icon for the Feeld app, I ignore the notification for now. Nothing ever comes from that venture into online dating. There had been one promising contact I made a while back, but she was all the way up in Raleigh nearly two hours away. And while I have my search results and my location set to be beyond our small town and the surrounding area on purpose, in an attempt to stay off the radar of anyone who might know me, two hours away would make it nearly impossible to have any type of real relationship.

While I've lost the hope of ever finding a submissive to collar and own 24/7—which to me would mean actually falling in love with a woman who would not only be my perfectly obedient sub but also my partner in life to spoil—it hasn't kept me from seeing what's out there in the vanilla world as myself.

When I first found the Feeld app, I had a feeling it was too good to be true. A dating app specifically for people who have similar desires and needs as my own? No having to find a way to bring up the subject of BDSM and how they feel about it?

Sure, there are plenty of posers on there, women who saw certain movies or read fictional books about the lifestyle and suddenly think they want to jump in headfirst to become someone's submissive. Nine times out of ten, they realize they just want some kinky sex every once in a while to liven things up. They have no idea what it means to be someone's full-time slave. But if they're on the app, I'd know I'd be in contact with women who at least have some knowledge of what they might be getting into, what might be expected in the bedroom.

Because surely you wouldn't join a dating site specifically

for kinksters if all you want is vanilla sex. That's what all the other sites are for.

Yes, it was risky, creating a profile as if it were on any other dating site. A quick selfie I took in my gym's parking lot before I headed to work as the main photo. I felt I had been in the BDSM community long enough to know there wasn't anyone local who knew me who would be on that specific app.

Anyone who knows me as a Dom has no clue who I am outside the club. I've taken tedious measures to make sure I can't be identified while I'm there.

It's why I haven't yet taken the steps to join the club's social media site one of the owners, Seth, created. Which I know would make it a hell of a lot easier to find someone single and looking, who lives the lifestyle, but the idea of my identity coming to light by revealing it to *anyone* at Club Alias keeps me from jumping in. Let the wrong person in on my secret, and it could mean the end of my career.

But more than anything, I'm not willing to risk losing Club Alias as my place of refuge.

As it stands, I have plenty of play partners at the club to keep me entertained for a lifetime. None of them know who I am in real life. I know this for a fact, because a couple of them have come into my ER. Neither of them showed any indication they knew I was the one who had them hogtied to a Sybian just the week before, or that I was the person who gave them the huge bruise on their ass they were being careful of sitting on when they came in for a cut on their finger that required stitches.

It's a heady feeling, powerful, knowing I'm completely anonymous at the club. I can be exactly who I want to be without the fear of judgement, without the worry of discrimination because of my alternative lifestyle. The black long-sleeved shirt, the black joggers that are actually scrub bottoms, the black hood and mask, the black leather fingerless gloves—not a single inch of me is recognizable. Especially when a ton of the Doms wear the exact same uniform for similar reasons.

So to take a chance of getting to know someone from the club and the relationship going south... the thought of her being able to so easily ruin everything I've worked so hard for in my life... it's enough to make me continue living my double life without a second's hesitation.

The vanilla world isn't educated on BDSM enough for me to be able to live openly as a Dominant. That word to a sickening percentage of people is synonymous with predator —and not the "Primal Predator" I identify as in our community, but the other kind. The kind who send innocents to my ER for me to do my best to fix. Those victims and survivors who are required to be sent to my friend Dr. Neil Walker to fix their minds that have been broken by psychopathic, sadistic bastards with no soul.

Not to be confused with sadists within our community— one can be a true sadist and still be safe, sane, and consensual. But *they* still have their conscience. They still have their heart and soul, their morals. They care about the masochist who is taking their sadism, if not romantically, then at least in a humane way.

At Club Alias, the masochists—people who derive sexual pleasure from *receiving* pain—can let go of all their inhibitions and trust that they are safe within those walls. The vetting process every single member is put through assures that even the ones who score 100% on the scale for Sadist— a person who derives sexual pleasure from *inflicting* pain— are of sane and sound mind; they're not there under false pretenses. Within the minimum of four therapy sessions, Doc always catches the slightest inconsistency or secret darkness someone tries to hide.

He's the one person at the club I never tried to hide my identity from. We've been colleagues for decades now. Went to med school together. He played a huge part in helping me realize who I am. People have always, always looked to me for guidance—even when I was just a kid and something chaotic happened, other kids would look to see what I was doing, how I would react first, instead of immediately panicking. But he's the one who helped me put two and two together that a Dominant isn't made. It's just who you are. One can learn to be a dominant person, whether at work being a boss or in a bedroom, topping their sexual partner. But a true Dominant… it's just who that person is right down to their very marrow, even without necessarily meaning to be.

Before Doc helped me become the D-type I am today,

way back before I knew anything about BDSM, my Dominance ruled every decision. Those kids who looked to me for guidance gave me the courage and confidence to take on the leadership role they placed me in without missing a beat. But I was always in the gifted classes—not being conceited, I was just born with a higher than average IQ—so I really thought about the consequences and outcomes of each and every choice before making a decision, especially when other people were looking up to me, counting on me.

It's also why my first job was as a firefighter. Yes, I probably could've done some incredible things with the opportunities my level of intelligence opened up for me, but becoming a firefighter called to something inside me. Peter Parker's uncle told him "With great power comes great responsibility." My power at that time was my IQ mixed with my Dominance. And what made me feel the most useful, the most helpful, was being a fireman, where making quick decisions with a clear mind was the difference between life and death for countless people, including myself in most rescues.

Then from there, I became an EMT, then leveled up to paramedic, then so on and so forth until I found myself years later shaking hands with the head of the hospital, when I signed on as their newest full-fledged medical doctor. And since that Dominance inside me never waned, never even took a step back, only got stronger and better and wiser, it's how I ended up where I am today, the head of the number-one emergency room in the state. If someone is hurt, they will risk life and limb to get to my ER, even if they'll pass several others on their way.

So to be associated with *the other* kind of predator just because of the control I desire over my *consensual* sexual partner and the need I have inside me to use her body in ways she never even considered before....

That's why I refuse to let anyone know the real me. On either side of the equation. The vanilla world who knows Felix, the medical doctor, has no idea of my sexual preferences. The BDSM community I hold so dear to me, they have no clue I'm the doctor who fixes them up in the emergency room at our local hospital. And on top of all that, no one knows I'm also the guy who works part-time at the home improvement store. Which at first was because I wanted to learn how to build certain things by surrounding myself with people who knew how, plus the bonus of a great employee discount. It just seemed logical to my logic-seeking mind.

But now I stay out of my need to fill time not spent at the hospital.

Because if I don't fill at least some of that time, it will be spent submersed in the other me, the real me. And I'm afraid if I'm allowed to linger too long in that mindset, I won't be able to keep the two people inside me separate any longer. I won't be able to stand living this double life anymore. It'll be self-sabotage, and I'll make my own life implode by being greedy, wanting to just be who I truly am all the time, when that's impossible. And it would be selfish of me to take away the doctor the people of this town needs in that ER just because I want to live openly as a Dom.

If only our culture was portrayed the way it *can* be—loving, healing, therapeutic, the greatest pleasure that can ever be felt by a human, both body and soul—instead of the dirty and taboo way it's shown in mainstream media and porn for shock value.

Maybe then, when a vanilla mom bringing her child in for their broken arm somehow finds out the doctor lives an alternate lifestyle, her first thought, her immediate worry, wouldn't be that they might be a pedophile.

Maybe then, if someone in a blissfully happy marriage that happens to consist of more than just two people, or consists of something other than a cis man and woman, other people's minds wouldn't instantly picture them in their bed. They'd meet their spouse or spouses or significant others and picture them the same way they do any other "normal" marriage—maybe sitting at their dinner table, or what their wedding might've been like, or what their kids might look like by combining their features.

If only more people had a brain like mine, with its touch of "mental illness." Then they'd be able to see reality without the haze of societal norms skewing their vision.

My phone lights up with another notification, pulling me out of my bitter thoughts. This time, it's an email, but as I pick up the cell, I can't ignore the orange icon below it on the screen. The what-if is enough to make me read the message preview instead of swiping it away without a second glance.

**You've received a 🩶 from someone within
2 miles of your current location.**

"Two miles? Jesus," I murmur, my heart speeding up with both worry it might be someone I know and the enticing possibility it could be someone I don't. I check my settings to see if my location got switched from the zip code I put in that's thirty miles away. Nope, it's still set, but there's fine print beneath it that says it lets me know the exact distance someone is by using my actual location, yet it won't tell the other person. Their end only shows the location you manually set if that's what you chose as your privacy.

"If it's someone you know, you can always say you thought this was just another Tinder," I say, even though I'm totally lying to myself. I had to choose what I was interested in from a multiple choice list. Obviously, my picks of kink, bdsm, foreplay, singles, and submissives would give me away.

But I can't stand the suspense any longer though, so I open up the app and click on the full message.

**You've received a 🩶 from someone within
2 miles of your current location.
Swipe through profiles and choose either (-) or 🩶
to see if you match up!**

**But don't worry. They won't be notified if you did
not choose to 🤍 them too.
Happy swiping!**

I've thumbed through this app so many times with no change in profiles that I'm pretty sure I'll be able to spot any new addition, especially since it shows how far away they are. Which reminds me....

I go into my *search* settings and switch the parameters to include people within a few miles, and then I move back to the home screen to start swiping. It's the same ole profiles I saw before I switched up my settings to show only people out of town. A swinger couple looking for a third or another couple. The same couple, but instead of it saying Male, it's a different profile with Female chosen. Different profiles women set up that are more for directing men to their Only-Fans accounts than to actually meet people to date.

Swipe. No.

Swipe. No.

Swipe. No.

Swipe. No.

I sigh as I just start swiping quickly without waiting to choose either the minus button or the heart.

Swipe.

Swipe.

Swipe.

Swipe.

Swi—

Wait.

I blink, my brow furrowing. Surely my mind is playing tricks on me.

I swipe again, but in the opposite direction, bringing back the profile that certainly doesn't actually exist. It's a figment of my imagination.

Seriously.

There's no fucking way.

But there is. She's right there, smiling back at me from the screen. When I can pull my eyes away from her face, then away from her body that's hardly recognizable in the green-leaf-covered mini dress—since the last time I saw it, it was covered in filthy black leggings and a hoodie that had seen better days—I look down at her username.

WillDive4Plants.

I don't even realize I'm grinning until my own laugh startles me in my quiet office.

What are the fucking odds?

It's the little hippy I rescued from the dumpster last week. I also know she's a member of Club Alias, since she never wears a mask and I've seen her several times over the years. But she's always been with a man, her husband I assumed, whenever I saw her at the edge of a public scene done in the common area of the club. She always watches so intently, as if studying them like a living, breathing work of art on display in a studio. And getting to see her reactions without the obstruction of a mask made her a rarity and hard to forget, especially her physiological responses when it's one of Sir Jeremy's scenes she's observing.

It's how I recognized her the very first time I saw her climbing into the dumpster. It's why I felt an odd sense of protectiveness over her while she did her thing, rescuing the plants. She's not only a woman, which automatically sets off my desire to keep her safe, but she's a true submissive. And while submissives are fucking badass, seeing as they hold all the power and are the ones *allowing* us Dominants to do what we wish to them, one does not become a submissive "just for funzies," as Seth so eloquently put it during one of his training sessions. There's always, always a psychological reason a person *is* a submissive. Like a Dominant, they can be submissive by nature, but to become *a sub*, as in within the BDSM lifestyle, I've never once come across one who *isn't* that way or in that role as a trauma response.

Therefore, ever since I learned more about the psychology of different kinks and identities in the community, I've been incredibly protective over submissives—female *or* male, doesn't matter.

I'm a Dominant through and through. It's just who I am. A natural-born leader who decided to lean in to my gifts instead of rebelling against them. Someone with my nature could easily use our "powers" for evil, but with my upbringing, I didn't have the luxury of making a bad choice that I could learn from and do better later. I knew I wouldn't have time to do penance for wrongdoings and have a character arc where I'd turn my life around. It was either do the right thing from the start, or the people who counted on me would be fucked. And there's no way I could let anything happen to my siblings when they were "blessed" with the same parents I was.

I snap myself out of those thoughts and focus on the screen in my hand. Now that I have access to her that's not just by chance, I feel an eagerness to learn more about the woman like I haven't felt in a long time.

WillDive4Plants
34 ~ Female ~ Straight
Single
I'm a bestselling BDSM romance author doing research for my next novel about a woman in her 30s who joins a dating site. I haven't been on one of these things in almost 15 years, so here I am, only here to see if anything has changed!
Desires below indicate things I'd like to interview other kinksters about.
Desires: friendship, bdsm, texting, kink, dominant, submissive

An author. Artistic-minded. Doing research. It explains so much about why it always felt like she was watching scenes at the club so closely. It makes me wonder if she used specific things she saw in one of her books. Did she picture the ones that I saw made her cheeks and chest flush red and her breaths speed up, as she wrote her bestselling stories?

The mere idea makes me hard.

I have the urge to dig until I find her books just to see if I can pick out the different nights at the club that inspired her. Because I can remember the way she pulled her bottom lip between her teeth as she watched Sir Jeremy tie the intricate knots of the harness created out of rope. I can still see her reddening chest rising and falling quickly as she panted for breath when the Magic Wand was attached to the harness and flipped on low.

I know from experience what it's like to be on that stage. What would it be like to have her eyes on *me*, whether from the crowd or up there with me? When I do a public scene, I like to stand back for a moment with my head tilted downward, my hood falling forward to hide my eyes that fixate on the audience, being the center of their attention taking my arousal even higher.

Though I have to hide my identity, I'm an exhibitionist —I like being watched. Maybe it's because I've always been put into a leadership position, so I just got used to eyes being on me. I've never been self-conscious, and not just because I take care of my body and understand I'm above average in attractiveness. Again, not being conceited, it's just a fact. Not only because I've been told so by people of all sexes my entire life, but because my features are near-perfect in symmetry, which scientifically registers as attractive in the human mind. But I've also never been self-conscious because, although I wasn't diagnosed when I was a child— Mom didn't care enough about us to take us to the doctor unless we were basically dying—I've heard more times than I can count that I'm definitely on the spectrum. And that's coming from colleagues whose job it is to recognize it. Most commonly known as Asperger Syndrome, it's now referred to as autism spectrum disorder, and I'm on the "high-functioning" end of the scale. It's hard for me to understand societal norms, and the part of one's brain that controls modesty just… got locked in the off position, I guess.

Things people pick up on easily that are "PC," I get stuck on, questioning them. Where most people can just go with the flow, do things "just because" that's how they're "supposed" to do something or act, I have to consciously make an effort to do those things if they don't make sense to me. People with Asperger's are quicker to see the lack of logic and even the unfairness in certain rules, which makes it harder to follow them just because they're rules.

I also do *this*… start with one thought and then end up somewhere else in my mind entirely, just like I do in conversations too. And while that's attributed to my ADHD, the ASD is to blame for how I rarely meet people's eyes. Mine flit around, not focusing on anything in particular because I'm usually looking inward, inside my head. And it's also to blame for how I've never quite perfected the art of initiating and leaving a conversation fluidly. I insert myself when I probably shouldn't, and I stay quiet when someone might normally speak up. But the latter has more to do with the fact that I don't have much of a filter and can come off blunt or rude, or even straight-up mean without doing it on purpose. So I've learned throughout my fifty years that sometimes it's better for me to stay completely silent and cut myself off from talking in that moment, until I can really think about what I want to say. Because you can't un-say things.

This is actually one of my quirks that made my colleagues give me their expert opinion without my asking. I have the ability to literally stab someone—or whip them, pierce them, choke them out, whatever—without feeling bad about it whatsoever if it's what they want, because I have the knowledge and capability to fix pretty much any physical wound. It makes me sound a little sociopathic, but I just don't feel empathy when it comes to physical pain. Especially when it's a masochist who's begged me for it.

Now, if I accidentally hurt a sub with a miss-swing or by being a bit too rough, I feel what I suppose is guilt, maybe shame that I wasn't more careful and didn't read my sub's cues well enough.

But what sets me apart from a sociopath—someone who has no conscience—is if I wound someone with my words, hurt their feelings, then *that's* when I feel bad. Like really, really bad. Because someone's emotions and mind are so much harder to heal than a physical wound. If I break someone down, I can't just sterilize them, spread some antibacterial ointment over them, and slap on a bandage. I can't just prescribe them some medication that'll take care of it in a week. You can't take back words once you speak them out loud. You can say you didn't mean them; you can apologize profusely. But once the other person hears what you've spoken, they can't erase it from their ears and mind.

Which, again, is why I choose to go silent sometimes, so I don't hurt people. And again with societal norms, "the silent treatment" is classified as either immature or can drive someone crazy if they want to talk something through. With nearly five decades under my belt, being called immature for anything is pretty annoying. But proving to someone my silence is much preferred over what could come out of my mouth always ends up with them in tears or severely pissed off, so I've learned to just deal with the annoyance. It feels less shitty than the guilt and shame.

My eyes come back into focus to see my screen has gone dark on my phone, so I tap it and swipe up to unlock it, where the picture of the pretty hippy is still up.

Do I heart her profile?

God, I want to.

But it's a risk in so many ways. She's seen my face now. So if we start getting to know each other, she could recognize me out in public. Hell, if she has an emergency, she'd come to my hospital. If she didn't come across me here, she could at least spot my photo on the wall next to the registration desk. Right now, she doesn't know my name. I'm only a face and a username with a short bio that doesn't give anything away.

I could click the minus sign, and she'd never even see my profile again. It would take me out of her search results completely. And unless for some reason she screenshot my picture—which, hell, I don't even know for sure she's the one who hearted me—then I doubt she'd be able to pick me out of a lineup just from glancing at my photo one time on a dating app.

But I don't *want* to hit the minus sign.

It's her. The little hippy who makes me smile just by rambling to herself while I listen outside the dumpster without her knowing it. The woman who fit so perfectly snug against me when I held her in my lap while I checked out her hand after she caught a fucking cactus and refused to let it go. The one who looked at me like I was a goddamn superhero before and after I fixed her up. And most memorably, she's the one who stirred up all those forgotten desires I had of ever one day collaring and owning a submissive who completes me. The other half of my soul. My perfect match.

No, not a match. I don't want someone who is the same as me. I want the other gear that goes with mine to complete our set, the one whose teeth fit just right between mine so that when one of us starts to move, the other does in perfect synchrony. Working together—not two of a kind, and not opposite either. Because while the age-old adage of "opposites attract" might be exciting in the beginning, later on down the road, once that initial exhilaration wears off, you'll want to have at least some of the same interests as your partner. Either that or you won't have *anything* in common, nothing that you both enjoy doing together. Then what's the point of the relationship at all?

"Let's think this through. Let's think this through," I murmur, trying to get my thoughts in order. "If I click the heart, it will immediately tell me if we matched up, if she *is* the one who hearted my profile. She won't know anything about me, not even my name. She won't know I'm a doctor. I'll just be some random guy on a dating app for kinksters. There's no way she can possibly know that I'm also a member of Club Alias." I take a deep breath and let it out slow, nodding as that train of thought makes me feel more secure about giving in to my urge to link up with her.

And then what?

"And then," I answer the internal question, "since she'll know what I look like, if we keep talking, I'll eventually have to tell her who I am. My name, my occupation. She still won't know I'm the employee who got her out of the dumpster, so she never has to find out I know who she is. I'll still be able to stay incognito there, and she also still won't know I'm a Club Alias member. She'll be meeting Dr. Felix Travers, and that's it. If things go south, the worst she could do is tell someone I was on a dating app. In fact...."

I quickly go into my settings and edit my profile so that my desires section only says singles and friendship. So again, as long as she didn't screenshot it before she clicked the heart button, there's no proof that I knew this app was specifically for kinksters.

I'm sure there are plenty of people out there who would think I'm being entirely too paranoid and cautious. They'd think keeping parts of me hidden is being dishonest. But if they went through what I did the one and only time I let a woman into all parts of my life, let her get to know the real me, every side, not just one or the other, then they'd be the same fucking way. Someone doesn't finally put all their trust into one person, have it completely demolished, and come out of it unscathed. And maybe it's unfair to let that shadow be cast over everyone who has and ever will come after her, but I look at it the way I would anything else—a lesson learned from experience.

If I touch a burner on a stove to see if it's hot and it singes my fingers, I wouldn't go back and touch the burner without being more cautious the next time, would I?

No. I might hover my fingers over it, get close enough to feel if there's heat radiating off it first. If there's no danger sensed, I might get a little closer, even tap the coil quickly before snatching them back, allowing the results of that test the time to register in my head. Then and only then, when I know it's safe—truly safe—would I relax enough to really give it a good, long feel with my whole hand.

With all the precautions I can think of lined out, I finally give in to the desire I know I was helpless against the moment I did a double take and saw that smile glowing from my screen.

My heart thudding in my chest, I hold my breath and click the heart button, my stomach bottoming out as if I'm on a roller coaster as the notification window pops up on the screen.

Chapter Eight

SIENNA

It's been a week since I first created the profiles on all the dating sites, and I've learned a lot in those seven days.

The number-one lesson: Being single in the digital age fucking sucks.

How can one feel lonelier with access to so many more people than ever before? It's like everyone has been jaded, become desensitized to taking other people's feelings into consideration because it's behind a screen and "not real-life," and you don't have to actually face the damage you're doing to someone's very real psyche.

They need to change the old saying from *plenty* of fish in the sea to *too many* fish in the sea. Because it's like everyone has taken the saying meant to make you feel better about getting back out there and trying again after heartbreak, and they've twisted it. Now, no one wants to put forth any type of effort to find something meaningful, to start slow, to get to know someone before trying to jump into bed with them.

There are too many fish in the sea, too many opportunities to skip to the "good" part, to cut to the chase. Instead of putting in all the work, they'd rather just copy, paste, copy, paste, copy, paste the same opening message to see how easy they think it'll be to get in someone's pants. Because they know there are people lonely enough, people desperate for any kind of connection, who will take whatever they can get, even if that's just a casual encounter, a meaningless one-night stand.

What's that other saying? Why buy the cow when you can get the milk for free?

I sigh and lean back into my couch cushions, opening the Feeld app on my phone, since I've already gone through all my messages on the sites I can on my laptop. I've talked to quite a few men this week, most of them blocking me the second I told them I was there for research and to actually get to know people and wasn't interested in just jumping into the sack.

I was, however, nicely surprised by a gentleman on the sugar daddy site who didn't question my profile right off the bat. While everyone before him had immediately asked if I'd reconsider what I was on the site for, as if I would see their photo and read their thrown-together About Me and fall so madly in love at first sight that I'd throw everything I believed I wanted right out the window. Because apparently, we little women can't possibly know what we truly need, right? So we should let the big, strong man who makes all the money tell us instead.

Well, guess what, assholes. I make plenty of fucking money on my own…

When I'm not too damn depressed to write.

And I know exactly what I truly need.

For some miracle to happen and for magic to suddenly be real. Then I could write my perfect Dom into existence. Because the men on all these sites… they ain't cuttin' it.

Anyway, whether this one guy really just has great game or if he's being sincere, there's no way to be sure. But I choose to believe there are still chivalrous gentlemen out there, so that's the option I'll go with. He messaged to say he's been on the site for quite some time and to let me know that I would most definitely get lots of messages from men who would ask if I was for real or not. Real, as in an intelligent woman with a career, an author, and if that was my real picture, and also real, as in really only on the site for research. He was correct on both of those counts. He said if I had any specific questions for my book, he'd be glad to answer what he could anonymously. As long as I didn't mention him in the story or the acknowledgments, he'd help with anything I needed to know.

We've had several messages back and forth this week, and when he slipped in one that offered to take things further, it made me smile rather than growl at my computer.

Because it was a respectful baby step and not the giant leap into bed like all the others tried.

> **Just throwing this out there. If you'd be open to asking these questions over coffee, I'd answer them still with the understanding you aren't interested in anything more. My treat, of course. After all, you know what this site was actually created for before it was taken over by the fakes. And I happen to be one of the rare few left who really does just want the company of a beautiful, intellectual woman for an hour or two to have a real and interesting conversation with.**

I'm still not ready to meet up with anyone in person, not even just for coffee. It set off my anxiety just thinking about meeting a complete stranger I'd never laid eyes on before in my life. So I did what I always do when I feel put on the spot but don't want to hurt anyone's feelings.

I made a self-deprecating joke and hardcore evaded the question like a fucking champ.

> **You must be under the impression I'm smart just because I'm an author and read a lot of books. What you must've missed was the fact that I write SMUT, and I have a great editor to fix up all my grammar and punctuation. So you'd probably be disappointed and ask for your money back for the**

coffee if you're really wanting to have an INTEL-LECTUAL conversation. But thank you so much for asking.

He took the rejection like the gentleman he's been the entire week and is still answering any random question I pop on to ask. If he keeps it up, even though I don't find him necessarily attractive from his photos, I think I'd be down to meet him for coffee eventually. Who knows, maybe there'd be tons of chemistry in person that I just can't feel through the computer screen. After all, I haven't felt even the slightest attraction to *any* of the men on these sites, so it could be possible I don't *have* that ability.

But when I decide to go into the settings of my Feeld app and finally try expanding the distance from ten miles up to thirty, I know that's not the case—I most definitely have that ability—the very moment I click on the search results.

I gasp and jerk back from my phone, which is pointless, because my head is already up against the couch.

"Holy shit. Holy fucking shit!" I squawk, glancing over at my cat with wide eyes, but he's so used to my outbursts he doesn't even open his to see what I'm freaking out over. So I turn back to my cell, reaching out blindly for my wine glass before guzzling down the rest of the sweet liquid courage.

Staring back at me from the screen, even if he is wearing silver thin-framed sunglasses with reflective blue lenses, is my freaking gym crush!

I let out a sigh, deflating closer to my phone, and it feels almost like he's here in person, since I've never actually seen him in such detail in real life. Always somewhat from afar unless he happens to be hurrying past me on the gym floor or out the door. And as powerful as all those quick glimpses were, they were nothing compared to this. My breathing has halted as I take in every detail of his devastatingly handsome face.

He must like to play around with his facial hair, since it's different from the last time I saw him, when he had a full, fluffy beard, and the time before that, when he had a goatee. Because in this photo, he's clean-shaven except for a very tidy, super-short salt-and-pepper beard just along his sexy sharp jawline. With no sideburns peeking out from beneath his faded bandana that was likely black at one time, his beard starts just at his earlobes, meeting in the middle of his chin, then grows up to the very edge of his full bottom lip.

He's not exactly smiling, but his face is relaxed, the corners of his lips barely upturned, which makes me inhale deeply, then let it out as yet another dreamy sigh. It's a rare occasion I ever spot a man with a resting pleasant face—the opposite of a resting bitch face. It always seems to me that men relax with an ever-present scowl.

But not my Gym Daddy.

Gym Daddy looks approachable, as if a stranger could ask him a question and he'd be quick to happily respond. Which I've noticed there before, actually. Other men go up to him all the time, everyone seeming to know him, and he always greets them with a friendly smile and an enthusiastic grip of hands.

I hate that his eyes are covered. Getting to see him in high-res is amazing, but the fact that he's wearing sunglasses, denying me the chance to study *all* of his beautiful features, is a fucking tease. I feel edged, like he got me right to the brink of ecstasy, then stole it away with a wicked grin.

And just like edging, it only makes me want more.

Yet the other pictures on his profile aren't even of him, as I click through them. But they most definitely add to the enticement. One is a photo of a nice little home dungeon, a St. Andrew's cross standing proudly in the center.

The other is of a coffee mug that says Romantic Sadist in bold black letters on a white background.

"Fuck," I breathe. "Another sadist." I glance at Kronk, and he must've sensed the rise in my blood pressure or something, because his eyes are actually open, and if I didn't know better, I'd say there's concern in the green orbs. I reach over and stroke between his ears, and he rolls onto his back to use his paws to push my hand away.

See? Knew better.

I click back to the selfie and focus on those upturned lips, my eyes going half-mast as my vivid imagination paints a picture of those lips coming closer as he leans down to press them against mine.

"But a romantic one," I whisper. "Maybe I could handle *his* sadism. He's Gym Daddy, after all."

Without much more thought, before my voices can start up with why I shouldn't, I click the heart next to his name.

And then the panic sets in as if that button was its On switch.

"Oh, God. What the fuck was I thinking?" I shout at Kronk, who has absolutely no words of consolation. In fact, he has no reaction whatsoever. He doesn't even blink. "Can I take it back? Can I find him on the app and undo the heart thingy?"

I hop on my laptop and open Google, then type in the question my cat has no answer for, finding there's no way to go back to Gym Daddy's profile. Apparently, once you either choose the minus sign or the heart, it takes that profile out of the list of ones they show you. They suggest only swiping through the people instead of choosing one of the buttons unless you know for sure whether or not you'd want them to have the ability to message you.

"But!" I turn my face more toward my lazy feline but keep my eyes on the screen to read aloud, "'They don't know you hearted their profile until they heart yours.' So that means he'll never know I marked him with a big ole **YES!** stamp, because he'd have to do the same to me while he's swiping through people on the app. And there ain't no way *that* man will give *this* chick a second glance. Hell, he wouldn't just swipe past me. He'd straight-up click the minus sign."

The thought is both depressing and a relief.

But that thought isn't able to go any further nor spin out

of control, because my phone makes a sound I've never heard from it before.

When I look down at my phone in my lap, I can't believe my fucking eyes yet again.

You've made a match!

I click on the notification, even though I know who the match I've made is, seeing as he's literally the only person I've hearted on the entire app.

Congratulations! RomanticSadist sent you a heart! Since you previously sent them one, that means your ability to message each other has been unlocked. You've taken the first step, now go for it! Start up a conversation now by clicking here.

Before I even have a chance to click on the little envelope icon, it turns red with a numeral 1 in the middle of it.

"I'm gonna pass out," I wheeze, blinking to make the world stop spinning so I can see the message I just opened.

ROMANTICSADIST:

VERY cool that you're an author! So just research? Or more?

WILLDIVE4PLANTS:

Oh holy hell...

"Fuck!" I bark, not meaning to type that out and send it to him. It was supposed to

either be just a thought or spoken aloud to Kronk—both those options to be met with the same response: Silence.

"Think, Sienna. Think, think, think," I tell myself, needing to focus on what to tell this man before he has a chance to read *that* as my only reply to his message. A message that makes me smile even as I panic.

Of course Gym Daddy wouldn't initiate a first conversation like all the douches who have contacted me. No "Hey." No "Pic for pic?" No "Are those real?" And most definitely not an empty message with only a dick pic attached.

His message means he actually *read* my profile.

His message means he read past my occupation to see I was on the app for research.

His message means that, although he saw I said I'm only on here for research, he knows I'm interested in him, seeing as he could only gain the ability to message me if I hearted his profile in the first place. Therefore, the "Or more?" part of his question is forgivable.

The real question now, though, becomes… do I tell him I know who he is? I mean, no, I don't know *who he is*, but I've seen him in real life before. I know he has a membership to the same gym as me, so if he wants to stay incognito on this app like so many of the other guys did on the dating sites, then I run the risk of him blocking me from Go if he knows I could easily approach him in person at any time.

But as I swipe back to see his photo, that pleasantly

relaxed face, and having seen his friendly demeanor with anyone who talks to him at the gym, something in me tells me I should be completely honest with him. Something tells me there's no need to ever lie to this man, not even by omission. So I take a deep breath, close my eyes to line up my words, then begin to type, letting my real personality out, because why the hell not.

WILLDIVE4PLANTS:

> Ok, full disclosure. I've totally drooled over you at our gym before. So if you need to go ahead and block me, I understand 😬

"There," I say, sinking back against the couch cushion as if I just ran a mile. Kronk barely opens one eye, enough to scold me for making him wobble. And then I sit right straight up as my phone rings out with a notification. "Holy shit."

ROMANTICSADIST:

> LOL That's nice of you to say, and I appreciate the offer. Will you also offer to meet and be discrete? 😉 Would be EXTREMELY nice to find just one sexy AF (which you are, btw), local, discrete-fun friend to play with. Not wanting just one time either.

I slouch down a little, wilted by his words. "Nooo," I groan. "Not Gym Daddy. Anyone but my Gym Daddy. Please, please, please don't be one of *those* guys." I swipe

666666666
66666666666

back to his profile. "Says he's single. But that could be a lie, of course. Why else would he be so adamant about the discrete thing right off the bat?"

As if he heard me, another message pops up.

ROMANTICSADIST:

But if discrete is a deal breaker, I understand as well.

I groan again. "What does that even mean? If I'm not discrete, he won't even talk to me?" I drum my fingers on my thigh as I hold the phone in my other hand, trying to figure out what to type.

And once more, as if he's listening in to my conversation with myself—I flip over my phone to make sure no weird light is on or something to indicate my microphone is in use —he adds:

ROMANTICSADIST:

Do you use Kik or anything? Mine is @RomanticSadistLL. But a platform to call on would be optional

I... I don't even know what to say, what to think. I need to wrap my head around the back-to-back messages. Actually, no. They weren't back-to-back, one after the other. It's almost like he sent the first one, and when I didn't respond quickly, he regretted what he said, so he backpedaled a bit. And again, when I didn't immediately reply, it's like he wanted to let me know he did still want to chat, no matter what my decision on the discrete thing would be.

And if that's the case, maybe there *is* another reason he wants to keep him being on the app, or talking to me, a secret other than he's not actually single.

Or maybe that's just my wishful thinking, my desire for this man I've crushed on from afar to live up to what I've built him up to be in my head. Because if he's not, it would be devastating. It would be like finally getting to meet your very favorite celebrity, your idol for years and years, and them being the biggest douche bag in history. I know from meeting some of the authors I once idolized that it's the letdown of the century.

But I'm getting ahead of myself. No matter the reason, there's nothing stopping me from keeping our conversation between him and me. I don't *need* to tell anyone I've spoken to him at all. I'll definitely want to tell Vi, but even if I do, she wouldn't tell a soul if I asked her not to. And if we start to progress further than just talking about things that would be in my books, then I'll ask what the reason for discretion is. If it has anything to do with him being in a relationship, I'll stop everything in their tracks right then.

I blow out a breath and finally type out my reply. And then another, and another. Unable to keep my fingers from word-vomiting.

WILLDIVE4PLANTS:

Discrete is perfectly fine! But I'm really here to research for my book. I've gotten blocked by every other person I've tried to talk to about it. 👀 I found this app finally after trying a couple of others, started swiping, and I saw you. I think I even squealed a little, because I knew you. 😄 Then I had an internal battle of "do I heart or not?" Then when I figured there was no way you'd heart back, I thought, what the hell. But then you did 😳 Then I was like, do I tell him I see him all the time at the gym? 😏

Sorry—fair warning number one: I have severe ADHD even medicated, and so I totally go off on squirrel tangents.

Oh, and just FYI, the others blocked me apparently because they were scared I'd mention them in my book or something—plus, why waste time on me, right? But I promise I won't.

I add the last message because I had this overwhelming fear he'd think they blocked me because I'm some crazy stalker or something. I'm doing my best not to sound like one, which is why I went ahead and confessed to recognizing him.

It takes a few minutes, but he replies, and I let out a huge sigh of relief.

ROMANTICSADIST:

Glad you're good with discrete. Why waste time on you? You mean because you're only in it for book research and not for meeting up? I mean, still an intelligent, hot friend. Don't get me wrong... I think it would be incredibly interesting to meet up with you soon to see if we vibe enough to have fun. But if it's not what you want...

My heart does a backflip, making my tummy feel funny. He made it known he's on the app to meet a play partner. His previous comment about not wanting it to be one time either makes me feel better, because that means he's less into fucking once and then ghosting. And the part about how I could still be an intelligent, hot friend and wouldn't be a waste of time—that... meant a lot to me to read. Sadly.

But I don't want to be one of those girls who basically catfishes a guy by posting their very best-looking photo, only for them to meet in person and find out it was from ten years ago. That's the second time he's mentioned finding me attractive, and seeing as it's my professional author photo Clarice took for me, in full hair and makeup and a cute-as-fuck ensemble, I don't want him to have the wrong impression.

WILLDIVE4PLANTS:

🩶 Well, that's nice to hear for sure. I wouldn't be surprised if you've seen me at the gym and just don't recognize me in my photo. I was there literally every day until recently, just hiding behind my laptop like a little cave creature. But I 100% do NOT look like my profile pic when I'm there. I'm always in workout/author mode and look like a swamp thing 😅

There. At least now he's been warned and won't have it in his head that he's talking to some supermodel. When his next message comes in, I snort out a laugh.

ROMANTICSADIST:

I always say if I meet you all done up, you've only really got one way to go... although I do appreciate a submissive going down 😂😭

"Aaawww... he's punny," I coo to Kronk, who actually gets up from his pillow and sidles up close to me, booping my hand holding my cell with the top of his head. I give him a scratch behind his ears with my other hand, then text Gym Daddy back.

WILLDIVE4PLANTS:

cackles 📝 Notes for future use.

With only a few messages, he's managed to put me at ease. Enough even that I decide to send him a more accurate depiction of me. I have to scroll for a good five minutes, because apparently I haven't taken any selfies in a fucking long time, yet I *have* taken a gazillion photos of plants and screenshots of random shit on the internet.

Finally, I come across a photo of Astrid and me in the women's locker room at the gym. She's sprawled in one of the lounge chairs wrapped up in a hundred towels from head to toe, fresh from the steam room. Even her face is covered with a sheet mask, but you can still see her grinning for the picture. I'm dressed in a comfy tank and leggings, hair in a messy bun, glasses on, my laptop sitting on my hips in a chair that matches Astrid's. I always loved writing in that spot, right between the steam room and the hot tub. Every time someone opens the door, a cloud of eucalyptus-scented steam comes pluming out, and it's heavenly.

I suddenly really miss going to the gym. It's always been a happy place for me. I just haven't had the motivation to go, especially with the weird schedule my body has gotten on as far as sleep goes. But what would it be like going to the gym now, knowing I could see Gym Daddy in person, and also knowing he's totally aware of his not-so-secret admirer? No more being just some random hot mess on the treadmill who could watch him all I wanted without him noticing.

As I attach the photo, I let my mind wander. What would it be like not only being someone he knows at the gym, but maybe… someone he talks to frequently? Like every day? He's fit as fuck. Do I have the balls to ask him if he's done personal training before? I send the picture along with my message, which does not include my wonderings.

> WILLDIVE4PLANTS:
>
> It took me forever, but I finally found a pic in my natural habitat.

But the second I hit the Send button, a notification pops up on the screen, and I growl.

> Oh, WTF? I have to pay to be able to send you photos? Dirty bastards.
>
> ROMANTICSADIST:
>
> Yeah, it sucks. But if you have Kik, we can just switch to that app and it would be free.

I grumble the way I always do when I have to download another damn app. I quickly check to see if there's a desktop version, but alas, of course there isn't. Only a mobile app is available.

But knowing it's to talk to Gym Daddy, I find it a lot less of a pain in the ass to fill out the form and go through the email verification process. When I'm all done and can finally send a message to someone, I type in the Kik username he gave me, and he pops right up.

> WILLDIVE4PLANTS:
>
> OK, I downloaded this just for you. Pray for my ADHD.

I send the photo too and pray he doesn't immediately block me.

I've been having a hell of a time trying to keep up with all the sites I signed up for, but I guess I'd be able to delete all of my profiles if Gym Daddy and I—

"Girl. Calm thy tits," I scold myself. "You don't even know his real name yet. Don't go planning y'all's future, you damn psycho."

A new tone dings from my phone, and my belly feels funny all over again.

> ROMANTICSADISTLL:
>
> LOL... thank you. I'm hoping you'll let me enjoy more than just speaking with you

I'm sure the thank-you was for my message and not the photo, but the fact that he's being persistent about wanting more *has* to be a good sign after seeing me not all dolled up.

Though, while I would pretty much give anything to lick this man's damn skin off, I really do want to take things slow. To enjoy the ride, I guess. I don't want to just jump into bed with him without there being much build-up. While I'm all for instalove in my books, in real-life, I want to feel all the anticipation. I want there to be meaning behind sleeping with a man. And most importantly, I have to be able to trust a Dom before I submit to him.

I decide to play coy—or dumb, whatever—and pretend

I don't know he's insinuating something naughty and physical.

WILLDIVE4PLANTS:

> I mean, if you're up for telling me stories, I'll totally meet with you. Our café at the gym has excellent smoothies. I even had a random thought a little while ago of you whipping my ass into shape.

"Ah, fuck, Sienna!"

> At the gym.

"Still not clear enough, you whore."

> Like... personal training.

"Goddammit. You're making his notifications go fucking apeshit. *Stop it!*"

> I really just said whip my ass to a Dom. 🙈

I clearly have no self-control. Either that or my fingers have a mind of their own.

Before I can embarrass myself any further, my app pings, and I grimace as I peek at the message, expecting him to admonish me in some way for blowing up his phone.

Instead, my face instantly morphs into a mask of pure sexual desire when I read his words.

ROMANTICSADISTLL:

I mean, meet me alone where no one can save you. You can get to your knees and bow your head, and I'll tell you stories about what I'm going to do to you, how I plan on enjoying you.

Chapter Nine

SIENNA

I don't know how long I stare at my screen or how many times I reread his message. I only know it's enough time for my mouth to go completely dry, to the point my throat clicks when I try to swallow, because I was doing both those things with my jaw slack.

Gym Daddy has turned me into a mouth-breather.

WILLDIVE4PLANTS:

I...

Have to go write now.

Inspiration suddenly struck.

Excuse me.

But I don't go anywhere. I stay right the hell where I am,

staring at my screen, my breath held to see what will come out of his mouth—fingers, whatever—next.

> ROMANTICSADISTLL:
>
> LOL. It'll be fun. What time will you be at the gym tomorrow? Before you go in, come meet me.

My entire body heats. One, because I'm embarrassed to admit just how long it's been since I've even gone to the gym. And two, because the thought of meeting him in person has sent a flush through my veins.

I type the first thing that pops into my head that isn't either "with or without clothes?" or "ain't no way in fuck I'm meeting you when I haven't had a brow wax in three months or even remember the last time I bought razors."

> WILLDIVE4PLANTS:
>
> •• That's how people get kidnapped.

There's a spa at the gym where you can get your eyebrows done, and there are disposable razors in the locker room, the little cunt voice inside my head suddenly decides to be helpful.

I ignore it and do my classic Sienna move. Deflect. Self-deprecate.

WILLDIVE4PLANTS:

Sidenote—for real though, do you do personal training? I just saw a picture of me in an open-back shirt my friend Vi took, and now I feel the desire to go do the row machine for like 83 hours 😅

He allows it.

ROMANTICSADISTLL:

83 hours would be impressive.

I let out a sigh of relief that he let me off the meet-him-tomorrow hook. My foot wiggles as I stare at my screen. I don't really know what to say now. It's been a long time since I tried flirting with a guy, and even though I've written more meet-cute scenes than I can count, my words just aren't lining up for real-life courting.

"Courting? Jesus fuck, Sienna. Get your life together. This isn't the 1800s," I grumble, my finger closing out the app to take off some of the pressure I feel to say anything just to keep the conversation going.

I open TikTok and decide to reply to some comments to distract me from the man on the other app. I go through the notifications to make sure I answer all questions first. I love that people have a way to so easily ask me anything they want, and if I can't get back to them right away, my followers jump in to help them out.

The reading order of one of my series? My amazing

reader **@christi_marxen** answered that three hours ago and even included all the short stories in her numbered list.

Which book should they start with? My sweet supporter **@ginarodriguezwells** gave them the rundown of which books are funny and which are dark, so they can pick depending on what mood they're in.

Where do I find inspiration? **@redhare05, @lookit-sjordy, and @1977photography** all pounce on that one, commenting with their favorite characters and who they've heard me say inspired him or her.

Do they need to read the books in order? **@amanda-vandemeulengraaf and @wholu2020** go back and forth about the pros and cons of reading them chronologically by how they were released. And **@whitneyreadsromance and @shaurinotsorry** assure that they're all standalones and can be read in any order.

And then I have tags from **@floweraura, @orithedraw, and @biblio_mama** to blind-duet with other TikTokkers' videos who remind them of my different characters, which I record immediately so I can see what they mean. My readers never fail to blow me away by totally nailing the image I had in my head when writing the hero or heroine or even a side character, and I love being able to give them a genuine reaction, when they took the time to tag me after thinking of me.

Getting near the end of my new notifications, I see **@cecesbooknook, @mishagalli, @cassiehargroveauthor, @afox1537, @huntersmoontrading,**

@brocococreations, and @drinker.belle have all tagged me in a comment under the same video, which I can tell because of the thumbnail next to each of their names. It always makes me super curious when this happens, because it either means my readers are giving me a shoutout under a booktokker's recommendation request —the best feeling ever!—or that there's a thirst trap—a post by a hottie meant to be attention-grabbing by using sex appeal—that really captures something from one of my books. This time, it's the latter, and I make sure to duet the video and reply to each one of their tags to thank them.

Finally, I'm elated to see **@shannon_hezakhai and @reasbooks_** have made review videos about two of my books. The fact that they always take the time to record their thoughts and showcase their excitement about the stories they read makes me proud that I have the ability to make a reader feel the same way I do when I read some of my favorite authors' books. It's still surreal to me when people call me their favorite author, and don't even get me started on the ones who now have my stories incorporated in tattoos permanently inked into their skin. That's just mind-boggling.

When I'm all caught up on notifications, I hop onto my own page to see what the last video I posted was. It's been a while, almost a week, because I just haven't felt up to being creative. And because filters only help so much. It almost makes me believe being on these dating sites and having zero luck even holding one exhilarating conversa-tion—until tonight—has made me feel worse than I already did.

It was one thing being single and lonely when I didn't even try to put myself out there. It's an entirely different thing being single and lonely and having put in a stupid number of hours scouring the internet for just one decent human male to chat with and coming up empty.

And while I've learned a lot from the one gentleman on the sugar daddy site, it's done nothing for my loneliness, which I know is my own fault, because I put up all the road-blocks that kept him detoured in the "book research only" zone.

Realizing that, why am I fighting tooth and nail to keep Gym Daddy between those same lines?

Because you want to be chased.

My face rearranges itself to ask a resounding *WTF?*

Go ahead. Try to deny it. Why else would you be pumping the brakes on the one guy you've had the hots for since you got dumped?

My head jerks back, even though the person being rude is inside of it, not in front of me.

"Um, first of all, I did not get dumped. It was a mutual agreement to go our separate ways when we realized we would be happier not married to each other. Second… I've had the hots for more than one guy. It just so happens that the other two are completely unrecognizable because I have no idea what they look like. Which should actually mean a lot, if that show *Love is Blind* is anything to go by. Being attracted to a man when you haven't even seen his face? Now that's something special."

So why don't you hop in your car and go to the store to see if Dumpster Daddy is there, if you're so... down in the dumps? the cunty voice cackles, and I roll my eyes, even though I know the dumb pun technically came from my own brain. Before I can respond... aloud... to my own thoughts—I let out a sigh at how crazy I sound even to myself—the voice speaks up again. *Or why don't you get your lazy ass off the couch, go shower for once, get dressed, and go to the club to see if Dream Daddy is there? Grow some fucking balls and approach him for once instead of standing on the sidelines watching some other ho get all his attention!*

I'm shaking my head... at myself... before the voice inside it even finishes taunting me.

"No way. Dumpster Daddy, okay. He seemed more approachable if I happen to run into him again. His vibe was... cautious but obliging. Like he was telling himself he shouldn't help me because I got myself into that whole mess on my own, but then he couldn't resist, because that's just the kind of person he is. But Dream Daddy?" I shake my head again, this time hastily. "That man, one does not approach unless you've received a written invitation. No, not even an invitation, because that would imply you can choose to decline. Nuh-uh. That guy... you don't get to be in his close proximity unless you've been *ordered* to be there."

Even though that makes him sound like either the biggest douche canoe on the face of the planet or just plain scary as shit, my body gives zero fucks. It still reacts the same way it always does when I think about the Dom at Club Alias known as Sir Jeremy. But I call him Dream Daddy nonetheless, because he's who I imagine would be the Dom of my dreams. The way he speaks to the subs he plays with, the way his glove-covered hands move along their skin with such care, such reverence, the way he never gives up until he's wrung every ounce of pleasure he possibly can out of their bodies…. That's only the tip of the iceberg of what makes my pussy always begin to ready itself, clenching and growing wet, as if waiting for a turn to experience such a Master.

So, no. I will not be hightailing it to the club like a cat in heat to go proposition a sex god who probably wouldn't even give me the time of day. Not to say he's one of *those* Doms. That's a rabbit hole I wish I would've never fallen down, because while I'm coming to terms with being a pleaser to a fault, Gorean Doms—at least for my own submission—take it too far.

Living the lifestyle 24/7 based on a science fiction novel from the '60s?

Sounds a little too culty for me.

And from what I read—which could be completely wrong, seeing as I've never actually spoken to Gorean kinksters—they take it even further than a Master/sex-slave relationship, in which a true Master still respects his sub who has given up her ability to set limits. *Those* Masters know their sub's likes and dislikes, what they truly enjoy and what they allow only because they want to please their Dom, and

CHAPTER NINE · 175

they keep their slave's trust by not taking things too far. They love to toe the line, even go past the boundary on occasion as a test of their sub's obedience, just to make sure the slave hasn't gotten too comfortable in the idea their Master won't still use their body the way it pleases them. But if they have that level of trust from another person, it's very hard for a good Master to do anything that would break it, that would break the person who has submitted to them so fully. It's the ultimate form of submission a Dom could earn, and it would be downright stupid for them to fuck that up for themselves.

From what I gathered about the Gorean ones though, all that trust stuff is bullshit. They don't give a damn about their slave's pleasure and comfort. The slave is there to be used however the Dom wants, and whether the sub gets any enjoyment out of it is of no concern to the Dom.

That's a no from me, dawg.

Going back to what I was doing before my voices did their usual distracting thing, I click on the video I posted last, and I'm not even ashamed to admit I laugh my ass off at myself. Well, I guess it's not me that's funny, seeing as I'm just lip syncing to someone else being funny, but it makes me laugh either way.

The sound is a person saying, "I just figured out why girls call each other 'sis.'" After a pause, they deliver the punchline. "It's because they're all calling the same dude 'daddy!'" And they let out a "gotcha" kind of laugh that's contagious every time I hear it.

"Jeez, maybe Vi was right and I do have some closet daddy kink," I murmur as I copy the link to the video. I don't even realize what I'm doing until I've already added a laughing emoji and pasted the link into a Kik message to Gym Daddy.

Before I send it, I ask myself why I've suddenly discovered myself in this position. And with wine flowing through my veins and the lingering adrenaline-fueled excitement from actually speaking to my crush for the first time, I'm able to be honest with myself when I answer.

I want to impress him. I want him to like me. I want him to see the real me, being my nerdy, goofy self, and I want him to want me. Not the hot-looking porn author on the kinkster dating app, but the real me, hair in a rat's nest on top of my head, glasses on, looking up from my laptop to deliver that punch line and make a goofball face during the laugh part, who enjoys being a dork and lip syncing songs and funny quotes.

I have nothing to lose, so I hit Send.

WILLDIVE4PLANTS:

*link attached

It takes a little while, which I hope means he's watching the video and finding me amusing, but he finally replies.

ROMANTICSADISTLL:

LOL you're awesome!

I grin like a fool. He could just be saying that and not

bothered to watch the TikTok, but just the idea of Gym Daddy laughing at my dorkiness and thinking I'm awesome because of it is such an uplifting feeling I choose to believe he's being sincere.

His next message reels in some of that good feeling though.

> ROMANTICSADISTLL:
>
> **Not sounding like I'll get to enjoy you though.**

I let out a heavy sigh.

I go back to my previous thoughts about why I'd still keep Gym Daddy at bay if I know it only amplifies my feeling of being so utterly alone. There's no reason for me to keep him in the same gated-off "book research only" compartment I put everyone else in, because I *am* attracted to him.

To an alarming degree.

Those other guys I spoke with, I felt nothing toward them. Not one single emotion. So I know a part of me kept them compartmentalized like that so I wouldn't let my loneliness overrule my true wants and needs, so I wouldn't give in and settle for just anyone to make that feeling go away. Because I know for a fact that it wouldn't work, and then I'd be disgusted with myself, making things ten times worse than they already were inside this tornado mind of mine.

But taking Gym Daddy out of that box? That wouldn't be settling. That wouldn't be just to relieve the solitude. It would be acting on what I want, putting myself out there, but by doing so, I'd open myself up for being hurt.

Because as one of my asshole voices is taunting at the moment, *Just because you'd be taking a giant step by letting him go further than everyone else doesn't mean it's going to be a big deal to him. You see how gorgeous he is? You see how charming and friendly he is at the gym? And you see how he has the ability to make even a best-selling romance novelist's jaw drop with that message about getting to your knees and bowing your head? This isn't his first rodeo, bitch. Be smart.*

But I'm so utterly exhausted, so tired of always being cautious and "smart." I want nothing more than to just give in to my desire, consequences be damned. My intrusive thoughts always make that damn near impossible. I never have time just to take a leap of faith and enjoy the moment, because the very second an idea pops into my head that seems like it would be so much fun or a YOLO experience, the voices jump on it like a swarm of hornets whose nest has been disturbed.

So being braver than ever before but still cautious enough to keep my voices from going into instant panic mode, I message Gym Daddy.

WILLDIVE4PLANTS:

That's something I'd have to psych myself up for, and it would not be quick. Soooo… just for research for now.

"There. Now he knows I'm interested but a little scared.

If he isn't receptive or is inconsiderate of that, then I shouldn't worry about taking things further with him anyway," I tell myself, more as a reminder to be strong in the face of such temptation.

To give him a little more transparency of my interest, I add to my last message.

WILLDIVE4PLANTS:

Writing a book is how I get my thoughts about something in order 🌱 And it just so happens that I'm doing research for a book about a woman who tries online dating for the first time. Up until I received your message, I had little hope of her story being a happily ever after. Either that, or I'd have to lie my ass off about what dating sites are really like. Which would be okay, I guess, since I write fiction.

I breathe a sigh of relief when his response comes in.

ROMANTICSADISTLL:

Not quick EVER. Friendship and desire first. Mind before body. Always. The things I enjoy and need make that a requirement. It's why I've pressed to meet you in person, because it's impossible to truly feel someone's energy over messaging.

I need to process what he just said, so I get back on my TikTok and mindlessly scroll through my own videos. If he's being honest and that's the real reason he wants to meet in person, then that's a totally valid explanation. He's right. I was literally just thinking that before I received his first message, that maybe I couldn't feel chemistry with anyone through a computer or phone screen.

But it would be so disheartening to finally meet him in person after crushing on him from afar for so long, and him decide there's no desire on his end. An unrequited love story is not what I had in mind for my first book idea in nine months.

"Instalove or die," I murmur Vi's and my mantra for our storylines.

But that's fiction. I'm not sure instalove exists in real life. I may be smitten kitten over Gym Daddy, but it's not a love at first sight thing, I don't think. I'm infatuated, for sure. Have a hardcore crush because of how fucking attractive he is. But insta*love*? If anything, that would definitely have to be discovered in an in-person situation.

Yet… is it *just* because I find him hot beyond belief that I'm so infatuated? I see ridiculously good-looking men all the time. At the gym. At the club. Hell, it's literally part of my job to be surrounded by gorgeous, Adonis-bodied male cover models. And never once has any of those men had the effect on me Gym Daddy does. His face is the only one I've consciously pictured as I made myself come.

His *face* is the only one.

That's not to say I haven't imagined Dream Daddy more times than could be considered respectful. No, I definitely fantasize about that man doing very disrespectful things to my body, but since I have no idea what he looks like, he's faceless while I imagine the filthy things he'd make me do.

But the man I'm currently messaging with, while his face and the rest of him are downright beautiful, that shouldn't be anything very special to me. That shouldn't be remarkable in any way, since I'm overexposed to hot guys, jaded, desensitized to the effects male beauty can have on a woman.

So there must be something more about him that I'm not consciously aware of. There must be something else at work when my eyes connect with him. Even across an entire gym, through all the equipment, between and past all the other stupidly fit and good-looking people, when my eyes land on Gym Daddy, I not only feel those infamous butterflies everyone always talks about, but I have an actual physiological response. My heart races, and it has nothing to do with moseying along on the treadmill without even an incline set. My skin prickles, and it's not because of the AC pumping out onto the workout floor. My breathing becomes quick and shallow, my panties are suddenly wet, and it's not a rare thing for a whimper or moan to come out of my mouth without my consent. All just from spotting that man I've never even spoken to in person before. I don't even know what his voice sounds like, since I've never been close to him while he's been speaking.

"I bet it's deep and rumbly, like what a bear-shifter

would sound like if they were real," I tell my cat, just now remembering he's been curled up beside me this entire time.

I read through comments for a few more minutes, and then I come across the TikTok I made about a St. Andrew's cross before the one I sent him earlier, and I snort. "What are the odds?" I copy the link and send it to him.

WILLDIVE4PLANTS:

Of all the things in the universe you could've posted a picture of on your profile, it just so happened to be this little contraption I said just a week and half ago that I'd love to try out.

"That was pretty flirty, right?" I scratch the back of my head, my broken nails getting caught in the strands.

ROMANTICSADISTLL:

Yes, you and I should definitely play.

"Psh!" The unladylike noise leaves my mouth as I pull a hair out of my nail that got yanked out of my messy bun. "You say that, but if you were to see what's on the other end of the phone at the moment, you'd never trust online dating ever again, good sir." But I don't text that. I still have a little time I can attempt to get my life together. I mean, I could definitely summon the energy to shower at some point.

WILLDIVE4PLANTS:

Well, hope you weren't just trying to be nice when you said that about a hot intelligent friend before, because you're talking to a chick who is terrified to even heart your profile. I'll probably hide if I ever see you at the gym again. I'm only brave on TikTok and in my books until I get to know someone.

ROMANTICSADISTLL:

LOL not kidding. Intelligence seems so rare these days. It would be a shame to end it already just because you're not interested physically.

"He's gotta be shitting me." Does he really think I have no desire to—

WILLDIVE4PLANTS:

There's a very big difference between "not interested" and "I am a giant pussy" 😂

Please take the reins. Please take the reins. Please take the reins.

I've come to the conclusion that it would be stupid of me to try to keep him at bay when that's the last thing I actually want. I wasn't playing hard to get before; I was trying to protect myself. But how will I know he won't hurt me if I don't open myself up enough to let him prove he won't?

But as a submissive through and through, it goes against every fiber of my being to assert myself in a way that would come off... bold. So from this point forward, I decide to make it known in my replies that I'm open to more than just talking about book research. We can still go slow. Like he said, mind before body. But I feel like if I keep my walls super high and reinforced so he only gets to peek in through a window, I'll lose my chance.

And I know if someone heard me say that out loud, I would be scolded, called a doormat and other lovely names that mean I'm weak. They'd tell me that if a man isn't willing to work hard to get to know me and earn my trust and attention, then they don't deserve me.

But in my mind, how the hell would he know I'm worth all the hard work if I don't let him see that? If I don't let him see what he'd be missing out on, then what would be his incentive to try winning it?

ROMANTICSADISTLL:

If you're interested, then that means I still have a chance😏 And who knows? I may end up being too boring for you.

That actually makes me laugh out loud. So loud it startles Kronk and he makes his little chirpy sound that means he's annoyed.

"Sorry, kitty boy. This man really said he might be too boring for me. Of course, he has no idea boring would be welcome in comparison to what my last partner needed in bed," I murmur, and when I look back at what my fingers typed and sent without my permission, I groan and follow it up with another message.

WILLDIVE4PLANTS:

I've seen your muscles in action. There's no way in hell you could ever be boring.

FML I said that out loud.

Chapter Ten

FELIX

This little sub has cast a spell on me. If I hadn't been sure before—listening to her from outside the dumpster—of just how vulnerable she is, how fragile her grip on normality is, then in the past week I've spent texting with her throughout the day would've confirmed it. It makes every single part of my very being want to protect her at all costs, to surround her and keep her safe.

But at the same time, I also want to be the one who breaks her. I want her to lose her death grip on what she thinks she *should* be, so I can awaken what I know she truly is inside.

The perfect little obedient slave.

And it has nothing to do with me wanting that to be true. With every message she sends, it just proves more and more that's what she yearns to be. Her true self. But her entire life has been spent with people trying to change that about her. For some reason I can't grasp, even with my above-average IQ, everyone seems to think it's the people pleasers who are in the wrong and need to be "fixed." They're told they're weak, that they need to toughen up and learn how to tell people no.

That doesn't make sense to me one bit.

Why would we want someone who gains pleasure from helping others to... stop being so eager... to help others?

In my mind, that's like telling an artist to stop painting because they're good at it and it makes them happy.

Or telling a doctor to stop healing patients with the skills they spent years upon years learning.

Or telling a fireman not to put out the burning building.

It's who she is. It's her personality. Why does anyone think they have the right to tell her that her personality is wrong, that it's bad, when it doesn't hurt anyone? In fact, it does the complete opposite of that. It helps someone, or a lot of people, depending on how she's using her pleasing skills.

And if they're so concerned about her that their argument is "it's for her own good, so people don't take advantage of her," then instead of trying to change *her*, why don't they put all that effort in scolding and trying to fix the ones who are *actually* the problem? The ones who would take advantage of her.

More than anything, I want to teach her that. I want to give *herself* back to her. I want her to be the sweet everyone has tried to turn bitter, because God knows we need to protect what little sweet is left in the world. Before everyone gets their way and convinces all the pleasers they should stop all that paltry kindness bullshit. That they can't just walk around throwing out "yeses" all willy-nilly. That they need to keep all that love and nurturing nature to themselves, just because someone undeserving could steal some of it.

Fuck that.

It's now my goal to undo the damage others have done to her. To erase the things people have made her believe about herself. All that anxiety she feels? She wouldn't have nearly as much if she wasn't spending all her energy fighting who she truly is inside. If she just embraced it, gave in to her own wants and traits, all the effort she puts into trying to do what the assholes are telling her to—suppress the desire to help people, to make others happy, to be there for someone who needs them—could be spent just... being fucking happy as herself.

Because in the end, isn't she just trying to please the people who are telling her she needs to stop being a people pleaser?

Hence why her mind seems to be in constant turmoil, manifesting as anxiety and depression, causing her actual *chemical* imbalances and hereditary disorders to be downright uncontrollable even with medication.

They've twisted this highly intelligent, artistic, empathetic, and deeply thoughtful brain until it's in knots. Add in the fact she has intrusive repetitive thoughts that aren't able to be quieted with meds, and it's no wonder she's been damn near comatose the past year. She's a child sitting between her two parents who are screaming at each other about things she doesn't understand. Only she's a grown woman, and the arguing is her own thoughts, taking place so loudly inside her mind she can't focus on anything else.

It fucking pisses me off.

And I won't allow it any longer.

For the sixth day in a row, the moment I wake up, I reach for my phone on the charger on my nightstand and send her a message I know she'll sweetly avoid instead of turning me down. Probably without even realizing it, she's unwilling to give me a flat-out no.

> ROMANTICSADISTLL:
>
> Good morning, pretty. Ready for a kiss yet?

> WILLDIVE4PLANTS:
>
> 🥹 Just got in my favorite chair at the gym! Gotta write 19k words in two days. Pray my Adderall kicks in soon!

The pleasure I felt a few days ago when the little writer told me she signed up to be in a charity anthology, inspired to write after almost ten months of being unable to, was surprising in its intensity. But I'm sure it had a lot to do with the way she didn't hesitate to tell me it was thanks to my attention. She's sent several messages stating in various ways that I was the reason her words were flowing again.

All I've done is answer her questions honestly and praised her whenever I possibly can. I feel her practically glow through the screen with each "good girl" she receives.

I take a shower and throw on my workout clothes, then grab my phone to send her a message. It's been about forty-five minutes since I got hers, which should've given her time to write a good chunk uninterrupted.

ROMANTICSADISTLL:

Then I should come by, and you can meet me outside.

This suggestion always gets the most creative diversions from my little wordsmith.

WILLDIVE4PLANTS:

That's what Ted Bundy used to tell women right before he threw them in his Volkswagen. 😊

I chuckle at that. I've learned without even asking about it that she's utterly obsessed with serial killers. My first clue was that time in the dumpster, when she named the coleus Edmond after Edmond Kemper. Next, she sent a photo of her in a T-shirt that read "Choke me like Bundy. Eat me like Dahmer." It opened up a whole world of filthy flirtation over texts with the little hippy.

ROMANTICSADISTLL:

That's not a no. I'll be by in about 15 minutes.

I taunt, even though she never actually tells me no. But I know she's not quite ready, so I really am only teasing. I'll still go to the gym to work out, but I won't see her, seeing as her favorite chair she mentioned is one in the women's locker room.

WILLDIVE4PLANTS:

Stooooop. I'm hiding!

I don't reply, knowing she won't be able to stand it and will continue to send more until I do.

WILLDIVE4PLANTS:

Don't you dare! 😬 I now have 18k left! Hunkering down.

No boys allowed in the women's locker room.

Meds have engaged!

K bye.

Wanting to give her enough peace of mind to be able to concentrate on her work, I finally respond.

ROMANTICSADISTLL:

No, I wouldn't. It's CNC, not just
NC. No means no. Maybe you'll
change your mind and let me know
we can play. Enjoy your day,
little one.

She asked me several questions about CNC—consensual non-consent—scenes for her research, and in that back and forth conversation, it was easy to pick up on the fact she was interested in it not only for the book but for herself. The idea that such sweetness desired such darkness was enough to send me into the shower of the men's locker room that day to jack off. And knowing she was just right across the hall, in the women's, made me come within mere seconds.

I focus on driving and my workout in order to force her to get her work done. The app tells us when the other has read the message, and I saw she opened my last one right after it went through. I closed out the app on my phone before she could type out a response. Whatever she sent, it's telling her I still haven't read it, which will be easier on her intrusive thoughts than if I read it without replying. She'll assume I'm busy and just can't check my phone, which is the boundary I've put in place so her anxiety won't eat her alive.

When I finally do check the app after a few hours at the hospital, a blissful feeling envelopes me like a hug. Message after message from her, with pictures too. She thought of me a lot in my absence, and I love that she makes that known instead of trying to hide it.

The first one was sent just a minute after mine.

WILLDIVE4PLANTS:

Had to go and hit me with the "little
one" 😊

The next was sent an hour later, as if she couldn't stop
thinking about something and had to go in search of it
for me.

*screenshot of Kindle page

This is from my very first book in a
nine-book BDSM series

I click on the photo and see she has a paragraph highlighted where a male character is calling someone "little
one." I grin, since I know she wrote that book almost six
years ago. That long ago, and her imagination had her hero
character using the same endearment I've been calling her
in my head since she sat in my lap the night I got her out of
the dumpster.

Has it really only been two weeks since I touched her? It
feels like years I've been craving to put my hands on her
again.

Her next message came in an hour ago, which makes
me smile again, because she obviously could not get it out of
her head that I called her the same name her heroes have
used.

WILLDIVE4PLANTS:

*screenshot of Kindle page

And also in book 4 😊

It's clear the nickname resonates with something inside her. The desire to be seen as small and fragile? As something to be cherished and taken care of? Or is it more about the person who is calling her that name? Does she crave someone who towers over her, who could take her, make her do things against her will because of how much bigger and stronger they are than she is?

If her curiosity about consensual non-consent is anything to go by, I'd bet it's more likely the latter.

I smirk as I begin to type out a message for my little author, knowing my words excite her even though that's *her* specialty.

ROMANTICSADISTLL:

Adorable. But you haven't felt the full effect of that name until I gently place the edge of my finger under your chin to raise your eyes to mine, lean in to give you a sweet kiss on the cheek, and then whisper into your ear "You please me greatly and make my heart smile. I am happy you're mine, sweet little one."

I press Send and tilt my head back to rest on the back of my leather office chair, closing my eyes and picturing what I illustrated in the message. In my head, she's on her knees, legs spread, her arms crossed behind her back as she grips her elbows. I'm knelt before her but still have to tilt her chin high because she really is a *little* thing.

Her eyes glisten with pleasure from just being in my presence, her anxiety about meeting in person long gone after all the training I've given her by then. I've barely even touched her, and I can already see her need for me as if it's written on her lightly tanned skin in bold black ink. I kiss her cheek just as I told her I would, taking in the softness of her skin there, the scent of whatever she put on that makes her seem to glow. And when I whisper those words in her ear, I focus more on her body's reaction to them than anything else in the world.

Shortness in breath.

An instant flush accompanied by goose bumps along her skin.

A shiver of her feminine shoulders.

And a seemingly unconscious rocking of her whole luscious body toward my own, as if pulled instinctively to the one who owns it.

I'm yanked out of the vision when my phone dings.

WILLDIVE4PLANTS:

> That, Sir, was completely uncalled for.

A growl rumbles up from my chest and out into my office as I read what she called me without ever being told to do so. My cock is instantly rock-hard from the little sub calling me Sir. And of course she capitalized it. She *would* know it's a sign of respect to a Dominant to capitalize whatever name you refer to them by.

WILLDIVE4PLANTS:

> My watch is now telling me to breathe, so thanks for that LOL

Same, little one, I think to myself, but I don't have time to reply as I'm paged for an incoming ambulance.

When I get back to my office two hours later, she's only sent one message. I'm surprised by the intensity of the disappointment I feel that there's not a string of her random thoughts for me to scroll through and enjoy, but when I read the one she sent, I get that she's trying to write under different circumstances than before.

WILLDIVE4PLANTS:

> Annoying not fun fact about our gym—no outlets by my locker room chair. Forced to sit with the peasants in the café instead of sprawled in a lounge chair by the hot tub 😂

I grin at her dramatics. From getting to know her this past week, it's easy to tell she's completely joking about the peasants comment. It's just her funny little way of telling me she had to move locations. Again, probably without being consciously aware of what she's doing, she informs me of things any 24/7 sub would be trained to tell their Dom, their Owner and Master. We always like to know exactly where our belongings are.

But I keep that to myself, allowing her to lie to herself that this thing between us is moving slowly, when really, I can already feel an attachment. From both sides. What I felt from the moment I heard her inside the dumpster that first night, the protectiveness and amusement, has grown exponentially. Not only that, but I enjoy the lightheartedness she brings out in me, when it seems like I've felt nothing but heaviness for years.

ROMANTICSADISTLL:

Ugh those BASTARDS

She replies within seconds, as if she's been waiting to hear from me with bated breath. It makes all remnants of the disappointment I felt moments ago completely disappear, especially when I perceive she must've been holding off on texting me more than she did because she's been so conditioned that it's annoying. She's sensitive to that feeling, more than anything else I've come across in our conversations so far. She's been told time and time again by people throughout her life that she's "too much," and she's been trying her best to keep herself reined in with me, when that's the very last thing I want.

I want every bit of her she has to give. I want her to lavish her attention on me. I want her obsessed with me. And when she finally breaks down all the barriers her past conditioning built inside her and allows herself to smother me with her fixation, I will never, ever reprimand her for that. I will give her nothing but the praise she craves like it's the air she breathes.

WILLDIVE4PLANTS:

Right?! As much as we pay for that place, you'd think they could at least provide ample enough electricity 😔

I'm paged for another patient, and by the time I get in my truck to go home and check her messages, the last one she sent an hour ago says she was going to get some sleep.

Pride fills me. Asleep before one in the morning? That's a big deal for the little sub. Writing all day, conversing with me, getting out of the house where she can't so easily lie down for a nap, her circadian rhythm might finally be on the mend without me even putting that much effort into it. I haven't even had to resort to slipping in tiny assignments, tasks for her to complete at random in order to keep her stimulated during the day to stay awake and for me to enjoy her unhesitant obedience. I have many in my pocket to pull out whenever the urge hits me.

A selfie wherever she happens to be at that moment— if she's lying down, nodding off, it would influence her to get up and moving again. She wouldn't want me to see her being unproductive. It goes against her entire personality.

A photo of what she's eating for lunch—it would force her to grab some food when I know sometimes she forgets to eat or doesn't bother because her medications kill her appetite.

A question that seems out of curiosity but actually has a purpose. Like "What brand of body wash do you use? I'm at the store and want to smell it, so I can pretend I'm inhaling you." If she doesn't know off the top of her head, she'd hurry to her bathroom to either read or take a picture of the label to send to me. And with the thought I put into her head about me inhaling her, it would encourage her to take the shower she hadn't felt the energy to before.

My suspicion the night I fixed up her hand has been confirmed several times over the last week. The little sub has Obsessive Compulsive Disorder along with her ADHD, and I'm entirely certain she's been in a depressive episode that's lasted quite some time.

The next morning, I throw on my workout clothes and head to the gym. I'm just pulling into a parking spot when my phone dings with a notification. And then another, and another, and another, and I chuckle, knowing without looking they're messages and exactly who they're from.

The little sub has arisen.

WILLDIVE4PLANTS:

So I had a dream last night that made something occur to me. How accurate is that little app I found you on? As far as location/distance? Because it definitely said you were only two miles away... while I was sitting in my living room. As in at home.

Which would be a whole new plot bunny in itself if the hero she meets on the site happens to live in her neighborhood. Could you imagine? 😅

Holy shit. Like... what if they kept passing each other every day and had no idea they were RIGHT THERE all along? I mean, I saw you a lot at the gym. But if you've been one of my neighbors all this time... not gonna lie, it'd kinda make me sad. Because it's almost like I could've known you all this time and missed out.

Sorry. Went a little Stage 5 Clinger on you there. I guess I'm just bummed I could've had a like-minded friend to talk to when I was alone all that time.

My gut clenches at her opening up and being vulnerable with me, feeling similar to what she probably does when she receives praise. It's like a reward, deeply touched by the trust she's giving me. I also feel... something I'm not very familiar with when it comes to empathy. While I know I experience guilt when I hurt someone's feelings with my seemingly careless words, I've never truly understood what people meant by the term "lying by omission." It doesn't compute in my head how you are *telling* someone a lie, if you aren't voicing anything. I've always chalked it up to one of those illogical societal norms my disorder will never let me grasp.

But for some reason, in this moment, I feel... uncomfortable? With the fact that she doesn't know I saw her long before we met on the app. Yet telling her could possibly change things, and I don't want that to happen. What's happening between us feels right, tantalizing our minds with the possibility of there being incredible chemistry once we meet in person.

Maybe that's it though.

I already *know* there's incredible chemistry between us when we're in each other's physical presence. My persistence comes from wanting to feel it *again*, knowing it's there and craving more of it. She, on the other hand, is still working up the courage for what she believes will be our first time meeting face-to-face. But until that happens, I'm getting to know a side of her that's most likely more carefree and unembarrassed to tell me her random "squirrel thoughts" as she calls them, than if she were to know I was the one who caught her in a dumpster.

She has yet to mention her nighttime hobby. Dumpster diving, that is. She would never reveal her other nighttime activities of being a member of our elite club. It's against the rules of Club Alias to speak about it to just anyone. So I haven't wasted time even awaiting a message that included something about that. But her "treasure hunting"? She hasn't said one word about it, and since she's revealed a lot about herself, including her love of gardening and going off on adorable tangents about different plants, for it to not be mentioned tells me it's not something she wants me to know about.

And the only real reason she wouldn't want me to know is she's embarrassed, maybe ashamed even, since a lot of people would draw parallels between dumpster diving and being poor, or homeless, or even just desperate. It would take an explanation for them to understand she does it more as a "fuck you" to "the man." She does it because her principles drive her compulsions. And with her disorder causing her to hyperfixate on whatever she's feeling compelled to do, her dumpster diving has become even more to her than just rescuing healthy plants from the garbage.

It's now become a part of her. She probably believes each one of those plants is her in some way, and if she has the form of OCD that includes rituals—God, my poor little one. In her head, she could possibly be telling herself that if she *doesn't* rescue the plants, something bad will happen to her. Add in the intrusive thoughts on repeat, and no wonder her sleep schedule has been fucked to hell and back. She can't sleep at night, because that's when she can dumpster dive. If she doesn't dumpster dive, something bad will happen to her. This makes her so tired that she has to sleep most of the day, which leaves no time for anything else.

No time to work.

No time to eat or work out.

No time nor energy to even worry about hygiene and self-care.

So it's a secret she wants to keep from me, and that's

perfectly fine. Because as long as it's a secret, she gets to show me the real her that's not fixated on her obsession. She gets to pretend it doesn't exist and finds other things to focus on and talk about with me. Which is therapeutic for her as well, since she's not fixating on it. I've interrupted that loop, which she desperately needed.

So although I feel a tinge of discomfort for not correcting her when she says anything about us meeting in person "for the first time," I feel it would hurt her more if I revealed the truth at this stage, when she's gaining so much more by not knowing.

The rest of our conversation this morning takes place between my sets on the different chest and triceps machines, giving me a reason to power through every rep so I can read her reply that never fails to come.

ROMANTICSADISTLL:

Stage 5 isn't even close to the level I WANT you to be, little one.

Not expecting your address, so let's go with... how far from the gym do you live? In minutes.

And the app says your 3 miles away right now. Where are you?

WILLDIVE4PLANTS:

LOL seeing as you have my real name and links from my TikToks I sent you, where you can clearly see everywhere I go around town, I think it's safe to say you could easily find me if you really wanted to. I live in the neighborhood by the lake. It's the only lake around here, so you know where, I'm sure.

It takes me nine minutes to get to the gym, since they opened that sweet little shortcut

ROMANTICSADISTLL:

I'm in the neighborhood off that "sweet little shortcut." So not far at all. Accurate enough, to answer your question.

I'm at the gym right now though.

WILLDIVE4PLANTS:

Just got here!

ROMANTICSADISTLL:

Friendly face-to-face? I'll behave.

WILLDIVE4PLANTS:

I'm so glad you said that. I was trying to get up the courage to ask.

I have some questions for my book, and I can't find anything but stupid fuck-boys in my search for someone to interview. You're literally the only person that doesn't give me the ick 🫣

ROMANTICSADISTLL:

Courage to ask me to behave?

Told you, has to be consensual unless CNC is agreed upon, then different rules. No matter what we state our kinks are, people are people and deserve respect. Unless we RESPECTFULLY change the rules based on agreement.

I mean, I still want you, will continue to ask you, might even test the waters and tempt you into changing your mind... but will always respect your boundaries.

Until it's time not to 😈

WILLDIVE4PLANTS:

I

I just meant... the courage to ask you for a friendly meet... where you'd behave 🫣

But you've been fairly warned how freaking awkward I am. I'm only cool on TikTok. There's a reason I am a reclusive author.

And see? You're literally the only person I've come across on these sites and apps who truly knows and follows the real aspects of BDSM. I bet if I asked any of these other fuckers what the three fundamental principles are, they wouldn't know what the hell I'm talking about.

I'm in the middle of typing out the story of the guy who brought the sub into my ER when I realize what I'm about to reveal.

It's the spell she's put on me. Without even thinking twice about it, I was going to tell her so many things that could identify who I am, and I'm not ready for that. Don't know if I ever will be, but this is the first time I've *wanted* to in several years.

I delete the message and start over.

ROMANTICSADISTLL:

That's why you should agree to play and be taught to submit. Call it research. No thought, no awkward, no wondering what is wanted or expected, because you will be told, shown, and taught. Your insecurities are called with knowledge that you are doing as I want and desire

WILLDIVE4PLANTS:

You're straight out of my books.

I'm just saying.

Also, I've been a sub for many, many years. But I've only had one Dom—my ex-husband. We divorced because I couldn't be what he needed, and he deserved to be with someone who could. But with that in mind, I really don't know how to be someone else's sub, because we never played that way. So thank you for being open to teaching a sorta-newb.

Now I have to get my legs to work to actually take me inside the gym.

FML.

Chapter Eleven

SIENNA

What the hell was I thinking?

The moment I had a solid plan for the plot of my book, I called Vi and told her the news. She was so excited, and she said something along the lines of "if only you were farther along in the process, you could be in the charity anthology we're putting out in a month."

A month in my authory brain from two years ago sounded like ages. Plenty of time to bust out a novella or a short novel, depending on what they needed for the project. When I stuck to my guns, I could write ten thousand words in one day. A fifty-thousand-word novel would take me a work week. Send it to my amazing editor Barb, who took maybe three days to work her grammar magic, then to Vanessa, to proofread and catch any booboos in the plot, then to Casey for one last round, because I'm anal, and she somehow catches the teensiest, tiniest typos, and boom! I was a published author once again.

So I jumped on the opportunity like I hadn't had writer's block for the past almost ten months, hadn't been out of the routine of sitting down to stare at a computer screen for twelve hours straight without coming up for air. Or maybe I just thought it would be like riding a bike. Muscle memory, ya know?

Twas not the case.

I was very, very wrong.

But still, it felt good. I felt a little more like myself, even though the words seemed to be coming much slower. I was made to feel even better when I hopped in my old group chat with my author besties, Vi, Tara, and Crystal. They welcomed me back with open arms, as if my last contribution to the silenced message thread wasn't while I was writing my last book almost a year ago. And when I confided I was a little discouraged because I was no longer a word machine, they also reminded me that the first ten thousand words always seem to take forever to write, and then the rest of the book flows much easier.

Now, I only have about fifteen thousand words left to make the fifty-thousand-word goal for the anthology. I have nothing else to contribute to it than Gym Daddy. His gentle motivation and easily given praise has been everything that's kept me going. Which is crazy, because I have yet to lay eyes on him again since we started talking. We've been at the gym at the same time several days now, and somehow, I haven't been able to catch even a glimpse of him. Not even when I've been forced to sit in the café so I can recharge my laptop.

I will never understand why people think they must hold their private conversations on speakerphone set to the loudest volume. So loud my noise-cancelling headphones pumping white noise into my brain can't even drown them out.

It makes my blood pressure crank up to the Boil setting.

But my laptop is fully charged as I set up shop in the café today, choosing a seat in a more secluded corner where it would be hard for inconsiderate jerks to pace right next to the chick clearly trying to get some work done while they scream back and forth with their buddy on speaker. Knowing Gym Daddy is in the same building, that we're breathing the same freaking air, is exhilarating. I'm right by a window that looks out to the front parking lot. If I don't catch sight of him walking past the café, I might still stand a chance of seeing him when he leaves and is walking to his vehicle.

I wonder what he drives. I know he has a motorcycle, but he also seems like maybe a truck type of guy. I don't get a sports car vibe from him. Definitely not sedan. I haven't asked him what he does for a living, but the neighborhood he lives in suggests he at least isn't a bum with a prepaid phone who's texting me using free Wifi. Plus, he has a membership *here*, which isn't one of those super-cheap gyms in shopping centers that are everywhere. Time of Your Life

Athletics is pretty bougee, if I'm being honest. It's one of my splurges I just refuse to give up, no matter how low my savings account goes.

Thankfully, a fellow Club Alias member I chat with whenever I see her works here, and I confided I hadn't been doing very well on the mental health front when I finally got my ass here a few days ago and she asked where I'd been. She was kind enough to pause my card from being charged for the next few cycles after seeing on my account I hadn't been in for five months.

When I check my notifications for the first time since leaving my car, I'm utterly thrilled to see Gym Daddy has not only sent me a couple of messages, but the first one is *super* long, my heartbeat skyrocketing as I sit back in the cushioned seat to devour his words.

ROMANTICSADISTLL:

The ones who understand (newbies are unfortunately preyed upon) what it is to be a true submissive are often very strong, powerful, intelligent, and independent women in real life and who offer and desire what they do to whoever they trust and feel deserve it. Because they need/crave the release they get from submitting. They want to feel a sort of freedom from the power, responsibility, decision-making, and those they view as weak. Speaking strictly of straight women who desire to submit, they want a man to be a MAN—strong, protective, decisive. a leader not to be

questioned, and physically and
mentally able to guide, control, and
correct by any means necessary.
But also a gentleman, nonetheless,
who knows how to treat someone
who gives themselves over and is
under their care and protection. Cis
female subs, slaves, pets,
princesses, masochists, brats...
these are egos I know and
understand. Different kinks have
different rules. True sadists just
torture, and that's what they are and
do. Their partners have different
mindsets and needs. *I* am a
hedonist... pleasure just for
pleasure as well. If a girl wants to
just fuck and play without anything
"other"—meaning other than they
just like to be used like some
nympho porn star slut and probably
fuck like one too—then by all
means, let's fuck. Because vanilla is
still ice cream. Not going to turn it
down if it's someone I desire, just
because she doesn't want to be
ruled 24/7. It's actually a very, very
rare thing to find someone who
wants to live the lifestyle all the
time.

Can't meet in gym, little one.
Discretion. I'll tell you where when
I'm done showering. You'll have to
just trust me... and you... to
behave.

Oh, fucking hell. I can't even spend a second dissecting what his long message means because he clearly wants me to meet him somewhere else. Somewhere that's not my safe place, my happy oasis, where lots of the employees recognize and would look out for me if I told them I needed them to. And while I feel an embarrassingly deep connection to Gym Daddy after chatting with him and opening up more and more over the past week, in reality, I still don't even know his name. Not even just his first name! I don't know his occupation. I don't know anything personal about him whatsoever.

And trust me, I've used all the FBI skills I've ever learned during book research to try to find this motherfucker. Reverse image search. Scouring the different social medias that are neighborhood and area based. Searching his screen-names on every search-engine site on the fucking internet.

Not one damn thing.

He does not exist.

If it wouldn't break the promise I've made to him about being discreet, I would totally ask my Club Alias acquaintance at the front desk who he is. I would walk up there and casually stand with her while we chat, letting her know that a hotty's about to walk by us and out the door and that I'd buy her a coffee or something if she'd tell me who he is. Just his name. That's all I'd need. And then I would deep-dive once again into the internet's depths to find out all I could about him.

But doing so would call attention to the two of us. It

would form an association, at least in that one employee's mind. And there's no way to be sure she wouldn't say something about my little crush to someone else. I've been burned too many times to trust any woman who is not Vivian Lowe or Astrid Walker with an actual important secret.

So my only options are to either do as he says and leave where I feel safe, which is what a younger, much more naïve Sienna would've done without a second thought, or I can be honest and tell him I'm not ready for that yet.

I choose neither of those two options and instead lie my ass off so I don't displease him, even though he's not actually my Dom. Right now, he's just a fellow kinkster I'm getting to know, and he has no actual dominance over me.

I have not gifted him my submission.

I have not given him permission to order me about.

He has not earned my trust yet, so it would be a rookie mistake to give him unquestioned obedience. No matter how devastatingly hot he is.

But being the people-pleaser I am to my very bones, I still don't want him to be disappointed, so a little lie to ease the rejection will do no harm to either one of us.

WILLDIVE4PLANTS:

I can't leave the gym. My best friend's little girl is in child care, and I told her she could run do some errands while I sit here in case she gets paged for a kiddo 911 🐾 I was hoping you and I could just chill in the café like friends. That's discreet, right?

ROMANTICSADISTLL:

Not quite discreet. Long story, but if this thing between us goes anywhere, I'll explain the whole thing. I promise. One day soon, I'll meet you in the café. Then you'll meet truly discreetly, where we can have longer.

Ominous… but at least he doesn't seem upset I'm not leaving to meet him somewhere else. I don't really know what to say, so I just send an acknowledgement.

WILLDIVE4PLANTS:

Noted.

And then the disappointment I was so worried about him feeling decides to come hang out on my shoulders instead.

I discover my desire to meet him in person after talking to him constantly for the past week is slightly stronger than the debilitating anxiety I feel overtake me whenever I try to imagine what it will be like actually looking him in the eye, speaking to him, hearing his voice and it being directed at me. Add in the idea of him actually touching me—like, at all, not even sexually—and I hardly recognize myself.

I may be a lot of things, but I have never in my life been shy when it comes to talking to *anyone*. My mom used to say I've never met a stranger, because even when I was little, I'd start up a conversation with anyone within hearing distance. Still to this day, when I'm at the grocery store for example, I can't help but start chatting with whoever is next to me. Whether it's to tell them whatever they have in their cart is delicious, or maybe to give them a random compliment—anything. Who knows? Maybe it's a nervous tic or some-thing, a way to avoid awkward silence. But I don't *feel* nervous when I talk with anybody; I really can't explain it.

So it's very strange for me to feel such anxiety about just trying to form words in his presence.

Or maybe it's different. Maybe it's not anxiety and instead it's... anxiousness? In my mind, those two things are not the same. Anxiety always has a negative connotation to it, while anxiousness seems more like you're just dying to do something, you're ready, chomping at the bit, can't sit still because you are so riled up to do whatever it is that's giving you that feeling. Not necessarily a positive connotation, but not definitively negative either.

Which makes more sense, as it's definitely disappoint-ment I'm feeling that he won't come to the café to meet. So, I try to reassure him, put his mind at ease that being seen with me will not be a big deal, hardly noteworthy, in an attempt to change his decision.

WILLDIVE4PLANTS:

I'm no one special at the gym. Everyone just knows me as that quiet author chick. I have named a couple of characters after some of the café employees for keeping me fed though LOL. But I'm no one you'd have to worry about being seen in public with.

Side Note: do you do personal training?

I ask once again, because he seems to always avoid answering. It would give us the perfect excuse to be seen together at the gym. His reply makes me laugh, because I totally didn't think of it the way he did.

ROMANTICSADISTLL:

So let's see... Sit with the girl who everyone knows writes kink novels 😊 The point of being discreet in my case is to avoid any association with the lifestyle. But as I said, that's a discussion for a later date.

To answer your question, I have trained people before, but in general, not really.

Why do you ask, little one? In your picture, you look amazing. But you haven't sent like... a lingerie pic or anything, soooo... 😈

I giggle like a damn schoolgirl at the compliment and at

the fact that he's fishing for a naughty picture.

Something I haven't taken in a few years, not just since I've been single.

WILLDIVE4PLANTS:

> LMAO! I said "across." Like acrooooss. Not *with* haha

> And they don't know I write kink, just romance. They probably think Hallmark channel 🙄

> And! I don't even know your name. Of course I haven't sent those 😬

"Ha! Take that, Mr. Fisherman. I can do that too," I tell my phone, forgetting I'm sitting in public for a second, and I glance up to make sure no one is looking at me funny. When I see I'm alone in my corner of the café, I suddenly have the urge to be a little brave. When was the last time I took a photo that wasn't in either workout clothes, comfy clothes I write in, or whatever I've been wearing for a week straight while under my cloud of depression?

Turns out, not as long ago as I thought.

I scroll my Instagram for only a moment when I see a picture I forgot I'd taken in my garden. It was hotter than Hades, so I only had my bathing suit on along with my fanny pack so I wouldn't have to keep up with my phone.

There's nothing better than putting in headphones and listening to an audiobook while weeding. It's 100 percent meditation for a mind not built for clearing. Instead, it's as close as someone like me can get—being able to focus on one single thing without effort. A mindless task like pulling weeds for my body to zero its hyperactivity in on, combined with all my conscious thoughts focusing on the book being read… it equals pure bliss. Producing a calmness I'd never felt before I accidentally fell in love with gardening.

Before I can talk myself out of it, I send him the link to the Instagram photo.

WILLDIVE4PLANTS:

> As close as I can get. I don't have anything else that's recent and shows more than just cleavage.

When the little checkmarks don't turn black to indicate he's seen the message, after a minute, I remember I have to get my ass to work finishing the book.

Four hours later, I'm more upset than I have been in the past year.

And there's only one person I want to tell about it and make me feel better.

WILLDIVE4PLANTS:

> OMG I'm sobbing in the locker room. I lost everything I wrote today. My laptop shut down, and it didn't autosave, even though I have it set! 😭 FML

Thank goodness, his response comes fast. There's no

solution in it, but just his attention is enough to calm the rising panic enough I can take a breath.

ROMANTICSADISTLL:

Holy crap, I didn't think that was even a thing anymore with all the autosave options.

I squawk before realizing he can't hear me, "Exactly! It shouldn't be a thing anymore. But it's—"

WILLDIVE4PLANTS:

Right?! But it's Mercury fucking Retrograde, so just... Fuck me. Of course this happened 😊

"Great, now he's going to think I'm extra-extra crazy when I go busting out my astrology shit. Great job, freak," I grumble to myself, ignoring the girls giving me weird looks as they go from the steam room to the sauna.

ROMANTICSADISTLL:

LOL! Poor little thing... Come sit on my lap, and I'll make it all better.

That makes my breath completely halt in my lungs.

First, I picture Gym Daddy... sitting on a workout bench upstairs, since that's the only setting I've actually seen him. He pats his thigh, and I enter the image as he reaches out with his other big hand, pulling me toward him when I go to sit on his knees. The move makes my ass nestle right up against his cock, which is easily felt through his gym shorts. I see my knees draw up, and his thickly muscled arm comes around them, wrapping my whole body up in his embrace as he hugs me tight.

And then I watch as something happens that I haven't allowed since my life began to slowly crack almost two years ago before it completely fell apart.

All the tension in my entire body dissolves, and as I deflate, his arms tighten even more, seeming to keep me held together while I allow myself to finally crumble, a dam not breaking but bombed on purpose. No longer needed to hold back a river of emotions and mental turmoil as it's permitted to flow freely, redirected and safe away from destroying anything innocent nearby. As long as I'm right here, in his arms, I can let it all out without the worry of it touching anyone else.

I snap out of it just long enough to send one message before I drift once again.

WILLDIVE4PLANTS:

No, I did not just read that and catch myself curling into fetal position.

Second, I picture Dumpster Daddy. Probably because that's the last time I actually sat on someone's lap. Before then, it had been a super-long time. I'm not a cuddler, and Art didn't mind I'd rather not be wrapped up, where I'd get all sticky and gross, especially at night in bed, since my Prozac gives me night sweats.

So sexy.

But I was happy on Dumpster Daddy's lap, comforted and comfortable as he first checked out my hand. Another big, strong, muscular man, clearly older than me, taking control of the situation and allowing me to follow his lead. What a relief it had been not to have to figure out how to get myself out of the mess I was in.

That's all I want.

That's all I crave.

My mind is too full, screaming with too many voices, to try to make wisely thought-out decisions. It makes me impulsive, where I just say "fuck it" and pick whatever is yelling the loudest, and then I have to deal with the consequences of that "make it stop" reaction.

Like right now, when I know I have work to do, but all I want to do is walk upstairs, say "fuck discretion," and sit on Gym Daddy's lap like he teasingly offered.

"What? I was only following your orders," I say aloud in a sultry tone, as if practicing how I'd voice it to him when he'd look at me with a face that said *What the fuck are you doing?*

But then I remember it's been several hours I've been writing in the café—all those words lost—and he's surely left by now. I shake my head, trying to get back on track. I pull out my laptop and get comfortable in the lounge chair.

WILLDIVE4PLANTS:
I have to write.

But all my mental disorders laugh directly in my face after I send the message, choosing to complete one full loop of my intrusive, repetitive thoughts about the three men I've been thinking about constantly.

Dream Daddy.

What would it be like to sit on Dream Daddy's lap?

Oh, I shall tell you, because it's been one of my most-repeated fantasies while I've Hitachi'd myself to sleep ever since I've been single.

Dream Daddy, aka Sir Jeremy at Club Alias, is infamous. Known at the club as the Pleasure Dom who sets records for how many times he can make a submissive orgasm. I've never been with a Pleasure Dom, but they sure are fun to write. Especially when I switch to their point of view and get to pretend like I have any clue what a person who gets off on making another person come as many times as physically possible could possibly be thinking.

It's dreamily entertaining to romanticize though.

But as frequently as Sir Jeremy is called forth from my spank bank when I need a spectacular image to send me over the edge, in reality, it's not the orgasms I'd pay money to experience.

Get this: You know how I literally just got through thinking about how I'm not a cuddler and hate feeling like I'm smothered—which is its own little quirk in itself, because I'm pretty into erotic asphyxiation?

Ya ready?

It's not the guaranteed ticket on a rocket straight to subspace that makes Dream Daddy so fucking... well, dreamy.

It's his aftercare.

Yeah.

Right?

WTF?

I can imagine telling him, "I don't like cuddling, but if you don't snuggle me right now, I'm gonna be big sad, Sir."

He makes even the thickest, curviest, the most Amazonian women look like little fragile puppets when he finally decides they've taken enough of his forced pleasure, picks up their ragdoll body, and carries them over to the overstuffed leather recliner to envelop them with all those black-fabric covered muscles. So when I picture myself in their place, 5'6" and 125 lbs., my weight pretty much evenly distributed, which means I'm not very curvy aside from my silicone boobs, it looks like one unintentional flex of his bicep could crush my entire ribcage.

But instead of all that power in one body scaring the shit out of me, it makes me want to tuck into myself meekly, tiptoe up to him, tilt my head back to look up at him with anime-wide eyes that glitter with begging words that don't need to be said aloud, and give myself over to him. Mind, body, and fucking soul.

Just take me, Dream Daddy. I'm yours to use as you see fit, as long as you cuddle me when you're through.

Jesus fuck, I'm pathetic.

I shake my head once more, this time forcing myself to type out my intentions so maybe I can get some fucking work done.

WILLDIVE4PLANTS:

My brain can't math right now, but whatever 50K minus 37,049 is, that's what I have to write today or I am royally fucked. And not the fun kind where I'm called princess. So, for my own self-motivation, I'm going to pretend you're my Dom who's just like the one my friend is married to and have given me a word count assignment, in which there would be consequences ON TOP of losing all my PREORDERS!!!

*Breathes heavily

OK. Now that I've panicked and freaked out... I apologize for the shouty caps 😅

The joys of being a creative type. K Bye.

I set my notifications to Do Not Disturb and do something my therapist, Doc, has told me repeatedly not to use as a form of motivation.

I tell myself I can't check my phone until I have two thousand words written, and if I do, then something terrible will happen.

Doing this on purpose when I have a disorder that forces

these awful thoughts on me anyway, and then puts them on replay, basically undoes any progress I've made in therapy to make it stop happening so frequently.

But I'm desperate, and I can work on fixing my permanently broken brain after I meet my deadline.

When I check my phone exactly 2,133 words later, I have a message waiting for me from Gym Daddy.

> ROMANTICSADISTLL:
>
> LOL. I'm nowhere near your level, but I've been known to be decent with the words I choose. Of course, there's much to be said for physical presence... and delivery. So you'll have to add that later.

I snort grumpily.

> WILLDIVE4PLANTS:
>
> CORRECTION! I was very physically present THIS MORNING. But SOMEONE must've taken one look at the nerd in the café and made his escape without saying hi 😩
>
> Or at least that's what my intrusive thoughts decided to pick on me with.
>
> See? *twirls finger by my head. I told you I was nuts 😩

But also, yes. I've been impressed as hell by the words you've chosen. Because 99.9999% of the time, men are cringe when they try to talk "NOT BEHAVINGLY." Hence why I didn't block you when you did it the first time. Everyone else got the boot when they didn't listen when I said I'm here for research only. You're... given special privileges.

Entirely for research purposes though 😏

I don't hear from him again while I go through the last chapter I wrote, fixing little typos and switching out repetitive words. When I get to the end of the document, I send it to Barb so she can go ahead and start editing it while I attempt to finish writing the ending. I pack up my bag and head out of the little area closed off with a pony door, and when I start to pass the showers, I come to a stop, staring into the brightly-lit alcove. Two long rows with individual, private shower stalls on either side of each row are separated by a wall of a seemingly endless supply of perfectly folded, pristine white towels and washcloths.

The sound of a couple of the faucets running along with the scent of clean steam coming from the alcove is enticing, when for the past several months the mere thought of forcing myself to shower was enough to make me bury my head in my pillow and take a long nap.

To anyone who has never had a depressive episode or

been diagnosed with any kind of mental illness, I'm pretty sure they wouldn't understand the idea of a shower feeling like a huge undertaking. Get in, soap up, rinse off, get out. Done.

Wrong.

Because in a disordered mind, it's aaall the steps leading up to the shower, every minute detail of what happens inside the shower, and then again, aaall the shit you have to do when you get out.

Like now, for instance, I'd have to walk about twelve feet ahead and find a locker that's not taken. I'd have to put my bag in and set a temporary code for the lock, then try my best to not only remember the code but also which locker it is, because they all look alike. Another number to try to remember. I'd have to go up to the long line of sinks beneath the beautifully lit mirror that runs twenty feet, where there are canisters set on the counter next to each faucet.

I could grab a disposable razor or two from a canister, take them into one of the shower stalls, but first, I need to grab two washcloths—one for my face and one for my body —and two towels—one for my body and one for my hair.

And then the real work begins.

I don't know when in the process it happened, but while I was lining out all the things I'd have to do first in order to take a shower, I unconsciously started doing them. Maybe when the idea flipped from being daunting to inviting, when I remembered I could shave my legs for the first time in God only knows how long, since I can never remember to add razors to my grocery delivery.

Whenever it may have happened, it doesn't matter. What matters is the fact that I've already completed the annoying task of hanging up my two washcloths, my two towels, undressed without getting my clothes damp with my wet bare feet, managed to hang all said clothes on the one little silver hook on the wall outside my stall, and am now spinning the handle to let out an endless supply of scalding water—just the way I like it.

It takes an embarrassing amount of time, but I finally get the hair tie untangled from where it was buried deep inside the rat's nest that made the top of my head its real estate. We won't talk about how much hair was ripped out in the process.

Nor will we acknowledge the amount of hair that comes out of my head just from ducking my head under the water to get it wet. Certainly not the strands that come out when I shampoo, rinse, and repeat three times, because why the hell not? And last, but definitely not least—because it's, in fact, the largest quantity of all—we will not pay any mind to the literal chunks of hair that come out as I condition, run my fingers through to get some of the tangles loose, and rinse.

Nope. We're just gonna take our big toe with the chipped off nail polish and sliiide that huge wad of my poor mane off the top of the drain it's covering in the middle of the floor and tuck it in the corner of the stall to be disposed of when this mission is complete.

I'm sure it's been close to an hour I've been under the spray, the heat of the water never dipping no matter how many other women have come in, showered in other stalls, and left within a couple of minutes like normal people do. I've got my eyes closed, head tilted back as I let the water cascade over my tender scalp, when my phone dings loudly off the tiles, making me jump. I dry off my hands on the towel hanging over the glass door and reach for my phone on the little shelf the disposable razors of sitting on, looking like they went through war and just want to be laid to rest in a recycling bin somewhere.

I smile when I see Gym Daddy's message.

ROMANTICSADISTLL:

I know. But I'm also different in the fact that I am artfully sensual in my sexual advances instead of clubbing you over the head by being oafishly blunt.

WILLDIVE4PLANTS:

It's very much appreciated. My head couldn't take much more. Also, how did you do that? It's like you sensed I was showering at the gym to get the writing troll look off me.

"Oh, what the hell, Sienna? Why would you even send that?"

WILLDIVE4PLANTS:

Aaaaaand just file that under things NOT to say when you're trying to be funny and instead sound like you're fishing. 🪨 You make smart girls stupid. Just in case you never noticed.

Chapter Twelve

SIENNA

The next morning, I'm back in my lounge chair in the women's locker room at the gym. I finally got home after my obscenely long round of hygiene at around midnight last night, and all that physical activity wore me out to the point I went right to sleep.

How sad that just taking a shower is that exhausting for me.

Moving along from that depressing thought, I do have to admit I'm in a tremendously uplifted mood. And it only gets higher when Gym Daddy's message lights up my phone.

> ROMANTICSADISTLL:
>
> LOL I prefer to call it putting them at ease so they feel comfortable and safe enough to be silly and free without judgment. I'm upstairs BTW.

I scroll up to see what message he was replying to and giggle when I realize he's talking about my "makes smart girls stupid" comment, trying my best to ignore the fact that only one floor separates me from him.

I go on the website to see how much time I have left before I must upload my completed manuscript and take a screenshot, attaching it to a message.

WILLDIVE4PLANTS:

This is a countdown of how much time I have left.

50K - 44456 is what I have to write and edit before that clock runs out in eight hours and 58 minutes. I have never not had my book fully completed at least two WEEKS before my deadline.

An hour later, I have to take a break or I feel like my head will explode. So of course I end up scrolling Reddit for inspiration. And the squirrels have joined the party.

WILLDIVE4PLANTS:

Fun fact—did you know there are actual ads on Reddit by men offering CNC fantasies to be fulfilled? Like, full on, "I'll meet you in a park at night and throw you in a van." 😊 Where was this shit 15 years ago?

I want to find someone who will pay me to let them clean my house. Is that a kink?

ROMANTICSADISTLL:

LOL that's funny. I've done it. Not
offered ads but had her give her
schedule for every morning for a
week and a half before I took her

My jaw drops, and I'm suddenly overcome with jealousy. Which is ridiculous, seeing as I haven't even met this man in person yet. His next message comes through right as I'm sending my reply.

ROMANTICSADISTLL:

Also, I'm jamming "Islands in the
Stream" as I lift 😋 just letting it ride.

WILLDIVE4PLANTS:

😊 seriously?! 😊 Guess what my
first BDSM book was about 😊

I laugh at the image he paints, the handsome, burly man covered in tattoos and a salt-and-pepper beard who looks like he could snap someone's neck with his bare hands, up there pumping iron to a Dolly Parton song.

WILLDIVE4PLANTS:

🎶 that is what we are... No one in
between🎶 My Daddy had that
record 😋

Now when I see you over on the big boy equipment when I'm on the pussy machines, I'll wonder if you're listening to like… ABBA when all the other dudes—and I—are listening to metal 😅🤭

ROMANTICSADISTLL:

LOL I was feeling 80s pop and that came on. But IDGAF 😜

WILLDIVE4PLANTS:

You're pretty fucking dreamy, huh?

Anyhoo, I just decided I'm changing what I plan to write for the final scene where she finally fulfills his fantasy, which was going to be just hot indoor voyeuristic sex. Instead, and this actually fits the plot way better anyway, with hints about her I didn't realize I was even dropping. It's going to fulfill both their fantasies. He still gets to watch, but he'll be watching her CNC scene.

ROMANTICSADISTLL:

Your pussy muddy be amazing if you're always on the pussy machines 😜

WILLDIVE4PLANTS:

LMAO! I don't know what made me laugh harder, what you said, or what you meant to say before typos got you. 😂

> While I am a crazy plant lady and enjoy getting super dirty in my garden, I don't believe it would be good for my pH balance to give my pussy a mud bath. 😜

ROMANTICSADISTLL:

LOL often I just leave the typos because well why not 😅

WILLDIVE4PLANTS:

> As a full-time author, I've gotten good at translating my own typos and autocorrect, so meh

Nine hours later, I sigh with resignation and open Kik to see I haven't gotten a message from him in all the time.

WILLDIVE4PLANTS:

> Well, I did not finish before my deadline. But! I uploaded a placeholder I can replace the second my book goes live on release day. So at least I won't lose all my pre-orders.

> Also, bright idea writing a freaking CNC scene in public. Now I have to wait for these other chicks to leave so they don't see the puddle I'm no doubt leaving in this damn chair 😂

When I haven't heard from him in another hour, I

decide I'm done writing for the day since I now have four more to complete the book.

With nothing else to do, since I don't want to get on Amazon or TikTok, which would certainly lead to me signing up for retail therapy, I decide to brave my email inbox.

I've been emptying it for close to twenty minutes when I come upon an email from Club Alias that arrived three days ago. I click on it and see it's from the social media site one of the owners created for the club a while back. Vi had signed me up for the beta version, to play around on the site and app and to report any glitches, but once it was opened up to all the members and I saw everyone's profiles, most of them happily paired off and linked to their partner's profile, I signed out and haven't been on but maybe a time or two since. Just to see if anyone new joined or if there were any interesting events coming up.

But this email, it's a notification saying someone from the club wants to be friends. And because Seth is an evil genius, he didn't allow any hints of who that member might be, which forces traffic to the actual site if you want to find anything out.

"Dirty bastard," I grumble, clicking on the link and signing back in to my account, which thankfully is effortless, since my computer remembers and fills in all my log-in information.

I see the little silhouette at the top has a 3 in a little flag, so I click on it to see who sent me a friend request.

And I can't even put a name to the sound that leaves my mouth when I read who the members are.

It's not Dixie, the sweet bartender at the club, who makes my peripheral vision go fuzzy.

It's not Evie, the high school librarian who put on my very first solo author signing at Club Alias when I published my first book.

No. It's not my friendly acquaintances with other subs from our lifestyle club who sent their requests *months* ago.

It's the request sent three days ago from a blacked-out profile picture with two words next to it, while the Accept and Reject buttons sit beneath them.

SIR JEREMY.

Chapter Thirteen

SIENNA

One month later

There's a big argument online about who first put the words "if these walls could talk" together in a published sentence. But who said it first and whether it was a poem, a movie title, or even song lyrics isn't important. What that phrase means to me now is.

Because I now see the intrusive thoughts I've worked a lifetime to quiet as the voices everyone so wishes their walls possessed. In fact, my voices *are* the walls, ones built up inside me, around my heart and soul, and they're fortified over and over again, strengthened every time they whisper their warnings and reminders.

I no longer see them as being unkind, as my own mind fucking with me.

They've been right far too many times now for me to have the desire to get rid of them anymore. While they bring me immeasurable pain with each repetition of their cruel words, I've learned that pain would be far worse had I not been fairly warned by my walls that talk to me.

They're that certified "blunt and unfiltered" friend people warn you about before you meet them.

Other people might have similar walls that speak to them. Only they might call them "intuition" or "instinct" or a "hunch."

They might "get a feeling," a "feeling in one's bones," a "gut feeling," or just feel "funny."

If someone doesn't care what anyone thinks about their word choice, or if they truly feel these voices are *more* than just their "Spidey sense" going off, then they might call it "divination" or "clairvoyance" or "second sight," or that they're having a premonition.

But most people feel a milder form of what I do, and they think of it as just an "inkling," a "sneaking suspicion," or they get the "impression" something is coming. They might even get an unexplainable sense of foreboding.

Yet what I feel, what I hear and see inside my head when my walls start whispering their bitter not-nothings, is so much... *more*. So much more intense and impossible to ignore. With my artistic mind—in which I use words to paint a picture instead of brushes and wet colors—I see what my voices are saying in vivid images, watch the images form a scene behind my eyelids, the scenes adding up to the length of a whole movie, and I'm sure if I let them continue on with their repetitive ramblings, they could show me every avenue and outcome of every decision of an entire lifetime.

If these walls could talk?

No. There's no *if*. They do. They don't shut up. And for the first time in my life, I don't want them to. Because I need those whispering walls to protect me.

Even if it's from myself.

Part 1: FIN

Please read this note from the author:

Dearest Reader,

If this is your first venture into my Club Alias World, welcome! If you are a longtime lover of my beloved series, thank you for sticking around through so many of my characters' stories. It means the world to me that y'all continue to beg for more and more of them.

This book, you might have noted, is a little different than the others. For one, it's a cliffhanger. I am so freaking sorry to those who hate cliffies, but it just had to be done, and here's why.

Even if you don't know a single personal thing about this little hippy author—oop! Sound vaguely familiar?—I'm sure you could tell that Sienna seems a bit... real? A bit more human than the average heroine? At least, that's the nice way of putting it, when my intrusive thoughts want to say things like "trainwreck" and a "should-be-padded-room resident."

This story is a passion project of mine.

This story isn't written like a lot of the others, with questions like "What will readers think?" "Will they hate that it's going to be a duet?" "What about my instalove enthusiasts? Will they hate that she has more than one prospect and hasn't even met any of them in person by the end of Part 1?" in mind.

Okay, that's a total lie. Of course I asked myself those questions. My brain forms questions inside my head without my consent all the time. But the difference is, I stuck to my guns—with the encouragement of my girls Barb and Vanessa, who kept reminding me this was a book I wanted to write for MYSELF, so I could read about a heroine like me and imagine her... not being "fixed" but learning she's not actually broken to begin with.

Because as much as we use words like "disorder" and "illness" when it comes to mental health, it does not change the fact that the person who has it is a HUMAN. And just like everyone in the world has a unique fingerprint, we need to remember that everyone in the world has a different mind. And I wanted to write about a heroine who goes through a not-so-instant process of realizing she's not LESS THAN, because of her mental health. She is also not TOO MUCH, as so many people have told her—me—throughout her life.

She's just fucking right.

The cute sign you see at HomeGoods that says "You are exactly who you are meant to be in the world" or whatever, may be cliche, but when you really think about it, they ain't lyin'. If we took away all the "mental illness" in the world, what would we be left with?

The answer is *not* perfect happiness.

It's actually pretty fucking boring.

All the art and stories and creativity that fills the world with color and excitement, there's a very high chance it came from someone who's "not quite right in the head."

I told a friend recently, "It's sad, but at this point, I don't know who I would be without my voices," talking about my Obsessive Compulsive Disorder and intrusive, repetitive thoughts. And they responded, "Nobody."

And of course my first reaction was to be slightly hurt. Like, damn, bruh. But then I remembered who I was talking to. My bestie with Asperger's Syndrome, who just tells me like it is and literally cannot concern themselves with things like tone and wording.

They continued, "Without your voices, who would've told you all your characters' stories? So you wouldn't be an author. Who would get you to do crazy shit like jump in a dumpster to rescue plants, when you couldn't even previously keep a cactus alive? So you wouldn't be a crazy plant lady. Who would've made you leave your brother's house in the middle of the night to go meet some guy off the internet at a Denny's, which eventually led to you falling in love with his best friend, having three daughters, and now being married for over twelve years? So you wouldn't be a wife and mom. You'd be nobody, because you wouldn't have anything telling you to LIVE." (Read the entire story of *that* insane-o time in my life in The Blogger Diaries)

And that, dear reader, is why you befriend people with these so-called "illnesses" instead of being awkwardly "kind" while trying to avoid us.

My mental illnesses have now gotten sexual assault survivors into therapy when before they said they had no hope of healing.

My mental illnesses have given women who once gave up on finding love because of their "weirdness" their second wind to try again, especially after seeing the hotty *this* dumpster fire landed. I mean, come on. Have you seen my hubby in my videos on TikTok? Phew!

And he likes me. He really, really likes me. No matter how fucking "sick" my brain is, he doesn't want me any other way. And that just proves there is someone out there for literally everyone. We just have to find the person whose demons play well with our own.

So if you were pissed off about the book ending this way, look, I'm sorry. That depressive episode Sienna was going through, how she hadn't written a word in nine months, lost all her "friends" in one fell swoop, and all that other shit? 100% real. This book is a goddamn diary of sorts.

But what's also real in it?

Vivian Lowe. Who, in this book, is really my real-life best friend Jamie Vest, my ride or die, then flavored with a little Aurora Rose Reynolds, Erin Noelle, and CC Monroe —my author besties turned family. Every word out of Vi's mouth in this book was spoken by one of these real-life goddesses, and like Sienna, I couldn't have made it through the past two years without them.

What's fiction?

I couldn't tell you to save my life. At this point in world building, it's hard for me to decipher between reality and what I've made up and submersed myself in for the past eight years. It was very confusing the other day when I walked into my husband's shop and saw he had built me a life-size replica of the St. Andrew's Cross from one of the playrooms at Club Alias.

But that's a tale for a different book.

There's another reason this is a Part 1 instead of one whole book—I fell in love with these characters SO HARD, and I wasn't ready to leave them yet. I could've easily made this an instalove, wham-bam, thank you, ma'am, but I. Didn't. Want. To. If I could guarantee my readers wouldn't disown me, I would stretch Sienna's story to be a whole damn series just to keep spending time with Gym Daddy, Dumpster Daddy, and Dream Daddy.

Just wait, y'all. You ain't seen nothin' yet.

Plant Daddy Part 2 will be available January 31st.

Promise.

And you'll see Sienna get her happily ever after.

But with who?

I don't know. The voices haven't even told ME yet!

Love,

KD

PLANT DADDY

PART 2

USA TODAY BESTSELLING AUTHOR

KD ROBICHAUX

CLUB ALIAS SERIES

Plant Daddy

PART TWO

IMPORTANT NOTE FROM THE AUTHOR

Dearest Reader,

Ya see… what happened was…

I'm what's known in the writing world as a "pantser."

You remember back in the day when our teachers tried to pound it into our heads the importance of outlining and planning your entire essay or story before you even wrote the first word of your actual manuscript? Everything from those bubble charts or the boxes with arrows leading to other boxes that spread across a page until it damn near looked like one of those walls they find in a conspiracy theorist's secret room hidden behind a Murphy door?

Yeah, well… we pantsers look at all that and say… 😐 "Nope!"

The lightbulb turns on in our head, illuminating this brilliant idea for a story, and we may flesh it out a little bit in our mind, letting it form enough that we sorta know where to begin the journey, but then we just jump right in and start writing.

The characters and their tales are revealed to us much the same way they are to you—we just happen to be the ones typing it out while they talk, so you don't have to.

Now that I've set the scene…

This storyline and these characters took on a life of their

own. What started out as this fun idea to have a crazy plant lady join a sugar daddy dating site in order to fund her plant addiction has turned into something so much more.

And it's not entirely my fault.

Okay, so the first part was totally my fault: What was supposed to be a standalone book in the Club Alias Series, Plant Daddy, ended up releasing as Plant Daddy Part 1, because there was way more depth to these people than what I first saw when my lightbulb turned on.

My bad.

It also morphed into this therapeutic release for me, much like Confession Duet did back in 2015, when real-life Dr. Walker assigned me the task of writing myself a sort-of closure to my past. With Plant Daddy though, it was fun to write and put everything I've gone to therapy for down on paper.

Because we should totally document all our crazy, right?

👀

Turns out, yes! At least in this case, because that's where my fault was overshadowed by that of my amazing readers.

If I thought it was startling, the number of women who connected with my heroines across all twenty-something of my books, that doesn't even begin to touch on the staggering amount of you who messaged, commented, emailed, said in your reviews—any way you could possibly let me know— that you'd never related to a character more than Sienna before.

Quite the plot twist when I totally released Part 1 thinking, Welp, gonna have to warn people this was a passion project I wrote just for myself, so I could read about a character like me, since I'm weird and don't know anyone who's brain is like mine.

I'm serious as a heart attack, y'all. I wasn't going to necessarily unpublish it, but I was really thinking about not even putting any sort of effort into spreading the word about PD1. Because while it was cathartic and fun to write and I was proud of the words I'd written, I was also super embarrassed to show the world how truly "ain't right in the head" I am. And it was too late to be all "she's a totally fictional character."

Nope, I made it perfectly clear Sienna is me. Totally coocoo for Cocoa Puffs… right down to dedicating the book to one of the voices inside my head.

Like… who freaking does that?!

But then the messages and reviews started rolling in, and I was a sobbing mess for an entire month, reading and listening to all my readers saying this was THE book. This was the story they'd been dying to read all their lives, because it had a heroine just like them. It wasn't a storyline about a woman with this quirky little "character flaw" that was touched on sporadically throughout the book.

No, that's not how real mental illness works.

It dictates every thought inside our head and every word out of our mouth, and that's how I wrote it.

That's why it took over fifty thousand words just to introduce you to the characters and set the scene, and by the end of Part 1, Sienna hadn't even met Felix in person yet!

Usually by fifty thousand words, my characters are already balls-deep and on their way to their happily ever after.

But Sienna isn't that lucky.

Girl gotta overthink every... fucking... thing.

Just like me.

And, I discovered, just like tons of you.

So this has been another 792 words (so far) to tell you, dearest reader, that this book is NOT the end it was supposed to be. In fact, this is still only the beginning. And for those of you who said you hoped their story would never end because you could read about them for the rest of your life... I've got you, boo.

I've decided—

Nope. Scratch that.

Sienna and Felix have decided to turn their standalone romance into an entire spin-off for themselves.

Felix is demanding like that. *smirks

It will take my readers on Sienna's full journey of balling up everything she's always been told was wrong with her and embracing every last bit of it like an extra-soft stuffie.

With the help of a delicious doctor Dominant blessed with a neurodiversity that allows him to see through all social norms, she'll truly be able to shed all the negativity the world loaded onto her shoulders. This is something I feel is important to put out there in the world, and to do it right, to make it really hit different, that can't be done properly in one little book. Because if you guys really are like me, if you truly think the way I think and crave all the information you can get in order to use it as ammo against the voices inside your head, then there can't be any skipping ahead in the timeline. There can't be any "Six weeks later" and suddenly she's a brand-new person.

No. We need to read every single second of what happens as if it's a step-by-step guide on How to Start Loving Your Hot-Mess Self.

So I present to you, Plant Daddy: Part 2, which completes Plant Daddy—Book 1 in Sienna's spin-off of the Club Alias Series. A spin-off that will now be known as The Submissive Diaries.

You guessed it—a nod to my very first trilogy, The Blogger Diaries, where my crazy real-life journey as a hot-mess author began.

I hope you'll stick around for the ride. After all, I always have loved rollercoasters. Ask Vi.

Love,

~~Sienna~~ KD

PS: Oh, and @Jeayness, yes. Yes, there is smut in this one. I promise.

Chapter One

SIENNA

"Vivian P. Urkel! What the fuck is happening?" I scream, my mouth right up to the front-facing camera, so my best friend probably has the perfect view of my uvula—the little dangly thing that swings in the back of your throat. When I pull back so I can see her expression, my suspicions are confirmed.

It's the wicked grin with the evil little twinkle in her pretty eyes that give her away.

"Why, bestie. Did you just so happen to get a friend request on the Club Alias Members Portal from a certain Pleasure Dom you've been drooling over for years, not long after joining a bunch of dating sites?" Her giggle would make me want to punch her in the face if she wasn't my favorite female in the world.

"Quite the coincidence, *bestie*." My eyes narrow as she

260 • PLANT DADDY

flips her hair over her shoulder with too much delight for it to be anything but for show. "What. Did you. Do?" I ask, my breath coming out in heaves between the words.

She shrugs one bare shoulder, and it's then I zoom my brain's focus out and realize the hussy is in her bathtub, the camera's view cutting off right above her nipples.

She has great boobs. It was Vi who talked me into getting mine enhanced when she couldn't say enough good things about what her augmentation did for her self-confidence. While it did do wonders for my willingness to flash people, it didn't have quite the miraculous effect on my psyche I'd hoped for. Which did a lot to help me understand my lack of self-esteem had less to do with my body image than I first believed.

"Ooh, nothing. I was just having lunch with Twyla yesterday, and we stumbled upon the subject of different public scenes that have taken place at the club recently. And you know as well as I do that when public scenes at Club Alias is the subject of conversation, a certain Master of forced orgasms *always* comes up in the discussion," she says, making her eyes extra wide with innocence.

I growl at her. "That may be true, dear, sweet friend of mine, but how the hell did that lead to me getting a friend request from a Dom who likely didn't know I even existed before he sent said request?"

Her grin takes over her entire face before she tries and fails to mask it. "I did not break any best-friend codes. I didn't reveal any secrets you've specified to keep between us.

You've made it clear in our little circle that if there was one Dom you'd smash if ever given the chance, it would be Sir Jeremy."

"One does not smash Sir Jeremy, Vi. Tis Sir Jeremy who does *all* the smashing. And—"

"*Any*waaay!" she cuts me off. "When he came up in the conversation, I mentioned to Twyla that you and I were just talking about him and how pouty you got when I recon-firmed I have no idea who he is nor have access to Club Alias member personal information. That's when our adorable confidante Facetimed her husband right then and there and gave him the most precious puppy-dog eyes through thick-framed glasses I've ever seen."

Okay, now I'm less panicked and more on the edge of my seat.

"What did she tell Seth?" I ask anxiously, wondering what the tech genius behind Club Alias and all its security had to say in response to his wife.

"She made a request for him to contact Sir Jeremy to see how one would go about setting up a scene with him. After Seth had an absolute shit-fit thinking Twyla was inquiring for herself—which was quite comical, seeing as she literally gave him her V-card and has never been with anyone else, nor has any desire to—she informed him it was our sub friend who has only had one Dom. She told him the sub had never been unowned before this, since her first Dom was her now ex-husband, and that Sir Jeremy is the only Dom who piqued her interest at the club. And that's when

Seth had the brilliant idea to have Sir Jeremy contact the sub on the club's social media site, so he could answer her questions directly instead of playing a very kinky game of telephone through multiple people." She giggles. "Would that technically be a telephone orgy?"

I swallow thickly, ignoring her question. "And that's when you guys told Seth it was me?"

She snorts out a laugh and shakes her head. "Didn't have to. He was a child prodigy, remember? An actual, honest-to-God mastermind—no BDSM pun intended. He took that little bit of information and combined it with what he's observed at the club and knew straight away it was you."

My face blanches. "Is there anyone who *doesn't* know about my crush on Dream Daddy?"

A banner notification pulls down from the top of my screen, letting me know @kristinreuterphoto duetted one of my TikToks, and it distracts me with enough "somebody loves me!" warmth that my embarrassment fades a little.

She grins at that. "Apparently, Sir Jeremy himself. Seth said the man was very flattered and interested to meet a woman so special she inspired friends to go full-on junior high school to let him know he had a secret admirer."

I groan, "Oh God. He probably thinks I'm an immature and completely inexperienced prude now. The complete opposite of the super-confident, masochistic submissives he always scenes with."

"Ha!" Vi squawks. "Yeah, right. I'm sure he knows if

someone has a crush on him, it's not because of his movie-star good looks, seeing as no one knows what the hell he looks like. And it's certainly not because of his charming personality, since the man only speaks to the sub he's sceneing with. If he finds out a woman is interested in him, I guarantee he's well aware it's because of his other... attributes. And a woman who's attracted to *those*? She ain't no fucking inexperienced prude, my girl."

I sink back into the couch, mollified by her reassurance, and while my blood pressure is slightly lower than it was, I reach for my trackpad on my laptop and hover the pointed finger over the Accept button by Sir Jeremy's friend request.

Should I click it? Should I start talking to another man, when I'm already feeling a connection with someone else? I enjoy the conversations I have with Gym Daddy. Not only am I sexually attracted to him, but he makes me laugh, and I actually *like* what I know about him so far. He makes the 24/7 sub in me feel seen and extremely validated.

Sir Jeremy speaks to the... I guess you'd call it the "scene submissive" part of me like no other. Playing with him would be intense and all-consuming. I have no idea what it'd be like around a man such as him all the time, to be owned by him, his to dominate every second of every day. It might be too much of a good thing.

No. I don't think I could handle being around such extreme power all the time. It might be judging a book by its cover, prejudice, whatever one would want to call it, but I couldn't imagine the man I've watched so closely at the club, the one who seems to suck all the oxygen out of the room while he literally brings his sub to her knees with pleasure, would be able to joke around and be goofy. There's no way there's a jovial sense of humor beneath that mask of his. And even though his aftercare looks like it would be heaven on earth to receive, I can't see any other form of gentleness coming from that man. He's too big, too strong, too... much.

I'm ashamed of myself the moment the thought enters my mind. How many times in my life have I been called "too much"? Too excitable. Too anxious. Too caring. Too scatterbrained. It hurts every single time it happens, my face heating with embarrassment, feeling like I've been slapped, because usually it happens when I'm being animated and showing my passion about a subject. I'll be full of so much joy and excitement for something, and then the second the person says "whoa, calm down" or "take it down a notch" or however they say it, it's an instant glass of ice water thrown on my happiness fire. A punch in the gut that takes me from maxed-out to negative. So I feel like a hypocrite thinking Sir Jeremy is "too much" just because he's so intense to watch at the club.

But still, I feel somewhat guilty considering talking to another man when I'm feeling something for another. I know that seems a bit premature, since Gym Daddy and I aren't even dating. Hell, we haven't even met in person yet.

I don't even know his freaking name!

But the fact of the matter is, anything with Sir Jeremy

would basically be an automatic sexual situation. He sent me the friend request after being told a fellow member of a BDSM club admires him, which can't mean anything other than I admire the way he Dominates a woman sexually, seeing as that's what we mainly do at Club Alias. It's not like I could admire him for his dancing skills, or his taste in food and beverage—since I've never seen him on the dance floor nor at one of the bars next to it.

Deciding not to accept or decline the request, since I have such mixed feelings at the moment, I sit up to tell Vi just that, when suddenly my phone dings loudly, making me jump... and click the mouse... which was still hovering over the Accept button.

"Fuck!" I cry, seeing the screen switch to Sir Jeremy's profile with the words **You are now friends** at the top of the page. And as I hear Vi asking what my deal is, my eyes turn to her but catch on the banner at the top of my phone screen, which dropped down to tell me that I have a message on Kik from Gym Daddy.

My heart feels like the cars on *Fast and the Furious* when they flip the NOS switch on. I don't know how much more of this I can take.

First, a minor stroke from Sir Jeremy's friend request.

Then the roller coaster of emotions from Vi's and my conversation about how that request came to be.

Then the bejeezus is scared out of me from my ringer being entirely too loud in my silent house.

Followed by whatever the panicked feeling is I'm experiencing from accidentally accepting said friend request when I *just* decided to hold off.

And *now* a cardiac episode from finally hearing from my gym crush for the first time since this morning, when it's almost midnight.

"What's that face?" Vi asks, her voice sounding echoey in my head as if from a distance.

But above all the crazy emotions swirling around inside me at the moment, I can't ignore the overwhelming need to give Gym Daddy my full attention. I've done my best not to let the voices in my head convince me I hadn't heard from him in eleven hours—and never would again—because I'd freaked him out with my last text. Now is my chance to put the bottled-up anxiety at ease over the matter.

"Uh… sorry! Just saw one of my favorite TikTokkers is Live. I'll call you back!" I hang up, close Facetime, and open Kik at the speed of light, my heart still racing as I glance over my last messages to him.

WILLDIVE4PLANTS:

> Well, I did not finish before my deadline. But! I uploaded a placeholder I can replace the second my book goes live on release day. So at least I won't lose all my pre-orders.

Also, bright idea writing a freaking CNC scene in public. Now I have to wait for these other chicks to leave so they don't see the puddle I'm no doubt leaving in this damn chair 😬

ROMANTICSADISTLL:

Very proud of you for coming up with a temporary solution to give yourself more time to finish, little one. Been a crazy day at work and still not off, but had to pop on to see if you made it.

Lucky chair.

The last message startles a laugh out of me after I'd been so worried all day I grossed him out. And with it, a tension I didn't realize was holding my muscles rigid leaves my body so abruptly I'm like a balloon deflating, feeling exhausted but relaxed.

Before the voices can start in on me, overthinking what I should say in response, I allow myself to enjoy this relief, sending off a quick message before finally hauling my ass off to bed.

Completely forgetting about my new Club Alias Members Portal friend.

Chapter Two

FELIX

WILLDIVE4PLANTS:

> I would just like it known that I changed out of my pajamas and into workout clothes today 🏋️ Kinda a big deal for me.

> 🙄 Doesn't mean I'm gonna work out. But hey. I changed out of my pajamas.

Baby steps 😅

The messages come in one behind the other, and I smile, sending her a reply from the gym's parking lot.

ROMANTICSADISTLL:

I've been sitting in my truck emailing stuff. Going in now.

It's an exhilaration I haven't felt in a long time, knowing I'll be in the same building as the woman I can't stop thinking about. I have yet to catch sight of her in person, but just the fact that we're so close has excitement making my blood run hot.

If she were mine, I'd be going on and on about how proud I am of her for getting dressed today. As an ER doctor, I see more than my fair share of people with depression, mainly those who fell too deeply into that dark place in their mind and came to the tragic decision to try to reach that final bright light.

To know I'm partly the reason this special woman felt good enough today, had more energy than she's had in quite some time, to not just haul herself out of bed and to her favorite chair in the women's locker room at our gym to work on her book she's writing, but to take the time to change clothes makes me feel... powerful. Powerful like I've never felt before.

I feel powerful often.

Being the head doc of a hospital's emergency room, saving lives.

Being a respected Dominant at an exclusive and elite BDSM club.

How far I've come through hard work and using my intelligence alone, knowing how close to the bottom I was when I started this life I was given.

But for some reason, all of that is eclipsed by helping this beautiful girl dig herself out of her dark place.

Literally and figuratively.

I wonder how she'd react if she knew I was the man who pulled her out of the dumpster a few weeks ago.

I get out of my truck and unhook my backpack from the carabiner I have tied to the headrest of my passenger seat with parachute cord, and I stick my arm through the padded strap. I hear three dings from the cell in my pocket as I make my way to the entrance of the gym, and when I pull it out to open the app with my member ID, I force myself to ignore the messages until the front desk attendant scans the barcode and I can finally give her my full attention. I set my backpack on the bench in the center of two rows of lockers in the men's locker room, sitting down beside it and opening Kik.

WILLDIVE4PLANTS:

> I swear I used to work out every single day. *sighs

> Two weeks to make a habit, right? Just got to start the two weeks 😅

> I mean, I guess I could tell myself, "You get to peek at the dude you drool over at the gym," as motivation 😳😋

I smile at the reminder of the very first message she ever sent me. The immediate openness and honesty, confessing she'd seen me in public before and could identify me at the gym we're both members of—she gave me the opportunity to block her, in case I wanted to take the precaution. A lot of people do this on dating apps, blocking anyone they know in "real-life," not wanting to risk being recognized for all sorts of reasons. But just the fact that she informed me of her recognition instead of keeping it a secret… it made me want to get to know her more.

Which I know is terribly ironic and hypocritical, seeing as I haven't told her I knew her outside of the dating app as well.

At least my reasons are honorable.

In my head, anyway.

ROMANTICSADISTLL:

> I mean, you've been showing up to write, so at least there's a habit of coming here 😊

WILLDIVE4PLANTS:

> Exactly why I do it 😊 See? You get me 😊

"More than you even know, little one," I murmur, seeing the dots dancing to inform me she's typing once again.

WILLDIVE4PLANTS:

> Sidenote, because my meds haven't kicked in yet: I want to know how the fuck Lowe's keeps all their crotons out in full sun on concrete all day, but when I bring the little fuckers home and try to put them in full sun, they croak. Such bullshit.

My response is automatic, and I wince, hoping it doesn't make her connect any dots between me and the man from the dumpster.

ROMANTICSADISTLL:

LOL fresh trucks, babe! Plants are only out in "full sun" for a couple of days at most, and they're watered every night at the store. Then people take them home and follow the watering suggestions on the tag, which is like once a week. So the plants go into shock. Especially crotons, which don't take being moved very well to begin with. Hard to establish them. Don't even bother trying to transplant them.

WILLDIVE4PLANTS:

> Well that makes me feel way better 😊 And also, I'm so hot for you right now. 😜 Talk planty to me.

I know she's joking, but the mere thought of making her hot and her someday being confident enough to admit it to me in a message makes my cock swell inside my workout shorts. Which doesn't go away in the slightest when I see her next message pop up, and it's a video.

"*I*... am going into the gym," she says matter-of-factly, her eyebrows raised in determination as she sits in her car. "And not only am I going into the gym, but *I*... am going to go up the stairs." Her stern face wavers a bit, and she lets out a nervous giggle. The movement allows me to see out her window and that she's in the parking lot. "And once I get up those *Godforsaken* stairs... I'm gonna work out." She nods once. "That's what I'm gonna do." She winces. "I'm gonna do it." She snorts and then gives a big grin to the camera. "'Kay, here I go."

I can't help the smile that spreads across my face at her silliness. Not to mention the fact that she took a video speaking to me directly. She's never done that before. Yes, she's sent links to various TikToks she's made, but this... it's her first time talking to *me* with her *voice*.

I watch it again... and again. She looks different. Her hair is in a long, damp ponytail, not in the wild messy bun she always wore when I saw her rescuing plants, and not down and curled to perfection like in her profile picture—her professional author photo. It means not only did she get dressed today, but she also felt up to at least showering and washing her hair. Her face is makeup-free, and she's in a simple black tank top, so no unnecessary, extra effort has been made as far as I can tell from the short video, but I know damn well how monumental the steps she *did* take this morning are.

And while I've been doing my very best not to praise her like I would if she were my sub, since we haven't established any kind of rules between us and she hasn't given me direct permission to use monikers with her, I can't help it. I'm just so fucking proud of her.

But just as I'm typing out the message, a voice calls from behind me, and I spin on the bench, clicking the button on my phone to shut my screen off.

"Dr. Travers!"

"Brian." I grin, standing quickly and reaching out to shake the big guy's hand he holds out before leaves. He's one of the co-owners of Club Alias and one of the very, very few people in existence who knows my true identity in and out of the establishment. But he of all people holds discretion to the utmost level of importance.

After all, he's a fucking mercenary.

There's a mutual understanding—one that's more take-it-to-the-grave than even the club's NDAs and the honor between people in the lifestyle can assure—between me and the four men who created Club Alias. The four men who also happen to run Imperium Security next door to it. Imperium Security being a cover business for what they truly are—vigilantes... mercenaries who take matters into their own hands when the system fails.

With my Asperger's, it was much easier for me to grasp what Doc, my long-time friend since med school, was telling me when he came to me for help. One of the main aspects of my particular spot on "the spectrum" is I have to actively keep myself from fighting against social norms. Things that most people can intentionally accept even if they don't make logical sense.

So there was no question when Doc confided he's the head of a mercenary team who makes rapists disappear when justice won't be served otherwise and asked if he could put me on the payroll as their on-call MD. It was an immediate yes.

I can't willfully take someone's life, not after the oath I made, no matter how evil they might be, but I can make damn sure the brave men who've made it their life's mission to wipe them from the earth stay healthy and get any injury fixed under the radar.

Especially when a few moments later, I get a photo of a treadmill screen with a caption.

WILLDIVE4PLANTS:

Day one, I guess.

What are we listening to today?

I love it when she speaks to me this way, like we're old friends who have known each other forever. But at the same time, I can't let it go on much longer this way, or she might not be able to see me as anything more than that. It's better to establish the tone and the way she should view me as an authority figure from the beginning, or else it'll be hard to get back there if she becomes too lax.

So, after I leave the locker room, I make my way up the staircase that leads to the workout floor, spotting her immediately on the treadmill closest to the glass wall—just mere feet away from me on the landing. I'm lower and slightly behind her, so unless she were to look over her shoulder and down at this exact moment, there's no way she'd see me before I disappear behind the solid wall the glass is attached to when the next set of stairs begins.

Though I can't see her face from this angle, I *can* see clearly how small she is, tall and slender but no muscle tone. I know from holding her on my lap for that brief minute outside the dumpster that she's soft in all the right places, but from the way she's asked over and over, practically begging me, if I've done personal training before, she's unhappy with her body. She wants to get back to the way she looked before the depression took hold of her and she fell off the workout wagon. As I climb the rest of the way up, I have the sudden urge to give her just a little taste of the praise I have the uncanny ability to dole out, so breaking my own rules, I give us what we *both* want before we've ever established our roles.

I lean against the wall next to the water fountain, mostly blocked by everyone on the exercise bikes, but I have the perfect view of her flushed face as her head bobs above the screen of her treadmill with every step. I type out the message, glancing up at her as I hit Send.

ROMANTICSADISTLL:

> Great job, little one. I'm very, very
> proud of you. *kisses forehead

I watch closely, my focus on her every microexpression I can pick out from this distance. Four rows of moving bodies on big machines separate us, but in that moment, it's like the rest of the world ceases to exist as I see her headphone-topped ponytail swing out from behind her when her head whips toward her phone propped in the cupholder. She smiles even before she picks it up, I assume recognizing the notification is from me, which I confirm when I glance down just long enough to see my message go from Delivered to Read. My eyes return to her, and her physical response corroborates everything I've built up in my head, everything I desire from her.

Her mouth drops open, her hand not holding her cell letting go of the treadmill's grip rail to cover her parted lips with her fingers, her eyes widening then going half-mast. She must read it over and over, because she stares at her screen for a full minute or two and the message was only two short sentences.

She stumbles, righting her stride before my foot can complete its first instinctive step toward her, and it snaps her out of her fog as her lips form a very clearly mouthed "fuck!" She replaces her hand on the railing, using her thumb to message me back.

WILLDIVE4PLANTS:

> I swear to God, if you could've just
> seen my face when I opened that—

Oh, I could, little one. I could and did, I think but don't type to her. I have the feeling that if she knew I'm watching her, it would make her self-conscious. It would make her feel uncomfortable and not relaxed enough to be herself. And I so want to see her be herself. While she's mentioned before how awkward and what a nerd she is, calling herself the typical clumsy heroine of any early 2000s rom-com, she's actually a breath of fresh air. So many subs have this aura about them, sexy seductresses with perfect and graceful movements, almost like a Geisha. And although that is beautiful and can be absolutely delightful at times, it's so formal and… uptight; it can be exhausting, something I'd never want to be twenty-four seven.

What I truly desire is someone who can make me smile even when her mouth *isn't* on my cock.

A feat for sure, but not entirely impossible. Especially since this woman makes me smile often from her messages alone.

I've completed my short workout for the day—shoulders are my easy day—and am back in the locker room when I receive her next messages.

WILLDIVE4PLANTS:

> I'm seeing pretty lights in front of my
> eyes at 1.09 miles.

Good enough.

Impressive for not working out for several months and being stagnant for just as long. I want to reward her, even though she's not my sub. I want to praise her, give her incentive to continue on and not give up—not today, but to come back tomorrow and do it again. I try to think of something to say or do. Maybe a video so she can hear me tell her I'm proud of her?

I decide to send her a picture, which is something I haven't done this whole time we've been talking, even though she's sent me several. I don't take many, since I don't really have anyone to send photos to.

I'm in nothing but a thin white towel wrapped around my hips, because I'm about to hop in the shower, and it's not until I flip my phone's camera around to take a selfie that I realize this will be the first time she's ever seen my body, at least shirtless. I'm not worried about her recognizing me from the club or from the dumpster incident, since at the club I'm always disguised from head to toe, and I was pretty much fully covered at work, with a mask and hat too. It's just something that occurs to me.

What will she think when she sees me? I know I'm fit, and not just for my age—by any standard. Not being conceited, it's just fact. I'm of Polish descent, so I'm hairier than a lot of men, but I keep it neatly trimmed, long enough to be soft and doesn't poke uncomfortably through the fabric of my shirts, but short enough it doesn't get bushy and make the material stand out from my skin. I have several tattoos on my arms and my back, but none on my front. I recently buzzed my beard all the way down to my usual scruff. It had gotten too long and looked silly when I wore masks at work, so I decided to start over. It won't take long before it's at a more manageable length.

I'm bald, cleanly shaved. My hair started thinning in my early thirties, and when my barber told me I had a nicely shaped head and would look much better with it completely smooth instead of with my "ring of knowledge" as I jokingly call it, I allowed him to shave it off and have never gone back. I mean, I've gone back to my barber, but not back to my unshaven head. I still visit him to treat myself to a professional shave once a month, taking care of the upkeep myself the rest of the time.

So what will she think of me? What is her opinion on body hair, the color of it, her opinion on tattoos? She has many of her own tats, and she's clearly seen the ones on my forearms while I work out in short-sleeved shirts.

I've never worried about anyone's preferences on my physical appearance before, and I'm not so much worried as I am… anxious. I'm anxious to hear what she'll say in response as I snap the selfie, the very top of it hitting just below my chin and the bottom stopping on the towel right above my cock. No need to send her something obscenely immature like a hard-on tent. I don't have a dick pic on my dating site profiles either. I find the practice vulgar and uncreative, and from what I've heard from previous subs, they do nothing to entice most women. I also find that the men who post dick pics as their profile picture need more validation, craving assurance that their cock is impressive enough to attract attention. I don't need such platitudes. Again, I'm Polish, and along with being hairy motherfuckers, we're also endowed as fuck. I have no need for anyone to tell me I have a larger-than-average penis. It's just a fact.

Plus, I only want to send her a taste, just enough to stimulate her appetite and want more. If I were to send her a photo that includes what's beneath my towel, it could have the opposite effect. It was hard to believe the first time it happened, but there are women who will decide against a man who is well endowed for fear it will be too much to take.

I upload the photo into our message thread and hit Send, her response coming soon after, but long enough after it switched to Read that I know she must've stared at me for a while.

WILLDIVE4PLANTS:

> You're much prettier than I am right now.

> I'm gonna go die in the café.

My chest swells, and I smile at her compliment, knowing damn well she's trying to play it cool. I'll put a stop to that shit right now.

ROMANTICSADISTLL:

> You almost got a video so you
> could hear me tell you how good
> you're being and that you make me
> smile.

I can practically hear her sexily whimper through her next message.

WILLDIVE4PLANTS:

> (Photo of the gym stairs aimed
> downward from the top)

> Let me make it down the stairs,
> pretty please. You can't be putting
> images like that in my head when
> I'm trying to do super-hard things...
> like walk.

That actually pulls a chuckle from me, and I put my phone in my locker so I can take a quick shower. When I return and get dressed, I then check my messages, seeing she didn't send anything else.

I wonder where she is. Is she still here at the gym, or did she leave while I was rinsing off? The idea of her being gone while I'm still here is weirdly unsettling. I don't want to be here without her. It's oddly comforting in a way, when I know she's in the same building as me, even though I've never even approached her in person. And I have the sudden urge to see her with my own eyes again. The brief minute I watched her on the treadmill wasn't nearly enough, and I realize she unknowingly gave me that same taste that sparked my appetite for more of her.

I grab my backpack out of the locker and my huge water jug's strap, slamming the door closed before striding out of the locker room and the short distance between it and the café, my eyes scouring all the couches over by the front wall of windows to my left. She's not there.

ROMANTICSADISTLL:

Where are you?

How is my mood sinking so quickly just from the idea that she's already left? This is ridiculous. No woman has ever had such an effect on me before, especially one I've never even spent any amount of time with in person before.

My phone vibrates twice in my hand.

WILLDIVE4PLANTS:

Right here 🥴

Dying. Look to your right.

And just like that, my mood lifts like a fog being blown away by a powerful wind. My head lifts and I follow her direction, my eyes darting right. And there she is. Sitting Indian-style with her laptop resting on her thighs, big rose-gold headphones over her ears, black thick-framed glasses perched on her cute nose, her eyes on me for a split second until I meet them, and then they lower to her computer screen. She wears a shaky closed-lipped smile, clearly unable to control her nerves.

Did she glance down out of respect for a Dom, or was it just another nervous reaction, unable to hold my gaze?

Either choice is delightful as fuck. And before I know it, my body takes control without my mind's consent, as I take a step in her direction.

Chapter Three

SIENNA

Oh holy fucking hell. He's here. He's. Right. There. And he looked at me! I think that in the past tense, because I have no idea if he's still looking at me. Shit, I don't even know if he's still standing there or if he took one look at me, did an about-face, and then ran away like a man being chased by a velociraptor.

With my noise-canceling headphones playing Stray-Kids's "Maniac" into my ears, I don't hear him approach, but my peripheral vision picks up the fact that he's close enough his legs are just above the top of my laptop screen. Even through my K-Pop music, I can clearly hear my heart-beat increase, my hands beginning to shake as my fingers tremble on my keyboard. I'm not typing anything at the moment, but I have my fingers in proper position across the middle row of letters, both thumbs on the spacebar like I was taught in Keyboarding back in high school. My breaths are shallow, and my throat won't listen to my brain when it tells it to swallow or I'm going to literally drool on my computer.

I feel my heart racing, the elastic of my sports bra suddenly too tight around my ribs as my breaths become quicker. And no matter how hard I try, I can't seem to lift my eyes to look at him up close. He damn near made me moan out loud the second I saw him step into the café, apparently looking for me over on the couches beneath the windows. Which I guess would make sense, a writer working on the comfy leather sofas. But it's too bright over there for me. I prefer it over here in the darker corner by the bar—not to be closer to the alcohol, even though I could really use a drink at the moment, but because I don't have a view of the parking lot or the many TV screens around the space. Meaning fewer distractions.

I lift my eyes just enough that they're aligned with my laptop's camera at the very top and centered in the screen. It allows my peripherals to absorb him setting his laptop and big water bottle on the table nearest me but mostly behind a rectangular column that stands from the cream-tiled floor to the white ceiling.

I'm concentrating so hard on watching him but not actually looking at him that I jump when my phone dings with a notification through my headphones, my fingers hitting a few keys and typing gibberish on the screen. I grab my phone from beside me and read the message quickly, knowing it's from him.

ROMANTICSADISTLL:

Getting a drink then I've got errands to do

Good. That's good. I need to write, and there's no way I'd be able to do that if he decided to chill at a table just a few feet away from me to do his own work or something. But at the same time, even though I'm growing nauseous with anxiety at his real-life closeness, I'm disappointed he won't be nearby for very long.

I play it cool like I've been trying to all day with him, when it's the furthest thing from what I feel.

WILLDIVE4PLANTS:

Vegan PB&B shake with espresso is the best.

I can feel him walk away, toward the line of refrigerators along the wall before it reaches the counter, like his presence alone is a physical touch.

ROMANTICSADISTLL:

LOL I'm sure. But not that healthy, just caffeine.

I read the message a few times, trying to make sense of it. Does he mean the shake isn't good for anything but the caffeine?

Before I can think of a response, three messages come in, rapid-fire.

> **ROMANTICSADISTLL:**
>
> If I whisper to you through those headphones, can you hear? 😈
>
> I'm just going to tell you good job.
>
> Without the kiss of course

Jesus Christ. He wants to whisper to me? Which means he'd have to get close to me in order to do that, especially if he's wondering if I'll hear him with my headphones still on. Like... not just sit beside me, but like... lean in and speak right next to my ear.

I swallow thickly, my anxiety setting off my defense mechanism to make jokes and kid around instead of sprinting out the exit door.

> **WILLDIVE4PLANTS:**
>
> I have Korean hotties singing to me at the moment, so no.
>
> **ROMANTICSADISTLL:**
>
> Ahhh Lucky girl. Thought you might want more to visualize for your writing.

I smile at that, but the muscles controlling my expression are acting like I've hooked them up to a TENS unit. What the fuck is wrong with me? Am I having a seizure? He's still up at the register, waiting in line to buy his drink, so I feel safe enough to be honest about my nervousness.

WILLDIVE4PLANTS:

I'm having problems controlling my face. Is that normal? 😂

And then my undeniable urge to relieve my stress through humor takes over my fingers yet again.

WILLDIVE4PLANTS:

And it's vegan! What do you mean the shake's not healthy?! I drink those fuckers every day!!!

I feel rather than see him walking back toward his table, and a moment later, I get two messages from him. The first one sends me into a panic so strong my instincts skip right over fight or flight and go directly to freeze. I think my heart even ceases its involuntary rhythm.

ROMANTICSADISTLL:

Turn off the music, tell me when it's done, keep your head down like you're looking at your laptop, close your eyes, and just listen. I'll come tell you, then I'll leave.

No, princess. The drink *I* am drinking isn't healthy.

I don't have the mental capacity to even decipher what the second message says, so I hope it's not important at the moment. All I can focus on are the orders he gave and how I have the compulsive need to follow them, even though I'm freaking petrified. My fingers unfreeze, apparently, because I feel them plucking along the keys of their own accord. I don't even know what I'm typing. I'll just apologize for the stupidity they're probably spewing when I can finally brain again.

WILLDIVE4PLANTS:

Oh God.

OK.

Fuck.

Imma faint.

I can't feel my face.

Somewhere between those messages, my right hand reached up to turn my headphones off. The music stops, but everything is still muffled. While the noise-canceling feature isn't active, just the shape of the headphones—the kind that fully encompasses your ears with thick padding—shuts part of the noisiness of the world out. But still, the switch in auditory stimulation and just the adrenaline the situation is causing to pump into my system is downright startling. Especially as a body suddenly appears on the bench next to me, only separated by the foot-wide piece of wood that acts as a table to set one's drink on that's built in between us.

He told me to close my eyes and just listen, but I can't. Closing my eyes feels too vulnerable, like it would leave me too exposed. So I stare at the bottom of my screen, hoping from his angle and height it looks like my eyes are shut.

"Hello, princess."

Oh my God. His voice.

Even with my headphones on, the two-word greeting sends a tingle up my neck, and I'm not sure what percentage is because of his voice alone versus him calling me yet another sweet nickname.

"I'm so happy I get to see you in person finally. It feels like I've known and been talking to you for a lot longer than reality."

I try out a small smile, and my cheeks twitch, so I attempt to relax my face instead, but that just makes my lips tremble, the corners fighting to pull downward into a frown as I try to keep them in a perfectly straight line.

What the fuck is wrong with my face? I ask myself once again.

I've been nervous to speak in front of people before—interviews, author panels, those sorts of things. My voice might quiver a little in the beginning, and then I relax and it gets easier the longer I speak until I'm not at all worried and end up chatting like we're lifelong friends. It's my nature to be an oversharer.

But I'm not trying to talk to this man. I've been directed to just listen. I'm not even supposed to *look* at him—eyes closed, in fact—yet all my senses seem to be shutting down except for one—my ears. As if my body is taking his demand to "just listen" literally—flipping the Off switch for all my other systems.

I've had full-on panic attacks before, and not even during those did I lose control of my facial expressions.

Am I having a stroke?

He's speaking lower now, so low I can't hear him through my headphones, and my heart aches at having missed a single word from this man's lips. The ache is enough to bring control of my hand back online. So without taking my eyes from where they stare unseeing at my word counter at the bottom of my document, I lift my right hand once again and move the headphone just slightly behind my ear canal, the pad still resting on my cartilage. Instead of dropping my hand completely, I slide it down my jaw to cover my mouth, propping my chin on my thumb. I do it so I can stop focusing so much on my twitching face, as if I didn't have enough things to be self-conscious about. My lips press to the center of my palm, my fingertips pointing toward my uncovered ear, where I can hear him perfectly clear now, his deep voice so close, so crisp. And just in time to hear words I've longed to receive.

"I'm very proud of you for coming today to write. I looked you up on Amazon, finally gave in to my curiosity, and I saw so many people look forward to your books. They bring your readers happiness and comfort, which makes your hard work *so important*. You like to make light of the books you release. But I know you put so much effort into your research and your stories, and your readers can tell.

What you do, what you bring to the world, means more than you realize, little one," he tells me, his voice unwavering. His speech isn't broken up by a bunch of pauses, ums, or likes.

How does he do that?

Even when I know damn well what I'm trying to say, my sentences are all sprinkled with an uh, an um, a like or four, and more than my fair share of cuss words. And it's literally my job to eloquently make use of the English language. So how the hell did he say all of that without a single stumble? I'm actually mesmerized, almost jealous of how articulate he is while talking aloud to me.

His words are concise. The tone serious but pleasantly so. Not at all patronizing, as if he were speaking to a child who needs to be reassured, but like a smart man using facts to make a point.

"And even more than that, I'm so proud of you for not only changing out of your pajamas and into workout clothes today, but you worked out for the first time in *six months*. You made it more than a mile, sweetheart, when I know sometimes just getting out of bed is too hard. I know every single day is a struggle. I understand the voices in your head do everything they can to bring you down, when all you want to do is raise everyone else up. And that's so hard, princess. It's hard to be who you truly are when it seems like everyone and everything is working against you."

If anyone else had said that to me, I would've scoffed. I would've thought they were making fun of me, sarcasm highlighting their words. But when he says it, I feel nothing but seen. I feel understood. I feel like he truly gets me.

"But I just wanted you to know I adore what you've shown me of yourself so far, and I hope I get the opportunity to see more. You've made me so happy today," he says, and I involuntarily gasp behind my hand, my eyes finally closing on their own. Such simple words after completing such an easy task for most people, yet they hit me like he wrote me a soul-deep sonnet. "And I know those voices will set in the minute I leave, if they haven't already, so I also want to say thank you for allowing me to sit here with you, to see you and speak to you in person, and that, from what I see, I wouldn't change a goddamn thing about you, pretty girl."

And with that, he stands, and my heart leaps toward him, as if it has hands that want to grasp his arm and make him stay. Make him continue to just murmur his sweet words to me all damn day and well into the night.

But instead, I just drop my hand from my mouth, not realizing until that moment that my cheek is wet when tears fall the rest of the way down to my jaw. I wipe the side of my pinky off on my leggings before using the same shaky hand to swipe the tears away, feeling silly for getting emotional without even noticing it when it happened.

I still can't make myself look up at him, even when he says one final thing, an order I want to follow immediately, "Keep writing, princess," but I do nod in agreement.

It's such a mix of feelings that hit me all at once as he

moves around the column back to the table with his back-pack and water bottle. While most of me wants to do anything to make him stay, to spend more time just sitting here with me, even if he doesn't keep talking the way he just did, there's also parts of me that keep me from putting that want into motion: like my lungs, which seem to finally be able to take a full, deep breath. My throat, which can finally swallow after my salvatory glands come back online. My shoulders and face, which relax and stop their incessant, tense twitching.

But my heart refuses to slow.

My hands continue to tremble on my keyboard.

And my mind suddenly begins to race as I try to go over and repeat every word he said so I don't forget a single sylla-ble. I want to write it all down, to keep forever, to pick apart and dissect, but my fingers won't do anything but quiver upon the keys.

If I can't type anything, I decide I'll just read over the last page I wrote to get back in the mindset of my story.

Ha! Fat chance. Instead, "you've made me so happy today" in his deep, soft voice plays on a loop inside my head, bringing me a sense of comfort that it's one positive thought my brain has decided to focus on instead of a clusterfuck of negativity for once. A calmness I don't recognize settles over me, one I've never felt even when I take my meds on time.

Several minutes later, the rest of my body returns to all hands on deck, and I reach for my cell to send Gym Daddy —I really fucking need to learn his name—a message. I don't know what, something… anything… just to let him know he didn't scare me away. I go with honesty.

> WILLDIVE4PLANTS:
>
> I just now unfroze.

It's embarrassing how many typos I had in that short sentence I took the time to fix before actually sending it.

> WILLDIVE4PLANTS:
>
> But not done shaking apparently.
>
> I've read the same sentence in my manuscript 14 times and still don't know WTF I wrote.

I smile as the messages go from Delivered to Read within seconds.

> ROMANTICSADISTLL:
>
> I apologize that you couldn't get the full effect. If you would've come to my car where I could get closer, you would've felt my breath as I whispered in your ear, felt my presence, close enough to sense but not enough to physically feel. With your eyes closed, and that closeness, my aura would caress you, then consume you until your body wanted to respond.

I literally gulp. After hearing the sound of his voice, I read his words in his tone in my head, and anything that might've sounded cheesy coming from any other man just makes me weak. Because there's only truth in what he said. I felt *exactly* what he meant. His aura radiated, a hum you heard and felt when it first flipped on, until you got used to it, and then weren't actively cognizant of it again until it flipped off. And if I weren't so overtaken by the inability to do *anything* but listen, my body would've responded by leaning closer to him, closing the short space between us.

I have never in my life reacted to a person like that before.

I have never once been struck speechless and immobile.

And although it was a terrifying feeling, it was exhilarating as fuck, and I want nothing more than to beg him to come back.

But I won't. No way. He said he had errands to run, and I don't want to come off as needy. So instead, I message him with a different bit of honesty.

WILLDIVE4PLANTS:

So what you're saying is... the fact that it did that anyway is... not typical? • •

ROMANTICSADISTLL:

I thought about making you say "yes, Sir" when I was done, asking if you understood your instructions. But when you covered your mouth, I didn't know if you could trust your voice to work.

So he noticed my hand, huh? That's not embarrassing at all.

WILLDIVE4PLANTS:

I'm pretty sure I hyperventilated.

He's right. If he would've told me when he was here to confirm verbally, it would've come out in a humiliating croak or a barely audible whisper if anything.

WILLDIVE4PLANTS:

And that would've been a challenge. I'm not sure I can even speak right now, actually.

And I definitely covered it because I lost all control of my facial muscles and started trembling.

Oh my God, Sienna, swallow some Pepto. We need to control your word-vomit!

When he still hasn't replied after a minute, I scoff at my almost immature physical response to the man. It's the same response a young teenager might have while talking to their biggest crush, or even just sitting next to them in class. Hell, it's the same exhilaration when meeting a celebrity, but even the several times that's happened in my life—since I'm a huge nerd and go to comicons—I was never too stunned to speak or just *look* at them.

I sigh at the realization.

WILLDIVE4PLANTS:

I am 34 fucking years old.

I am ridiculous. 🙈

Finally, the messages switch to Read and the dots do their dance for quite some time before his finally comes through.

ROMANTICSADISTLL:

It is typical with a true submissive who desires their Dom, but submissives who are artists at heart are especially excitable when you gently kiss their mind's eye. By nature, your imagination is stronger, and you feel what you imagine with more intensity than if someone tries to merely physically excite you.

A warning dings and pops up on my laptop, letting me know my battery is about to die, so I pull my cord out of my backpack, plug it into the outlet built into the bench, and connect it to my computer. Back on my phone, I scroll up through my messages to remind myself what he's responding to, rereading my question about being able to feel him so strongly without him actually touching me.

WILLDIVE4PLANTS:

Hm! That's actually pretty fascinating and makes perfect sense.

I adjust in my seat, and the feel of my tight compression leggings pressed against my now overly sensitive flesh is too distracting to ignore. It demands attention, yet there's nothing I'd be able to do about it here. I'm unable to have orgasms without my vibrator, and even then, it's a lot of fucking work to reach climax when you're on an anti-anxiety medication. And since I don't seem to have a filter between my wandering thoughts and my fingers, I type out a message about that conundrum without thinking and hit Send.

WILLDIVE4PLANTS:

> If only I wasn't broken, I'd just jump in a shower stall to take care of this ache that's not going away no matter which way I sit. But alas.

I must have been super distracted by being able to feel my heartbeat in my clit, because I didn't notice he was also typing out a message at the same time. It comes in at the exact moment mine is delivered to him.

ROMANTICSADISTLL:

> In fact... a man you're slightly attracted to has a better chance of creating your orgasms through a mastery of language, creating imagery and suggestion, than if they try just physical stimulation. And if you have someone who can read your body, knows your mind and desires, you will experience it so profoundly that your body may quiver at even a fleeting thought of what you had become in those moments.

Jesus on a cracker. The most delicious man I've ever seen in real life talking *to me* about orgasms and my body quivering… it's not helping the situation in my pants whatsoever. I have never—*never*—talked to a man who sounded anywhere close to the way the heroes in my books speak. The ones I've written *and* the ones I've read by others. Ever. Obviously, since they're fictional men written by women, our fantasies brought to life only on the written page. There have been guys who managed to not make me cringe while "spitting their game," but the vast majority, yeah, total eye-rollers.

But this man….

Is it the age difference? Fourteen years between us, if his profile stating he's forty-eight is the truth. Could that be why he sounds so much more mature than men I've talked to in the past? So much more eloquent and articulate?

So… confidently intelligent without being overly cocky.

I don't know how much time passes, but when I blink out of my pondering, I discover my laptop has gone to sleep.

I swipe my fingers over the touchpad.

Scratch that. My laptop is dead as a doornail. It doesn't turn on no matter what button I push, and finally the little empty battery symbol flashes across the screen for a second before going black again.

I sigh, unplugging my cord from the useless socket.

WILLDIVE4PLANTS:

Just realized, because I was so spaced out, this plug doesn't work and my laptop has been dead for a good 10 minutes now while I just stared at the blank screen. 😂

I'd say your assessment is accurate.

At least for me. Since I keep hearing "you've made me so happy today" on repeat and my heart starts pounding like I'm climbing the stairs again.

Why had that specific line had such an effect on me? He's messaged and spoke way deeper and more lyrical words to me since I started talking to him, so why is him telling me I made him happy today sticking out to me like some sort of milestone, or like a neon sign glowing for attention?

ROMANTICSADISTLL:

Well, thank you for allowing that. For research's sake. I believe it might help you better understand a submissive's mindset and desire to serve, what they get from kindness and affirmation that they are appreciated by someone, valued, and that what they do for someone DOES matter and make their day.

I never want him to stop.

I don't ever want him to stop explaining things to me,

teaching me in a way I can absorb and understand with no more effort than reading his words.

Nothing pisses me off more than a guy mansplaining something to me, speaking to me like I'm an idiot and won't grasp what he means just because I'm a woman. More often than I care to remember, a man has broken something down to a condescending degree, as if I'm a sheltered child instead of a grown woman who has experienced plenty in her three and a half decades on this earth.

But that's not his tone with me. He's chosen to delve deeper, go past what I've told him I already have knowledge on. He's trusting I did my research for my past books, either my reviews or the answers I've given to his direct questions proof enough I'm not some presumptuous poser. He's chosen to further my education on a subject I've been fascinated by and lived for years and years, like a professor who teaches at the highest level, with students becoming masters of their topic instead of one filled with a classroom of fresh-out-of-high schoolers.

And most of all, he's making me understand myself in a way I never could before. He's making me feel like I'm not so weird, not so mentally high maintenance, which is more than I could've ever asked for when I signed up for dating sites looking for a sugar daddy to buy me plants.

ROMANTICSADISTLL:

> When you climb the stairs next time, your mind will go to those words as well. Whether you mean for them to or not. The rest of your body will begin to respond along with it. Allow me to tell you how much you make me smile by staying on top of your workout, and you'll feel your body respond even when driving to the gym, looking forward to those stairs.

I almost snort in response, but something stops me. It rings true, looking forward to those godawful stairs, if I know he's somewhere at the top of them. So it's hard to doubt I'd look forward to climbing them if it got me the praise it did earlier. I'd climb a million steps to get to experience *that* again.

WILLDIVE4PLANTS:

> I've 100% always felt that way, submissive with an actual desire to please. And everything you said (what a sub gets from kindness and affirmation that they are appreciated, valued, and that what they do for someone truly matters and makes their day) is exactly what I've always desired.

> Every single one of my heroines is me in a lot of ways. Their backstories change, but the baseline of their personalities, it's all me. And all my heroes are my dream Dom. I just didn't think one existed in reality, since I've only ever had one Dominant in my life, and we weren't a good match.

And then the beginning of his last sentence finally registers in my head.

WILLDIVE4PLANTS:

> Allow you to? Is that a request? Like, you'd want to do that?

Just the possibility fills me with yearning. Above all, this is what I've craved from a Dom of my own. Being a people pleaser, I feel if someone ordered me to do things for myself, I would be more likely to actually do them. I put others before me always. I will choose to use my time and energy on bettering someone else's life than on my own every single time. So if I had a Dom who ordered me to take care of myself, then I wouldn't be doing it for me. I'd be doing it to obey him, which is way more acceptable.

I'm fucked in the head. I know. And I waste no time letting him in on that.

WILLDIVE4PLANTS:

My best friend is also a writer, and her Dom gives her assignments to help her complete her work. Before that though, he started out by giving her orders to take care of herself, things that are simple for most people, like showering, brushing teeth, regular hygiene stuff. But then it progressed to things like primping and pampering, things she never would've wasted time doing on her own for herself. But because it was to impress and look good for HIM, she jumped at the chance. I've always craved that.

I'm shocked how easy it is to tell him things I've never told anyone before. Not even Dr. Walker. Sure, we got to the root of why I'm a submissive, but because Art and I were already an established D/s couple who was also married, we didn't go quite as far into depth as I believe other members might when going through the process to join. And later on, when we went into counseling with him to figure out if we could still work, whether as Dom and sub and/or husband and wife, we focused more on Art and his sadism, his need to inflict pain and humiliate, and why it had grown over the past couple of years.

Yet all this time I thought I stayed exactly the same in my submissive needs while Art's sadistic nature grew, I'm starting to think we might've been going more in conflicting directions than I originally believed. My desire to be coddled and loved on, to be sweet to, praised, and cherished were getting stronger and stronger, while his desire to do the complete opposite became clearer and clearer.

One thing was certain through it all though. Art might be a sadist, but he's a good man. That's one thing I try my best to educate readers on with my novels. Just because someone needs to physically or mentally hurt someone, it doesn't mean they're a bad person. Especially when there is the perfect Yin to their Yang, someone who needs them to physically or mentally hurt them for whatever reason they may have. As long as they follow the three fundamentals of our lifestyle, to be safe, sane, and consensual during all their scenes, then there are perfectly healthy matches for sadists and masochists.

My phone dings through my headphones, making me jump I'd been daydreaming so deeply.

ROMANTICSADISTLL:

I would love to give you assignments and commands, tasks to complete. But you would require the promise and threat of consequence, both good and bad. I fear you will not allow me these privileges.

You would have to feel my praises more intently and deeply. Then I would have to be allowed to correct you for a request not completed.

Jesus.

Mary.

Joseph.

And all the saints.

I gulp and catch myself trembling as I read his messages over and over. So much to unpack there. Not only is he explaining how that dynamic would work, but he said he would love to do that for me. And of course he would need to be able to either reprimand or reward, or what would be the point?

I cross my legs and discover I'm wet, my face warming as I look around the café, feeling as if everyone is suddenly staring at me like they know everything that's happened and all my reactions in the last hour.

Is my body really readying itself for a man who so far is completely nameless other than a goofy nickname I gave him nearly a year ago?

WILLDIVE4PLANTS:

Sidenote while I compartmentalize so I don't embarrass myself: I don't even know your name! And believe me, I've lost a stupid number of hours trying to discreetly find it out. My usual amazing FBI skills have failed me, and it's probably why I missed my deadline.

And here I was trying not to embarrass myself. Well there you go 😂

It's true. I've used every search engine in existence to

seek out anything containing bits and pieces of his user-name and what little I know about him. I went on our town's Facebook page and scoured the members, looking for anyone with the initials LL who could possibly be my gym crush. Nada! I even downloaded a few photo lookup apps, trying to see if there was some sort of facial recognition feature that would pop him up on Instagram or something. Again, nothing!

And with my making it known how desperately I searched him out, I'd bet money he won't just tell me now. Especially since he hasn't offered it up before now.

ROMANTICSADISTLL:

Well then, that will make this next part even easier for you. From now on, you will call me Sir. If it helps, you may think of it as my name. Use it so often that it feels odd to end a sentence or thought without saying it to me. Am I understood, sweet princess?

"Called it," I grumble.

WILLDIVE4PLANTS:

I had a feeling you were going to say that—*sighs—Sir.

I read his message again, and a smile takes over my face, knowing I've written so many books in which the Dom hero first tells his sub what he likes to be referred to as.

Yes, Master.

Yes, Professor.

Yes, Doctor.

Yes, Husband.

And, in a few stories: Yes, Sir.

A reader might find the moniker simple, too generic, especially if they're from the South, where we're raised to refer to any man as sir.

But this isn't that same sir.

This is Sir.

More relative to knighthood, like Sir Lancelot, a great hero embodying alpha leadership and demanding of respect.

And also capitalized to show it pertains to a Dom.

It fits him beautifully. Gym Daddy transforms into Sir in my mind with little effort, and I'm grateful to have something else to call him, a name he finally gave me to use to address him with when I need one.

I still wish I knew his name though.

WILLDIVE4PLANTS:

But that is so not fair. I'm just saying... Sir. And this gives me the best memories of writing one of my books, Sir.

I jump onto my Kindle app and search the word "sir" in said book, screenshotting the Dom telling his sub to call him by that name. I attach it to the message and send it, receiving one from him at the same time, and my face falls, literally, going from a big grin to an open-mouthed whimper as I read it.

ROMANTICSADISTLL:

Sweet girl, if your first response to calling me Sir is sighs and sadness, then I don't want it. A true Dom is not a bully, and I get no pleasure out of forced submission. There are other kinks that enjoy that. If my sub enjoys that, then that changes things, but a sub serves so much better and honestly when she gives it freely. Submission is a gift. It has to make you happy to do it, or there is no pleasure in it for me either. My name is Felix.

My heart is pounding in my chest while I reread the message again and again, but it's not from excitement at learning his name. The emotion I'm feeling at the moment, with my scalp tingling and my neck breaking out in a cold sweat as my tummy turns… is shame. This is my instinctive response to the disappointment I read woven throughout his words.

I want to take back my message, erase it and resend it without the playful sigh I included before.

"Idiot," I snap at myself.

He doesn't know you. He doesn't know you're just being goofy when you say shit like that. He can't hear your tone in a written message, dumbass. Now he thinks you're an argumentative bitch who doesn't want to submit, when that's the exact opposite of who you are, the cunty voice inside my head reprimands, kicking me when I'm already down like she's known to do.

I have to correct him. I have to let him know that's not at all what I meant.

WILLDIVE4PLANTS:

I promise the sigh was only from frustration that I couldn't find out your name on my own, Sir.

I hope he can decipher my sincerity. I can't dwell on it too long or I'll send myself into a panic, imagining how disappointed I've made him, so I skip down to the last sentence of his message, letting his real name finally deposit into my memory bank.

WILLDIVE4PLANTS:

Felix? 😳

I wasn't expecting that. Two hours of my life scouring Fort Vanter residents on Facebook with LL initials. You suck, Sir 😅😭

I erase and retype the last sentence thrice before finally hitting Send. I want him to get to know my personality so in the future when I'm being playful, he'll be able to recognize it and not be offended or disappointed.

I try to ignore the fact that I'm already thinking of a future with him, when I've technically never even spoken a solitary word to the man.

When I just fucking learned his real first name.

> **ROMANTICSADISTLL:**
>
> No Facebook. Those initials were out of frustration. I was like "fuck it" when I was starting the account and just hit a letter.

Oh, how badly I want to question what frustrated him while making his username, but I can actually feel the irritation coming off his message as if he's sitting right next to me again, so I try to lighten the mood.

> **WILLDIVE4PLANTS:**
>
> That "just hit a letter" thing really fucked with my FBI mission, Sir 😑😂

His response doesn't seem to be any lighter, but at least it's not short and clipped sentences like the last one.

> **ROMANTICSADISTLL:**
>
> And just know that it wasn't your displeasure that made you get your way. Forcing you to say Sir won't work. It's like the person above you forcing you to call them boss when addressing them, when they are obviously less intelligent, skilled, or deserving. Leads to disdain and the title itself becoming a form of mockery.

> Well, my rookie mistake of forcing
> the Sir got you your name. Mission
> accomplished. You are free from
> using it. If you don't want to say it,
> then don't.

I want my flirty Gym Daddy back. I want to exorcise whatever is making him push me away. At least, that's what it feels like he's doing. It's then I realize I crave the way he chases me, not like a depraved madman but with a stealthy prowl.

And my natural response is to fly into people-pleaser mode.

WILLDIVE4PLANTS:

> And FYI, reverse image search
> sucks a bag of dicktips too. But
> Google could tell me where you got
> your sunglasses, Sir 😄

> I fucking love how you KNOW that.

> Like, you're real.

> That right there is all the more
> reason to call you Sir.

> I'm glad I didn't chicken out when I
> saw your pic, Sir. Something told
> me just to say fuck it and heart
> your pic.

Nope, you're stuck with it now. You earned it, Sir. You're going to get tired of hearing it, Sir. 🐶 Lost puppy eager to please, remember, Sir?

He must get tired of my incessant notifications, because he finally puts me out of my misery.

ROMANTICSADISTLL:

You'll know when you feel it. It's like knowing someone is the leader just because that's who they ARE. You WANT to follow them, because you know they will take you where you want to go, that they will have your back when you need it and pick you up when you fall. Carry you if they have to, and stand in the hole to get you out, even if it means they can't get out themselves. You'll know, because when you say it, type it, or think it, you will smile inside, and some of that breathless, shaky, heart-racing feeling will begin to sit just below the surface, because you know what saying it means, who I am, and what I can have you feel, and you'll want me to do so.

"Fuuuck," I breathe. I damn near send him a message saying "I want to sit on your face, please and thanks," but

my hands are thankfully too uncontrollable at the moment.
When I can, I stick with honesty.

WILLDIVE4PLANTS:

I'm all shaky again, Sir.

ROMANTICSADISTLL:

I will never tire of hearing it from
you. You can never use it enough.
Use it at the front and end of your
interactions. If you feel it, and it
makes you quiver a little, it excites
me to hear it from you when I know
what it means to you as well.

WILLDIVE4PLANTS:

So riddle me this, Sir.

I'm at the gym every single day. I'm
attracted to literally no one. Maybe
just jaded, because I spend 24/7
writing and reading about dreamy
heroes no one can compare to. Yet I
always, ALWAYS saw you and
thought you were... 😔

Yeah. And then... I'm scrolling
through the stupid sites and apps,
frustrated beyond words because
they're all douchecanoes... and
boom! Your face. I recognized you
immediately. Like, not this "why
does he look familiar?" or "he kinda
looks like...." No. It was "OMFG, it's
HIM."

I see a message from him come through before I'm done

with my thought, but I'm so eager to read what he said I go ahead and send mine.

ROMANTICSADISTLL:

Oh, and that "Stuck with it now" is a bratty side of sub-flirting playfulness. Daring the "what you gonna do about it?" Just enough to be playfully bent over my knee, shorts pulled down, and spanked quickly, sharply, giving that cute little ass a handprint. Then your shorts pulled back up as you're given your feet again.

I clench so hard my eyes cross at the image he paints. I'm pretty sure I whimper too, but I can't hear it, because my computer finally rebooted a while ago, and my music turned on through my headphones.

WILLDIVE4PLANTS:

Note to self: start doing squats again to toughen up the booty, because I was the baby and only girl out of four, so I can't help when the bratty comes out. Got it, Sir.

I don't remember what my question was going to be, Sir, so just take my previous message as a confession, I guess

ROMANTICSADISTLL:

Then I thank you for the compliment

WILLDIVE4PLANTS:

You're very welcome, Sir

I finally focus on my computer. Seeing my document on the screen, I snap a picture of it with my phone, sending him an excerpt of what I'd written last.

WILLDIVE4PLANTS:

For when you're bored, Sir.

A message from him pops up, and then a couple minutes later, another one that makes me smile harder than I can remember ever smiling in my lifetime.

ROMANTICSADISTLL:

But the answer to your unspoken question is simple and complex. There's someone for everyone... or chemistry, pheromones. The "I don't know, there's just something about him."

Then I should allow myself time to be bored more often, little one.

The excerpt I sent him was the heroine telling the hero she finally had the energy to change out of her pajamas for the first time in three days. I always like to include bits and pieces of my real life in my stories, to let readers know they're not alone in their struggles. I hid behind some of these things at first, embarrassed and scared what people would say about these "fictional" characters, but in a shocking turn of events, those were the parts so many of the reviews gushed about. People gave tearful responses to the books, saying how much they related to the heroines' hardships and that they would continue to read my stories if I planned to be so inclusive when it came to characters with mental health issues.

I'm no longer embarrassed to admit my characters' disorders or plights are ones I experience in real life, because nothing feels more validating and like I'm not alone in the world than these women—and a few men—writing me things like "I've never left a review before, but I just had to tell the author thank you from the bottom of my heart for writing a character I can actually relate to."

WILLDIVE4PLANTS:

Sounds vaguely familiar, something like "I changed out of my pajamas today," doesn't it, Sir? 😏

ROMANTICSADISTLL:

I'm happy and impressed with the ease at which you are adapting to saying Sir. You have been practicing using the written form in your books. We will see if your lips form the words as well as your writing.

WILLDIVE4PLANTS:

I've been training for this my whole life. I'm from a military town, Sir 😌

ROMANTICSADISTLL:

> And I know there are days you don't change out of your pajamas, sweet girl. I hope you'll give me the chance to help you see your true self-worth and that you deserve to spend time pampering yourself with more care.

I fight of the sudden urge to cry and read through our messages we've sent back and forth today. I haven't spoken to any one person like this in ages. God, years upon years ago, as far back as when Art and I were dating. Even friends I've had throughout that time, or hell, family members to catch up with, it was always sporadic messages here and there. Nothing so in depth, where I was hanging on their every word, so eager for the next text to be delivered.

I don't know how much time passes, but when my ass feels like it's gone numb from sitting on the café bench seat, I glance at the time in the top right corner of my laptop, gasping and sitting up straight.

WILLDIVE4PLANTS:

> I have a request, seeing as it's apparently not going to happen otherwise, since I've now just read our conversation thrice instead of working, Sir.

I take a deep breath and type out my message. I try to be playful with it, but I hope so deeply that he'll read into it and know what my request actually means.

WILLDIVE4PLANTS:

Can you just like... tell me to go
fucking write? 😂

Even my Adderall doesn't stand a
chance against you otherwise, Sir😳

I bite my lip and cross my fingers, and I gulp as the dots on his side of the thread start to bounce while he types.

Please, please, please. I need your orders, Sir. You basically said you wouldn't give me any unless I agreed to allow you to praise or reprimand in return. Meaning in person. Please, read my request and know it's my chickenshit way of agreeing to your terms. I'm still too scared to say what I truly desire. Please, plea— Oh shit!

Chapter Four

FELIX

ROMANTICSADISTLL:

What time can I see you tonight?

She's an intelligent woman who lacks confidence. The way she reads deeply into my messages lets me know not only that she's aware of the stipulations I mentioned but that I should also look deeper into her request as well.

Her *request.*

Before, she had outright asked me about personal training, about Domination from a distance, things like that. But to phrase what she wanted as an actual request, a way a submissive politely makes her Dom aware of her needs, I know she's giving me the green light for what I require in return. And the way she made jokes during said request shows she's just too riddled with self-doubt and the fear of

326 · PLANT DADDY

rejection that she can't outright ask for what she desires with conviction.

I can't wait to see the confident woman she'll no doubt become under my hands.

Instead of an answer to my question, she sends me a short excerpt from her book. And where I'd find this annoying coming from submissives in the past, it only makes Sienna more intriguing, like a puzzle I have to figure out but with the guarantee of a prize unlike any other inside.

"What to do with you now," he murmurs, his voice bringing me back to the present.

I swallow thickly, my own voice coming out weak. "Please, just let me go."

He lifts a brow at me, a look I allow myself to admit is sexy as fuck, and my pussy clenches as his hand just stays... right... there... against it, barely touching me but not moving away. And now that I'm conscious of that, my hips rock of their own accord, even as I try to keep them still. My body's instincts are starting to take over, feeling his gentle touch between my legs and reacting the way my brain has taught it to—soft and warm pressure... on clitoris... equals pleasure. Must get closer. Must have more.

And he allows it. He literally has to be, because if he didn't want me to move, I would not have the choice. Where my husband already makes me feel tiny, his muscular frame taller and wider and stronger than my own, this Dom makes me feel fragile, downright breakable, like he'd be able to hurt me without even exerting a fraction of all that size and strength.

It's a fact that suddenly makes me so wet I should be mortified. I can feel the wetness seeping from me, trickling between my cheeks there's so much of it. There has to be, seeing as he still has the gusset of my panties pressed against my slit, which means I'm so aroused I've already soaked through the cotton.

I can't look away as his head lowers, and I feel his hot breath on the tip of one breast. My body, choosing a different instinct to react to this time, flinches away from it, somehow recognizing that breath doesn't belong to its master, but that doesn't stop my nipples from tightening to an almost painful degree. Another shiver works its way from my chest to my neck and up through my trapped arms, and I hear him hum, as if in approval.

"So responsive, little one. Your mouth might be begging me to let you go, but the rest of your body? It's begging for something completely different," he purrs, and to my utter shame, my vision goes blurry, my eyes unfocusing in order to concentrate more closely on my other senses—the sound of his deep, quiet voice, the scent of his intoxicating, crisp cologne, the feel of his heavy body on top of me, my mind trying to pick out the specific parts of him and where they've aligned with the different parts of me.

I read the page, seeing the heroine in her story is too scared to speak. From what Sienna told me about the backstory, it's a heroine's CNC—consensual non-consent— fantasy being brought to life by her husband and another Dom. She wants to tell the Dom yes—anything he wants from her, he can have—but she craves for him to take the lead. There's a need in her to run, but she wants more than anything to be chased, to be caught, and to be forced to submit to the powerful male.

And she's also told me countless times her stories are filled with parts of herself.

So my little hippie with the gentle and nurturing soul yearns to be dominated by darkness and filth. By roughness and animalistic hunger. She wants more than anything to be released of all responsibility, to just give herself over with blind faith to her Master.

But in order to be able to do that, a Dom must earn her trust, or she won't fully surrender to the experience.

I'll give her a taste of what she thirsts for. I'll allow her to see I'm a man worthy of such a woman so eager to please and shower them with affection, only wanting to be loved and praised properly in return. But then I'll take my time training her, at the same time building a bond between us and stoking her belief in me. Then and only then will she truly be able to become everything she craves to be—a twenty-four seven owned and collared slave.

I read the excerpt again, and with the heroine's desires in mind, I give Sienna her first order as my prospective submissive.

ROMANTICSADISTLL:

Little princess, I need you to listen carefully. I want you to write for me today. You have procrastinated long enough. I desire proof of what should've been done and what you have accomplished. I enjoy that you are so skilled and are able to move people with your words, so they must be written. You will meet me tonight, and you can hear me tell you how proud I am of you with your own ears, and I will keep my promise to behave. Should you not achieve your goal, I will still keep my promise and you may keep covered, but you will be bent over my knee and receive the spanking you deserve. Am I clear, princess?

The message shows it's been read for quite some time before I see she's typing her reply. And even then, several minutes go by before I'm notified I've received a message from her.

WILLDIVE4PLANTS:

Hm. 🙄 My throat just did that thing where it swallows by itself when your fight-or-flight goes off. Oh, and look. The shaking is back, Sir. And I hear my heartbeat in my eardrums. FML, Sir.

I can't help but smile. Subs have told me they were nervous or excited before. They've told me they were quivering with desire or wet with need for me. I've had a couple admit they had anxiety over meeting me or playing, submitting during a scene we discussed. But never has someone described so in detail how I make her feel. I love knowing I have such a profound physiological effect on this woman. And the fact that I've never even touched her before makes it all the more intoxicating.

She didn't give me a straight answer though. Yet I haven't told her how I prefer my orders to be acknowledged before they're carried out. Which is the only reason she doesn't get scolded when I see the picture of her word count pop up in our thread as I'm typing out my response to her.

ROMANTICSADISTLL:

> That fight-or-flight had better be what sets you in motion to write. It'll so greatly lift my spirits to be able to praise you for your obedience and hard work, but a disobedient princess needs to be taught a lesson, even though it will pain me to do so.

WILLDIVE4PLANTS:

> IDK if you can read it clearly, but it says 48,549 words, Sir. I had to take that pic three times because it was so blurry 😂 That Allstate Mayhem commercial "shaky shakyyyy" just popped into my head 😂

> I have to have 50k, Sir. 😅

God, she's fallen into the habit of addressing me with

the respectful name so beautifully. I can't wait to hear her voice, to listen to it and watch the word form on her pouty lips.

ROMANTICSADISTLL:

And what do I expect it to be?

The answer I'm looking for from her is a simple "completed by the deadline you set, Sir" but I've quickly learned the little author doesn't answer anything simply. Yet her responses bring too many smiles to my face and makes me chuckle aloud far too frequently to order her to change her ways.

WILLDIVE4PLANTS:

🐿 1: My ass is numb from sitting here all day, so a spanking wouldn't be all that bad.

🐿 2: I was never spanked as a child, so it wasn't associated as a punishment, so go ahead 🐷

🐿 3: Shut the hell up! Why would you admit that?!

You expect it to beeeee... not shitty? • •

No.

Um.

Fuck.

Done by the time our gym closes, Sir?

> It's a sex scene, and those take me the longest, because I'm super anal about getting every word perfect and non-repetitive.

> And now I'm panicking, Sir 🙈

> Did I really mention anal to a Dom AGAIN?! Jesus H. Roosevelt Christ, Sienna. Get your life together.

I'm actually curious how long she'll keep this up, sending me her random, fleeting thoughts in short messages as quickly as they enter her mind and can exit her fingers. One, it's pretty fascinating to see a manifestation of what it's like inside my own mind. We're more alike than she'd ever believe. And two, I like the feeling it brings me, knowing I'm at the forefront of her mind so often. If she's messaging me, it means she's thinking of me, and I desire that more than any amount of physical pleasure a sub could bring to the table.

I tell myself I'm not going to message her for a full hour, just to see how many she'll send me within that time without a response.

I won't be cruel though. I won't open the app, marking them as Read. That would be close to evil if I were to do that to someone with her intrusive, repetitive thoughts and her need to please. It would drive her to insanity trying to figure out why I was reading her messages but not responding. So instead, I just read what I can when the preview of each message pops up on my phone's lock screen.

I busy myself by folding a load of scrubs, then I go to my truck in my garage and open up the back. I *will* be seeing her tonight. I'll keep my promise and behave, just like I told her I would, but that doesn't mean I can't be prepared for the possibility of something more. After all, we didn't clearly define what "behave" meant. So to me, that tells me to do what I've done in our messages this whole time, gently pushing, testing her limits, provoking and enticing until she stops me or pushes back. Because I don't think even she knows what she wants and doesn't want.

After all my adjustments and preparations have been made, turning my SUV into something so much more than a vehicle to get from one place to another, I fill my time with landscaping I've been putting off for a week.

My notifications have been quiet long enough I think she might have finally given up and forced herself to get back to work. So it draws my attention when it dings once again close to the end of the hour I was letting run out, and I open the app to read the rest when the preview cuts off her words.

WILLDIVE4PLANTS:

Shit. Hopefully you get this pretty quickly: my phone is about to die, but my computer is fully charged. Is there some other site I can talk to you on? I just looked to see if I can still do it on Kik, but it's a mobile app only, Sir.

A screenshot of her phone's home screen comes through, and my brows furrow, wondering what I'm supposed to be looking at. And then my slight scowl lifts when I see the little pleaser's explanation.

WILLDIVE4PLANTS:

> so you can see I'm not being flaky, Sir. Just irresponsible and used up all my battery reading your messages an embarrassing number of times 🌱

Sure enough, the battery icon in the top right corner of her phone has barely a sliver of red left. And all because she couldn't get enough of *me*.

Her self-deprecation indicates she wants attention, any attention, even if it's negative. A masochist's silent plea, though I don't believe she truly falls into that role. But I refuse to acknowledge her speaking badly of herself and instead give her what she wants with a gentle reminder, a nudge in the training a prospective sub direction.

ROMANTICSADISTLL:

Google Chat. Here's my email.
Don't start forgetting your Sirs now.
You're doing so well.

WILLDIVE4PLANTS:

I'm sorry! Panicking, Sir. I wasn't exaggerating when I said I'm unstable. 😅 Not in a psycho way, but like, just a hot mess express, Sir.

ROMANTICSADISTLL:

What is your Gmail, princess?

She's long past keeping her identity hidden from me, so I'm not surprised when she sends me her personal Gmail address instead of one that's been created specifically for secrecy.

WILLDIVE4PLANTS:

Had to type that a stupid number of times to get it right, Sir 😅 That's how badly I'm freaking out.

It's time to get her back on track. If she's stays at this heightened level of stress, her creativity will likely go to shit, and then our night won't go the way I'd like it to. Yes, I'd still get to meet up with her, but I don't want that first time to be sullied with a punishment for an incomplete task. She needs to be praised for her efforts, and I set the bar just high enough that she'll have to push herself, enough she'll really feel accomplished when she completes it. Otherwise, it will feel too easy to her. It won't give her the motivation she requested so sweetly.

ROMANTICSADISTLL:

How many words are you at now?

Check the Google Chat and send answer there.

I switch to that app, which is still using my anonymous

username and not my personal information. She's openly admitted she's done everything she can to find out anything about me, and I have no doubt she could do that if given just one more hint about me.

She never looked at me at the café. I doubt she'd be able to recognize I'm the one who pulled her out of the dumpster those weeks ago even if she did peer at me up close, but it's not impossible. Thankfully though, she seems entirely too respectful of privacy to come to my second workplace and out me like a woman scorned if things were to go south.

No, when I walked into the gym's café and spotted her sitting with her back against the wall, sequestered in a way that wouldn't allow anyone too close to her, I had to blink twice.

I know she warned me she didn't look like her profile picture in real life, especially at the gym, and even though she'd sent me pictures of herself not all dolled up like her professional author photo, I hadn't expected *that*.

Was it a costume? Was she role playing? Or was that really the woman I'd been talking to day and night for so many days now?

I had my doubts she was showing me her true self... until I approached her and she became stiff yet twitchy with nerves.

The many books she's written, her profile stating she was there to interview people in the lifestyle for research, the reviewers mentioning just how explicit and "filthy" the sex scenes are... I expected something much different than the almost mousy woman huddled beneath her huge laptop, which put it in my head that maybe she was playing the part of the nerdy librarian countless men fantasize about. A bun on top of her head, glasses so big they kept sliding down her pert little nose, long legs wrapped in workout tights that fit her like a second skin.

But then I looked more closely and purposefully shed any preconceived notions I had about her from knowing her occupation and hearing her vast knowledge about BDSM.

The bun on top of her head was messy, as in it looked like it was actually thrown up quickly just to get her hair out of her face—not the artfully twisted hairstyle young women like to *call* a messy bun. There was even a couple of pens sticking out of it, either being used to actually hold it up or to keep them handy for her to write with.

The glasses were prescription, not costume ones or the kind people bought just to protect their eyes from blue light coming off their devices. Her real, everyday glasses, not anything fake.

The pert little nose they slid down was completely makeup-free, along with the rest of her pretty face. Not even a swipe of mascara to bleed down flushed cheeks if I were to make her orgasm to the point of tears as she begged me to stop.

If this was an act, a put-on to look like the nerd fantasy brought to life, then she would've certainly at least worn gloss to draw a man's attention to her pillowy lips. Yet another check in the Genuinely Her column.

Those long-ass stems in the tight-as-fuck leggings weren't posed to entice when I was to get my first real look at her. They weren't positioned in a way to make a man imagine being between them upon their first impression. They were actually drawn up onto the bench, where she sat Indian style. The only reason I knew how long they were was because of her photos and TikToks I'd seen. She was practically folded in on herself, using that big computer as a shield to keep between her and the rest of the world.

Or more likely, in her mind, without her even realizing it, she kept the world she created on that laptop screen between her and reality.

This was no super-experienced, well-trained sub who was so versed in the art of submission she could know how delightful an intelligent librarian type would be to a man like me. That would take an impossible amount of sociological skill to decipher from our messages alone. After all, she has no idea what I do for a living. No, this wasn't a role-playing game. I had just walked into the café to find a real-life *She's All That* situation. And realizing that, all her messages warning me of what a "hot mess" she is flashed through my mind, and I understood she wasn't just being playful or exaggerating her cuteness and submissive personality. She truly was the dorky heroine of a '90s teen rom-com come to life. She truly was the sweet, self-conscious, caring, awkward, artsy, clumsy girl on the outside with the straight-up naughty vixen thoughts on the inside.

She knows so fucking much about BDSM from her

obsessive researching, and she may have lived it as her ex's sub, even seriously enough to be a member of Club Alias. But she clearly had not been given the opportunity to find herself in her role as a submissive. She hadn't been taught or given the space to play in order to discover who she is in the lifestyle. Probably, she'd just gone along with whatever her ex wanted, allowing him to take the lead as she knew a submissive would, but he hadn't given her the chance to find out what she enjoyed herself. A Dominant can still keep their submissive on a leash, but they should give them enough slack to dance around, play, and have fun. Otherwise, what's the point? It's not a true power exchange if she's not enjoying what she's giving. Sure, there are times to choke up on the sub's leash, to rein her back in and use a firmer hand and take a more controlling tone, but in return, she's rewarded with time to be who she likes being.

How fair would it be to have a sub be everything you could possibly dream of, perfectly obedient and your every fantasy brought to life, but then you're unwilling to turn the tables and be the Dom she craves? A submissive yearns for things just as much as a Dominant does. She—or he—has desires that should be validated and fulfilled.

A D/s relationship isn't just an exchange of power. It's an exchange of being everything the other person needs. A perfect give and take.

I used all the self-control I could muster to focus on that and not the admittedly dark thought tiptoeing along the edges of my mind:

Mm… this is going to be fun.

I snap out of the memory from hours ago as her response to the message I sent on Google Chat dings through.

ROMANTICSADIST:

Hello, princess

SIENNA:

48,809 words, Sir.

She also attached a photo of her laptop screen. At the bottom of it, she circled the word count in red. I flip to the other app to see what her previous count was, doing the quick math in my head, and my brow furrows. She hasn't even made it to three hundred words this past hour. I need to snap her out of whatever is distracting her. Maybe a tougher task is in order to make her focus. Some people work better under pressure.

ROMANTICSADIST:

Good girl! You're on track to barely make it by when it closes 🎰

I smirk, a plan forming as I check the time—8:37 p.m. I want to see if she will rise to a challenge if it's harder than what she had in mind for herself. I expect her to melt at my praise, for her to be relieved she'll make it by her self-imposed deadline, at which time I would've hit her with a plot twist—pun intended. But her reply couldn't be further from my assumption.

SIENNA:

Fuck! Why you gotta say it like that, Sir? lmao!

Of course this woman wouldn't just take the atta girl at face value. I'll need to remember she reads further into the specific words someone uses than the average person. After all, it is her specialty.

ROMANTICSADIST:

Barely is still on time. Keep it up. But you'll have to push a little. You will meet me at 9:30. I may push it till 10, but only IF you're in the middle of a scene.

Because you SHOULD be almost done at that time. If you're not at 49,500 by 9:30, you WILL take your spanking. Do you understand?

That means just under 700 words in a little under an hour. She said she used to average a thousand an hour, so it shouldn't send her into the "that's impossible" zone where she'll give up before she even tries.

SIENNA:

Wait... the gym closes at midnight, Sir!

Oh hell. Yes, Sir.

I smile as her second message comes in hot on the heels of the one before it, like the first was an automatic, unfiltered outburst before she could catch herself, then quickly correcting herself. But it's important for her to know from the beginning what will and won't be tolerated, based on the type of submissive she is, no matter how amusing she may be.

> ROMANTICSADIST:
>
> I'm HOPING you're letting me know that as a courtesy and not because you think I didn't previously check or have my reasons. You keep this up and I'm going to question if you're not more brat or other kind of masochist than I thought.

I'll have to adjust the way I speak to her and what I allow, depending on her sub identity. A brat needs to be allowed to talk back, to tease and provoke her Dom. Being mouthy and poking the bear is part of what gives them the release they desire. So therefore, their Dom has to permit more insubordination than they would a sub who identifies as a perfectly obedient slave. But the other part of that type of submissive's needs, why they want that moment of "bratting," is the punishment they desire in return. Brats are masochists because they crave to be put in their place by a stronger hand. They want their time to mouth off and sass, to get that cathartic relief of arguing, and they most likely enjoy when ordinarily they'd "win" said argument, but it's the result of it they truly yearn for. The darker, heavier-handed domination, the physical manifestation of the answer "because I said so" that a parent might use when their kid is right about something.

I wouldn't peg Sienna as a brat. They don't normally have praise kinks, which is what she craves the most. But she could have more brattish tendencies, wanting to banter as her way of flirting, which would make sense for someone intelligent like she is. She'd want to impress me with her thought process if she was on the opposite side of a debate than me. I don't believe she'd give her input as a way to provoke a negative response like a true bratty sub would.

SIENNA:

My throat did that thingy again, Sir lol

I... don't know how to respond to that, Sir.

Just as I thought. I wasn't even that stern with her and it already has her fumbling with nerves. I want her to get her work done, so I put her out of her misery.

ROMANTICSADIST:

Yes. The gym closes at midnight. I am planning to leave my house and drive there just for you. That can only be done so late, because I have to work early in the morning. By the math (not the reality of how an artist's mind works), you should hit my number and be on track.

When in doubt, just try "Yes, Sir" or "Sorry, Sir" or "I'll try harder" (or "won't happen again." Whichever is more appropriate)

And after you see me and either get your praises or punishments... Maybe you'll be inspired

SIENNA:

Yes, Sir. And do with this what you please, Sir.

A screenshot of a BDSM personality test comes through, and I recognize the page immediately. It's a scary-accurate sliding scale test Seth created that uses the results to show what percentage of each role or type a person is within the kink community.

I click the photo to make it full screen and see she cropped out anything that would've identified Club Alias, and a sense of pride comes over me that even in all the chaos of her mind, she still remembers her vow of secrecy. The results screen is so generic, with only white typeface on a plain black background, that if I were to ask where she took this quiz, she could send me to any random BDSM test on the internet.

Good girl.

Test Results:
100% SUBMISSIVE
100% ROPE BUNNY

88% VOYEUR

80% MASOCHIST

68% EXPERIMENTALIST

63% BRAT

62% PRIMAL (PREY)

60% SLAVE

50% EXHIBITIONIST

48% VANILLA

39% DEGRADEE

34% SADIST

33% PET

23% RIGGER

19% SWITCH

0% AGEPLAYER

0% OWNER

0% NON-MONOGAMIST

0% MASTER/MISTRESS

0% BOY/GIRL

0% DOMINANT

0% DEGRADER

0% DADDY/MOMMY

0% BRAT TAMER

0% PRIMAL (HUNTER)

SIENNA:

No idea what a "rope bunny" is, Sir, but apparently I'm a closet one.

> But maybe like... adjust it with a learning curve? Since technically ALL my education has NOT been applied in real-life situations and you're my first super-experienced Dom, Sir. Like... I'm book smart, not street smart? But I will do my damnedest not to disappoint you, because my therapist never was able to fix my "disease to please."

Her first message is somewhat shocking. She's been submersed in this lifestyle for years now, through researching her books and as a sub to her then-husband at Club Alias. How has she never heard the term Rope Bunny before?

Or maybe it's only a common term in my mind, because as fate would have it, I'm 100% a Rigger, a Rope Bunny's counterpart, the Yin to her Yang.

I'm suddenly even more excited to start teaching her more and more about herself.

ROMANTICSADIST:

> When we meet, you're getting some rules and info.

SIENNA:

> PS: I'm the super-adorable light-gray SUV on the tennis side of the lot, Sir. It was my present to myself when I hit USA Today Bestseller. I've never really cared about what I drive, but I saw it and fell in love, Sir 😊

I smile once more as the filter between her busy mind and her fingers ceases to stop anything.

RomanticSadist:

You deserve to reward yourself for a job well done. I'm glad you enjoy your ride, little one 🖤

SIENNA:

And I meant adjust the TEST RESULTS with a learning curve, Sir 😂 Not the reward/punishment.

ROMANTICSADIST:

The message before my last one was just a statement. When we meet, and if the vibe between us is anything near the connection we have just in text conversation, you will be given some rules and information to help you learn and be taught to please me, how I'd enjoy you to behave. If you desire to be taught and trained, decide you want to fully serve… you'll never be the same, little one. I can promise you that.

Now, focus on writing. I'll message you before long and tell you where to be. And don't worry… you'll get to speak freely to ask questions as well. And if you ask nicely, you can get a spanking even when you do well 😊

I add the last part, because even though she danced

around answering before, I can confirm from her test results she's not adverse to roughness and a little pain to go with her pleasure.

SIENNA:

You say that, but I'm sitting here wondering how the hell I'll be able to walk outside to meet you, when I couldn't gather up the courage to even look up at you, Sir. I mean, I'm going to. I'd never not come out, with you out there waiting for me. But just know I'm nervous as fuck, Sir.

God, the innocence. Everything she says, the way she says it…. It just confirms my belief that what I saw in the café this morning was genuinely *her*, not an act.

ROMANTICSADIST:

I will lead you through it, little princess. I've got you.

I've been calling her princess as a stand-in until I decide on who she will be for me. One of my greatest pleasures as a Dom has been giving a sub the name she'll answer to when she's serving me. Seeing their eyes light up, knowing I put a lot of thought into their names, skimming through choices of what might fit them the best according to who they truly are as a submissive, their reactions are always like I've handed them a physical gift, something special and meaningful—which is exactly what it is. In return, I've always enjoyed the names they've come up with for me as well. Yes, they're commanded to use the respectful moniker of Sir when speaking to me, but I don't demand them to use it in place of a name when referring to me. A lot of the Doms at the club came up with their own Dominant name, which is what I also did for simplicity sake while I'm there. But between my sub and me, who I am to her and her alone, she gets the honor of giving me that same gift—a name. Because as most everyone knows, names hold power.

SIENNA:

Hm, a discovery just occurred, Sir. Apparently, I'm one of those who gets emotional and choked up when I'm told things like that. Who knew. 😢

A feeling I'm unfamiliar with makes my chest hurt at her response to me telling her I'll help her through everything.

SIENNA:

Panicky? Yes, Sir. Make jokes at inappropriate times to redirect anxiety? Most definitely, Sir. People pleaser to a fault with no care given whether it hurts me or not? Oh, you betcha, Sir. It's why I have no friends. They got what they needed me for and ditched me once they used me for "clout," or whatever the kids call it these days. But weepy and choked up? Fuck no, Sir. I only do that when dogs die in movies. Cry? After being married to a Sadist discovering who he truly is and allowing him to use me, because I thought that's what I was supposed to do as his wife and sub, I don't do that, Sir. Soooo... that's interesting.

But before your hackles rise, Art never actually HURT-hurt me. I would grin and bear it until I couldn't anymore, then use my safeword. And he'd always, ALWAYS respect it. Since the female body sometimes has an instinctive reaction that someone on the outside would view as pleasure, I don't blame him one bit for continuing until I tapped out. A Dom has to be able to trust his sub to tell him when something is wrong. Y'all are not mind readers.

Even though sometimes it seems like YOU are, Sir.

ROMANTICSADIST:

Dogs... loyal to a fault and deserve
the best and all your tears.

Jokes? Learned coping mechanism.

People pleaser? GOLDEN. What a
Dom yearns for in a sub.

The people who used you THINK
they won and are CLUELESS to the
treasure they threw away and left
behind.

And OF COURSE physical pain
means little to you. You suffer such
mental anguish that nothing
physical can touch it.

She reads everything immediately, but there's nothing to indicate she's even typing for quite some time. I fight the urge to prompt a response, allowing her the time to process instead.

SIENNA:

Oh... kay. I.... Yes, Sir.

I nod with pride, the emotion filling my chest and shoving that previous painful feeling out.

ROMANTICSADIST:

Good call. Not everything needs a
response, sweetheart. I talk a lot
and often state my opinion as if it's
fact. I might learn to control it if I
weren't right most of the time.

> But I must admit, it saddens me that
> someone having your back chokes
> you up.

I confess that to her, since she's been so freely sharing insight into her feelings. I seldom feel that emotion strongly —any emotion, really—that something in me wants to let her in on the fact that she made my chest ache for her.

SIENNA:
> I was just caught off guard that
> anyone could "get" me like that, Sir.

Trying to put on a brave face. She still fears she's "too much" and doesn't want to turn me off with how deeply she feels things. Only time will convince her that's one of her most attractive traits, in my opinion. It takes someone like her—sensitive, empathetic, deeply emotional even though she's learned to hide it—to be able to submerse themselves in the skills I've learned and naturally always had, to the point they lose themselves to the pleasure and reach a level of bliss so few can.

ROMANTICSADIST:
> I see you, princess. Deep inside. I
> can see.

I silence my phone, leaving her on that comforting note, because she needs to work. If I hear her notifications, I won't be able to resist checking them. And to be sure I don't physically check my phone to see if she's messaged me, I leave it on my charger in my bedroom after setting an alarm for the time I gave her, then stride into the attached bathroom to take a shower.

It wouldn't do to meet the sweet sub face-to-face and touch her the first time while I'm covered in grass clippings from mowing my lawn.

Although the sexy little plant lover might find that arousing, I think with a chuckle as I brush my teeth. Then I soap up, take the time to thoroughly manscape—after all, it's the respectful thing to do for a woman who might agree to come anywhere near your cock—and rinse off. I trimmed the rest of my body hair with clippers just a couple of days ago, so I don't need to waste any more time on preparing myself other than getting dressed.

When my alarm goes off, I snatch it off the nightstand, almost embarrassed by my level of anxiousness to check on Sienna. It's too close to feeling out of control, and I can't allow that.

I see she recently wrote two long messages, and I dive into them like I'm on fire and her words are the only thing that can extinguish me.

SIENNA:

> Obviously, you probably come in contact with a lot of "weirdos," because no one "normal" is drawn to this sort of stuff. And so I figured you probably went into chatting with me knowing I'd be at least a little nuts. But I'm diagnosed OCD with intrusive, repetitive thoughts, so I fully 100% expected you to read the emotional thing and be like... "deuces, I'm out." 🫠 Your response was not even on my radar, Sir.

> I literally had to invent a whole-ass person, the center of my entire 9-book series, a fictional fucking character, this all-knowing, superhero-like priest—don't judge me—to be able to write out ME getting to interact with someone who gets me... and you did it in like, a day. So there's that, Sir. And no, schizophrenia is not one of my adorable personality traits, Sir. LOL! Just trauma that happened when my very naive self was finally released into the wild, Sir.

My answer flies from my fingers before I can stop it.

ROMANTICSADIST:

> You poor thing. What has society done to you?

Nothing pisses me the fuck off more than people feeling

beaten down because of societal norms. I know it's because of my Level 1 autism, which used to be called Asperger's, that I can see the bullshit more clearly than someone who's not on the spectrum, but because of that, it's even more frustrating to me when someone else allows "normalcy" to greatly affect how they live their life. People go through their entire life suppressing who they are and what brings them joy and pleasure, even dying without letting their real self have a single day in the light, just because they fear being judged and how others might treat them after knowing the truth.

But then, I can't fault them. Because I do the same thing every day. I'm no "better" than they are just because I've found a way to live a secret double life. I understand exactly why they hide, yet I'm no less frustrated with myself than I am with them, which means I'm not a hypocrite, just more of a sheep than I wish I was.

SIENNA:

Society, Sir? LOL! Nah, I just have a terrible sense for choosing the people I get close to, Sir. So like... I really hope you're the same in person as you are in my DMs, Sir.

Wow... you were right, Sir! It is starting to feel weird NOT to put the Sir. Here... let me try.... Nope. Don't like that, Sir. *The Office gif

Also, this just happened. #overachiever

I was just about to ask for her word count to see whether she met the deadline or not, so I could get in the mindset needed for either reward or punishment, and my heart explodes with pride when I read the number in her screenshot.

ROMANTICSADIST:

50945!

I KNEW you would have no problems.

In all honesty, I was a little worried, since she was spending so much time texting me. But not only did she meet my demand, she blew it out of the water by more than doubling it. What better way to enforce good behavior than to meet it with confidence she'll then take on herself.

SIENNA:

Oh, look, Sir. There's my heartbeat in my eardrums again.

ROMANTICSADIST:

You definitely have earned the right to not be bent over my knee.

This is where you are conflicted, by the way. IS this the reward you worked so hard for?

I grin as I watch her typing bubble appear then disappear several times, questioning herself, questioning how right my observation is, before she finally replies.

SIENNA:

Yes, Sir.

ROMANTICSADIST:

LOL! You typed... erased.. typed... erased, then did a rewrite to Yes, Sir. I'm so impressed with you, princess.

SIENNA:

I just whimpered out loud. Thank you, Sir.

ROMANTICSADIST:

You almost wrote yourself into being bent over and given things you may not yet fully want. You'll learn soon enough I'm very protective by nature, and not only does that make me want to take out whoever hurt someone I care about, but it also makes me want to fix and make my person happy again. And the fastest, most efficient way I know how to do that is with physical pleasure.

SIENNA:

Oversharer, Sir. 😊

I try my very best not to trauma dump, but you have a weird effect on me, Sir.

I don't say so, because it's way too soon to admit to the feelings she provokes in me, to her or myself, but she has the same weird effect on me. I share things with her I don't normally tell people until I've known them for a very long time.

SIENNA:

> I just remembered I got a pizza kids meal from the cafe before they closed, and it's just been sitting here while I hyperfocused.

> That's both sad and incredible, Sir.

> Cold pizza, I'm fine with, Sir. But SMELLING like pizza? Great first impression, Sienna 😌

> And now I'm starting to panic, because I'm like, "Is he going to let me know when he's here, or am I supposed to be out there already?" Are you sure you want to deal with me, Sir? lol

She needs direction. She's begging for it without actually asking. And I want nothing more than to give her instructions I have no doubt she'll obey without hesitation. Because a pleaser who begs for direction has no desire to question or deny. They just *do*.

ROMANTICSADIST:

> Get your pizza.

SIENNA:

> I did, Sir. Figured it might help the shaking.

> Who needs cardio, when they have you, Sir? lol

ROMANTICSADIST:

Good girl. I'll be there in about 10.
Stay until I tell you I'm there.

You may also go use the
mouthwash in the locker room by
the sinks

SIENNA:

OMG! I totally forgot we had that!
Thank you for the reminder, Sir.

God, she's sweet. If she agrees to be trained as my sub, then I'll do everything I can to keep all that sweetness intact for me to enjoy while also bringing out the vixen I know she longs to be for the right Dom.

ROMANTICSADIST:

Of course. And I'll also remind you
that you asked me to behave. Your
breath can smell of delicious pizza,
and I'll never know.

SIENNA:

You would if you're close enough to
talk in my ear with that sexy-ass
voice, Sir. I'm just sayin', Sir.

A grunt escapes my suddenly puffed-up chest at her forward compliment. Knowing she thinks my voice is sexy, the otherwise shy woman feeling it strongly enough to tell me so is quite a big deal. It makes me think back to the first compliment she ever gave me, the first words she ever said to me, the first message she ever sent me—*I've **totally***

drooled over you at our gym before. Technically, it was her second message. The first was a response to my greeting, one I look back on and smile, now that I've gotten to know her. Such a "Sienna" reaction. ***Oh holy hell…***

ROMANTICSADIST:

> I will give you this choice. I will meet you at your parking spot at the gym, OR you can drive a block so the parking lot security won't bother us while we talk.

I send her a screenshot of my Map app where I've circled the abandoned bank near the gym. I scoped it out when I left her this morning, knowing she'd feel more comfortable staying close by. But the security fucker at our gym rides around on his golf cart, checking in on anyone who stays in their car longer than a couple of minutes, thinking they're casing cars to break into. I call him a fucker because although he sees me there every single day, he still comes and taps on my window to question me when I spend a while checking emails and fucking off on my phone.

I may wear graphic tees with a backward cap, have five silver hoops in my ears, and a shitload of tattoos encase my hard-earned muscularity. Not to mention a demeaner that makes people either run from or gravitate toward for safety with no in-between. But while I've been told countless times that I look like a modern-day pirate, I'm not one. I don't need to steal anything. I make plenty… as a fucking emergency room doctor. I'd love to throw it in the prejudice motherfucker's face, but at the same time, I value being underestimated even more. It's too great of a card to have in one's pocket to just throw it down without waiting for the opportune moment.

And yes, that was a Jack Sparrow pun.

SIENNA:

Fuuuuuck. Um... And you promise to behave, Sir? I'm sorry to question you, but like... you just read my trauma dump. Never mind. Yes, I'll meet you there, Sir. Should I leave now, Sir?

She makes it so easy to see inside her mind when she sends me her every thought leading to her final decision. It'll help me learn even more about her way of thinking before I help her gain the confidence that'll turn her answers clear and concise.

ROMANTICSADIST:

No... I want you to wait.

Sit there a bit. Be nervous. Let your anxiety in, your fight-or-flight kick in, your heart race, your breathing turn fast and shallow.

Her message comes at the same time mine sends, and then her reply not long after.

SIENNA:

FML it just dawned on me I'm going
to have to actually speak to you...
and look at you... IN PERSON, Sir.
My whole body is literally vibrating.

No problem, Sir lol

In order to learn how to beat her anxiety, she first has to face it in all it's overwhelming glory. You don't beat cancer by only treating a tiny piece of it. No, you have to get rid of it entirely, as much as you can all at once, even taking extra just in case. And then whatever you couldn't quite reach, you hit it with all the ammunition you have as a fallback. Otherwise, that shit will just spread and keep on coming back.

ROMANTICSADIST:

Sit and let your imagination—
fantasies and fears, both—run wild.

SIENNA:

I'm very, very, very good at that, Sir.

I know, little one. And I can't wait to teach you all the pleasures that wild imagination can conjure.

ROMANTICSADIST:

Are you beginning to think you're
not the only word wizard? 😊

I've been told throughout my life I have a way with words. I just shrugged it off as a kid, not understanding what they meant, because I just spoke and wrote the words the way they popped into my head. It's not like I was taking the time to make my speech poetic or witty on purpose. But then when I got older, seeing the effect the way I talk had on women, I learned to harness it. I admit I went through a period of time I used my power for evil, getting things I wanted with coercion or by spinning questions and answers in a way that made others believe it was all their idea. But after becoming a part of the BDSM community, I hung up that hat and chose to only use that power for good—or at least in a way that wouldn't hurt anyone if they realized my special abilities.

SIENNA:

I knew that from "go," Sir. It's why you weren't blocked after message #2.

It's both awesome and terrifying meeting someone who's actually smarter than me, Sir.

I pull my lips between my teeth, biting down to keep from laughing out loud. I can't count the number of times I've thought to myself—learning early on that saying it aloud was frowned upon by societal norms—how frustrating it is that I'm always surrounded by idiots. Not being conceited, just a fact. My IQ is almost always the highest in the room, and combined with my people-reading skills, it's probably a good thing I was born on the spectrum. Otherwise, I would've probably ended up as a serial killer instead of taking the opposite route as a healer. I'm at just a far enough distance from "normal" people's emotions to think on the spot and make split-second decisions without feelings being involved, but not so far that I don't truly *feel* emotions. A move in either direction would've been dangerous for everyone. All sorts of things in my past could've made me snap, and I would've had the intelligence and skillset to never be caught. But since I had that tiny "flaw" in my brain, it acted as a safety buffer, a filter that kept me at a safe distance from feeling things too intensely.

In Sienna's case, she is incredibly intelligent. But instead of having my ability to read people by watching them and listening to their words, she's opposite. She feels "too deeply." Meaning she's an empath and can know a person by feeling their emotions. I suspect that's where most of her anxiety comes from without her even realizing it. She's an introvert, so while she *wants* to be surrounded by friends and people, she inadvertently takes in all the chaos when a big group gets together, and it drains her.

She's never asked what I do for a living, and I wouldn't be able to give her the whole truth without it leading to her discovering my identity. So I go with one of my favorite quotes.

> ROMANTICSADIST:
>
> Thank you for the compliment. But there are different kinds of intelligence. The mechanic is no less intelligent than the doctor. They just know different skills.

Everyone is a master of something.

SIENNA:

Does that mean I'm a master of
writing Masters, Sir? hehe

Her go-to when she's overwhelmed—making jokes.

ROMANTICSADIST:

Possibly, little one.

An honest answer, not one to feed the ego. I've never read her books, so I wouldn't know how accurately or lyrically she writes a Dominant's story.

SIENNA:

OMG I'm so ridiculous, Sir. WTF.
Men don't make me nervous, Sir. I
can walk up to literally ANYONE and
talk their ear off. But I'm about to
have a freaking heart attack thinking
about just *looking* at you in
person, Sir.

What she doesn't say is men don't make her nervous because she's not normally attracted to them, to *anyone*. She's said it before. The fact that she's this nervous goes to show just how attracted to me the little sub is.

SIENNA:

> I wonder how much it would cost to outfit an entire room in padding. If I sit here letting my mind wander much longer, I'm going to need to get a free estimate.

More jokes. It's time to let her off the hook... or at least give her something in reality to worry about instead of just marinating in her vivid imagination.

ROMANTICSADIST:

> Start walking to your car and go there now. I will find you. Park next to you. Then

I see her message pop up as I'm in the middle of typing her instructions, but it's the perfect opportunity to show her what a caring Dom should be when a sub is feeling the most vulnerable. So I go ahead and send what I have written so she can start preparing, then respond to hers.

SIENNA:

> I may expire right there when I get out of my car, Sir. So like, use those big muscles to catch me, kay? K.

ROMANTICSADIST:

> I'll carry you, little one. Hold you above all else.

SIENNA:

> I just whimpered out loud again, Sir.

I have to see all your instructions first, while I have WiFi, Sir. Am I good to go?

Ah, her phone is dead. Right.

ROMANTICSADIST:

I'll come to your driver side door. And since the idea makes you so nervous, you don't have to look up at me. I'll open the door for you, and you'll get out. I'll guide you to my truck, and you'll get in like you're told. You'll have concerns, but you'll trust and get in.

That's all for now. You'll hear the rest in person.

Gray Hummer

I add the last part quickly in hopes she hasn't already closed her laptop. I know she received it though when her rapid-fire messages pop into our thread.

SIENNA:

Is it too late to take up drinking?

Shit!

Ok. Leaving now, Sir.

fuck fuck fuck fuck...

Chapter Five

SIENNA

"Oh my God, oh my God, oh my God… what am I doing?" I ask myself as my foot presses on the brake pedal and I push the ignition button. "You can do this. You can totally do this. He's just a man. You've been talking to him for three weeks now. He knows some of your deepest, darkest secrets that you've never told anyone before. And he said you don't even have to look up. Just park and turn your mind off. He'll do the rest. That's what you've always wanted."

My entire body is filled with terrified anticipation. It's that feeling when you're not quite next in line for a turn on the biggest rollercoaster in the amusement park. Where you're looking between the people getting off the ride, their expressions, and deciding if you should jump out of the queue and follow them out the exit gate. Once you're at the head of the line, there's really no turning back—or maybe that's just me. I don't want to piss anyone off by chickening out last second and screwing them up if they've carefully counted out heads and rides to make sure they get to take their turn in the same car with their family or friends.

But there is another feeling making itself very known inside me, one that has to be strong as hell in order to be noticed over the fear that can't be ignored.

Desire.

I, Sienna Brookes, am horny as *fuck*.

I can't ever remember being this aroused in my whole life. I can feel my pulse between my legs, and I have no doubt I'm already soaked just from the anticipation I've felt all day.

He was insightful as hell to ask me if I truly *had* worked my ass off in order to not be turned over his knee and spanked. Seeing my word count grow, I had the thought— multiple times—to slow down so I wouldn't reach my goal on purpose, just so I could experience laying across his lap and feeling his hand come down on such an intimate place. And bare too. He'd described pulling my shorts down to make the smack count, skin-on-skin, not even a thin layer of spandex to separate us... to protect my flesh.

When I read that message, my hand had a mind of its own, as I discovered it beneath my laptop, the four fingers of my right hand cupping my aching pussy and my thumb hooking in the leg of my shorts. I was so turned on I unconsciously reached down to touch myself right there in the locker room, and when I realized what I was doing, my face flamed as I snatched my hand back, and I took a quick glance around. Thank God there was no one else there.

I didn't know how to respond to his question.

> ROMANTICSADIST:
>
> You definitely have earned the right to not be bent over my knee.
>
> This is where you are conflicted, by the way. IS this the reward you worked so hard for?

How honest should I be with this man I, in reality, hardly know but feel I've known for countless years?

I had typed out the whole truth at first—**I want to be bent over your knee more than I want my next Venti Peppermint Mocha with extra Vanilla Sweet Cream Cold Foam, Sir. And there's never been anything I've wanted more than THAT before.**

But then I erased it. Chickened out. My voices talking me out of speaking what I truly desired.

You've never even looked the man in the eye before and you're gonna tell him you want him to spank your ass?

He's gonna think you're too easy, you ho.

Have some dignity. Jesus.

A spanking isn't a reward, remember, Miss Not-Masochist-Enough-To-Keep-Your-Sadist-Husband-Happy? You busted your ass for a REWARD, not to get your ass busted!

God knows he's already going to think you're a little slut for meeting up with him to play just a few weeks after meeting him.

"That's not necessarily true. People at Club Alias play together without having even met before that night. It's an exchange of power, an understanding between two consenting adults," I argued aloud with the intrusive thoughts badgering me like they constantly did. "Two people fulfilling each other's needs without shame."

Yeah, well, he's not a member of the club, now is he? No. He's some random dude off the internet you just so happened to recognize from the gym. You have no idea if he's safe to play with. He hasn't been put through psychological testing from a professional to make sure he's sane and not some psycho who's just really good at manipulation.

That was the thought that made me forcibly shut the voices down.

I felt oddly protective over Gym Daddy. I never got a single bad vibe from him when he was just my gym crush, and he's been nothing but kind, understanding, and uplifting while I've talked to him constantly over the last few weeks. I'm sensitive to people's auras. It's an annoying characteristic I wish I could either turn off or be able to read more accurately, because there are some who are so good at masking their true intentions that they can fool an empathetic person like me, who wants to always see the good in people.

Most often, it's other women.

Case in point: my ex-best friends.

Now, my hands tremble on the steering wheel as I turn out of the gym's parking lot, and before I know it, I'm pulling into the lot of the abandoned bank. Just as he promised, his dark-gray Hummer is parked in the back of the lot.

A jolt of unimaginable energy zips through my entire body at the sight.

He's really here.

It wasn't until this moment I recognize there was a tiny voice teasing in the background, behind all the louder, more annoying ones, mocking me in a whisper, *He's not gonna show up. Why would he waste time on you? There are so many better options out there. You're just a fun experiment, someone to pass time until a submissive worthy of a man like him comes his way. He said over and over that he didn't think you'd actually give him what he desires. Sure, he disguised it, worded it in a way that made it sound like you just wouldn't give in to your desire to play, but really, if you go back and read his exact messages, I'm sure you could translate it differently. So much is lost over texts, remember? I bet you anything he really meant you weren't good enough for him. I bet you he won't even be there when you go to meet him. I bet you… I bet you….*

And as I see just a glimpse of the light beard turn my way, I may avert my eyes on instinct, but inside, I want to shout, "Ha! See! He wasn't just toying with me. He didn't stand me up. He really does want to see me!"

But even as I think the sad little "pick me" comeback, that bitch voice already has a rebuttal.

You go to the same gym. Of course he showed up. He wouldn't want you confronting him in public, dumbass.

I don't park directly next to him. I'm so nervous I'm afraid I'll park too close to open my door, or too far away, taking up more than my space. So I leave just one spot between us, shift into Park, and turn off my car, placing my hands in my lap just as he instructed. Even though he didn't tell me to, I stare down into my hands, my head lowered like so many of my heroines I've written. But where they were doing it out of obedience, a classic submissive pose, my body does it of its own accord, because for some reason, I'm terrified to look up at this man as much as I crave his attention.

Yet the feeling that beats out everything else, the one that stands out above all the voices, all the emotions, all the reasoning and reality of the situation I've found myself in…

Is desire.

I've never wanted something more in my entire life than for this to actually happen.

For this to be real.

For *him* to be real.

There's nothing I wouldn't give, nothing in the world I crave more, than for this man to live up to the fantasy I've built him up to be in my head.

My gym crush.

The guy I was insanely attracted to without knowing a damn thing about him.

My attention just being pulled toward him as if his soul was calling out to mine.

And then boom, there he was on a dating app specifically for people like me, people who have an alternative perspective, desires and needs that aren't "the norm". How was it possible the one man I had been drawn to "out in the wild" also craved a D/s relationship like I did?

Or is that *why* I was drawn to him so strongly in the first place?

Is there something about him that screams Dominant, even without any obvious identifiers? Hell, even without any discreet identifiers?

I'd never noticed him wearing a triskelion—the symbol of the BDSM community—either on a piece of clothing or jewelry. Nothing about the way he dressed at the gym marked him as a Dom. I don't really know what could, off the top of my head, but surely a funny graphic tee or something would give a slight hint. Hell, even I have shirts that say things like **BDSM: Bees Do So Much (for the environment)**. My favorite though is a smiling potted plant with a watering can tilted above it, and it reads **Oh yes, all over my face, Daddy.**

If I wasn't known at our gym as that author who writes her dirty books in the locker room, I'd be easily pegged as freaky-deaky by my decidedly immature but hilarious sense of style… or lack thereof.

A submissive would be much easier to pick out in a crowd than a Dom, and that's by design. A collar, maybe a bracelet or anklet with a lock, whether it be a fake one just for show, like a charm, or an actual locking clasp that couldn't be opened without their Master's key. We wear these different little tokens—or big, super-loud ones—to make it known to people who know what to look for and would recognize what we are, to say "Here I am! You're not alone! I get you! I'm one of you!" but also, "I'm taken. I'm under my Dominant's protection. Yes, we are part of this amazing small community, in this together, and get each other on another level, but one wrong move, one step in a disrespectful direction, out of your proper place, and you will face the wrath of the one who owns me."

I crave that more than anything else, I think. Being owned, feeling powerful myself because I have a powerful Dom to protect me, even when he's not there. The collar is a symbol of him, his ownership, his strength. It lives inside the leather or metal or whatever material it's made of. And as long as it's around his sub's neck, or wrist, or ankle, or finger, or wherever the two of them have deemed the most meaningful between them, then the submissive harnesses all their Dominant's strength that they lack on their own.

God, I wish I had even an ounce of that.

Because God knows I have very little strength of my own.

I'm the weakest person I know.

Physically *and* mentally.

I don't know how much time passes. I either sit there for a tremendous amount of time stewing in my anxiety and in my ever-growing anticipation, wondering just how long it'll take for him to come open my door like he said he would. Or, I sit there for mere seconds—too quickly, it seems—by the time I hear the handle clicking, the door opening simultaneously with my car's lights turning on, my eyes closing against the sudden brightness.

But they startle back open as a zap of electricity wraps itself around my bicep. It takes me a moment to realize it's his hand, and then he's helping me out of the car. His softly spoken words are there in my ear just like they were when he came to speak to me in the café this morning. "There you go, little one. I've got you. Just watch your feet. I won't let you fall."

I feel like I'm floating, a balloon on a string tied to his finger. I can't explain it, but it's like his voice makes me weightless. I give myself over to it, and everything that's dragged me down for who knows how long poofs into inexistence, and I'm above every single bit of it with him as my safety line.

Yet even as I feel damn near high and deliciously thoughtless, blissfully unaware of almost everything but this man's dominating presence, I still sense the longing inside me. The desire growing by the millisecond the more I breathe the same air as him.

God, I want him.

I want him so desperately my core actually throbs, aching for him, making me feel empty both physically and emotionally, as if *I* might be the thing that poofs into inexistence if he doesn't slide some part of him into some part of me. I don't care what. I just want him to fill me up with himself so I can feel what it's like to connect with someone I crave like oxygen.

No, not like oxygen.

More like a *lack* of oxygen.

Because it's a darker, more sinister and filthy need I feel for him, like a hand wrapped around my throat, cutting off my air to give me something way more explosive and erotic than simply the ability to breathe.

And feeling his strong hand around the top of my arm, it makes it oh-so easy to imagine what it would feel like just inches higher up my body, that hot palm branding my neck as it tightens... tightens until I can't even whimper through the intoxicating pleasure it causes.

I'm vaguely aware of reality for a moment when I hear my car door close, and suddenly my breath really is stolen as I feel him take hold of my hips from behind, my knees damn near buckling as it sends an immediate image of what it would be like for him to take me this way—*God, yes, please... take me this way... right now*—until I gather he's just helping me up into the backseat of his SUV.

And that's when the fear kicks back in, battling my arousal for which feeling will reign supreme.

Oh, and in pops confusion's little head... because there is no actual seat. Either they've been removed or they fold down flat, making a perfectly level surface.

That's the moment I realize I should've paid more attention to all my serial killer documentaries as cautionary tales rather than story inspirations for my anti-heroes.

Chapter Six

SIENNA

"That's a good girl. Just slide to the back a bit, sit on your knees, ass on your ankles, and rest your hands in your lap. That's right, sweet girl. Just like that. You're doing so good."

His gentle coaxing somehow keeps my fight-or-flight reaction from making any rash decisions. As much as my mind and all its residents are telling me I'm an idiot for the current situation I've put myself in, that's the only part of me with any sort of negative feelings at the moment. Everything else—my instincts, my heart, right down to my soul—is telling me to give in to this opportunity. It feels like it could be everything I've ever dreamed of and then lived out vicariously through my characters in my books.

Because even though I'd been in a D/s relationship with my ex-husband, it just wasn't the same. It didn't feel like *this*. It always felt like we were role-playing, putting on an act for each other, since BDSM was something we discovered and tried to incorporate after our relationship was already set as something else, something vanilla, something that made it nearly impossible to view the other person as anything else other than what we knew each other as for years.

It would be really hard to see a man as this powerful, all-knowing, worship-worthy being... when for the previous three years you'd been washing the shit stains out of his tighty-whities.

But I don't want to think about anyone else or any other moment in my life than this one right here. This man right here. The one who has consumed my every thought made by each and every one of my voices for nearly a month now.

As long as I do exactly what he says, I'll be okay. There's no guesswork; there's no making hard decisions. I just have to do what he tells me to do, and I'll be safe, I remind myself.

I'll make him happy.

The dim light inside his SUV shuts off at the same time I hear him pull his door closed. My eyes don't lift to meet his, but they do go so far as to see the way he sits directly in front of me. No matter how hard I try, I just can't make myself look at his face. But just the way he sits reminds me of a sex god lounging across a bed of satin sheets and pillows, even though in reality, his broad back just rests against the back of his driver seat, one leg stretched out, the other knee up, where his forearm rests atop it.

Arousal Level: 43%

Fear Level: 37%

Confusion Level: 20%

His fingertips rub against his thumb in circles, and I can feel his eyes on me, making my breath catch in my lungs and my gaze lower to my lap once again.

I have the overwhelming urge to fill the silence with questions or a joke, but I cannot for the life of me pull my tongue from where it's glued itself to the roof of my mouth. Which is probably for the best.

But soon, he answers the questions I would've asked anyway, as if I voiced them after all.

"You might find it odd to be meeting this way. I'm sorry to disappoint my little serial-killer enthusiast, but I won't be kidnapping you… tonight, at least." I can hear the teasing in his tone, but all I can do is nod. "But I'd like you to know this is one of my sanctuaries. It's a place I can be my true self and completely at ease. You yourself have to be weary of the type of person you might be confronted with when meeting someone new face-to-face for the first time. In the vanilla world, a woman has to be extremely careful when she meets up with a man she doesn't know in person. As a submissive, you have to be even more cautious that the man claiming to be a Dominant truly is a member of the community. And on top of that, you have to pray he actually knows what he's doing," he says, and the more he speaks, the more relaxed I feel.

Just the fact that he's telling me all this, that he's aware of why I'm nervous aside from it being specifically *him*, makes me feel better.

"You've told me before how much you enjoy writing from the hero's point of view, so here's something for your books you may not have considered. A Dominant has to be just as cautious, if not more, when meeting a new submissive. Speaking specifically of a male Dominant and a female submissive, we too have to worry about our own safety, because a woman can be just as dangerous as a man. And just like a man, they can not only be *physically* dangerous, but in many other ways too. It's why I don't allow anyone to know where I live." He pauses, already knowing me well enough to give me a moment to process what he's saying. When I nod again, still looking down, he continues.

"But we Doms also have to worry about the sub herself, her state of mind, any triggers she might have. We can't just jump in 100 percent and be who we are as a Dominant. That would be irresponsible and not at all what a true Dom should be, how a true Dom should act. It is a Dominant's job, first and foremost, to keep a submissive safe. Everything else is just a bonus. Which is why I created this safe space, this sanctuary, for me *and* for my sub."

I take a quick peek around, even though it's dark, and I notice little things he could be talking about. Small, different-shaped pillows, a box of tissues, a stack of neatly folded towels, a soft-looking blanket… things that could easily be in one's vehicle as a just-in-case.

"It's not lost on me that meeting up and climbing into the back of a truck could feel not only scary but also cheap.

It could feel trashy. I've even been told it made her feel like a prostitute, just asking her to get into my car. But it soon becomes a haven for a submissive. Not only my truck, but anywhere a sub might serve their Dom. It's all about association. If a certain spot on the map is where only pleasure is given and received, then it automatically fills a person with positive feelings. It becomes their 'happy place.' And even those who admitted feeling negatively about serving me in what I like to think of as a mobile playroom but others might view as a fuckpad on wheels... they started *choosing* to meet in my vehicle, even when other options became available."

In the past, a man speaking of former girlfriends and relationships would've sparked my jealousy. It's an unfortunate character flaw I've never had any sort of control over. But for some reason, it's not like that with him. It's actually reassuring he's done this what I assume are many times before. It means he's experienced and more likely knows what he's doing. He's speaking and teaching from experience and not just from what he's read or heard. This is a huge weight off my shoulders.

I was Art's first submissive, and it was a lot of trial and error that was absolutely exhausting at times. Once we felt we had a handle on it, that's when we really started diving into the community. I met Vi, who eventually introduced us to Doc and Club Alias, and it was there we got a formal education on Bondage, Discipline, Dominance and Submission, and Sadism and Masochism. It's such a relief to know this man isn't an amateur and seems as if he's had that same formal education of his own.

It makes me wonder if he's a member of the club.

Surely, he'd somehow know about Club Alias if he's devout enough to the lifestyle that he has a fancy "mobile playroom" as he called it. While the club feels like an exclusive and secret society on the inside, as if no one knows anything unless you're a member, there's no way to keep rumors from spreading. Sure, it has an unmarked door, no sign in glowing neon lights screaming **BDSM CLUB** right in the middle of our little town square. If anyone shows up, thinking they're going to check out what they believe is just a nightclub, they'd never be able to see what's really going on, because it's on the second level of the building.

The first floor entrance, guarded by two scary-looking guards—who are actually a super-sweet gay couple who own a mobile dog grooming boutique—only shows a dark staircase leading to even more darkness. Not until you reach the very top of those steps can you pick up the sexy lighting, the thump of the music, the sight of men, women, and everything in between. And we're not just talking about everything in between as in gender identifiers. We're talking people are walking around in everything from extravagant ballgowns to nothing but a bunny tail attached to their ass by a butt plug. There's a woman I see almost every time I visit—she's always in a tuxedo and walks with a man on all fours, and he wears nothing but kneepads and a collar attached to a chain, the other end held in the woman's hand.

And that naked man could very well be one of the top dogs in the Special Forces.

Pun *totally* intended.

Either way... while no one can see what's really going on up those stairs, it doesn't take a rocket scientist to know *something* is. One would only have to be on the same street and see a person or the couples or throuples trickling in and not coming out for hours. No business hours during the day, so it's locked down until the sun sets unless an appointment has been made for a special occasion or situation.

So of course rumors would spread.

Anyone curious and intelligent enough could gather all the rumors and figure out it's at least some kind of members-only club. A little deeper with a fine tooth comb and they might pick up on things like "weird-looking chokers" or "masks, but not the medical kind." But most vanilla people would just chalk it up to being some kind of goth or alternative dance club. They wouldn't have the mind to think it's one of the most world-renowned BDSM sanctuaries in existence—

"What's that smile for, little one?" he asks, and it startles me from my wondering thoughts enough that my eyes finally lift to meet his for the first time, only to discover he's wearing the sunglasses from his profile picture, and I lower my gaze once again.

How odd.

It's pitch-dark outside, and there's very little light inside the truck.

I have the sudden urge to sing *"I wear my sunglasses at night…"* but don't want to offend him if it's something he does for his own comfort, a way to feel secure, the way some Club Alias members wear masks even if their identity is known on the outside. It helps them, for lack of a better term, get into character. To help them slip into their D/s persona and stay in that mindset. Or just like a submissive and her collar.

I can't think of a stealthy way to ask him if he's a fellow member of the club, so instead, I go with the other thought dancing around in my head. "I… I understand what you're talking about. Associations, I mean," I stutter out, my voice not sounding like my own. "Scent is a big one for me. To this day, if I smell lawn clippings and gasoline, I instantly think of my dad. He was a klutz and never managed to refill the lawn mower without spilling any gas. It was always super fun and a great day when he'd let me sit on his lap and steer the riding mower while he controlled the pedals."

I clear my throat, my face heating from rambling about my late father when I'm currently in the back of an SUV waiting to hear rules and information from a Dominant to see if I feel we'd fit what each other needs. All while dying for him to skip that very important step—that should never, ever, *ever* be skipped—and just ravage my fucking brains out instead.

"Well, if I knew it would bring such a sweet smile to

your face, I wouldn't have showered after all the yardwork I did before I came," he says, and the gentleness in his tone lures my eyes from my lap once more. One corner of his full lips is pulled up, easily seen in the dim lighting because they're framed by the bright-white "salt" of his salt-and-pepper beard. That verbal response in conjunction with his little half smile does wonders to settle my nerves to a more manageable level.

He must see me relax, or sense it, because he continues on as if we hadn't taken a detour in our conversation. If he can tolerate that happening about a trillion times per conversation without getting frustrated with me, there might be a chance we can at least be friends if we don't make a D/s match. One of the things my ex-best friend threw in my face not long before she and the other ladies in our friend group ditched me—all except my ride-or-die, Vi—was how annoying I am to try to talk with, because I would always interrupt her or seemed like I was trying to one-up her.

In reality, interrupting is one of the most common characteristics of ADHD. We have impulse control issues, so if we connect with something in a discussion, we insert it without much thought about anything else, like waiting until the other person is done speaking. Also, we've learned time after time that we'll most likely forget what we were going to say, so we blurt things to just put them out there in the dialogue.

And the one-up thing? Same thing. People with ADHD try desperately to pay attention to what their friends are saying, and we want that person to feel heard and validated. The way a lot of us try to show that is by telling them about something that happened to us as well, so they know they're not alone and that their situation is relatable.

But if we're unfortunate enough to be chosen as someone's completely silent shoulder to cry on or *only* all-ears for them to vent to when they're pissed... we can easily be made to seem like a rude asshole, when really, we're just trying to make them feel better about what they're going through.

"So... learning that from experience—my truck being seen as a haven for a sub and not just a way to keep myself safe—I decided to... take up a new hobby. A project, more like it. And you're actually the first person to get to see it completed."

With this, I hear a click, my head jerking to the side as the interior of the Hummer starts to convert into something else entirely.

My eyes widen and my mouth drops open as I take in what it has to be like inside Bumblebee or some other Transformer's vehicle disguise as they twist and turn into their alien robot counterpart. The nerd in me is delighted as I watch black screens lower from slim wooden boxes along the ceiling, staying so close to the doors, hatch, and windshield that barely an inch of space seems to close in around us. I hear another click, and I can see this time that it's a remote in his hand. My body instinctively rocks toward him on my knees before I catch myself when he sits up straight, leaning closer to me, as the two front seats fold forward and sink until the rest of the interior is a flat surface like the back.

And as if all that wasn't startling enough, his phone has magically appeared in his hand, and suddenly we're no longer in a Hummer, nor a blacked-out playroom on wheels. No, instead, we're under water, deep in the ocean, schools of fish swimming past us as the sun far above our heads makes swirls in their wake. It's all enhanced and submerses you so deeply in the image surrounding you as the noise of lapping liquid comes from a sound system you can literally feel vibrating the tiny hairs on your body.

A shocked laugh escapes me, and I face him once again to tell him how freaking cool this is. But the words halt in my throat as, right then, the shimmering lights glint off something to the right and left of—but just a bit lower than —his sunglasses-covered eyes, drawing my attention to his ears.

Silver hoops—three in one ear, two in the other.

And while I counted the tiny pieces of jewelry in his lobes, my eyes had narrowed, but as realization fills my mind, I'm sure they go comically wide. A gasp fills my lungs so quickly, so sharply, that I start to cough, because of course I choke on my own spit in front of not only Gym Daddy…

But who I now recognize is Dumpster Daddy.

I shake my head and wave my hand between us when he starts to reach for me, most likely to pat me on the back, and he stops. I'm embarrassed and confused enough already. I don't want to ruin this even more by having the first time he *really* touches me be to dislodge saliva that went down the wrong pipe.

With my eyes watering, and when I can finally take a deep breath, I use the fresh oxygen to croak out, "It's you!"

When his expression doesn't change, I think maybe he doesn't recognize me, even though that night I wasn't wearing a mask and a hat like he was, nothing that would hide any of my traits that could be easily spotted in pictures.

So I word-vomit something I had been purposely avoiding talking about because I wasn't ready for him to know my exact level of craziness. I at least had to try to seduce him with my awkwardness first. "You're Dumpster Daddy!"

I shake my head at myself—*Idiot*.

"I mean, you're the hottie who rescued me from the dumpster a few weekends ago. How...?" I shake my head. "Did I look like such a hot mess that night that you didn't recognize me at the gym this morning? Heck, not even in any of my pictures?" I question, my brows furrowing.

He finally gives me a little smile, a mischievous one that's tinted blue from the projected light. "I did recognize you, little one. But since you never brought up your nighttime activities during any of our conversations, I didn't want to somehow embarrass you or make you in any way uncomfortable. I didn't want to risk that you wouldn't still be yourself, when *yourself* has been *so* delightful to get to know."

I have such a mix of emotions from my discovery and from what he just said that my mind kind of short-circuits, and I just stare at him blankly, my lips still parted. I don't know which ingredient of the mixture should be the main focus of this dish.

Jubilation? *Oh my God! Gym Daddy is Dumpster Daddy! My gym crush is also the man who fixed my hand and made the butterflies set flight inside my lady garden!*

Confusion? *What are the freaking odds?*

Excitement? *Holy shit, I can't wait to tell Vi!*

Hurt? *He couldn't have told me he knew who I was? The first thing I said to the man was that I recognized him from the gym. It would've been so easy for his response to be "Hey! I know you too!"*

Understanding? *He's totally right though. I would've definitely acted different, been less open in our conversations, if I first went into them with the knowledge he already knew just how weird I am. It was comforting to think I was revealing that fact only little by little, showing him my crazy parts one at a time instead of just punching him in the face with all of them at once.*

And of course, we can't leave out—turned on AF! *As if I didn't want to fuck Gym Daddy's brains out to begin with, let's add on the fact that everything that aroused me about him is now combined with everything that I felt that night I met Dumpster Daddy. And I am by no means a mathematician, but somehow the lust I feel for him now, is more than the sum of those two separate men. Or whatever that Aristotle guy said.*

"That's actually a common misquote, but I'm very impressed with the way your mind works, as always, little one. And Aristotle was a philosopher who sometimes used mathematics to work out theorems about ratios and infinite magnitudes, but he wasn't actually a mathematician. But I'm curious, princess," he says.

I blink, because that's all I can do. I don't want to think about what I said out loud, when my thoughts went from being internal to external without me meaning for them to. I do that often, actually voicing my thoughts as they come to my mind. I was told it's another lovely feature of ADHD, categorized under the H—hyperactivity—since it's a mostly unconscious way we expend some of our energy, by talking to ourselves out loud.

"What was it that gave me away? How did you recognize it was me?" His expression seems amused, but I can feel the leery, cautious vibe coming off him in waves.

"The five hoops, Sir. Three in one ear, and two in the other, all perfectly symmetrical. They weren't visible in your profile picture, and they're so small I never noticed them at the gym before. And since I was too scared to look at you up close this morning, now is the first time I spotted them in your ears." I tilt my head, speaking to those little silver rings in his lobes, finding it much easier to use my voice when I'm not looking him in the eye.

Even though they're still covered, I can feel them boring into me, and the lenses gleam sporadically as the ocean scene projected on the screens around us reflect the sun as realistically as if we're just beneath the surface of the *real*

Atlantic Ocean two hours away. I'm too… the only word I can think of to describe it is *intimidated*.

"The night you helped me, they were one of the only things that were remotely identifiable. I remember very clearly you were wearing a backward baseball cap… I think this one, actually"—I lift my chin to indicate the dark but faded hat, spun around once again on his shaved head—"with your mask. So I could see your ears but nothing else besides a little bit of your beard. I couldn't even tell the real color of your eyes because of the annoyingly but also conveniently dim streetlights." The last part sounds gripey even to my own ears.

"Would you like to, princess?"

I swallow reflexively at his question, my pulse picking up rapidly enough my watch lets out a trill. It's the perfect excuse to look back down and busy myself for a few seconds to turn its notifications to silent.

"When I ask you a question, I'll expect an answer," he tells me, but while the words are stern and blunt, spoken as a clear rule, there's no harshness in his tone.

I pull in a breath through my tight throat and stutter out, "I… I…. It's very hard for me to talk out loud to you for some reason."

"…for some reason…?" he prompts, and I know what he wants.

It comes out as a whisper. "Sir." I swallow again, even though there's absolutely no saliva in my entire body, it seems. I choked on the last of it a few minutes ago.

"Very good girl," he praises gently, and I'm almost embarrassed by the way my whole mind, body, and soul breathes out a sigh of relief... because I've pleased him just by using the moniker. "It *is* a bit surprising how much you struggle to talk to me after the way you speak so freely in our messages. But at the same time, it makes perfect sense. When we're chatting over messages, you don't have to look me in the eye. You don't have to worry about the way you sit or the tone or volume of your voice. All you have to pay attention to is the words themselves, which is what you are so gifted at."

My face heats, and the warmth travels to my chest. He's exactly right—about the why of it—and his compliment makes me bashful. I've never been good at receiving compliments, but from him, I can't even get a thank-you to come out that I always muster up for my sweet readers. My automatic, natural reaction to a commendation is *always* to downplay it, wave it off, basically hide from it. But being a reader myself and telling my favorite authors how much their books mean to me, I realized how important it is for the writer to know how much I adore them.

If I had told Vi that first time how her books made me feel validated and seen, way less alone in the world, and that her talent was inspiring like nothing else ever had been for me before, and then her response had been "Nah, I'm just all right" or "You need to raise your standards" or something equally as self-deprecating, it would've dulled some of the light it brought me by actually putting myself out there enough to *tell her* how much I loved her. It brings me joy to make others feel accomplished and proud of their work.

So knowing *that* prospective, I trained myself to fight my urge to blow off compliments and to truly absorb them instead. I know how hard it is for introverts like me to come out of the shadows as social media "lurkers" and not only like or heart a post but to actually comment and praise someone. So when I can pull together enough energy to even check my notifications, the first thing I do is genuinely thank everyone I can before I'm depleted once again.

It's the number-one thing I hate about myself. The one thing I wish I could change more than anything. I wish I wasn't the type of person who feels completely drained just from interacting with other humans. I don't remember always feeling this way. But then again, I'm old and social media didn't always exist. In my younger years, the only interaction with the rest of the world was literally either in person or by talking on the phone. Now, unless you go off into the wilderness, completely unplug, and basically hibernate by yourself, there's no escaping "connecting" with other people.

And when you try to do that, you're looked at as rude and selfish.

What the fuck.

But on the other hand, if I were to check my notifications and not have anyone to thank, I would feel like the biggest loser ever. It's a double-edged sword. If you make it known that social media fucks with your anxiety, then there are those kind and nurturing followers who will think "I'm not going to bother her or freak her out by sending her a message or a comment she'll feel she has to reply to."

I don't know which one's worse.

Wait, yes, I do.

It feels way worse checking my socials and seeing I don't have any likes or comments. When all I have are notifications from Marketplace and the automatic keyword search I set up for when someone posts anything about plants, gardening, and boho décor for resale.

Yes, that totally sends me straight to Loser Town, which is way more anxiety-inducing than thanking my sweet followers.

"It all has to do with your desire to please, little one. You gain the most enjoyment from making other people happy. When they try to steer the focus toward you, it makes you uncomfortable, because your happiness comes from giving, not receiving," he tells me matter-of-factly, and my brows furrow, wondering if he read my mind. But then I sigh, because I did it a-fucking-gain. I mumbled out every one of my thoughts that entered my head in the last couple of minutes as I sat here mindlessly rubbing my finger across my watch face.

"Right when I think I've lost myself, oop! There I am." I shake my head. "I usually ramble when I'm nervous, Sir. So the inability to speak to you thing is slightly freaking me out."

"I know. That's what you've always done in our

messages, princess. And it's as endearing in person as it is when I open my texts to find all sorts of your clever and thought-provoking... well... thoughts." He chuckles, and my eyes go to his mouth.

Fuck me.

His smile is adorable and hot at the same time.

Up until now, I'd only seen it in person at a distance, across the gym, given to other members who approached him like they might be good friends as they shook hands or clapped each other on the back. In his profile picture, he wasn't exactly smiling, but the corners of his lips were lifted enough that it was a relaxed and pleasant expression. But his full-on smile makes my breath come out in a pant as I catch sight of the little gap between his two front teeth.

Everything about Gym-slash-Dumpster Daddy—I refuse to think of him by his real name—is incredibly masculine... powerful... and screams "sexy older man" and "alpha." But that tiny space in the center of his smile gives him a hint of boyishness that makes him even more irresistible. It makes me want to do everything I can to put that smile on his face as often as possible just so I can get a glimpse of that small imperfection that makes him all the more perfect in my eyes.

"Now, as I asked previously, would you like me to take off my shades? You couldn't meet my eyes this morning, and you said in our messages the idea of looking at me face-to-face made you exceptionally nervous. If I weren't who I am, that might've given me a complex," he says, and I open my mouth to explain it has absolutely nothing to do with his looks, but then I see that teensy gap between his teeth again and know he's just teasing me. When I close my mouth and press my lips into an embarrassed smile, he continues. "You're not the first person to have an issue with my eyes, little one. You've never been close enough to see why though. Yours has everything to do with your submissiveness, whether it's been ingrained in you as a sign of respect not to meet a Dom's eyes—which I'm not one of those who require it—or maybe it's just the intimidation factor alone. Others, mostly people outside the community, have admitted my eyes make them uncomfortable. So I wore the shades tonight to put you at ease... so you'd feel a little braver if there was this small barrier between us."

My brows furrow at this, and even though I know it's impossible, I try to make out his eyes behind the sunglasses he wears. They're the same silver frames with the blue-tinted reflective lenses he was wearing in his profile picture, the same ones I saw on him a number of times at the gym when he was either coming in or leaving through the front door. What could possibly be so weird about his eyes that I wouldn't have noticed it at a distance? Even that night he carried me out of the dumpster, I saw them up close. I just couldn't tell what color they were.

I'm just curious enough, and have been dying to discover their true color for weeks now, that I'm finally able to voice an answer to his question. "Yes, Sir. I'd like you to take off the shades. Thank you for the consideration.

That's... pretty amazing of you to do something like that just to make me more comfortable, Sir."

Again, such a small thing, like certain messages he's sent, that make it hard to swallow because of the lump in my throat as my eyes prickle, and I don't even realize I've lowered my head until I feel crackling energy beneath my chin and hear his voice much closer but softer than it was just a moment ago. "Do I have permission to touch you, princess?"

My breathing has sped up as my eyes focus on his hand hovering right in front of my throat. I can feel it on my flesh just as clearly as if it was actually caressing my skin, but he hasn't even laid a finger on me since he helped me into the truck. I want him to touch much, much more than just my chin or jaw or throat. I want him to touch me everywhere his hands and mouth could possibly reach and then some.

But I can't say that. God, I could never say something so bold out loud to a real person. All that is saved up until I can type them out in one of my books. I'd never be brave enough to voice my desires so openly.

He requires a verbal response to his question though, and I don't want this to end. I feel like I would literally die if he were to drop his hand away and tell me that's all for tonight. I need to at least tell him, or somehow show him, that I crave for this to go further, that I want more than anything in this entire universe for him to take control as I give him my submission. And I know that won't happen unless I give him clear, undeniable consent.

I nod quick and shallow several times, whispering, "Yes, Sir."

And then I'm melting, because the moment I get those two words out, his big, warm hand cups my jaw as he practically purrs, "That's a good girl."

He lifts my face, my eyes closing, but not out of my fear of meeting his, but because they roll back in my head at how much pleasure the small touch causes. One of his fingertips sits right beneath my ear, sending tingles all the way down my neck, while his thumb rests on the other side of my chin, stroking my jawline with the gentlest caress. Without meaning to, I sink into it, pressing myself into his hand, feeling him spread his fingers wider and brace his wrist to support the weight I give him.

With my head tilted to the side and resting in that big palm, the other side of my neck is fully exposed, and a delighted breath leaves me in a moan when I feel his other hand start to trail up and down the sensitive line between my ear and the top of my shoulder on that side. My eyes open then, wide with embarrassment that such a simple touch could pull the erotic noise from my throat. And that's when I see he's no longer wearing his shades, his face so very close to my own as he cups my neck with both of his hands.

My lips are parted, my breaths coming out in shallow puffs, and my gaze flickers up and down then back again between his light eyes and his full lips framed in that delicious gray and white facial hair.

I still can't tell what color those irises are, because the truck's interior is an oceanscape surrounding us in blue, but in this moment, I couldn't care less about that. The only thing I desire in this entire world is for him to press those perfect lips to mine so I can finally feel what I've been fantasizing about for ages.

Chapter Seven

FELIX

God, what I would do to this woman if we were more established in this thing between us. She's so easy to read, and it's not just because she speaks tons of her thoughts out loud without meaning to. Just like all those times I stood outside the dumpster, listening to her musings and grumbles as she hunted for her treasures.

Even if she didn't talk to herself.

Even if she didn't send excerpts from her books that were literal guides she's written on how she wants to be treated and what she desires.

Even if she didn't answer my every question in our messages with a thoroughness that would make the great philosophers proud.

Even if she didn't do all of that, I would still be able to decode every animated expression, change in breathing, and instinctive, involuntary reaction she has as if she's got an instruction manual tattooed on her impossibly soft skin.

Her body is screaming at me to take her in every way imaginable. She's open and willing to allow me to do absolutely anything I want, to use her in any way that would please me. She wants me so badly, craves me in a way that makes me feel more desired than I've ever felt before. Which is saying something, because I've never had any issue in the female department.

Not being conceited, just a fact.

I have symmetrical facial features.

I take care of my body and have defined muscle tone.

I'm a nonsmoker.

I'm a few inches taller than the average American male.

I have incredible hygiene, and not just because I'm a doctor.

The whites of my eyes are bright and clear.

And the list goes on.

Everything a woman sees when she first glances at me screams "strong, healthy, virile male." And that's usually all it takes to have at least one female aroused by me at any given time. It's just human nature.

What's not human nature is this woman clearly fighting her every instinct telling her to run—from what could easily be a very dangerous situation if she were in it with anyone other than me. She may think she's being a nervous wreck right now, embarrassed that she's panicky and skittish instead of whatever sensual vixen she thinks she should be behaving like, but she's wrong. Oh-so fucking wrong. This seemingly vulnerable and fragile girl riddled with anxiety disorders and scars from being burned by people in the past is showing so much bravery and strength right now it's intoxicating.

Because the fact is, she's going against everything she is and believes about herself... for me. Because her desire for me is stronger than any other facet of her personality and who she is.

And that is what makes me feel more wanted than anything ever before.

No one has ever waged war within themselves just to be in my presence.

When I saw her in the café this morning, I had that moment of thinking, *Oh, this is going to be fun*, imagining molding this woman into the irresistibly sexy temptress she could so easily be if she had the confidence and experience to allow it. Her nervous and awkward physicality, and her internal anxiety, all stem from her lack of experience. If properly trained and given the opportunity to practice what she's taught, along with lots of praise when she progresses and a loving but firm hand when she messes up, this little sub could very well be the perfect partner in a D/s dynamic.

She already knows so much about BDSM, the psychology of it. She's researched, seen, and even partially lived the lifestyle, so that cuts out so much of the task of introducing someone, a vanilla, to what I need and want, which had grown tedious over the years. Most probably because I hadn't come across a woman I found intriguing enough outside the bedroom to want to spend the time with that it would take to educate a true novice, a beginner who didn't even have the "book smarts" on the subject, much less the "street smarts"—aka having learned from experience.

But with Sienna, that is not the case in either situation. If I had met her in everyday life, she intrigues me on a level that would've put her in a league of her own, worth the time and energy it would take to introduce and teach a vanilla all about this alternative lifestyle. And not only did she have that going for her, but as an added—huge—bonus, she isn't a novice at all. I may have to touch on some things any Dom and sub would have to discuss, things talked about by even the most experienced and formally educated people who come together to either be in a relationship or just play. But I won't have to go so far back in "the book" that I'd have to give her a glossary, definitions of common BDSM terms, or a list of dos and don'ts everyone learns on day one. I won't have to hand her a syllabus of what to expect by entering into this world.

She's already landed and gone through baggage claim. She's already been to visit. She's learned the language and the culture. But now she just needs the immersive experience by getting to live it and practice it with help from a long-time resident, someone who has her best interest at heart.

Which is the decision I had to make today after I left the café.

I had that slightly sinister thought of *This is going to be fun*, and in my younger years, it could've gone either way—I could've used my abilities for good *or* evil. But at almost fifty years old and with this soul-deep desire to find the one and only woman who could be the perfect submissive for me, I had to decide what I was going to do.

I had to either stop things right then and there, cut myself off from her so I wouldn't risk hurting more than just her feelings from three and a half weeks of online friendship coming to an end.

Or…

I had to be all-in. I had to be willing to care for her on a soul-deep level, keep her safe mentally and physically. I had to be up for the incredibly important responsibility of owning a 24/7 slave, because the more I get to know her, it's becoming more and more apparent that's exactly what she desires the most. It's the highest level of submission, at least that I've ever witnessed or heard of. A submissive who gives her mind, body, and soul over to her Dominant with no hard limits.

And there are kinksters out there who would jump on that with pitchforks, yelling "Red flag! Red flag!" But there's a big difference in what their automatic thought process leads them to—"never trust anyone who says you shouldn't have any hard limits"—and what a proper and true Dominant who follows the real meaning of this lifestyle is talking about when they say "submission with no hard limits."

What I mean by that is I'd learn and know her limits,

allow her to voice her likes and dislikes, and then eventually she'd relinquish the ability to set those limits formally, which is a pledge of her trust in me as her Dom. In return, I would never break that trust by forcing her or even asking her to do something I know she would've set as a hard limit if she were allowed to. It's the purest form of exchanging power, the most blatant show of trust between a submissive and their Dominant. She'd have to trust me not to take her too far, and I have to trust she'll be honest and allow me to see her true reaction to whatever we're doing.

But it's too soon for all that right now.

I just had to think things all the way through after seeing her this morning, to be honest with myself and decide if I was ready to open myself up, to take the first steps in making my ultimate dream a reality. If there was any kind of doubt in my mind, I wouldn't even take this first stride forward, meeting her tonight to test the vibe between us, to see if what I felt for her online would even translate in person.

Sure, I'd stood close to her at Club Alias before and felt the static energy crackling between us. And yes, sitting next to her and speaking to her in the café had my heart pounding and adrenaline filling my veins. Plus, I couldn't forget the night I helped her out of the dumpster, held her on my lap, and doctored her hand that was full of cactus needles. Just the act of taking care of her when she was hurt filled me with the intoxicating rush of being needed I had become desensitized to after having worked in an ER for so long.

But this meeting would be different than all those other encounters. This would be the first time we'd come face-to-face as each other's prospective partner in a relationship that had the potential to be deeper than even a marriage.

This would be the real test, when everything before were just warmups.

With her head cradled in my hands, I feel like I have the whole universe held within my palms. George R.R. Martin once said "A reader lives a thousand lives before he dies." But what would he say about the authors themselves? God only knows how many characters and stories, along with her intrusive voices, actually live inside this mind of hers. Countless more than she'd ever have the time, energy, or concentration to put down on paper.

If nothing else, I can help her with that. She craves the focus she was born without, replaced, it seems, with unharnessed creativity and an ability to weave together words with articulated magic that reach her readers on a soul-deep level. I've scrolled through reviews of her books, and the thing people kept saying over and over no matter which title it was under was how connected they felt to the little sub's characters. She writes them in a way that brings them to life, makes them feel real, even giving the person reading the story a sense of longing that the fictional people on the pages were alive and walking amongst us, so they could find them and be their friends.

Little do they know, every single one of those heroines is Sienna herself. Maybe not entirely. Maybe they had a different backstory or family dynamic or lived in a different place and time. Maybe theirs looked entirely unlike the pretty face gripped gently between my fingers. Short hair instead of her lengthy mess of dark strands with highlights long grown out while she couldn't move, weighed down by her broken heart and heavy thoughts. But however different she made the female lead from her reality, all those books were autobiographical, whether she meant for them to be or not.

Pushing all other thoughts aside to focus on the here and now, I take in the way she shivers each time my fingers make a pass up and down the column of her neck. Before she gave me all control to position her as I pleased, she had tilted her head into my hand, baring her throat to me in a purely animalistic and instinctive ritual that primal-prey submissives naturally revert to.

I try to remember what her test results said, how high her percentage was for that specific role, which would've been calculated from answers she gave based on her limited experience.

Just like this morning at the gym, I have the fleeting thought she's playing a part. In the café, it was the role of the sexy librarian hidden inside the shy nerd. In this moment, it's the vixen portraying the vulnerable little mouse for the prowling and ferocious feline, or pretending to be the kitten cornered by the salivating wolf.

But as I said, the thought is fleeting, quickly dissipating when I remember who this woman is, what she's shown me time and time again what she truly feels and believes. This is no skilled actress trying to please a Dom by faking what she thinks he wants.

Instead, this woman is a geode that has yet to be split in two, raw and unpolished on the outside but valuable all the same. Because right now, she may seem contained, only what's visible on the surface, what you see before she's been cracked open, but there's no doubt what's clearly awaiting inside.

All she needs is a strong hand to reveal the wonderous beauty that lives within that shell.

I lean closer to her, so close my temple rests against her jaw so I can speak against her neck, keeping my voice low but clear. "I'm so proud of you, little one. You got more than your goal written, and you earned your reward. You've been so brave and so perfectly obedient, doing exactly as I asked even though you're scared of the unknown, of what might happen. But something is telling you to just trust me, to just summon all your courage and take a leap of faith, because you want what you so desperately hope I can give you. Isn't that right, princess?"

She nods almost imperceptibly, but I feel it because of the hold I still have on one side of her head and my forehead now pressed to her chin as I made my way along her sensitive flesh. I could feel the chills rising on her skin where my lips barely grazed as I spoke.

"Yes, Sir?" I prompt.

"Yes, Sir," she corrects herself on an exhale.

"That's a good girl," I praise, feeling her immediate shudder at the words she longs to hear above all others. And then she moves, no longer tilting away to bare her throat to me but the opposite—trying to get closer to me, to press her soft cheek against the thick hair covering mine. It reminds me of a cat when it's being sweet and rubs the side of its face against you as it starts to purr, and I have no doubt it's a mindless movement on her part, her body acting on its own.

I press a soft kiss to her neck, and when she whimpers and follows when I start to move away, I accept that as her unspoken permission to keep touching her with my mouth and not just my hands. So I continue to pepper kisses along the column that leads to the top of her shoulder, closing my eyes and listening to the way her breaths come quicker, her heartbeat loud in my ears.

Or maybe that's just my imagination playing tricks on me. I can feel her pulse pounding against my fingers, against my lips and cheek—whichever is pressed to her at any given moment—and combined with my own thumping steadily but hard, it seems just like I can hear hers as if I have my stethoscope against her chest.

I continue to murmur her earned praises, feeling her both melt and grow more excited by the second, and it would be so easy to take things all the way right here and right now, gently coaxing her inch by inch until it's all *my* inches filling up her pussy. But I'm no twenty-something-year-old boy who's just trying to get his rocks off.

I'm a grown-ass man who craves to enjoy every moment of this journey and not just the destination. I've had half a century on this earth to realize this kind of connection is not a race to win—trying to get to that finish line as fast as humanly possible. This is a backpacking adventure to remember every step of the way in order to find one's true self and share it all with another.

So no, I won't be using her reward as an excuse to feel her willing cunt milk my cock tonight, though I know I have the uncanny ability to make that happen even if she came here with the solemn promise to "behave."

Oh, I'm well aware it was technically her asking *me* to behave, to contain and keep control over "myself" when we finally met. But what she was truly asking me, what she was really begging for, was for me to keep *her* from sleeping with me the first time we're alone together. She's stated time and time again how much she desires me, and she knows human nature could take over, throwing all good intentions to the wind to get the instant gratification good sex can bring. But it's as important to her to do this right as it is for me, which is why she asked me to behave, and that makes her even more what I long for.

But that doesn't mean there aren't other physically plea-surable rewards to be had.

I drop my hands from her slowly, allowing her to come back to herself so she doesn't topple over from being immediately released. Her eyes open gradually, but only to half-mast, and I can imagine this is the same expression she wears when she's had a few drinks or maybe a little high. But she's completely sober now, aside from being a bit love drunk, or intoxicated by a different kind of dope—dopamine, that is.

I file that away to work in with my colleagues when they're all tossing around dad jokes at the hospital. I usually have to memorize some off the internet in order to not make them uncomfortable with the things I personally find funny.

Asperger's strikes again.

"Take off your shirt," I order, but I don't move away from her to sit back and enjoy the show. I stay close, close enough it gives her an illusion of privacy as she uses me as a shield. All while giving her the feeling I'm too near to see much of her.

But she surprises me. I expect her to at least hesitate, to need a minute to work up the courage to follow the order, or at least to come out of the pleasure fog she was in before her mind could make her body listen. Instead, she's the one who scoots back a little, not shy at all—in fact, quite the opposite. She looks damn near giddy to take hold of the bottom hem of her T-shirt with crisscrossed hands before wiggling just a little as she pulls it up and over her head.

And fuck me, she's not wearing a bra.

Even I have to consciously control the gruffness of my voice when I tell her, "Very good, princess." When I finally lift my stare from her breasts—probably one of the most perfect pairs of tits I've ever seen—she's actually looking at me, her expression telling me she's watching closely for my reaction, my opinion of what she's revealed to me. As always, she wants my approval, but this is different. This is something she actually has confidence in, and her self-consciousness has lifted enough to not weigh her gaze down to her lap. So she can actually try to read the effect her body has on me instead of waiting to hear about it while she hides her head in the sand.

I need to finally warn her that I won't have the typical cues to look for.

"You're stunning," I tell her, lifting my hand to trace one finger from her collarbone down to the center of her chest, where I can feel her heart beating wildly. I can sense her struggling to sit perfectly still, but her body wants to rock into my light touch, to feel more of it. "Absolutely beautiful, little one." I angle my hand just enough that my knuckles graze her left breast as I skim down the center of her cleavage, and I hear her tiny gasp that lifts her chest an extra inch.

"As I told you before, my eyes are strange to a lot of people," I begin as I watch goose bumps form in the wake of my gentle touch. "If you try to read what I'm thinking as you would someone neurotypical, I can promise your comprehension will be wrong."

"Neurotypical? You mean you're not?" she asks, and by the look on her face, she's surprised herself that she voiced the question so easily, especially as I continue to trace a figure-8 around and between her breasts.

I shake my head. "My face is normally unreadable unless I make the purposeful effort to change my expression. It's the exact opposite of my eyes, which never stop moving. They don't settle on one object unless I consciously force them to quit shifting, like to look someone deep in their eyes. Or what they perceive is deep in their eyes. Really, it's a trick we Aspie's use to make it seem like we're meeting someone's gaze, but in fact we're looking at one's nose or maybe the spot between their eyebrows."

I lift one shoulder in the learned gesture that puts others at ease, a shrug to relax the tension of confusion or to move forward in a conversation that would typically go nowhere. "Most people read that as a sign of dishonesty, my 'shifty eyes,'" I say the last part as if I'm telling a spooky story, even stealing my hand from her soft skin to wiggle my fingers in her face, lifting my eyebrows and flaring my eyes dramatically before giving her a smile and shaking my head.

My hand goes back to what it was doing, petting her as she leans forward into my touch. I wonder if she realizes she's practically crawled into my lap—to either get a closer look at my eyes, at what I'm talking about, or to press her tits together in an attempt to trap my hand between them. Or maybe both. Her nipples have pebbled so tightly, and I haven't even allowed myself to graze them, still just drawing patterns around and between the perfect globes.

Too perfect to be natural, in fact, but I literally could not care less about that. They fit her beautifully, not overdone in the slightest. If I were an average man, or maybe just not a doctor, it would've been difficult to tell she's had an augmentation at all. That's how well they were done. But the learned dead-giveaway is the fact that they *are* perfectly symmetrical, exactly the same size and shape. I could practically use her nipples if I didn't have a level handy.

But who am I kidding? I always have a level handy, along with every other tool I might possibly need in any situation. In a toolbox built into the floor at the very back of the Hummer. It's where I had grabbed the medical supplies to treat her hand the night she decided to catch a falling cactus in her palm.

Anyway, natural breasts always, *always* have at least one difference among each set, and hers do not. Minus the dark freckle on her left one nearing her cleavage, which would be there whether she got a boob job or not.

"That's all?" she asks, pulling my gaze from her mesmerizing tits to move back and forth between her green irises. "Sir, I mean. That's all, Sir?"

The corner of my lips quirks up. "Good girl for correcting yourself."

Her chin tilts down the slightest hint, but her eyes don't leave mine.

"What do you mean, little one?" I ask.

She swallows, her lashes fluttering as my fingertips come ever closer to touching the hardened tip of her breast. "I mean... umm... your eyes. That's what people get uncomfortable about, Sir? Just the fact they move around when you talk to them? That seems... silly." She shakes her head. "Isn't it—" She gasps as I circle right around her areola, torturously close but still not giving in to where we both want to feel my touch. "—microexpressions or something? Everyone looks up and left or up and right... to either access memories or to make up a story to answer someone's question?" She's practically panting now. "I... I can't remember which one is which at the moment, Sir," she whispers, and fuck me, hearing her call me that with her growing desperate for a firmer hand actually makes me have to exert some self-control.

This woman is setting off the Primal Dom within me, the part of me I keep contained except for on very rare occasions, because it's the only time I give up my tight grip on the reins of my control and allow my instincts to take over. It takes a strong and very special kind of woman to take it when it's unleashed. There's a violence, an inhuman strength, that lives inside me, and when it's given permission to rip free of its restraints, things can go bad very quickly if I'm with the wrong person.

If I've judged a submissive incorrectly.

Or if she's done what I was suspicious Sienna was doing before, pretending to be something she's not in order to seem more desirable.

It's why it's just as important that a Dom can trust his sub. He has to be able to trust she's been honest about her limitations, because if she isn't, he could hurt her when he was sincerely taking great care not to. A genuinely good Dominant can be made to look like a bad one, a careless one, if a sub is dishonest with them.

And that's not to say a sub who's being dishonest is doing it to trick a Dom, to cause something negative to happen. They think of it like a little white lie; no harm could come of it. A sub could be fibbing about their pain tolerance because they want to make their Dom happy. Or they could say they enjoy something—a toy, a position, a scene, what have you—when really they just grin and bear it, because they think it brings their Dom joy. Their dishonesty could be as simple and well-meaning as giving in to something they don't care for in order to be a "good submissive." Or maybe they fear they won't be good enough and their partner will leave them if they set too many boundaries. Whatever the case may be, it's downright dangerous for a sub to keep the full truth from their Dom. And lying by omission is just as precarious.

"Of course you'd know about microexpressions, my smart girl," I rumble against her ear.

She lets out a puff of air that was probably meant to be a laugh. "I don't know about smart, Sir. I just binge-watch a lot of TV. It was on that show *Lie to Me*."

And here's an example of when I'm even more different from most men.

Whether she's consciously fishing for a compliment or reassurance with that little self-deprecating stab, I don't acknowledge it when a woman does this. I know a lot of people's automatic response would be to say something about her intelligence level being much higher than merely remembering something off the television. I've observed this my entire life, and it's one of those social norms I just can't get behind.

That's not to say if my sub or even just a colleague or acquaintance came to me and asked for reassurance, I wouldn't give it to them. That's completely different. In that situation, they're being honest with their intentions, open about what they feel they are lacking, and I can in turn reward that honesty and openness with the validation they crave.

I've found this practice much more effective when teaching someone to be more self-confident. Not only does it cut off their reason to talk shit about themselves if they don't get the positive reinforcement when they do it, but it also forces them to summon the courage to voice and/or ask for what they want.

So instead of doing what most people would, or even what a lot of Doms would in this situation—reprimand her for putting herself down—I continue on as if she never spoke, ignoring what she said completely. "I have Asperger's. Well, that's the antiquated name for my disorder. It's now technically known as high-functioning autism disorder, but I prefer its original moniker, because it sets it apart with what to expect, instead of grouping it all together with something that has symptoms that don't even apply to me. But one of the symptoms, or characteristics, I *do* have is the tendency to unconsciously avoid eye contact. And I say unconsciously, because I don't do it on purpose, and when I realize I'm not meeting someone's eyes during a conversation, I make the effort to fix that."

"Asperger's. Isn't that what one of the cardiologists on *Grey's Anatomy* had?" she asks.

"A very dramatic portrayal of every symptom of the disorder set on Maximum Level," I tell her. "If an Aspie had all the documented characteristics at the highest degree, then that's what it might've looked like. A stereotypical representation. In reality, just like your ADHD or your OCD, each characteristic of the disorder is on a sliding scale of how much it affects you. You have 100 percent of the intrusive thoughts, but I haven't heard you say anything about symmetry or germs or having to do things a certain number of times. That's not to say you don't experience those things with your disorders, but they're on a much lower level than your voices."

As I've spoken, I watched her face relax while her own eyes shifted back and forth. She'd occasionally glance up at my eyes, but her focus was drawn more to my mouth and then up and to one side or the other as she thought about and filed away what I was telling her for future use.

"I swear I could listen to you read the phone book to me out loud, and I'd be completely content," she murmurs, and by the flush that rises up her face, she didn't mean to say it out loud. It's something I'll have to be lax on in the beginning if she agrees to be mine. Just like in her messages, where she tends not to think much about what she's typing before she's already sent it. But for now, I want her to speak her mind as openly as possible. Nothing could be more important at this stage between us, because it allows me to really get to know her—as a person and as a submissive.

"Which is kind of funny, because another aspect of Asperger's is our voices tend to be quite monotone, without inflections. Over time, we learn to mimic typical voice patterns, but until we get really good at faking it, until it's basically muscle memory, we can seem extra strange while we figure out volume control and things like... a question ending on a higher note than the rest of a sentence. Some people even get offended because they think we're making fun of their accent or the colloquialisms they use, when really we're trying to make them feel comfortable by speaking more neurotypically." I've been told often that I overexplain things, so usually I cut myself off long before this, when I recognize the haze that comes over people's expressions when their just being polite. Another social norm I had to learn instead of just interrupting someone's conversation I found boring or redundant. But in Sienna's case, I keep up with the flow of memorized knowledge, because that haze never comes. Just this... dreamy expression, like a live-action version of a Disney princess when she's falling for her hero.

Taking things another step forward, I order her, "Take off your bottoms," but this time, my command isn't so readily followed. She doesn't look as excited to bare this part of herself to me. Her movements are slower, unsure.

And she leaves her panties on.

This is an easy test to see how comfortable a submissive is with getting naked in front of a new Dom. It's also a way to see just how comfortable a woman is with her body, period. Some women have no problem taking off all their clothes, defining "bottoms" as everything they're wearing from the waist down including underwear. Or maybe they're only wearing shorts or pants with nothing underneath. Either way, complete nudity is the end result.

And then there are those like Sienna. She pauses but then chooses to follow the order without questioning, but she keeps herself covered to the best of her ability by leaving on her panties.

This is the test, as if I've asked a question without actually having to speak nor requiring her to answer. By leaving her panties on, it's a clear sign of her boundaries for tonight. This is something I won't push her on. I'll give her this bit of modesty, and it might have the effect of opening her up to things she wouldn't be willing to do if she were totally naked.

I praise her for following the order with only a slight hesitation. And since she seems to like being petted, after telling her where to set her clothes and shoes so they're out of the way, I go back to tracing patterns along her skin, the top of her chest, down her arms and back up, lightly grazing over her throat, between her cleavage... until she completely forgets about the sudden nervousness she felt being ordered to take off her shorts.

I lean forward once again to speak softly next to her ear, and as I do, I feel her forehead come down to rest on my shoulder. It's such a sweet, innocent slip, her giving in to her desire to get closer to me, that I allow it, even pressing my cheek next to hers to squeeze her in a sort of arm-less hug. "I enjoy finally seeing this beautiful body of yours, little one. Thank you for giving me this gift."

She exhales. "I feel silly for saying you're welcome, Sir. But it seems like it would be rude not to, so you're welcome."

I can't help but smile, and I bring my hand up to trace more patterns along her nape then down her back, catching on quickly to the fact that it soothes her, putting her more at ease. Which she'll need in order to face the next step.

"Would you like to explore mine as well?"

I hear her swallow, and I can feel her mouth open and close a few times since my jaw is still lightly pressed to hers. She tries to answer verbally, but no sound comes out, her nerves stealing her ability to speak, so I attempt a joke to calm her.

"I promise you won't hurt my feelings if the answer is no. Who'd want to see an old, bald guy naked, am I right?"

She lifts her head from my shoulder slowly, and when she's up and back far enough for me to see her expression, it's an almost comical mix of horror and disbelief.

Who knows if she's ever been with someone like me

before, who has no issue with letting a potential partner inspect them closely to see if they're someone they want to be intimate with.

I might've had that moment or two earlier... not necessarily of doubt but of curiosity... of what she would think of my body. But sensing her strong positive reaction to my closeness, to my voice, to this whole situation, and knowing she had a crush on me before she ever even knew anything about me—so purely based on my looks, there's really no sense in worrying about something so trivial.

I'm wildly curious what will come out of her mouth in response to my teasing. She looks utterly flabbergasted. I might not have used enough of a joking tone, if her face and her mouth mimicking a fish are anything to go by.

What she finally does unleash makes me both hard and want to spank her ass for using such a sassy tone.

"Um. Sir. One... you are not old. You are deliciously aged to perfection, and I would even go so far as to say that if you were any younger, I wouldn't be more than half naked in the back of your truck at the moment. And two, bald is sexy as fuck. Hello? Bruce Willis? The Rock? Jason Statham? Men like y'all don't need hair on your head. It would just distract from all the yummy you've already got going on everywhere else." She says the last part while moving her hand in a circle to indicate she's talking about from my face down, and I feel a sense of pride that she's grouping me in with some of my favorite action heroes.

Instead of reprimanding her for the brattiness, since she

was defending me against myself and giving me huge compliments, I slide back from her just enough to give myself room to pull my olive-green Grunt Style T-shirt up and over my head so I don't accidentally hit her. I hear her sharp intake of breath as I fold my tee in half, then once again, then set it to the side before I glance at her to assess her reaction. I can tell she's trying not to gawk, trying to hold on to some semblance of keeping her cool, but the way her breaths have sped up, and from the flush that has come back to her face, she can't hide the fact that just my bare torso has spiked her arousal.

I guess that answers the question about what she'd think of my body hair.

"Would you like me to stop there, or continue, princess?"

This time, I *will* make her respond directly to the question. A chest is one thing, but a man exposing himself to a woman who hasn't given explicit consent is not something I'm willing to overlook.

She looks away—to the side, not down this time— nibbling on her lip for a moment. I haven't moved, giving her time to make her decision. I don't prompt her either. I won't do anything to coerce her in either direction. This will be all up to her.

When she faces me once again, she nods. "Y-yes, Sir. Continue, please," she stutters but recovers.

"Very good girl," I praise. "Earlier, I let you choose how to define the word 'bottoms.' I gave you the choice to keep your panties on, and I'm going to give you the choice now whether or not you'd prefer I match you and keep my underwear on, or if you want to see all of me."

For some reason, this question makes her much more fidgety than the previous, and her face morphs into an expression that clearly says "well... FML." This choice is harder for her to voice than if she wanted me to undress at all.

Is it because... before I was more specific with my question, she was going to have *me* make the decision, like I allowed her to do?

Or is it because she knows exactly what her answer is, but she's too ashamed to admit it?

I can tell by her quick glances down between my legs what she'd been hoping I would choose as my definition of "bottoms." But instead of leaving it up to me, she's the one who has to voice her desires. And this time, I won't be teasing a response out of her.

We're at a standstill. The longer I stay dead-silent and unmoving, the more uncomfortable she grows, until I sense her panic rising and not just a little nervousness. So I give in just enough to startle her out of her spiral. "Which is it, little one? Underwear on or off?"

She jumps on the lead like I was hoping she would, using the opportunity to state her multiple choice answer instead of having to come up with something to fill in the blank herself. "Off, Sir."

I bounce my eyebrows once as I tell her, "Off it is," just

to get her to smile, wanting this part to feel more like a fun discovery, getting to see each other this way for the first time, instead of overtly sexual and heavy, as if to lead to a night of hot sex. It might seem counterintuitive, but it's my way of keeping my promise to make us both "behave" tonight.

It's also an attempt to keep things *light* when she sees my cock for the first time, which is anything but.

Not being conceited, just facts.

In my younger years, I was one of those guys who posted dick pics. Even set one as my profile picture for a while, because that's what it seemed like everyone was doing. I learned pretty quickly it did not attract the sort of attention I wanted. Quite the opposite, actually—like for example, lots of propositions from men. And I even had some subs tell me they weren't interested because they didn't want the "huge responsibility" of keeping a man of my size properly serviced.

They took pity on me, women who had been in the community for much longer than I had, when I asked what exactly that meant. Basically, they said a Dom with such a big dick could be daunting, depending on how much sexual activity he'd require from a sub. It took no time for me to understand once they said it, because girlfriends in the past would need breaks from sex in order to recover. I learned quickly after I lost my virginity that I'd have to educate myself on how to fuck without unintentionally hurting someone. I had to pay special attention to a partner's reaction to everything we did, how deep I could go, how fast and how hard—which all men *should* do with each and every partner throughout their life, but to my knowledge, most men don't have to worry about bruising a woman's uterus or ripping the walls of her vagina when they're not even being slightly rough.

During my self-education, I saw many women complain that it seemed men with larger-than-average penises relied completely on their size, thinking they didn't need any sort of technique or skill to "bring to the table, since they were providing all the meat"—a line I read that really stuck with me.

And I decided right then and there I would not be one of those well-endowed guys who didn't know how to wield the potentially powerful weapon he was blessed with—a line I came up with on my own, since I'm a proud nerd who, to this day, plays Dungeons and Dragons when the opportunity arises.

It's also the same moment I took down all photos of my cock.

I didn't want what was between my legs to be what enticed nor scared away someone, when I was craving to connect on a much deeper level.

No pun intended.

Now, I slip off my black-and-gray-checkered Vans and get up on my knees, grabbing the remote that controls all the mechanical parts of my truck's interior. I push a button that should distract the little sub while I remove the rest of my clothes until I can sit back down in a less intimidating position. As I predicted, her attention turns to the cushion that rises at an angle, a special hinge with hours of upholstery work that turned the back of the driver seat into an adjustable headboard of sorts. Or maybe the seat back of a throne, depending on the scene we play that day. Whatever the case may be, as it clicks into place at the angle I like, one that will keep me mostly upright but tilted just enough to look down my body and see—

"Holy shit," she breathes, and I turn my head quickly from where I had undone the string of my joggers and pushed the waistband and my boxer briefs halfway down my thighs, expecting to see her eyes wide with fear at what I just revealed.

But instead, they're wide with wonder... as she still stares at the seat cushion.

"That is so cool!" she chirps, a big smile spreading across her face just as she tilts her head back to look up at me at the same moment I sit down and slide to rest my back against the soft leather.

I feel myself growing harder by the second, but I use every ounce of self-control I possess not to have a raging boner the first time she catches sight of me. I tug my clothes the rest of the way down my calves and off my feet, keeping the fabric between her and my lap as I fold all of it up, blocking her line of vision. It's not until I set all my clothes in a stack on top of my shoes next to hers that I give her a clear shot of my half-erect cock.

But I shouldn't have been so worried, because she does

something that makes much more sense for her. Her eyes drop to her lap, and she begins to fidget again, messing with her watch, then straightening the waistband of her panties. I cut all of that off, though, because I don't want there to be enough time for her anxiety level to rise any higher.

With my back against the cushion, I stretch my legs out straight and then spread them shoulder-width apart. "Come here, little one," I command but keep my tone soft, an order that sounds more like an offering. At that, her head lifts, and her eyes catch on my thick cock hanging between my thighs for only a moment—so quick I would have missed it if I hadn't been watching her so closely—before she focuses her eyes on the center of my chest.

There's a period where the world seems to stop, and it's a very rare occasion in which I lose all sense of time as I wait for her to make the next move. I hold my breath, willing even my heart to stop pounding to give her all the stillness she requires to make her decision. I zero in on her every microexpression.

The smallest flare of her nostrils as her breaths speed up again.

Her full lips starting to twitch, just like she described in her messages after I saw her this morning.

Her eyes going almost glossy as she stares at that same spot in the dead-center of my chest, so fixated I have the urge to glance down to see what exactly she's focusing on, but I don't. She hasn't even blinked, and that's what clicks it into place in my mind that she's dissociating.

If we were an established D/s couple who knew each other much better than we do at this point, her ability to dissociate would be an amazing attribute to play with. It's that capability that allows someone to enter subspace, which not every submissive can reach. And I wonder if she knows it's her disorder she hates so much that gives her this incredible superpower.

But that's something we'll have to discuss later, and it's a power she'll have to flex later on as well, because right now, I need her all here in this moment. Because while it's a mechanism that's infinitely positive, it's also the defense someone's mind uses when they want to escape a situation. It's how sexual assault *victims* become *survivors*, by dissociating from what's happening to them during that perilous event, protecting their mind while there's nothing they can do to protect their body. In some cases, the survivor will remember very few of the specifics that happened while they were dissociated. And that carries over to those who can do it even when they're not in a fight-or-flight state— where a chunk of time just seems to have disappeared from existence, no memory left behind.

I don't want any of that for Sienna tonight.

I want her to be all-in. I want her to be cognizant of everything happening between us. I want her to remember every detail, whether it's just for her to look back on and have a fond recollection of the experience or if she wants to use any of it in one of her books. It's what gave me extra motivation to make sure everything about this first meeting was as perfect as I possibly could.

So in order to "snap her out of it," as people like to call it when you bring someone out of a "daydream," I say in a sharper tone, "Little one," and when she blinks a couple of times, then lifts her eyes from my chest, I pat the top of my right thigh twice with the fingers of my right hand as I finish repeating the order. "Come here."

Here is where a submissive's role is truly tested.

In my experience, her response could go one of four ways.

Total indignation at being called over like a pet, which would—one—send her either into haughty-but-playful brat mode, or—two—into a rage, telling me to straight-up go fuck myself as she realizes she's not a sub after all.

Three, her flight instinct could finally win out and send her running.

Or, four—

And of course this is how the sweet little sub I'm so lucky to have found me reacts—

Her palms immediately drop to the floor between her slightly spread knees, her ass lifts off her heels, and she gingerly crawls toward me between my legs.

Chapter Eight

SIENNA

Sweet Jesus in a handbasket.

Again, what the fuck have I gotten myself into?

But even as that thought repeats over and over in my mind, my body's response is all the same. I want him with every fiber of my being. Plus, seeing how massive he is, when he's not even fully erect…? Yes, anxiety fills me, but also excited anticipation.

What would it feel like to have all of that inside me? And along the edges of all those thoughts, there's a voice doing cartwheels and merrily sing-songing, *Holy shit, I just now realized we never saw a photo of his dick! What a thrilling surprise! Of course this man has a monster cock. He's got Big. Dick. Energyyy!*

How have we been talking for this long and him not

send me an unsolicited dick pic like every other man on the face of the planet?

There has never been a male in my past who either hadn't already put a photo of his cock up on his dating profile or who hadn't just gone ahead and sent one to me at some point before we had sex for the first time.

Even my ex-husband, Art, had gotten drunk at his fraternity's party and sent me a dick pic—albeit a blurry one taken in his inebriated state—a couple of dates into our relationship, before we had gone all the way. So I always, always knew what to expect, what I was getting into, before I was ever faced with a penis in person.

But it's not until my eyes land on Mjölnir—that's Thor's goddamn *hammer*, for all the non-nerds out there—that it dawns on me I hadn't seen *this* man's. It hangs so long and thick the crown of it damn near touches the leather he sits on, which is quite a feat, since he's not leaning forward. He's relaxed back against his fancy seat.

"Little one" comes his voice, bringing my eyes back to focus on the deliciously wide expanse of his chest. Though I hear him add, "Come here," it's the movement of his hand, patting his thigh, that catches my attention and has the instant effect of setting me in motion.

I don't even think. My body just does as it's told. And while I'm sure it would've been annoying to some women, would cause them to scoff and fight against the idea of some man treating them as if they're a dog, it's only a sense of calm, of *relief*, that settles over me. The voices have shut up their incessant chatter, and inside my mind, it's blissfully quiet for the first time in as long as I can remember.

Only my mantra floats around like white noise, whispering encouragingly, *Just do as he says and everything will be okay. He'll keep you safe. You'll receive the reward you earned, and you'll make him happy by allowing him to give it to you. Win-win. The perfect exchange. No need to think. No need for thoughts on top of thoughts on top of thoughts. Just do.*

As I've crawled, he lifted one of his knees to give me more room, and when I'm as close to his body as I can get between his legs without actually getting up and straddling his lap, I stop, because I don't know what I should do. But I don't have time to worry about that—to try to think up all the options and then choose one, which could be the wrong one and not what he wants—because his next instruction comes right on the tail of praise that makes me want to continue doing whatever he orders.

"That's my good girl. Now, sit on your heels like you were before. No, little one, don't lean back. Pull your legs up underneath you so you'll stay close to me. That's it. Just like that. Hands in your lap."

I feel his hand on the inside of my knee and realize I closed my eyes at some point, so I force them open, not wanting to be afraid of looking him in the eye anymore, when he said he's not a Dom who wants that. When he said others had the audacity to tell him his beautiful eyes made them uncomfortable.

His voice is a constant flow of easy commands, gentle

corrections, and genuine-sounding praise, and again I'm struck by how soothing it is. How could anyone have told him he talks too much? I never want him to stop.

"It pleases me most when your knees are spread as you sit and wait for my command. You should always be open, presenting yourself to me, so I can easily access any part of you I want," he says, and I do spread my legs an inch apart, but sitting between his, I don't have much more room. "It's okay to touch me, sweet girl. You won't get in trouble for your legs pressing against mine."

I nod, nudging them another inch apart, the outside of my knees now pressed to the inside of his thighs, and the feel of his hairy legs against my smooth ones seems incredibly intimate for some reason. Even more than when he was touching my naked breasts.

He leans closer then, the way he did before, putting his mouth right by my ear so all I'm aware of is his presence. "You won't get into trouble for touching me wherever and however you like, and unless you've been given an order otherwise, you have permission to do just that. In fact, it's welcome. If it were up to me, I'd have your hands, mouth, and pussy wrapped around parts of me every minute of every day. It's your obedience and willingness to please and nurture that I crave most in this world. It's what makes me feel alive. It's what makes me feel loved and wanted, a sub who can't get enough of me, who feels like a part of her is missing if her hand can't reach out and touch me."

His voice drops even lower, his lips even closer, as he tells me, "But right now, tonight, it's not about my pleasure. It's about yours. It's about the reward you earned by being such a good girl and getting your work done to please me. And it's about you exploring and deciding if I might be worthy of your submission someday, princess."

With that, he picks up my right hand that was resting on top of my right thigh and places my palm against the side of his face, his hand covering mine to mold it to his cheek and beneath it. The move means I'm now cupping his chiseled, salt-and-pepper beard-covered jaw, holding him, pressing the other side of his face to mine now, since he never moved backward from where he'd been speaking in my ear. Which also means I'm hidden from his view and free to explore without being self-conscious, since he can't watch whatever involuntary reactions and expressions that might take control of me.

But I don't explore just yet, because this feels too nice.

For so long, I crushed on this man at the gym.

And now I know he's also the man who was so caring when he carried me out of the dumpster and bandaged up my hand.

And then I've gotten to know him over the past few weeks, and everything he's said, every message he's sent, has done nothing but confirm he's not only the real deal but special. Yes, he knows all about the lifestyle. He understands the psychology of BDSM and is experienced in the practice, not just knowledgeable from studying it. But he himself is a special man. A special Dominant. I know a lot of experienced Doms who are righteous and deserving of respect, since I'm lucky enough to be a part of a club that insures those are the only Dominants allowed in. But on top of all that, my Gym Daddy has something extra. Something about him that sets him apart from even the best of the best.

There's a passion in him when it comes to the lifestyle. There's... it's almost like he has a belief in it, as if it's a religion and he's a loyal disciple of its teachings. And that's so fucking *attractive* to me. I can't pinpoint why. Maybe because I also know the psychology of it, the depth one has to dive into it to "get it" like we do, and because I know the positive effect it can have on someone's life. So if someone believes in BDSM that soul-deep, then that is a person I can trust. That is a man I can open up to and safely connect with on a deeper level.

That is a Dom I want to submit to.

But right now, it's a much more innocent act that's filling me to the brim with positive emotions. Just finally, finally simply embracing this man brings me so much joy I could cry happy tears.

And I realize it's because I'm hugging my *friend* for the first time.

He's become my friend over these weeks of chatting.

And as a hugger, I'm so incredibly fulfilled in this moment getting to wrap my arms around the person who's made me smile more in the past three weeks than I did in the last year combined.

Just like I get super excited and happy when I get to hug

my readers in person after talking to them and getting to know them on my social medias.

But different. Very, very different. Because embracing Gym Daddy feels like I've finally come home after a long, hard journey.

Hugging him feels like I'm taking a deep breath of clean, fresh air after being milliseconds away from drowning.

Holding him close feels like I have the key to my true, soul-deep happiness in my very hands.

And I never want to let him go.

Yet after a minute, even though I could stay like this for the rest of my life and be perfectly content, I don't want to make it weird. I don't want to make him feel awkward by just freezing in place, by not moving a muscle, when he's given me the opportunity to explore all of him. He couldn't have come up with a better reward to be given the first time we're alone together. Free rein to admire and touch and kiss and discover whatever I want on his body? A body I've drooled over and fantasized about too many times to count?

This is major.

This is such a big deal.

And so fucking smart of him.

It's a reward, because it allows me to do what I want at my own pace and can focus and spend extra time on parts that *I* find exciting, and it's also the perfect way for me to grow comfortable in his presence, so eventually he can command me to touch him the way *he* wants.

A weapon isn't so scary to be around if you know the ins and outs of it, if you know exactly what each part looks like and how they all fit together to work. The more you handle it, the more confident you become in working with it, in using it, in making it do what you want it to.

His body is a weapon I need to learn and practice with. And once I discover how to work each part, I'll be able to bring him the same amount of pleasure I feel from just hugging him.

So my first step in my exploration is lifting my other hand from my lap to place right in the middle of that glorious chest of his I've been absolutely dying to touch. It's the most attractive chest I've ever seen in my life, and the feel of it does not disappoint. In fact, it's even better than what I imagined it would feel like. The thick but trimmed hair, the heat of his skin, the firmness of his pectoral muscles... I want to press my face in the center of all of that pure maleness and inhale him. I'd have him wrap his strong arms around my head to smother me against him. And I would fucking die happy if that's the way I went.

With his face still held to mine, I tilt mine downward to watch as my hand skims over the surface, my fingers press to test hardness, and my palm practically gropes until I could write an entire novel about every single detail of his chest alone. And then I finally remove my other hand from his face but keep mine against his so he knows I want him to stay there. I just want to explore his incredible torso with both of my hands while I have this utterly delightful opportunity.

He's wonderfully thick but lean at the same time. I can feel every one of his muscles down to each individual ridge of his abdominals, but there's also this layer of comforting softness between all that hard strength and just below the furry surface of his skin. It's even more arousing than if he had zero-percent body fat. A brick wall isn't the most comfy thing to wrap yourself around and cuddle with. But a body like this? It's like some kind of beast's... a wolf... or a bear —they may feel soft and snuggly as you run your hand over them, but the second you apply any pressure and dig your fingers in, you discover they are solid as fuck and should definitely not be judged by their healthy amount of fat and cuddly fur.

I balance on my knees to run my flattened palms around his sides to his back, wanting to discover the muscles he has hidden back there as well. But in doing so, I lean so close to him my nipples brush against that chest hair I could write sonnets about, and it's like I've finally been thrown in my rightful place in the loony bin and have just undergone my first round of electric-shock therapy. Only they attached the paddles right to my boobs and not my temples. An involuntary gasp fills my lungs with the clean scent of him, and I freeze in place once again.

Sensory overload.

The wheel in the center of my brain's screen that indicates data-processing fills my mind's eye, spinning smoothly, then getting a little choppy, then stopping altogether, stuck there for God only knows how long, before it kicks into motion again, whirling faster than normal as it plays catch-up before evening out into a steady rotation once more.

And when it clears, a pop-up takes its place with big, bold letters:

W... T... F?!

When I got my breast augmentation, I lost sensitivity in my nipples. It wasn't a big deal because I wasn't particularly fond of them being messed with anyway. I never got the sexually pleasurable feelings I always read about other women getting from their nipples being stimulated. I was always more aroused by their fingers skimming lightly along the skin beneath them, enjoying the almost ticklish, teasing sensation *around* them rather than direct contact with the bullseye in the center.

So to have such a strong positive physical response to something I never cared about before is startling to say the least, and then add breathing in—deep and fast—his scent to discover the fresh and uplifting aroma of eucalyptus, I'm damn near intoxicated.

And immediately so wet my knees try to come together as if I might drip.

But it turns out his hand is still... right... there.

How was I oblivious to the fact that he never removed his hand from the inside of my knee when he instructed me how to sit?

But now it's all I'm aware of as his grip there tightens,

not allowing my legs to close even an inch, and my face flames at the idea I might leave a fucking puddle in his truck just from petting his chest.

"Keep them open. I told you how I like for you to sit. Don't receive your first punishment by ignoring such a simple command," he says, his voice gruffer than it was before, and that combined with the words he spoke makes me clench, which makes my blush spread down my neck and heat my chest. In turn, instincts take over, and my legs try to close again of their own accord.

I whimper, trying my best to hold still and will my pussy not to produce any more wetness. Yes, I'm wearing panties, but it's just one of the little thongs I wear beneath my workout shorts or leggings so I don't walk around with a freaking camel toe. They're not exactly made for absorbency. I will literally die if he feels how fucking embar-rassingly wet I am right now, when we haven't even freaking done anything to warrant such a biological response!

And then I panic.

With that tone of his promising a punishment if my legs don't stay open to him, but my body closing in on itself, trying to go full-on fetal position at this moment, I do the only thing I can think of to distract this completely over-whelming man from the fact that I literally cannot make my legs follow his order.

Instead of fighting against my instincts, I lean into them, trying to make it seem like I'm actually just repositioning myself—not closing my knees—as I lift my ass off my heels and my upper body continues to curl forward. It dislodges his firm grip on my leg, not by my own strength, but because what man is going to block a mostly naked woman from coming face-to-face with their now very much fully-erect cock?

For once, a decision I made in a state of panic is actually the right one... as in I succeeded in my goal of him not discovering the leak I've sprung. But as a result, I have skipped far ahead in the delightful process of learning each and every inch of his body.

It's just like me to be so self-conscious or embarrassed of something about myself that I completely give up a hard-earned reward just to save face.

I've spent countless hours fantasizing about asking him the story behind every one of his tattoos, and I was going to get to do just that... in reality... right here and right now. I was oh-so close... literally holding the prize right in my hands, and then it was snatched away. This somehow always happens to me. I think I've lucked out and will get to do something I want to so badly, and then some bullshit ends up throwing a wrench in my plan, fucking up my opportunity.

But while I'm bummed that's the case, I also can't be too upset about the predicament I've found myself in now— eye-to-eye with the one-eyed monster that lives in Gym Daddy's gym shorts. The monster that is no longer half-asleep and lounging comfortably between Gym Daddy's muscular thighs but is now standing as tall and big around as a 40-ounce Monster can—go figure. And I am not even exaggerating.

If I thought I knew how big he would be when I saw him at what I figured was half-mast, I was very, very mistaken. I had grossly underestimated the elasticity of this particular appendage belonging to this particular man.

There's that joke about a guy being a grower not a show-er. This man is a show-er *and* a grower.

And now I'm frozen yet again, as my elbows come down to the floor in front of my knees before I scoot them back, my ass now in the air, putting my soaked pussy as far away from his reach as I can figure out how to right now. My brain can only focus on what is in my line of sight, and the only thing within that constraint—because it is that big and fills up the entirety of my visual capabilities, is his cock. Which is now mere millimeters away from my face.

He doesn't move either—either because he is shocked at this turn of events or because he doesn't know what the little psycho between his legs is going to do this close to his manhood.

No sudden movements.

I don't know why—maybe it's still the adrenaline coursing through my veins, or maybe it's something along the lines of how they say your life flashes before your eyes right before you die—but the most random thought pops into my head while I figure out what the hell to do next.

W.W.C.D?

What. Would. *Clarice*. Do?

For the longest time now, Vi's and my photographer friend has been someone I've looked up to, even though I'm a few inches taller than her. I'm forever telling her she's my girl crush, that she's my spirit animal, the woman I wish I was inside. She always waves me off like she doesn't think I'm being serious, but that woman is a total baddie. She is a switch with her husband, Brian, a nearly seven-foot-tall giant of a man who she has wrapped around her dainty little finger. She could look him in the eye and tell him "You will sit down when you pee," and that man's ass would immediately perch upon a porcelain pot.

So, in this moment, that is what comes to mind, and channeling my badass, I-am-all-that-is-woman friend, I lean that last inch forward, closing the space between me and this fantasy lover brought to life.

My eyes automatically close the moment my lips press against the scalding skin that feels like velvet-upholstered steel. And at that same moment, for the first time ever in real life, I hear an actual growl come out of a human male.

It doesn't sound like a grumble.

It's not the rumbling sound a man makes when he's pissed off.

It doesn't even sound like a guttural groan some men vocalize when they're experiencing mind-numbing pleasure.

This is 100-percent the sound of a soul-deep growl that belongs to a beast with thick fur, deadly canines, and claws that could rip someone's throat out.

And it too has the automatic effect of—shocker—making me even wetter.

Is there anything about this man that's not arousing?

Everything about him is a goddamn aphrodisiac.

There's not one trait that doesn't add to how completely infatuating he is, how utterly desirable and... *exciting* he is.

All of him—his body, his intelligence, the way he speaks to me, his voice itself—is pure sex.

And at this point, I'm counting on him to keep his word about behaving, because if he doesn't, I can tell you right now I would not try to stop him. Not even a "maybe we should slow down." Nope. If he were to say "Climb up here and take a seat on my dick," by God, that's exactly what I would do, no question. Not because my body would do its thing and follow his command on its own. And not because it took one look at what he was packing and said "We're gonna need a bigger boat"—well, in this case, more lubrication—and readied itself for him. No. It's because I'd freaking want to!

I'm horny as hell!

I don't think I've ever been this turned on in my entire life, and I'm a fucking award-winning porn author!

I'm a member of a world-renowned kinky sex club, and yet I have never so badly wanted a man to tell me to mount him than I do right here in this one's truck in an abandoned bank's parking lot.

"If you weren't ready for me to touch anything below the waist, all you had to do was tell me, little one," he says, his voice traveling down over the plains and ridges of his chest and stomach to fill my ears.

I almost snort. Of course he wasn't fooled! I should have known what I thought was a stealthy move to divert his attention from touching me would be laughably transparent to him. When am I going to learn what he's told me about himself is the truth? He said he's been in the lifestyle for twenty years. That's two decades as a Dominant learning to read subtle body language in order to be everything a woman needs to hand herself over and safely submit to him.

He's literally done this long enough he could officially retire, and I thought I suddenly had cat-like reflexes that could throw him off my scent.

Ew.

Bad analogy.

As wet as I am, I do *not* want to think about any sort of scent I might have at this exact moment.

I have no words to give him, and by now I'm sure it's getting awkward, me down here just breathing on his dick, yet he's not giving me any sort of instructions. Even the last thing he said didn't give me a clue of what *he* would like me to do, so it seems as if we're still in the midst of my reward. I'm still the one driving this party bus; he had just been informing me of how I was to sit in order to please him while I was at the wheel.

But it feels like it would be super weird to sit up and go back to what I was doing before, to pick up where I left off stroking his chest and back. Like, "oh, ya know, I was just taking a quick detour to kiss your cock hello, but now I've returned to more innocent territory. Doesn't everyone do that?"

Nope. I'm already down here, so there's no turning back now. This party bus ran a few redlights and arrived at the nightclub ahead of schedule.

Fuck it. Let's dance.

I lift up from my elbows, brace myself with my left hand on the soft leather cushion beneath us, and reach forward with my right, wrapping it around him for the first time. Surprisingly, but also not so surprisingly, the tip of my middle finger doesn't reach the end of my thumb on the other side. I've read and even written about cock this thick, where the heroine's hand couldn't wrap all the way around it, but seeing as I'm pretty tall with hands made for playing the piano in my younger years, I never thought I would actually be one of those girls in real life.

So I guess I can check off something on my bucket list I didn't realize should've been included.

He doesn't growl again, and he doesn't make any other sound per se, but it's actually the absence of sound—a catch in his breathing, a split second where his exhale stutters in his chest—that lets me know I have an effect on him as well. He's still not giving me instructions, any guidance, so I take that to mean he expects me to explore the way I want, and so that's exactly what I do.

Chapter Nine

FELIX

Every second I spend with Sienna, the more and more she solidifies my earlier thought about her being the lead in an early-2000s rom-com. She really is the charmingly klutzy diamond-in-the-rough. But I wouldn't even call her "rough." We're not talking a full-on Anne Hathaway playing Mia in *The Princess Diaries* makeover. Not quite a Sandra Bullock in *Miss Congeniality*. I think I pretty much nailed it with my first reference; she reminds me of Lainey from *She's All That*. Not a total head transplant, but just a change of outfit, a little boost in confidence, and this girl could be my own personal porn star.

A man who wasn't so well versed in reading people wouldn't have picked up on the fact that the little maneuver she pulled wasn't actually because she was so cock-hungry she lunged for my dick the first chance she got. He'd want to believe that; He'd want to feel so irresistible this pretty little thing had to have him and couldn't stop herself from diving face-first into his lap.

But I was well aware of everything going on inside that busy mind of hers, as it all played across her body as clearly as the projector still tinting everything blue. The panic in her eyes when I tightened my grip and rose just an inch up the inside of her soft thigh. A test, of course. I never would've actually gone all the way up, not when she left an unmistakable barrier between me and her pussy. It might as well be a stainless steel chastity belt instead of the scrap of thin fabric it actually is, as far as I'm concerned. I won't touch her in such an intimate place until she gives explicit consent.

Yet I was expecting her to either try to close her legs again or to finally do what I was really after—use her voice to establish a boundary. But alas, she's even lower on the confidence scale than I first thought.

I went into getting to know her with my first impression of her being that of the sassy and outspoken woman talking shit about big corporations and their mistreatment of plants while she dug in the dumpster I stood outside of. The more she ran her mouth, the haughtier she got, which gave me the impression she wouldn't have too much of an issue standing up to people. But as time goes on, it's plain to see it's much more likely she's one who just talks a big game. Well, not even that, really. She believed she was alone and just talking to herself all those times I heard her. Who knows if she'd ever voice those things to another person? Probably only someone she trusted implicitly, who she wouldn't worry about whether they'd rat her out.

So this means I gave that sassy mouth too much credit when it came to reading how self-assured she is in reality.

Which means I need to delete that variable from the equation when I'm picking out things to keep in mind about her, to remember when choosing my next move. Otherwise, her reactions—like trying to protect her pussy and keep it out of my reach by giving up on something she truly wanted and worked so hard for—will come as a surprise each and every time. And that's not good when it comes to a D/s relationship. Yes, there are times when surprises will be pleasant... after we know each other much, much better. That's when the surprises will count for something special. But right now, in order to make all this run smoothly, in order for her to feel comfortable enough to trust me and softly submit until rules and limits are established and I can push her, I have to use the skills I've mastered over the past twenty years, not only as a Dominant but as a doctor whose job it is to quickly assess if a person is dying.

Nothing teaches you to read people faster than having to use tiny clues to figure out what's wrong with a patient in the ER who can't—or won't—tell you anything.

So from here on out, my decisions will be made based off the person I've actually spoken to back and forth for almost a month, the person I'll now get to read face-to-face. The girl who was dumpster diving doesn't exist, as far as my potential submissive is concerned. Not until she feels comfortable to even *talk* about that girl—the one she is when she believes no one is watching or listening.

Honestly, I can't wait for her to show me that side of her. Not only because it's completely entertaining, but because if she ever does, it'll mean she trusts me beyond anything she can comprehend right now. For her to show me the pieces of her she hides from literally everyone else in the entire universe would be the ultimate gift, the sweetest submission.

Unlike those rom-coms, I don't want to *change* anything about her. I want her to be herself, her true self, the woman she would've been if she hadn't been taught and conditioned to hide the best parts of her by the rest of the world. Her quirkiness portrays an innocence that's refreshing and genuine, not covering up the naughty vixen I can tell lives inside her but living in there alongside it. It would be a shame to dull that sweetness in her personality, when the world doesn't have enough sweetness left as it is. I just want to train her on the way I like to be pleased, and with her desire to do just that—please someone to the best of her ability—it wouldn't take long for her confidence to grow. She's intelligent as hell, and I have no doubt once she's taught then given the chance to practice until she gets the hang of it, she'll be a brand-new woman.

Well, the brand-new she craves to be.

She has a strong desire to feel self-assured.

She wishes she didn't have to rely on other people to feel like she's doing something correctly.

But that's part of that people-pleasing personality. Someone like her can do something incredible for another person, absolutely astonishing and mind-blowing, believing they did a great job. But if that person isn't impressed, doesn't say thank you or show any appreciation, then the pleaser takes a blow. Because the whole reason for putting all that effort in and doing everything they could to make that job great... was to impress and please the other person. If that doesn't happen, then all of it was for nothing, and that translates to them being a failure.

If John buys Jane a mansion in the Hollywood Hills, and Jane doesn't appear to like it, no matter how gorgeous and expensive and hard-earned the mansion is, John—if he's a people pleaser—will feel like he presented Jane with a cardboard box on Skid Row instead. He'll feel like he was the one who messed up, didn't get the right gift, and even worry he offended her with his "bad decision."

My goal with this little sub is to take all the guesswork out of it, teach her everything I like and inform her of everything I don't. And with that knowledge, those guidelines, she can use that wild imagination of hers to no doubt please me in ways I've never even thought about. I have a feeling she'd come up with all sorts of little surprises, thoughtful gifts or tasks completed just for me, just to make me happy, and she'd succeed beyond all expectations. The praise she'd earn from me would be 100 percent genuine, brought forth from being truly impressed and made to feel cared about... and even loved.

Above all things, that's what I crave.

Yes, all the sexual acts and power plays are not too far behind, but the number-one reason, the psychological reason I choose to be an active Dominant, is because I have a need to feel important to someone, loved to a point I'm damn-near worshipped.

My disorder allowed me at a younger age than most men to cut the bullshit and denial to realize this stemmed from "Mommy Issues." I didn't go through much of time period trying to figure out why I had these desires, this craving to feel like I was the center of someone's universe. I don't have the same ego as a man who isn't neurodiverse, so it was always very clear to me, made perfect sense, that it was because my mom—to put it lightly—wasn't the nurturing kind. In fact, she seemed to make it her mission to make me feel as much like a burden as humanly possible.

But with my personality and the way my not-so-typical mind worked, while it did hurt my feelings and cause obvious emotional damage, I also saw our relationship and my upbringing as just another obstacle to overcome by myself. I signed *myself* up for the gifted and talented program at school. I figured out ways to bring extra food and necessities into the house, when all she would do is complain that we kids ate too much and that's why we didn't have enough to make the groceries last. It had nothing to do with the fact that there were five of us siblings, including growing, teenage boys.

I could go on and on for hours about how being born to

that woman and growing up with her as my "caregiver" is the sole basis for the particular needs I have in a D/s relationship. Hell, in any romantic relationship, really. Doc said it was odd but not unpleasant, during my sessions for club membership, to speak to someone so level-headed and self-aware when it comes to where their desires stem from.

I've allowed my mind to wander this long so the little sub between my legs could decide on her own what she'll do next. If I were to focus on how she's now tightened her grip on my cock as she looms over the tip, so close I can fill the little puffs of her breath along the crown, the need to take control would rise up, when I need it to take a back seat. I exerted too much of my dominance on her a few minutes ago, wanting her knees open for me, and damn near ruined a reward she rightly earned. I refuse to do that.

So in order to not push her, not hurry her along so she can do exactly as she pleases at *her* pace, I try to keep my own breathing steady and think back to John and Joan and their Hollywood Hills mansion. But only because I want to allow her the chance to get acquainted with a part of me I hope she becomes very attached to, both physically and emotionally.

A lot of people would say that Jane is an ungrateful bitch. They'd place all the blame on her for not liking the mansion John bought her. But this is actually one of those societal norms that's been shoved down everyone's throat since the first person on earth ever tried to give the second person a gift they ended up not liking. It's one of the social cues I had to learn when I was very little. Otherwise, I was accused of being extremely rude, when actually I was being politely honest.

A girlfriend once got me Cane's chicken tenders for lunch.

I don't eat Cane's.

Most men, even if they don't like a certain food, will choke it down just so they don't hurt their girlfriend's feelings. In this case, it's not that I don't *like* Cane's; it's that their breading makes my stomach extremely upset. In fact, I had to have my gallbladder removed and I can't eat certain things or I will be so sick I won't be able to do my job.

But when I said to her, still politely, "That was very kind of you, but no, thank you," my ex-girlfriend went up in arms, pissed off that I wouldn't just eat the food she had gotten, because now it would go to waste. Therefore, I had to take the time to explain why I couldn't eat the food she had brought me.

I had to pacify her, give her a reason why I didn't want to eat the Cane's.

Afterward, she felt it was okay that I wouldn't eat it then, but only because it would make me physically ill if I did.

This ended up being a social experiment, a learning experience, I didn't realize I was playing out at the time. Not until I'd revert back to that specific event over and over again, trying to understand why all of that had to go down.

Why would a person have to give such a long and drawn

out explanation for not wanting to accept a gift they didn't want, just to make the other person feel better?

Why would a person be considered rude just for saying "no thank you"?

Why was it my fault that I couldn't eat what she had surprised me with on her own?

Why was I suddenly the bad guy, when I didn't ask her to get me anything, much less a meal from a restaurant I knew I couldn't eat from?

In my head, it made more sense, if we were to place blame, that it would be on *her*.

She didn't ask me if I wanted chicken tenders for lunch.

She didn't ask me if I wanted *anything* to eat at all.

In fact, I can go so far as to say it was her fault for having never noticed I only eat *grilled* chicken. I don't eat anything fried, because there are serious repercussions.

I still took the time to show my appreciation for her thoughtfulness, for wanting to do something nice for me, so why did she react the way she did?

And no, she wasn't a bitch at all. Her reaction to variations of that situation is actually the societal norm.

So going back to my hypothetical couple and their mansion in the Hollywood Hills, most people would say that the person being gifted something so extravagant and not loving it is an ungrateful asshole.

But what if later, they were to discover that Jane would've been much happier in a nice one-bedroom apartment with all the amenities like a pool and gym included?

What if that was her *dream* living situation she'd been working toward for years? It would've cost much, much less than a mansion in one of the most expensive real estate markets in the world, and now the burden of taking care of that mansion, the property, the pool, plus a separate gym membership payment, is suddenly going to be expected from her. Since it was a gift bought *for her*, right?

Why can't she just say "That was so sweet of you for wanting to be so incredibly generous to me, but no thank you"?

Why would everyone's first reaction be "Gasp! What a cunt! I'd kill for what she has, and she's just turning it down?!"

Why is she obligated to accept and show nothing but love for a "gift," when really, what she should be thinking is, *Thanks for all this exhausting work you have now gifted me with, on top of all the other shit I've got going on in my life. We've obviously been together a long enough time if you want to purchase me a home, but that also means we've been together long enough you know I'm a minimalist who only wants what I personally need to survive. I was going to go a teensy bit crazy and give myself the luxury of that small space—that small footprint I want to take up in the world—being in a nice, safe part of town, maybe even a gated complex with a pool and grounds that are maintained by someone else. But you know what? Just because you completely neglected everything I wanted, everything I stood for, and shelled out millions of dollars for all this space that I did not want to take up in the first place, I must smile and thank you and tell you how grateful I am... for such a thoughtless gift.*

But I digress.

As I do often.

Getting sidetracked and off on a tangent that leads far enough away from the original thought or conversation that I don't know where it began or how to get back there. It's the reason many people find it so frustrating to talk to me.

But not the woman who finally just dipped her head to take a tentative taste of the very tip of my dick with her shy little tongue. No, she tells me all the time how much she enjoys listening to my ramblings. I blink, my eyes refocusing on what's actually before me instead of turning inward, and God, what a sight it is.

Sienna's eyes are closed, her long lashes making two dark fans atop her cheekbones from my angle. Beneath and between, her perfect nose releases an exhale, long and audible even over the ocean sounds playing throughout the truck. It sounds like a sigh of relief, maybe excitement, but it's positive either way, and that's confirmed when her tongue disappears back inside her mouth, followed by the head of my cock before she wraps her full lips around me, just below the ridge.

The words start pouring out of me before I can stop them, but her reaction to them is all the consent I need to keep them flowing.

"That's a good girl." Her hand around my shaft tightens. "I'm so proud of you, sweetheart. You worked so hard to get your writing done so we could see each other tonight." The inner end of each eyebrow lifts as her lashes flutter, but her eyes stay closed. If they were open, I'd look for welling tears. "You've made me so happy today. You can't even imagine. First, getting to see you this morning, and then you sent me lots of messages throughout the day, which let me know you were constantly thinking of me, even while you were getting your work done. And now, my brave little princess, fighting your nervousness and following orders just to please me. And you have, sweet girl. You've pleased me so, so much tonight. And you're pleasing me even more now, getting to feel that hot little mouth wrapped around me. Can you take me deeper, little one?"

Her immediate response is to slide her hand farther down my shaft, leading the way for her lips. I hear her jaw pop as she opens her mouth wide enough to fit around my girth, and even with the projectors turning everything blue, I see her cheeks darken as she blushes, clearly having heard the sound too.

"That's a good girl," I tell her again, reaching my hand up from where it'd been resting on my thigh to push the hair that had come loose from her bun back behind her ear. She shudders at the gentle touch, the reaction genuine, clearly not just an act for my benefit, because every inch of her exposed flesh rises with goose bumps. So I leave my hand there, my fingertips toying with the extra-soft bit of skin right behind her ear, and she whimpers, tilting her head into my hand the way she did before. But she doesn't pull me from her mouth. Her grip on my cock tugs me along with her, slowly starting to jack me up and down as her lips circling my girth keep the same rhythm, my dick diagonal to the rest of me now as she tries to get closer to my touch. It's the same move every pet on earth makes when their master scratches that sweet spot where the back of their ear and their neck blends. If she wasn't currently using my erection as a handhold along with the suction of her mouth at the end of it, I have no doubt she'd have the same end result as all those cats and dogs too—toppling from leaning too far over and falling, both trapping Master's hand to keep up the scratches and using it as a pillow.

I wonder if the sweet sub knows all her instinctive reactions mirror those of a "little," a role in the BDSM community that's grouped along with the "Daddy kink"—aka ageplay—and with petplay. It didn't escape my notice earlier when she realized who I was that she called me "Dumpster Daddy," and while she was unknowingly speaking her thoughts aloud, I'm pretty sure I heard her call me Gym Daddy as well. It made me smirk, even though I've never been big on being called "Daddy." Not because it's a turn-off, but because it's so overused—and incorrectly. Everywhere you look, there are girls on the internet and TV and in songs calling just anyone "Daddy," whether it's just because he's an older man or because he has money, or both I guess. And it frustrates me that a part of this lifestyle I believe in so wholeheartedly is becoming the butt of a joke, when before it was "cool," not many people took the time to understand the DDlg—Daddy Dom and little girl relationship.

It's one of the most healing D/s relationships there is, for both parties involved. For the longest time, and actually still to this day, more often than not, people don't "get" the Daddy kink. Their mind inevitably turns the relationship between the Dom and sub filthier than it really is—as in they think more along the lines of pedophilia and incest, when that is not that case at all. Not even close.

And having a Daddy kink doesn't automatically mean "Daddy Issues" either... but... I can't concentrate on that line of thinking when this particular little sub is working her mouth and hand in tandem and in a way that is highly distracting and even more pleasurable.

"Fuck, sweet girl," I growl, and her next pass up and down my cock steals my breath it's so exquisite. Her hips have begun to move, so now she's putting her whole body into it, and it's so easy to imagine her riding me, the picture so delicious I know without a doubt I won't be giving this woman up, no matter how hard she tries to scare me away. "Just like that. I love the way your hips are moving, pretty one. Can you arch your back more while you.... That's a good girl. Fuck." The last word is a groan as her hand tries to strangle my dick at the same time she moans when she takes me deeper into her mouth. I've seen countless women respond positively to being called a good girl in my lifetime, but none have had the unconscious and immediate strong reaction this one does. It's like the words send a surge of power through her, a defibrillator to her soul, taking her from flatline to perfect rhythm with one whispered endearment.

"God, your ass with your back arched like that makes the perfect heart shape," I tell her, and I slide my palm down her body, spreading my fingers wide to touch as much of her skin as I can as I travel toward the softly rounded cheeks that are moving in an enticing dance a short distance in front of me. I have to sit up farther and lean forward, but I reach her ass, feeling her immediately stop any movement on my cock. Her head is now snuggled up against my abs and chest, so all I have to do is tilt my face down to speak right into her ear again.

"Keep going, princess. I'm just going to pet you. Trust me not touch what your body has made it clear you're not ready for yet." After a moment, she gives a tiny nod, then resumes a slower pace with a lighter grip than she had before I moved. "Yes, Sir?" I prompt, my big palm caressing her ass cheek, and she surges closer to me.

Her mouth leaves the tip just long enough to whisper, "Yes, Sir," and before she can even fill her mouth with me again, I praise her in a lilting but clear tone, "Good girl."

And just like before, the effect it has on her physical response is undeniable. She doesn't just take me deep in her mouth but sucks me—so much suction and with such a tight grip I groan. "Fuck, little one. Just like that. I want you ravenous for my cock. Squeeze with all your strength. Suck like you're trying to pull every last drop of cum out of me.

That's right. God, you follow directions so exquisitely, sweet-heart. So obedient. Such a good little sub for me."

That last sentence murmured low but clear right into her ear actually makes her whimper, a tremor taking over her whole body, and a moment later, I feel something hot and wet hit the lowest part of my stomach. And then again, and once more before I feel the liquid drip down my body toward my shaft like they no doubt would be doing to her cheeks if she weren't hovering face-down.

So much to unpack there, but at this moment, I have one final quick test for the night, and then I need to take care of the little submissive crying so sweetly on my cock.

I lean back slowly, dragging my palms from her ass and up her body until I'm resting against the cushion once again and take her head in both my hands, my fingers burying themselves beneath the wild bun and deep between the pulled back strands to massage her scalp. She sighs, swirling her tongue around my tip, but before she can take me in her mouth once more, I order, "Lick me up and down, princess. And then I want to see just how deep you can take me in your mouth. Yes, Sir?" I go ahead and prompt the answer I expect, to remind her I want a verbal response when I give a direct command. It's also a simple way to see if she *doesn't* want to submit to the order, without her having to say a word—literally. If she goes silent instead of parroting my cue, then I'll know she's at a soft limit for the night.

But I have nothing to worry about.

"Yes, Sir," comes her whispered reply, an exhale I feel hit everywhere her saliva and my precum has coated.

"Good girl. Now show me," I urge, pulling my left hand from her hair but leaving my right buried in the mass, closing it until my fingers have all of it in a fisted grip I use to tilt her head just so... in order to see her follow my command.

With her grip still wrapped around my shaft, I see her make a wider opening between her thumb and the rest of her fingers for her tongue to travel from the very tip of my cock, blazing a path downward that seems to take an obscene amount of time, until she reaches the very root of me. At the base, right where the anatomy switches from penis to balls, her full, wet lips join her tongue, making my cock jerk at the unexpected but welcome addition of sensation as she drags her mouth back upward.

Her eyes are still closed, her cheeks wet from her tears, but there is an expression of delicious appreciation, of pure bliss, on her face that's unmistakable. She's enjoying this just as much as I am, and that's a trait in a submissive a Dom should treasure and do everything possible to hold onto for as long as they can. A sub who gains just as much gratification from giving as receiving is a gift herself, and because of that, I'll make her feel like the treasure she is, and she'll soon learn what it means to submit to a Pleasure Dom.

Because just like everything else between us, like fate decided to have a hand in this serendipitous match, our roles and desires mesh perfectly, and as much as she clearly loves and gains from following my commands, giving me that obedience I crave more than anything, it's a reflection of my own passion, which is making a sub experience so much intoxicating pleasure she begs me to stop, unable to take another second of it.

It's how I got my nickname from a former sub of mine —Romantic Sadist. Because truly, I'm not sadistic. I don't gain sexual gratification from doling out pain, even when the sub is a masochist who needs it. I have no problem providing that for them, even find it amusing, and their appreciation makes me happy, especially when it makes them want to be even more obedient and please me the way *I* want, but *sexual arousal* from hurting someone? No.

However, the begging. The sweet, sweet sound of desperation for mercy—that's what gives me a sexual high like nothing else, but only when it's a plea for me to stop overwhelming them with "too much" pleasure. Enough pleasure, with so many orgasms, can feel as intense as pain-inducing torture, and it's that intensity that will make a submissive cry out for help, make promises of unfailing servitude, swear fealty, and offer up their very soul to me, and I never once have to lift a violent or sadistic finger.

A *Romantic* Sadist. Pleasurable torture. An oxymoron that just works beautifully and makes perfect sense.

Just like the little sub between my legs, who's still taking her time licking me up and down as she summons the courage to try to deep-throat me for the first time.

Beautiful. And she makes perfect sense. At least to me. I

get her in a way I believe no one probably has before, given the way she's so surprised every time I understand and provide an explanation for anything she tries to clarify about herself. Which tells me, just like she has told me many times now, that I understand her better than she does *herself*.

And God, I want more than anything for her to allow me inside her, to give me full consent and her submission, so I can truly start helping her learn, understand, and believe what a gift she is, not the burden the world has spent the last thirty-odd years convincing her she is. Because if there's anything I've learned in my almost fifty years on this earth, it's that a person who genuinely wants nothing more than to make you happy is a rarity, and you should let them be exactly themselves, who they truly are, and protect them at all costs—not break them down and try to kill that desire they have to please others.

"But she's going to get hurt. Someone is going to take advantage of her kindness, and then she'll be heartbroken."

That may be true, but what would be worse? That, or not allowing her to experience joy in the first place by making others happy? People can agree with that saying *"I'd rather have loved and lost than never to have loved at all."* So why is it so hard for them to understand that same concept when applied to a people-pleaser?

Because if you kill off all the genuine kindness in the world, replacing it with suspicion and selfishness, what will we have left?

I can tell you what we most certainly would *not* have left.

Sienna Brookes.

The woman who just inhaled a great-big breath and is letting it out slowly, an attempt to relax her muscles and her anxiety, as she finally starts to lower her mouth wrapped around the head of my cock. Her hand retightens around the fully erect rod she coaxed to life with sweet licks of her teasing tongue. I'm harder than I can remember being in a very long time, and my breath catches on an exhale, then continues outward in a groan as her other hand leaves the cushion beneath us to grip around the bottom few inches of my cock.

With her two fists now stacked on top of each other, she only has about four inches of my length to take into her mouth—clever girl. It makes me smile that she figured out how to pleasure more of me without actually having to take me down her throat. She thinks I'll be fooled by this trick, I'm sure, and when we're more established, I'll set her straight. She'll be reprimanded for not following my direct order—which was to show me just how deep she could take me in her mouth, not how much of me she could stimulate at once with both her hands and mouth.

I will give her credit though. From her concentrated expression—gone is that relaxed, almost blissed-out look from earlier—and the tug of her head I feel against her hair wrapped around my hand, it shows she actually is trying to push herself, to take more of my thick inches as she slides both her fists down my shaft as far as they will go. But then she gives in to her need for oxygen and slides back up and off me quickly to gasp in a breath.

The whole scene is sexy as fuck, the little sub trying so hard to please me past her actual level of comfort, the sound of her sharp inhale, the sight of her swollen wet lips still parted to take in more air, the sheen of saliva around her mouth—which I see she's lifting a hand to wipe away. But with my tight grip still on her hair, I stop that from happening when I pull her up toward me, a little squeal coming out of her as she falls forward, her wet hands landing flat against my chest to catch herself. Yet when I wrap my other arm all the way around her back and squeeze her tightly at the same time I tug upward on her hair, her arms buckle as all that soft, warm, naked flesh of hers presses tightly to my front, and I steal our first kiss from her cock-reddened mouth.

The feel of those deliciously messy, pillowy lips against my own is enough to pull another growl from my chest, and I dip my tongue into her mouth so for just a split-second taste. I feel her try to match my kiss, to meet my tongue with hers, but I don't allow it. I tease her, using my mouth to make her desperate for more. I suck her bottom lip between mine, biting gently but firm enough it makes her gasp, and with her mouth open, I swipe inside with my tongue again, making her give chase with hers once more, only to come up against my closed lips, which I press to hers one final time once her tongue retreats back behind her teeth. I can tell my actions both arouse and frustrate her, and she grows even more frustrated when it clicks in her mind there's absolutely nothing she can do about it.

She's submitting, and trying to take control of the kiss to force my lips and tongue to dance with hers in a gracefully choreographed way she probably got used to with anyone else she's ever kissed would go against everything she wants between us, because she'd be topping. Totally out of her jurisdiction.

But all that frustration leaves her body the second I speak against her lips, "I'm so proud of you, little one. You did so good. Excellent for the first time ever sucking my cock." She melts against my chest, and I let go of her hair and tighten both my arms around her, since the tension leaving her muscles makes her go soft and start to slide down my front. "Such a good girl for me. Such an obedient little sub already. And if you let me, I'll train you to be perfect, everything I could possibly ever want or need, sweet princess. Would you like that?"

She's gone even more lax the longer I've spoken in my deep but clear voice, softened until her face is now nuzzled into the crook of my neck, where I feel her breaths evening out, and she nods.

I find my hands running up and down the long, smooth, naked line of her back. I don't know when they started the firm but soothing back-and-forth motion of their own accord, but the effect it's having on the submissive I suspect more strongly than ever is a "little"—as in the counterpart to a Daddy Dom—brings me a sense of power that wielding whips and chains never could. Because the woman now blanketing me, more relaxed and anxiety-free than I've ever seen her or heard her talk about being, is telling me without words how much she wants and needs this... needs *me*.

She didn't want to give anyone else the chance to feel this deep sense of worth she's providing me in this moment. Said it herself—I'm the only one she was pulled toward, attracted to. I'm the only one she was willing to risk getting hurt over.

I don't know if it's just coincidence or if all these stars aligned to create this perfect moment in time. But what I do know is I will do anything and everything I have to in order to Own and Master Sienna Brookes.

Chapter Ten

FROM SIENNA AND FELIX'S GOOGLE CHAT

12:20 a.m. - 3:58 a.m.

ROMANTICSADIST:

I'm extremely proud of you. You did
AMAZING. You were scared and
nervous and still made my soul
smile more than you can imagine.
Thank you, princess.

SIENNA:

Thank you, Sir. But also, dis me, Sir.

Gif: Thumbs-up sinking into lake

ROMANTICSADIST:

Ummm... you're drowning 😅

SIENNA:

> LOL!!! No, Sir. Just a part of me.

ROMANTICSADIST:

You can call a timeout, little one...
ask some—SOME—of your
questions going through your head.

LOL! Drowning is generally not seen
as good, but yours has a thumbs-
up, so really could've gone
either way.

SIENNA:

> Ok. 1: WHERE THE HELL DID YOU
> LEARN THAT?

> "You get that on Amazon?"

> If you don't have Tiktok, you're not
> gonna know what the hell that last
> sentence is from lol

> 2: Well, that's really it. Because the
> other ones fully stem from my
> intrusive thoughts and low self-
> esteem, so we'll just ignore those
> and let the Prozac take care of them
> in the morning.

ROMANTICSADIST:

LOL so out of everything tonight, and after being told to ask the thoughts I know are running through your head—given EXPLICIT permission and carte blanche to say whatever you want—you choose a vague question and a comment I won't understand 😌

How high was the brat score again?

Let's hear the intrusive thoughts. And the low self-esteem should be good. *grabs popcorn and sits

SIENNA:

Ha! You fell for my TikTok play on the old figure-out-if-he's-single trick, Sir. So you don't have one? Bummer.

But also, I'm writing this: (Photo of Excerpt)

The question wasn't vague. I'm serious. Where did you learn REAL Domination and not the fake shit on pornos?

ROMANTICSADIST:

Oh, I have TikTok. But let me break it down: 48-year-old male who looks up DIY ways to fix things, tools, weaponry, and Viking cosplay costume ideas for the next RenFest. So obviously, the algorithm decisively fills my For You Page with girls in their 20s just shaking their ass and tits. Needless to say, I don't waste time on that app unless I just want to use the search feature.

I meant vague, because I wasn't sure exactly what you were talking about lol.

And for some reason, it's not letting me pull the pic up to expand and read.

SIENNA:

Hm. Interesting. I look up plants, cleaning, and people turning lame crybaby music into badass rock covers. But the algorithm insists I want to know everything about this chick in Utah who outted a whole Mormon swinger ring.

Uno momento, Sir <3

"So responsive, little one. Your mouth might be begging me to let you go, but the rest of your body? It's begging for something completely different," he purrs, and to my utter shame, my vision goes blurry, my eyes unfocusing in order to concentrate more closely on my other senses—the sound of his deep, quiet voice, the scent of his intoxicating, crisp cologne, the feel of his heavy body on top of me, my mind trying to pick out the specific parts of him and where they've aligned with the different parts of me. My senses magnify even more from there.

I can smell the lumber stacked not too far away, the grass all around me, but laced through all of it is something spicy... dangerous. I'm at this man's mercy, and he's right; my body is turning on me, and if any normal woman experiences that, surely she doesn't feel what I'm feeling. She absolutely doesn't use all her mental capacity to take a snapshot of this moment so she can remember it for all time.

The way my skin feels like it has an electric current running over it.

The way my blood feels like it's boiling, expanding inside my veins, making them vibrate from being overfull and like I'll soon be proof that spontaneous combustion can really happen.

The way I can hear my heart thumping inside my head, my eardrums being pounded to its beat.

The metallic taste in my mouth from breathing so heavily, panting so uncontrollably my throat has gone dry.

And so many other tiny little details that should not be making me needier and needier. They should not be making my pussy beg to be roughly filled with something long and hard... ravaged... fucked until its raw.

I should be fighting with every ounce of strength in my

body, and I want to do that, crave it. But a normal woman wouldn't also still hope to be fucked while she struggles; she'd want to get away.

When my eyes refocus, I look away from his, unable to take all the things reflected in them at once. Maybe if it was only the throat-gripping desire, but not that while it's combined with the artfully put-on evilness along with the genuine care I've always seen there, acting as the base.

RomanticSadist:

> Oh you're SO lucky I don't have the verbal ability you possess.

> You wrote that when you got home? Trying to get a head start on tomorrow to avoid a proper spanking? Lol

> Help me understand your question, and I will honestly answer, if you would like. What did I do that you consider "real Domination," as opposed to what you've see in porn?

Sienna:

> Mother FUCKER. GRRRRR! My stupid computer died, and when I plugged back in, my whole message I wrote out was gone.

RomanticSadist:

Oh for fuck's sake lol

Sienna:

Probably for the best. I would've definitely gotten bent over your knee for it. I was answering your question about my self-esteem. I get the feeling you wouldn't like the things my brain tells me.

RomanticSadist:

I don't have to like it. That's part of the freedom.

Sienna:

Let me try to remember what I said. Oh wait, that should be easy, because I was just telling you what goes on repetitively as like... background noise 24/7

RomanticSadist:

What's funny is... what I wouldn't like hearing is something to the effect of "never seeing you again," but that can't be it, because you wouldn't be able to be bent over for it.

Then let me have it full force, little one. I want to know what those voices are telling you.

🙂I feel like I just dared the wicked word witch to do her worst.

Like lashing myself to the mast at the siren's call.

(Heads up: I really enjoy alliteration)

Ok, let me attempt some sort of answer on the "real Domination" for you. Porn Doms portray a Dom as a greedy, spoiled child, barking orders and expecting to be followed. There's no connection between them. There's no sense of his control or her will. The Domination of your body by triggering your mind and emotion is not shown.

SIENNA:

The most fun part about intrusive thoughts is I am aware they are bullshit, but what fucks with me is the repetitive part. Anyone can have a bad thought about themselves, but then they can wave it away and that be the end of it.

With my particular brand of OCD, I get the bad thought, can tell myself "He so wouldn't be here doing this with you if he found you repulsive, dumbass," but then my brain claps back with "You worked out for the first time in ages, got all sweaty, then put on a hoodie, and sat by the hot tub and sauna all day. You look and smell like a swamp creature. Oh, and do you see how perfect he is? Now, look at you. Nice skinny-fat bod. Oh, you thought you were feeling good about it after dropping those 15 lbs. while gardening? Lest we forget, it KEPT dropping, until it took all your ass that used to be AWESOME when you worked out every day. But alas, you had to go and be a crybaby for months because you're 'overwhelmed.' Well, boo-hoo."

And so on, and so forth, until my little "But like... he really wouldn't be here if he found me repulsive" gets drowned out.

Good times. Great oldies.

ROMANTICSADIST:

Now there IS a place for the physical brute Dom... oh shit

Give me a minute to read what you sent.

SIENNA:

And your alliteration gives me butterflies in my vagina.

ROMANTICSADIST:

You mean vaginal vibrations? Pussy pulsations?

SIENNA:

hahahahahaha clam clenches?

Kitty Kegels? Ok, that's all I've got. LOL

ROMANTICSADIST:

DAMNIT I was going to go with clitoral, but you went a little low brow lol

Oooo, I think you got me with the kitty kegels

Oh, and I have done the physical brute Dom, girls in chains and leashes, but it was by request. I'm not against it when it's wanted.

SIENNA:

YOU, Sir, have a very strange effect on me. You pull shit out of me that I learned through conditioning a long time ago that you don't say to people you want to stick around.

ROMANTICSADIST:

So here is where the timeout crosses. Would you like me to just hear out your confessions of inner thoughts? Give my opinion? Or is your timeout over?

SIENNA:

> Dis me:

> Gif: Harley Quinn in Suicide Squad. "Sorry... the voices."

ROMANTICSADIST:

There's the difference. You might not be entirely convinced you WANT me to stick around.

You may be *trying* to get me to not stay, so you don't go deeper down this rabbit hole...

Or me deeper into yours 😈

Whatever you say, you are safe.

You can tucker it up and then just pull taboo fantasies that you want to do, just be a play partner, and it would not change a thing about me wanting you.

SIENNA:

> It's more like the opposite, I think— or maybe a mix? Idk. I'm still a little endorphin-drunk at the moment.

I keep expecting, since it's happened SO MANY TIMES, that I'll open up too much, and that'll be it. It's why the very first message I ever sent you was "block me now if you need to."

And so, suddenly, you're this person who GETS the crazy shit coming out of my mouth, and it's like when you find a fellow conspiracy theory friend, and you go back and forth just letting all your conspiracies out of your mouth no matter how stupid or twisted they are. But I digress.

I'm trying to give you fair warning of what you'd be getting into with me, that way you can't later say some bullshit like "she was really good at hiding her insanity in the beginning."

Nope, it's all here in black-and-white screenshots for photographic evidence, Sir. You've been properly notified, and by continuing, you are agreeing to the Terms of Service.

ROMANTICSADIST:

That's exactly what I was hoping you'd say, little one.

Nothing you say can scare me away.

So here are my rules:

No messing with real life. Family and career first.

If we are to meet and something comes up, just tell the other. It's no big deal. It happens. There will always be another time.

Limited questions or comments about past relationships. This is usually a very solid rule for me, but I know the main reason you were even on that app was to research and gain knowledge for your books from experienced people in the community, so I will make an exception and allow you to ask whatever you need. But that doesn't necessarily mean I will answer everything you ask.

In public, for now, we'll have to pretend like we don't know each other. I will rethink this later perhaps, but this is best for now, since people at the gym know me from work, and they may talk to or be the same people who know the little kink author who writes her dirty books in the locker room and café. I can't have them make that connection between us, because that could potentially break rule #1: No messing with each other's career.

SIENNA:

> Soooo... I'll just slide my personal trainer hopes to the back burner then.

ROMANTICSADIST:

And the crazier and more twisted you are, the better, sweet girl. I want you porn-star dirty, fucked in the head, cock crazy, obedient to the point of just wanting to be told what to do and how to be so you can just shut your mind off and go to work pleasing me like you've been taught.

No... I WILL be your trainer.

SIENNA:

AT THE GYM lol

ROMANTICSADIST:

Yes, I was also speaking of that.

But your motivation will be very different than what most people seek out a personal trainer for.

SIENNA:

As in getting my ass back. Full of MUSCLE... that I grow MYSELF hahaha

ROMANTICSADIST:

Ok. Your timeout is officially over, princess. No more speaking freely without the Sir... unless you don't agree to my rules.

SIENNA:

Aaaaand there it is.

ROMANTICSADIST:

?

SIENNA:

Shit, I sent mine before yours came through. Let me fix: Aaaaaand there it is, *Sir*. Also, yes. I agree to your rules.

ROMANTICSADIST:

Oh cheese and rice ☺

SIENNA:

I had an epiphany moment, Sir.

ROMANTICSADIST:

Please... share with the rest of the class

SIENNA:

I had an epiphany? Epiphany moment? Whatever.

The porn star thing you said, Sir.

THAT HAS to be the fucking reason I'm so drawn to this lifestyle. Because my OCD doesn't let my brain STOP. The appeal of submission has always been so I can't think anymore.

ROMANTICSADIST:

You're so pretty LOL. I'd say just epiphany covers it.

And you're only partly right on the lifestyle/OCD thing.

SIENNA:

Seven years of research and a gajillion fucking books on it later, it just now clicked for MYSELF. Even after making that the same goddamn reason for my heroines. I swear to God, Sir.

ROMANTICSADIST:

Told you. Strong, intelligent, decision-making, successful women are drawn to it. They do "male mentality" all day and just want to be a "woman" and have a man be the man. Yes. Your brain constantly running falls into the please-shut-my-brain-off category. But—

SIENNA:

> The praise kink, I totally always got about myself. That was kind of a duh, Sir. I have all these intrusive, repetitive thoughts, and a Dom giving praise is like getting reassurance over and over. It's... fucking blissful, Sir. 10/10.

ROMANTICSADIST:

—that's just purely submission. Your desire to PLEASE is from something else. Sometimes, someone just TRULY enjoys pleasing others, being the bright spot in their day.

Lol! That was what I was going to type next, but I knew you had to know that one.

SIENNA:

> Oooo, interesting. Ok, let me overthink this right quick, Sir...

ROMANTICSADIST:

Can't wait...

SIENNA:

> LMAO!!!!!!

ROMANTICSADIST:

*counting the seconds

SIENNA:

I just scared my cat I laughed so suddenly, Sir hahaha

ROMANTICSADIST:

Here's something for you to overthink then. Let's say your desire for praise and reassurance comes from intrusive thoughts and insecurity.

BUT as time goes on... I train and teach you to be what I want... AND you start to believe and KNOW it in your OWN mind to be true, because I tell you and I trained you to be my fantasy...

The intrusive ones are still there, but the trained thoughts slowly get louder.

You'll still have many voices in that crazy head of yours, princess, but I'm going to be the one telling them what to say.

SIENNA:

I...

I just screenshot that last message to set as my background on my phone so I can read it like a mantra whenever I need to look forward to something.

That sounds like everything I've ever wanted, Sir.

Storytime:

So, originally, I went to college to be an Executive Assistant. It was always super appealing to me, the movies where she's the assistant and she keeps the big CEO all organized, and picks up all his dry cleaning, and is the one he relies on. Like, that's "what I wanted to be when I grew up."

A fucking assistant.

Had no clue why that was so alluring, especially being that young. I was 19! Like, aim a little higher, right?

And then fast-forward to adulthood, and I'm sent to therapy for "the disease to please" because I will literally do absolutely ANYTHING my "friends" would ask of me, and it always just fucked me over.

ROMANTICSADIST:

🐿 Please tell me you watched The Secretary

SIENNA:

Is that a serious question, Sir?

ROMANTICSADIST:

I just want to be sure.

496 • PLANT DADDY

I actually WOULD be disappointed if you said no.

SIENNA:

I'm sorry, Sir. Yes, it's very high in my spank bank, Sir.

The only thing I think I've orgasmed to more is the priest from Stigmata.

And yes, I was raised Catholic, Sir.

ROMANTICSADIST:

REALLY?!

SIENNA:

👀

ROMANTICSADIST:

Stigmata, not the Catholic thing

SIENNA:

Yes, Sir lol

ROMANTICSADIST:

I was raised Catholic, altar boy, boy scout...

Honors classes, played D&D

SIENNA:

CHAPTER TEN · 497

🐿️ I fainted on the altar the first time I served, because I got too hot in the robes under the lights. They fed me a banana. I still remember that LOL

But side note: I have a request, Sir. I don't want to call you by your real name, even in my head. I'm sure you know the psychology, how it takes you out of the world you're trying to stay submersed in and places you back in reality. And I know you like to be called Sir, but like... it always seemed weird to me to think of it as someone's name. Like if I were to talk about you to my best friend, it feels odd to say "Sir turned me into a puddle of goo on his chest, and I definitely left behind drool when I finally came out of my stupor."

Oh, are we competing to see who was the biggest nerd/good girl/boy, Sir? Because I was the district champion in BOWLING in high school, Sir. It's the only sport I was ever good at lol

ROMANTICSADIST:

Hmm... then your grip on my dick should've been more impressive.

And yes, little one. I haven't completely decided on your official nickname yet, so that's why you've gotten lots of generic endearments while I get to know you and pick one that fits you perfectly. But you are more than welcome to do the same for me. In fact, I'd love to know what a chart-topping wordsmith would choose to call me.

SIENNA:

Rude, Sir. I was having issues with my heart rate.

So hear me out, because I want you to know what a big deal this is, Sir. At first, I was thinking "Doc," because you remind me so much of my amazing therapist Dr. Neil Walker. Like, it's kind of eerie how alike y'all are as far as this... I don't really know how to put it. This "all-knowing" protector sort of vibe? It's very, very attractive.

But don't worry, he's extremely happily married, and his wife is one of my good friends. IDK if you're the jealous type or not... but just in case, yeah. Nothing to worry about there, Sir.

Anyway, so I thought about calling you my very own Doc, but that could get weird, ya know? Two Docs? Totally confusing. Especially since you work at a home improvement store and aren't actually a medical professional. That would be strange, right?

But I digress. Again. So! I nixed that idea, but I also can't keep thinking of you as Gym-slash-Dumpster Daddy. That's way too much. And I don't have a Daddy kink, so Daddy by itself would just be weird. Plus, too generic. Totally overused.

So finally, what you just said about being an altar boy finally gave me my lightbulb moment, Sir. Do you happen to remember how I told you my series is about a hot priest who hears confessions and talks with those in his parish needing guidance after being terribly hurt, and then he formed this group of men of the church who... help the people heading to hell to move along a bit faster than their natural pace? I always say he's my favorite voice in my head, my fictional guardian angel.

Before I met you, no one truly seemed to get me. Yes, my best friend loves me despite all my... quirks, but not even she truly understands me the way you do, Sir. So, as sad as it sounds, I had to write myself an imaginary friend, and I made him talk to and understand these heroines who go through some of the shit I do. And you're like my favorite voice, my guardian angel, my imaginary friend who really gets me, has been brought to life. So if you like it, I'd really love to call you by his name, because I mean that as the HIGHEST compliment I could possibly give a real person, Sir.

ROMANTICSADIST:

Sweet girl, I'd be honored to take that name, whatever it is. If it means that much to you, if I really give you the same positive feelings that character—essentially your perfect dream person—does, then I couldn't want any other name more. What is it? I'm so curious now.

Oh, and heart rate my ass. Don't think I didn't notice you could've FULLY deep-throated AND were totally sandbagging your chick sucking abilities!

Well shit... that loses some effect with the typo 😳

FUCK YOU, TECHNOLOGY

SIENNA:

His name is Zen, Sir. Before I fleshed out the characters and started writing their books, I called him Zen in my head, because that's what he felt like to me every time his voice would start talking to me. He gave me a sense of peace, of validation and calm. So, yeah. Zen.

*cackles

CHICK sucking abilities? Sorry, Sir. I'm strictly dickly.

And as I recall, my first lesson you ever taught me was if I show up looking all perfect on day one, then there's only one direction to go from there, Sir. Therefore, if I bust out all my best moves on Day 1...

ROMANTICSADIST:

I fucking love it, little one. Zen. It embodies what I want to provide you, but at the same time sounds totally badass lol. Thank you, sweet girl.

So I will forgive the "Rude, Sir" outburst COMPLETELY... if you come clean about why you were so jumpy when I came near that precious pussy of yours.

HELL YES!! Ok, you just got HUGE points with that.

SIENNA:

If you could've seen my face just now, Sir haha

ROMANTICSADIST:

NOOOOOO very, VERY well played.

You let just enough skill through, but I didn't see the play.

At first, I thought it was so I would feel like I taught you. But I knew you'd know I wouldn't fall for that.

SIENNA:

Gif: Rhianna putting on a crown

I feel so accomplished lol

ROMANTICSADIST:

Gif: Wayne's World. "I'm not worthy!"

SIENNA:

Inside voice: oooooooh, God. This is gonna be so, so bad. SO bad.

ROMANTICSADIST:

Hmm so based on this behavior, if you pretend to only take me a little in anal... I SHOULD BURY IT TILL MY COCK TOUCHES THE BACKSIDE OF YOUR TONGUE.

If your answer is anywhere NEAR "I dare you," I might faint.

SIENNA:

Gif: Schitt's Creek, Alexis. "Please don't stress me out about this!"

I don't know CPR, Sir.

ROMANTICSADIST:

SIENNA:

Gif: "Don't touch me there. That is my no no square."

Ok, I'm having way too much fun with the gifs, Sir. Lemme stop lol

ROMANTICSADIST:

I actually appreciate the gifs

Wait... so DON'T fuck your asshole?

SIENNA:

But back to your question, Sir, before I apparently blew your mind better than your cock... 😈 I have a request for you to ACTUALLY BEHAVE when it comes to "the no-no square."

ROMANTICSADIST:

Ok what the hell is a no-no square?

SIENNA:

ANAL IS WITHIN THE PERAMETERS OF THE NO-NO SQUARE. So that would be correct, Sir lol

ROMANTICSADIST:

You really DO have great tits btw

SIENNA:

LMFAOOO! It's a song "Stop! Don't touch me there. That is... my no-no square." I think it's something they teach kids so they know adults don't go there. IDK.

Thank you, Sir. Interesting that compliment came up when I put the lower region off-limits haha

ROMANTICSADIST:

The WHOLE lower region...

Or just the asshole?

SIENNA:

HOLY SHIT. It just dawned on me... you're the only other man to touch the tatas. All the ones before my ex got my sad little A-cups.

As you could probably tell, I had NO qualms with you going there, Sir. These bitches are AWESOME lol.

ROMANTICSADIST:

You know, when you say it like that... it sounds like there was a LOT of other ones before your ex.

And yes, they really, really are. I'm looking forward to visiting them frequently.

SIENNA:

Excuse me while I find a gif to accurately portray my reaction to your previous message, Sir.

ROMANTICSADIST:

It's like even your intrusive voices had to step back and say "Ok, you're making terrible decisions right now with this guy, but your tits are BANGIN."

SIENNA:

*offended gif

ROMANTICSADIST:

Lol I almost chose that one earlier

SIENNA:

EXACTLY. I got the best fucking surgeon on the East Coast. I know these things are phenomenal. But then my intrusive thoughts would be like "The best part about you is 100% fake." So there we have it, Sir. LOL

ROMANTICSADIST:

Fake?!? Does your car run? Can you ride in it? It was man-made. Does that make it fake?

SIENNA:

I 100% know how absolutely exhausting I am, Sir. I wish I could escape me. Trust me. LOL

ROMANTICSADIST:

Perception is truth. I can touch, taste, smell, feel, fuck, and cum on your tits, which equals real to me.

SIENNA:

haha! I prefer the "Yeah, they're real. Real expensive."

ROMANTICSADIST:

Lol I haven't heard that in a while. Oldie but goodie.

SIENNA:

Aaaaaand there's my Zen.

ROMANTICSADIST:

I actually went back to see just how much of a brat your test says you are.

SIENNA:

How is there not a gif of Bartok saying "That fell right out there, sir!" ???

ROMANTICSADIST:

Seriously? Surely there is.

SIENNA:

And what for?! There's been no sarcasm!! I actually felt pretty shy to throw out the "my Zen" and almost deleted it but said fuck it.

Boom, baby!

*Bartok gif

ROMANTICSADIST:

Are you certain these voices don't just sometimes take over your mouth?

NICE!! I KNEW YOU COULD DO IT!

Excellent reference grab as well.

> SIENNA:
>
> Obsessive COMPUUUUUULSIVE Disorder, Sir. They 100% do.
>
> Did you see my cup today when you sat beside me, Sir?

ROMANTICSADIST:

No, little one

> SIENNA:
>
> My reader made it for me. It says "I speak fluent movie quotes." It's because I had to create a whole-ass character just to be able to say all my dumb pop culture references, with a heavy emphasis on Disney."
>
> You just made me clench, Sir. You calling me that will never get old.

ROMANTICSADIST:

Good. Because I kind of feel like you're a Dom slayer and completely played me.

> SIENNA:
>
> 😌 I wouldn't know, Sir. You're my first experienced one.

All my other ones were either an amateur or imaginary lol

Shit! I mean... if you *want* to be my first experienced one, that is, Sir. 🙇 That's not embarrassing at all.

ROMANTICSADIST:

And I had to Google the fucking no-no square since you didn't answer, nor why I'm not to skewer you there.

GREAT. Played and beaten by a novice. I need to turn in my Dom card.

Sweet girl, when I told you my rules and asked if you agreed to them, you didn't take that as me wanting you to be mine? Or when I accepted your awesome name you wanted to give me?

SIENNA:

I did answer! I said I think they teach it to kids! Scroll... Nope. Wait... Too bossy. I request you scroll up so you can see I TOTALLY answered, Sir.

Oh. Well. When you put it like that... I guess I could've used context clues. Glad we cleared that up, Sir.

ROMANTICSADIST:

We were talking about fucking your asshole at the time, so I was a little distracted and didn't see your answer.

SIENNA:

Gif: Thumbs-up sinking into lake

This time, it means please drown me lol

ROMANTICSADIST:

And it all comes full circle. I bet your plots are amazing, little one.

ROMANTICSADIST:

I'm going to go to sleep, princess. I work tomorrow.

Here are your first official tasks as my sub-in-training.

1. Send me a good-morning text every morning with your schedule.

2. I want and need to know your hard limits.

3. Start logging what you eat and drink all day.

4. Tomorrow, you'll work out legs. Squats, hip thrusts, lunges, stairclimbers.

5. Write at least 500 words over what you think you were supposed to write.

6. Meet me when I get off from work. It would really make my night to enjoy your company.

SIENNA:

I'm taking my bestie and her kids to see Lady Gaga tomorrow evening and will be out late with them, but other than that last task, Yes, Sir.

ROMANTICSADIST:

Ok VERY cool

SIENNA:

Gif: Mean Girls. "I'm not a regular mom. I'm a cool mom."

*aunt

ROMANTICSADIST:

Sweet dreams, little one.

SIENNA:

Goodnight, Sir 🙇

***

9:23 a.m. – 4:12 p.m.

Kik app

ROMANTICSADISTLL:

Good morning, sweet girl! How are you today? I'm still smiling from you last night.

WILLDIVE4PLANTS:

Good morning, Sir. I just pulled up to the gym, and this was on the radio:

(Video: Sienna grinning and lip syncing, "I'll keep you my dirty little secret...")

Google Chat app

SIENNA:

Just download this on my phone, Sir. Idk which app you prefer, so now I have both.

Schedule~

10:58 mini kolache and one glazed doughnut so I can take my meds

11:00 finish my goddamn book. No choice. It goes live at midnight.

3:00 Second dose or I'll sleep. Narcolepsy—a super-fun side effect of ADHD and OCD

3:01 Continue finishing book

4:00 Do my workout if I haven't squirreled and already done it

5:00 Costco for gas and cat food

6:00 leave for Lady Gaga

Kik app

ROMANTICSADISTLL:

I very much enjoy that you send images and videos. It makes me smile even more. And yes, I TOTALLY appreciate the apparently innocent but definitely knowing cleavage you displayed in the video for me. I've always loved that song 🩶

Send a picture of what you're planning to wear to Gaga. Give me an option, and I will choose for you.

WILLDIVE4PLANTS:

👀 There's that damn choked-up feeling again. Thank you, and yes, Sir.

Also, I sent my schedule to the other app. Do you prefer this one, Sir?

ROMANTICSADISTLL:

I'm thinking of scrapping both apps. Signal should be good for PC and phone and looks like we can call and video. Which I do enjoy HEARING you say Yes, Sir 🩶

WILLDIVE4PLANTS:

Oh! K! Sounds good. So that means you have no reason to check the OTHER-other app then. (*cough Feeld app *cough) So you can just like… forget that one exists and just go straight to this BRILLIANT idea of yours, since you have absolutely no need to check the other one anymore, Sir. 😄

I took a break to run to the café and get a shake, and there was a guy there on his computer wearing a backward cap like you, and I definitely almost had a heart attack, Sir 😌

ROMANTICSADISTLL:

LOL that means things are going well. I want your body to react at the very thought of me.

And nope. Nooooo reason at all. In fact, I'll just delete it without even opening it again.

WILLDIVE4PLANTS:

Gif: Marie from Aristocrats fluffing her fur

*screenshot of Feeld app screen

Terminate Account

What was the main reason to terminate your Feeld account?

() I had some Privacy or Safety concerns

() I had some issues with my connections or Feeld community

() I don't understand how Feeld works or what it can do for me

() I've found something that better caters to my need

(✔) Other: I manifested one of my fictional Doms into a real person and he happened to be the guy I had a crush on at the gym. Nothing could possibly top that, so time to go 🖐

ROMANTICSADISTLL:

Gif: Fifty Shades of Gray. Christian lifting Ana's chin.

LOL I gotta do that

WILLDIVE4PLANTS:

🫠 I just know me, Sir. I won't do this again, so no need to take up space on my phone.

Also, you're damn right I screenshot your profile photo to keep before I deleted my account, since you're also like my heroes who for all intents and purposes don't exist, their identities completely erased from the internet by the all-powerful tech guru at the Vatican, Sir 😜

ROMANTICSADISTLL:

LOL! Of course. But I'll also send you all the selfies you want, little one.

Chapter Eleven

SIENNA

"What are you going to wear?" Vi asks, and my face heats, but it's definitely not because of the blow dryer I have aimed at my head as I brush my hair straight.

"Uhhh… I'm not sure," I reply, thinking, *Because Zen hasn't picked which one he likes best yet.* The thought brings a secret smile to my lips, because I can't remember how many times I've written this exact situation, a Dom choosing which outfit for his sub to wear, either because he enjoyed that extra little bit of control and receiving obedience, or because—like in my case—*decisions are fucking hard, and I don't wanna!*

So just like my fantasy Doms, as if I manifested one and brought him to life, without me saying a single thing about having to pick what to wear to see Lady Gaga tonight, he just *knew*. He knew this was a decision I'd eventually spend a stupid amount of time struggling over, and he just cut that right out before I even had a chance to think about it and took it off my plate.

I swear to God.

I wonder if this man has actually secretly read my books and is getting ideas from them for Dominating me.

"Me neither," Vi replies from my phone, where she's doing her makeup at her vanity while we're on FaceTime.

"The black one," comes a deep, familiar voice through the earbuds I have in, so I can hear what Vi's saying while my blow dryer is making its loud ruckus, and I glance at the screen propped against my bathroom mirror.

Vi is now looking over her shoulder, and in the background, I can make out her husband on the opposite side of their bed. He's got his hands on his hips, a serious look on his face as he stares down at whatever's on top of their fluffy white comforter. His black baseball cap—facing forward, unlike the way Zen wears his—tilts up then, and I watch his face immediately go soft when he sees Vi is looking back at him.

"The black catsuit, baby girl," he repeats, and I turn off my dryer. "It'll look great with your dark hair pulled back in a super-straight ponytail. And then after the concert, when you drop the kids off at your parents', then all you'll have to do is put on the cat mask and come straight to the club." And then his eyes leave her to look at me on her screen.

"She's gonna look smokin', Sienna. You won't leave her side, will ya?"

I grin at him. "You can count on me, Corb. Should I be her incognito bodyguard, or should I play her fake lesbian lover? It *is* a Lady Gaga concert after all, bro. We were born this way, babe." I hold my hands up in the claw-like gesture all Lady Gaga fans use to show they're her "Little Monsters."

He chuckles. "I saw you trying out that kickboxing class at the gym earlier. 'Lesbian lover' would be much more convincing, so we'll go with that. But only because I know you'd never actually try to touch my girl that way."

"I'm right here, you two," Vi inserts, but we both pretend to ignore her.

I shake my head. "Nope. I might try to steal her from you, but I'd have to give her back every once in a while for her to get any sort of sexual satisfaction. Vaginas creep me out. That's all up to you, dude." I lean toward my phone so I fill the camera, looking at Vi now when she spins to face me again. "I'm an ally, a total advocate for all humans—and I guess those who identify as non-human too—but Vi, please keep your nether regions away from me, please and thanks."

Vi lets out a laugh she covers with her hand before shaking her head. "I can take care of myself. Jeez. I'll be in mama bear mode, remember? The kids will be with us."

Corbin's head pops up over her shoulder, making me let out a laugh of my own.

"All I'm saying is all of us guys have to be on duty this evening until we can meet up with you two at Club Alias after your show, so there won't be anyone watching over you from a distance," he says for the twenty-sixth time in the past two days, ever since he got booked for a security gig. "Like, for real this time. Not just saying that so you don't get annoyed that you have security in stealth mode. So stay together, keep your pepper spray in your hand while walking outside all the way from and back to your car, and remember to always scream every cuss word you can think of instead of 'help,' because people will always look *toward* fighting words before anything that might make their own flight instinct go off."

"Yes, Daddy," Vi replies sassily, looking at me while she says it before rolling her eyes, knowing damn well her husband can see every bit of that on her phone.

Before I can even blink, Corbin's tattooed hand is wrapped around my bestie's throat, her eyes widening for a split second before closing as he uses the grip to tilt her head all the way back to look at him upside down. I smirk, not feeling awkward in the slightest, because this is *so* them all the freaking time. Plus, when you're a member of a BDSM club and see people doing literally every sex act you can think of—and some you never even imagined before seeing it right in front of you—PDA doesn't exactly set off your "Look away!" button anymore.

"What was that, baby girl?" he prompts, his voice a low

timbre that sends chills up my arms as I watch Vi practically melt into her chair.

The same way I melted on Zen's chest last night after he pulled me up his body and kissed me in a way that had me panting and so slick I had to immediately come home and use my vibrator for the first time in *months*.

"We'll be careful, Sir," she murmurs, and this does make my face heat and glance away, because she says that respectful moniker in a voice as breathy as I'm sure mine was when Zen had me say it while following his orders less than twenty-four hours ago.

Naked.

In his fancy Transformers truck.

While he told me nonstop how much I was pleasing him.

As I gave him a blowjob that *I* freaking initiated.

Because, Jesus on a cracker, I just had to know what *he* felt like, what that monster between his legs felt like, and just my hands wasn't enough to fully appreciate the man I was obscenely attracted to. So my mouth was added to get a better sense—literally, by adding taste to touch—of the overwhelming Dom I was now officially a sub-in-training to.

Just the fact he asked that of me was astounding in itself —*He really knows his shit!*—and made me want to take this amazing journey with him.

A lot of BDSM romance novels don't lay out the different steps of a D/s relationship, but I try to include bits and pieces in each of my novels so my readers can learn a little something about the reality of this lifestyle, not just read it for the smut. There are guidelines that can be followed. They're not necessary; nothing in this lifestyle is.

It's not like the community will kick you out if you don't stick to a regimented list of rules, when that's the beauty of a D/s relationship in the first place. The rules are completely created by the people in it, and they're agreed upon by both (or all) of them. No one else can tell them something is wrong in their partnership if they've laid out exactly what is and isn't allowed.

But in a traditional guidelines sense, there are levels they can be on, or steps their relationship can take, especially if it doesn't start as a romantic relationship first. These can also be identified by the types of collar the submissive wears.

First, there's the Collar of Consideration. To apply a vanilla-world term to this D/s stage, one could call this "talking." Not quite dating, but the getting to know you stage. This collar can be used when an already established vanilla couple is considering adding a D/s element to their relationship. A lot of times, it's a Play Collar the potential sub will wear while role playing. But most of the time, at least from what I've seen, there's not an actual collar at all. Maybe a necklace or some other piece of jewelry that's symbolic to the couple.

A Collar of Consideration can also be used when a Dominant and submissive who are not in a vanilla/romantic relationship are first learning about each other, the courting part before anything sexual happens between them, until after they've tested their chemistry in some way to decide whether they'd like to be in a partnership. Zen and I had this stage—just without an actual collar—but it was an online courtship before our "vibe test" last night.

And then during our conversation into the wee early-morning hours after I got home, that's when he offered me his rules to become his sub-in-training, and I accepted. Which means I accepted to metaphorically wear his "Training Collar" and took our relationship to the next level.

In the BDSM community, this would be considered the equivalent to a boyfriend and girlfriend relationship. Officially dating. No awkward stage of wondering "what are we?" For him to lay out his rules and me to agree, and then for him to accept the nickname I wanted to call him, that placed the "Training Collar" securely around my neck, no question about it. And it means I'm now in the phase where I get to learn everything there is to know about Zen, as far as what he wants from a submissive goes, and at the same time, he'll be doing the same, learning what I like and what my needs are from a Dominant.

In a perfect world, he'd tell me what he desires, and if it's not something I consider any kind of limit—something I don't like or just plain will not do—he'd teach me exactly how he'd like that certain desire to be fulfilled. He'd leave no room for confusion, so I can't "mess up." Utterly blissful for a submissive like me, who doesn't want the burden of making decisions.

Tell me exactly how you want it, and I'll do it. Don't make me ask a million questions to get the full picture of what you need from me. Spell it out, step by step, and by God, I will do it in a heartbeat, happily, and present it to you on a silver platter.

But I better get my fucking praise after you see I did it perfectly.

Which is something a Dom is learning from his sub while she's in training—how she wants to be treated, what she considers a reward or a punishment... not to be confused with a *fun*ishment. It's an incredibly important stage in any D/s relationship, because it will establish whether or not they *fit*.

Art and I... we didn't fit. He's a true sadist, and I don't have enough masochistic wants to *take* what he needs to *give*. I was holding him back, and at the same time, I was also trying hard to be something I'm not, just to please him. We weren't a good match.

By agreeing to be Zen's sub in training, I'll get a fresh start in more than one way. We aren't a boyfriend and girl-friend who are now going to try to add some kinky fuckery to our already established relationship. There's not going to be any situation where I put a limit on something, and he goes "What do you mean you don't wanna do that? We've been doing it for years!" I also won't have to feel awkward about trying something new, because I'm not in this set mold where everything would seem out of my element.

It's like the kid with the bad reputation—or the one who's constantly bullied—getting to move to a whole new school to start over, to reinvent themselves. But while a lot of people would use that as a chance to keep hidden what they let show that didn't have a good reception previously, this is the perfect opportunity for me to just *be me*. I won't be trying to mold myself to fit what someone else wants. I'll just be *myself*, be honest about my likes and dislikes, and we'll see if what I'm happily willing to give lines up with what Zen needs to receive—and vice versa, since it's a power *exchange*, not just a one-sided job with no benefits.

And that's when the relationship can move to the next level.

That's when a Dom can offer their sub-in-training a Permanent Collar.

While a lot of people take this literally, as in a 24/7, locking collar they can't take off without a key, it's also the term used to describe "being officially collared." It has the same significance as a wedding ring. It means you belong to one another, a bond as strong if not stronger than marriage. I say this because there are some D/s relationships I've seen that transcend anything I've ever seen in a vanilla marriage before, even if that marriage has lasted a happy fifty years. They know and trust each other so deeply they don't even have to speak to understand exactly what the other person is thinking.

Being collared this way is a big deal. It's not something one just jumps into for funzies. And it's to be taken seriously, not just by the people in the relationship, but by everyone in the community. That collar is a symbol of ownership, in a way that's much stricter than a wedding ring. Lots of people see a wedding ring and blow it off, not caring if someone they want is married. They'll still go after them, try to get them to cheat, with no respect for the piece of metal on their finger.

In the BDSM community, though, a collar around a sub's neck is not something to fuck with. People who live this lifestyle understand that a permanent collar is not something given lightly. It's not a friendship bracelet. It's not something that can be faked. It's not something to be done for any type of convenience, like an arranged marriage might be. That collar was given and accepted because that's what both people wanted, so it should be respected.

And I freaking love that about this world I'm a part of, because everyone I've ever met in it understands that and lives by it. If someone doesn't, word spreads fast. The openness of this community also means it's very hard to keep bad behavior hidden. All I'd have to do as a sub-in-training—or even before this stage—is ask one of Zen's former subs if he's someone I can trust. I could ask her things like if he respects safewords, if there are red flags I should watch out for, and personal things like why they went their separate ways, if it's something I should be aware of.

I mean… that is, *if* he weren't in total stealth mode on the internet and I could find a damn thing about him.

Just then, my phone dings, and I see the banner pull down from the top of my screen showing it's a notification from the man himself.

ROMANTICSADIST:

The green floral one… with the red wig I see hanging in the background. It's Gaga, so might as well go all out and have a hot Poison Ivy vibe. I expect pictures, my little plant princess.

"What's that face?" Vi asks me like she always does when I turn off my ears and instead start listening to the voices inside my head.

But this time, that's not what happened. A giddy smile took over my expression when I saw his name and what he chose, and I didn't bother trying to hide it. Observant and considerate as fuck, and he just so happened to choose the perfect partner-in-crime outfit to go with Vi's Catwoman that Corbin picked out for her without even knowing it.

"I have a lot to catch you up on tonight, bestie. But for now, just know Plant Daddy has been procured," I tell her, because earlier, before I snapped a pic of the three outfits I have laying across my bed and sent them to Zen, he ordered that I wasn't to dumpster dive anymore. And before I could very promptly revoke all consent for him to tell me what to do when I'm not naked, he informed me it was because he'd just stick all the plants that were to be thrown away in his truck instead of tossing them in the trash.

Somehow he knew that would mean more to me than buying me fresh ones.

But instead of looking giddy right along with me, her face falls, and she pouts. "But what about Sir Jeremy? I thought you were going to talk to him. That meet cute would've been freaking adorable to tell at your wedding, and it would've all been thanks to me if y'all got your happily ever after!"

"Baby, this isn't one of your books. If Sienna found someone she likes without your help, you shouldn't give her shit for it. You should be happy for her," Corbin tells her, and she glares at him in the reflection of her mirror.

Before my BFF can get herself into trouble, I jump in and let her know, "It'll still be thanks to you if we get a happily ever after, Vi. I met him on one of the dating sites, and it was your idea for me to join them." I don't tell her it also happens to be Gym Daddy... who also turned out to be Dumpster Daddy, because I have *got* to see her face in person to get the full effect of her reaction when she finds out.

That seems to pacify her enough I feel I'm in the clear to hang up without her receiving a spanking that would have her complaining all night about how uncomfortable it is to sit at the concert later.

But I gotta leave her with a little teaser, because after all,

I'm not called the Cliffhanger Queen by my readers for no reason.

"Gotta go. Need to put on what *Zaddy* chose for me to wear!"

I click the End button just as her eyes go wide and she squawks something I don't hear clearly. But she's probably dying, now that she knows whoever I found on a dating site is a Dom, and not only that, but he's a Dom I've given consent to, to send me orders.

Chapter Twelve

SIENNA

Just after midnight, Vi and I strut into Club Alias and strike a pose as if we expect paparazzi to start swarming. Really, it's just her husband Corbin—Sarge, since we're inside where we use our aliases—Seth, aka Seven, his wife Twyla, aka Doll, Brian, aka Knight, and Clarice, aka... well... I don't know which of her two roles she is tonight. And now that I think about it, I don't know what she prefers other people to call her at the club, because usually she and the big guy disappear into a playroom too quickly to worry about it. I know he calls her Mistress whenever she's topping, but I've never actually heard what he refers to her as whenever she's bottoming.

Weird.

Brian is Knight to me either way, since I'm a full-time submissive, and his role as a part-time Dom—plus the fact that he's like ten feet tall and could squish me like a bug—automatically keeps him in that Dominant position when it comes to what I respectfully refer to him as.

Also, now that my mind is off on this tangent, us girls don't really call each other by our given nicknames at all. I don't think I've ever spoken to Twyla here at Club Alias and been like, "Want a drink, Doll?" That would feel awkward for some reason. It's like... that's *her husband's* special name for her, so no one else should call her that. No, I'd just ask her without a moniker. But falling deeper into this rabbit hole, if I needed to find her, I *would* ask someone, "Have you seen Seven's Doll anywhere?"

Double weird.

Anyway, *squirrel.* No paparazzi, just the whole gang hanging out in one of the huge leather booths next to the dance floor. But Clarice doesn't disappoint. Being the professional photographer she is, she pulls out her ever-present camera and snaps photos of Vi—who's just "bestie" in my head no matter where we are—and me as we pose, then turn and strike another, and another, and we all burst out laughing when suddenly Madonna's "Vogue" starts playing throughout the club. We turn to look over at the DJ booth, smiling and waving back when Dixie, one of the bartenders, and her husband Mikolas lift their hands to greet us with big grins.

Vi slides into the booth next to Sarge, bumping his hip to make him scoot enough I can sit on the end.

"How was the show? You two look great!" Twyla chirps across the table.

"Freaking awesome!" we yell in unison, laughing once again. I swear, sometimes, it's like we're the same person.

"That woman can sing her ass off," Vi says, and I nod.

"And speaking of her ass, holy hell. She's now my booty goals. I never noticed what a great one she has until it was displaying across all the big screens in the stadium in all her crazy costumes. I googled it on the way here, and it's actually a thing. People ask her all the time in interviews what her booty workout routine is!" I say as I take out my phone, click on the picture I saved of Lady Gaga's butt, and then spin it around to show everyone at the table.

"Daaamn," Twyla and Clarice drawl, leaning in to take a closer look, but the guys pay no attention. Apparently they have no interest in another woman's ass, even if it is just a photo of a celebrity's.

That's sweet, I think, a teensy spark of jealousy mixed in with the genuine happiness I feel for the other ladies.

I wish I had someone who was so completely happy with me that they didn't feel the temptation to even glimpse at anyone else.

And more than that, I wish I wasn't so insecure that I even give a shit if my man simply looks at another woman. That's just being a human. I can see and appreciate the way a guy looks without feeling a single twinge of attraction, so why is it so hard for me to believe a man can do the same thing?

Or maybe I can, but just not when that man is mine.

I have no problem believing Corbin, Seth, and Brian can be surrounded by all these incredibly beautiful, erotically sexy, and literally freaking *naked* women, and not pop a boner once. But if it were a guy here with *me?* It's impossible for me to think they'd even remember I'm in the building.

I'm suddenly jarred from my self-deprecating thoughts when Vi elbows me, and I click the button to put my cell to sleep as I turn my head to look at her.

"What?" I prompt, seeing the wicked sparkle in her eyes surrounded by the black cat mask.

She nudges her chin in the direction of the bar. "Look who's here."

My brows furrow beneath my green mask made of lace that looks like foliage, and I turn my head quickly enough a few strands of my red wig get stuck in my lip gloss. I'm blowing air our between my lips, making spitting raspberry sounds as I try to get the hair out of my mouth, when my eyes finally land on who she's most definitely referring to up at the bar.

Because they're currently angled in our direction as they lean against the gleaming wooden countertop, the nightclub lighting playing across that exact spot at the same moment our eyes meet.

Well... not exactly. I can't see the eyes hidden inside the sexy black hood that hangs all the way down to the impossibly wide shoulders. But I can feel them on me as if they were mere inches away in the bright sunlight.

I gulp.

Literally gulp.

And my heart gives a hard thump before it feels like it just stops beating all together.

Sir Jeremy.

And he's staring right at me, no question about it.

I don't know how I know his attention is directed solely on me. Maybe because I'm the weirdo in the bright, almost neon-green getup in an ocean of pitch-black and blood-red. Or maybe it's the flaming red wig covering my dark length and blonde tips. But suddenly I feel like I stand out like a sore thumb instead of blending right in while I was in this same outfit at the concert just an hour ago, and I immediately start to fold in on myself.

Stopping mid-slump when my phone buzzes in my hand, scaring the shit out of me.

Everyone at the booth is mid-conversation, including Vi, so God only knows how long I was actually staring over at Sir Jeremy like a freaking psycho. But I open my cell with my code, since it doesn't recognize me with my mask on, and see it's a message from Zen.

And then my heart that had given up on its duty to keep me alive mere minutes ago suddenly explodes into action as if my nipples were connected to jumper cables when I read what it says.

ROMANTICSADIST:

Uh, uh, uh, little one. Sit up tall and
proud. A sub represents her Dom at
all times, even when he's not around
her. And my beautiful girl doesn't
want anyone to view her Dom as
meek and insecure, does she?

My eyes widen, my mouth falling open as I read the
message again and again.

He's here? That's what that means, right? Zen is here,
and he's watching me?

My head snaps up, and I look around to see if any of
the Doms have a phone in their hand. When my sight lands
on Sir Jeremy once again, he's still facing my direction, and
I still get the feeling his eyes are on me. No one up at the bar
is using their phone, but there are a few men in the all-black
uniform the Dominants here wear, standing along the edges
of the dancefloor and sitting at the different tables and
booths, I see with their phone screens alighting the masks
over their faces.

My attention is pulled back to my own screen when it
vibrates in my hand.

ROMANTICSADIST:

Out of your head, princess. There's
only room for me in here right now.
Just do as your told and enjoy the
quiet, knowing I've got you.
Understand?

My mind immediately fills with the image of me lying

atop Zen's chest after he gave me our first kiss. The feel of his strong arms wrapped around me, his hands stroking my back and lulling me into a state of relaxation I'd never been able to reach before. The blissful silence inside my mind, no voices, just the dull recognition of the ocean sounds still lightly playing over his truck's system.

A smile tugs at my lips, and I type out my response. I can overthink this later. Right now, I need to follow my Dom's order.

SIENNA:

Yes, Sir.

ROMANTICSADIST:

That's my good girl.

The quick, simple message makes me feel floaty, as if I fill with helium and lift up toward the ceiling. Really though, I just sit up tall, my back nice and straight like he told me to.

Chapter Thirteen

FROM FELIX AND SIENNA'S MESSAGES

7:10 a.m. – 11:11 a.m.

Google Chat

ROMANTICSADIST:

Message me on signal. (phone number)

SIENNA:

Umm... I texted the phone number you sent, and it started acting weird, Sir.

ROMANTICSADIST:

INVITE: Message Me on Signal

SIENNA:

Oh that's a thing. I thought you were saying when I got signal yesterday, as in my signal sucks in the locker room. 🙈

Signal app

SIENNA:

Good morning, Sir.

I just opened one eye so far, Sir

ZEN:

VERY good girl, little one! Now we can text, call, and maybe video chat all in one place, and I can delete all these other apps off my phone. Too many places to check could mean missing something important, so better to keep it all together.

SIENNA:

Aww! Your profile name says Zen?! Now it can be like I'm actually talking to my favorite voice in my head, and I'll have evidence when he talks back! LOL! Fancy, sir 😌

ZEN:

Thought you might like that.

SIENNA:

I have a question, Sir. Yesterday, you sent me a selfie, and it looked like you were wearing scrubs. May I ask, Sir, what your occupation was before you started working at the hardware store?

I mean, you could tell me a taxidermist, and I wouldn't care. Just, you know, artistic minds, Sir. Helps me paint a picture of you in my head.

ZEN:

Work in the ER. Still do. Day job.

Just got to the gym

SIENNA:

On my way now! But I need to shower. I just went straight to bed when I got home last night.

I mean, of course you did, Sir *gulps

Now the whole fixing my hand thing makes way more sense. Never thought I'd be the one with a hot nurse fantasy.

I can't believe you're a Club Alias member! I mean, I totally can. I had the thought from the beginning that you should've been, but holy hell. That was the best surprise ever, Sir!

Ok, you haven't checked your messages in a while, so ummm... I'll just... be in the shower, Sir.

ZEN:

You failed to send your schedule and goals today. Every morning, you are to send a good morning along with your proposed schedule and goals.

SIENNA:

Oh shit. I'm sorry, Sir. I just now pulled myself out of a shower breakdown. I'll promise I'll do better tomorrow, Sir.

I'm fine now, Sir, just so you know. Auditory overload while waiting for my meds to kick in. I warned you I should be in a padded room, Sir.

Well, I *said* I was fine... until I just discovered my noise-canceling headphones are dead. FML.

At least they quiet shit down a little bit just by being over my ears, Sir. Coming up to the workout floor now.

ZEN:

I'm glad you agreed to meet that first time. Are you telling me without words that you don't want to meet again? Bratty comments, not meeting goals or following commands... That doesn't sound like a sub who wants to be mastered. But if that's not what you're trying to convey, and you continue on that path, your jaw will be sore from the amount of dick sucking it'll take to make up for your disobedience. Might not be able to sit down from that little ass being bright red, then you'll placed in what I like to call "forced focus." Mouth open, hands tied behind your back, cock down your throat as far as I can right before you gag. Almost can't breathe around it. Definitely can't swallow your spit. You will sit like that... not sucking, just my dick deep in your mouth and your eyes focused up to me (which itself is difficult and uncomfortable in that position). And you'll sit just like that while I reiterate how you are to behave and what is expected of you. Then, as your neck strains from the position, jaw starts to lock, drool persistently running from your mouth, your mind and body screaming in your head to move, hands wishing to be free, if you fight your instincts and stay still as commanded, you will be freed. If you cannot properly repeat what you were told and graciously thank me for your lesson, then eagerly work that skilled little mouth of yours to best please me, I will have to unfortunately come up with something not so pleasant. Am I crystal, little girl?

SIENNA:

Super green, sir.

ZEN:

It's a good thing your mouth gets such a workout and is so, so strong from all your bratty responses, because getting oral is my favorite. And by hard-limiting your no-no, you'll be putting that porn-star upper half to work to please me. I expect you to say you're eager and happy to do so.

SIENNA:

It's not my mouth, Sir. It's these damn fingers. I'd never be able to speak this shit out loud, Sir.

I just almost fell off the treadmill laughing at no-no How you gonna use that name for it in the midst of all the filth?

And I'm eager and happy to do so, Sir, but also fucking terrified. That's... a lot. And I'm not just talking about a lot of cock, Sir. That's just a bonus.

ZEN:

SIENNA:

How did you almost make me pee with just one emoji?!

ZEN:

See? I'm going to take this as you're nervous joking sarcasm instead of backtalk... Because if that were the case, you might be in that position until you damn near black out. But being in my field, I have no fear about making you pass out, since I can just as easily bring you back.

SIENNA:

Fuck.

You made me clench, Sir

100% nervous joking, Sir

I'm already shaking

I just thought of a hard limit, but I don't see you doing it anyway, Sir

ZEN:

You will eventually behave and be taught to please me appropriately with enthusiasm, even if I have to tie you in position, harness you, and take my pleasure until your body is on autopilot, with your mind trapped just watching and asking for the ride.

SIENNA:

THAT. Yes, Sir.

Hard limit: I can't stand being yelled at. It freaks me the fuck out... like instantly, Sir. I think that's why I really, really, really enjoyed the way you spoke to me in person, Sir.

ZEN:

FML

SIENNA:

What?!

Physical pain doesn't scare me, Sir.

But after just coming out of a panic attack in the shower from being overstimulated with too much noise, it made me realize I can voice that to you, and I'm allowed to set it as a limit. I've never had that opportunity before to just be like, don't do that.

I mean, I guess I could've, but I would've felt bad about it.

ZEN:

Your ass is asking for your mind to be trapped. I knew that it never shuts off, but you spiral faster than I first thought.

Are you allowed bruises? Enjoy needles? Do you like to bleed?

SIENNA:

Well... Yes, Sir.

See? I just showed way more improvement, if you knew what I *wanted* to say, Sir.

Whatever you want, Sir. I freak out when I have to get my blood drawn, but now that I think about it, if it were you doing it, I don't think it'd be so bad. Never tried any of it for pleasure, but I'm not much of a masochist, Sir.

ZEN:

LOL carte blanche, say you're pierced

SIENNA:

Fuck no! I have a hard enough battle trying to orgasm. I wouldn't risk hitting a nerve that would take away all possibility, Sir.

ZEN:

What nerve? Hitting one of mine or yours?

SIENNA:

Mine! You asked if I was pierced, Sir 😆

ZEN:

Say your PIECE is what it was supposed to say, as in I was going to allow your remark.

SIENNA:

Oh!

I thought "DUH!" to "your mind doesn't shut off" or however you said it.

But that would've been too disrespectful, even for my fingers, Sir

Oh hey, look! I just did double what I did on day one, thanks to your distraction, Sir. But now I see the pretty lights again, so I'm going to sit.

Know that feeling when you get off a trampoline and you try to jump, Sir? FML

ZEN:

Sweet girl... you did so good. And no, I can't completely shut off your mind, but I can do things to you that will make the voices quiet and your head get all fuzzy 😈

Yelling won't happen. It's a brutish, uncontrolled, mindless response. I prefer quiet with the deepening of the voice and direct eye contact, looking into your soul so that even in the afterlife you will not forget what you were told.

SIENNA:

Jesus fuck. I think I just came.

So like... you're pretty perfect, huh, Sir?

Someone just sat down in front of me while I was looking down at my phone, and I definitely had another heart attack thinking it was you, Sir

ZEN:

Not perfect by a long shot. Don't
have to be. My crazy just has to
align with yours.

SIENNA:

Well then what's that saying, Sir?
Your demons would play well with
mine?

ZEN:

I hope so. I kinda like yours so far.

SIENNA:

Well that's reassuring, Sir. 😊

ZEN:

I'm finishing up in the shower. Get
us coffee, cream and sugar for me
with two cubes of ice.

SIENNA:

Gasp! A task! I just perked right up
from where I was dying in the cafe.
Which cream and how many/what
kind of sugar, Sir?

ZEN:

Good girl. Vanilla, actually LOL!
Regular sugar. The ice is because
it'll be too hot 🐱

SIENNA:

Same flavor for mine, Sir. OMG 🐱
Not the princess emoji! Lol!

And I normally forget about hot
coffee so long it turns cold anyway,
so I just skip straight to iced, Sir.

ZEN:

Walk out the door... straight back.

SIENNA:

Adding caffeine to the shakes. Lezz gooo! 😅

ZEN:

Don't worry. Can't keep you long, little one.

And your lesson for your brattiness will not be today, since I know you have to finish your book. Back of the Hummer, and you'll just start my day off right 🤍

Chapter Fourteen

FELIX

She had caught me off guard with her question. How could I have made such a reckless mistake, snapping her a selfie and sending it to the little sub when she said she missed my face yesterday. I hadn't thought twice about it, just hit the camera button right on the app, took the picture, and sent it through.

It didn't even occur to me who I was dealing with.

Literally the most observant person I've ever met in my life. Some would call that a superpower, but Sienna finds it a curse. She'd love nothing more than to be mindless to every minor detail her brain hyperfixates on.

So of course she would notice the cut of my solid black shirt—a scrub top—and now that I pull up the selfie itself, I can make out there are blurry white words at the very bottom edge of the photo that are easily recognized as an embroidered nametag, even though you can't actually tell what it says.

I was pissed at myself for the slip, but I refused to lie to her.

I'm just relieved she mistakenly thought I meant I'm a nurse, I assume because I called it my "day job." It wouldn't occur to her that a full-time medical doctor would work as much as one does and then also have an evening job at a home improvement store.

But my anger at myself simmered in my blood while I worked out. I pushed myself harder than I usually go on my chest, trying to burn off the frustration, but it didn't work. And ended up taking it out on the one who has me so caught up in her that I wasn't as careful as I always, *always* am.

I had been typing out my long-ass message when hers about panicking in the shower came through, so I didn't see it until I'd worked myself up even more with all things I wanted to do to her. I spelled it all out, everything I'd enjoy putting her through, if only I had a good enough excuse. I'd never wanted a sub to be disobedient before.

But then when I finally did read her message and her following responses, the anger and frustration at myself fizzled, my focus turning more toward the woman who needed her Dom's attention on helping her, not on him getting twisted pleasure from giving her a taste of what I'm capable of.

So I shook off the lingering tension and switched my

mindset from overpowering alpha to protective Primal Dom, distracting her from what was overwhelming and crippling her and activating her need to please. A task of getting coffee would give her something simple to focus on, something nearly impossible for her to mess up—especially when she impressively asked how I like my coffee instead of guessing or wasting a bunch of time worrying about it once she was trying to walk out the door to meet me. This way I can give her lots of earned praise, not reward her bad behavior of not following her everyday command to send me her schedule and goals.

Now, I look out my window to see the little sub balancing two stacked coffee cups in one hand, holding them steady with her chin, while she reads my message on her phone in the other. I hold my breath, knowing my girl is the embodiment of an early-2000s rom-com heroine, and pray she doesn't trip.

Literally the only way she could fail this task—dropping the coffee.

By the time she makes it to the car parked two spots away from me, I can't stand it any longer. But one would never be able to tell the anxiety I feel before I reach out and take the top coffee from beneath her chin, smoothly reaching out my other arm to open the back door for her.

She gives me a nervous smile, apparently unable to speak again now that we're face-to-face, and I take the other coffee out of her hand without a word as she gets up into the Hummer, the back seats flat like they were a couple of nights ago but with the front seats still in their upright position. When she crawls to the back and gets into position, on her knees, ass on her heels, I lift a brow, my eyes purposefully pausing on her closed legs before meeting her shy gaze.

"Oh! Sorry," she murmurs, her knees spreading a few inches apart, and then she reaches out both her arms toward me.

Something about it makes me go soft toward the woman. The innocent mistake she immediately fixed, remembering the command and knowing what she wasn't doing correctly, the sweet, makeup-free face that looks up at me with awe but also unease, not knowing what to expect. And when she opened her arms like that, holding them out to me, my first instinct was to lean forward and let her wrap them around my neck, to bury my face in the side of hers and breathe her in, to murmur in her ear that I missed her presence and am happy I get to see her before I have to go to work.

But I'm able to catch myself before I even move an inch, because she makes a grabbing motion with her hands, and I realize she's actually just offering to hold the two coffees while I climb inside the truck.

I don't know what's going on with my careful control of every aspect of my life. I don't know how this woman catches me off guard, plays and beats me without even really meaning to, and entices me more with her genuine eagerness to learn and please than any perfectly trained sub before her.

But there have been too many coincidences along this path.

I don't have the same mind as someone who fights and fights against something being real just because they can't see it clearly right before their eyes.

That doesn't make sense to me.

One or two "coincidences" between people, okay. Reasonable doubt.

More than that though—like I said, it doesn't make sense to me.

It makes *more* sense that other forces are at play, since I'm not one to care I can't see the force with my shifty eyes.

Perception is reality, just like I told her.

And right now, what I want to perceive more than anything—as she smiles sweetly when I hand her the two paper cups—is this little sub as *mine*.

Chapter Fifteen

A GLIMPSE INTO THE FUTURE

Club Alias Members Community
Sienna's Public Diary Entry #3

I have to write this down before my intrusive thoughts ruin it. I want to remember how it really happened forever.

I was so excited to see Zen today, craving his presence, that my usual shyness didn't even bother popping up her ridiculous little head when she sensed he was near. I got his command ("Get in, little one" 😊) and hopped out of my car and over to his, juggling his hot coffee, my iced Chai, and a cup of ice in case his drink was too hot. (Star Student)

Like the fucking gentleman he is (*dreamy sigh) he got out and opened the door for me, taking the hot coffee from me so I could climb in without disaster happening—which he knows I'm prone to, yet he still adores me for some reason. 🌿

Like the good girl he's training me to be, I took off my top and my shorts, leaving me in a new set of undies I bought to wear just for him. It's almost a bubble-gum-pink, maybe a little lighter, and I must say I felt a little confident in it. Weird for me—the only thing I'm usually self-confident in is my job. The bralette, in its pretty pink, is sheer, completely unlined, and with him so close, standing... right... there... my nipples were hard and clearly visible. Yet somehow I didn't feel the urge to cover myself.

Normally, I'm to undress down to my panties and get into the position he taught me he likes—on my knees, legs spread, head down (although I think he added that one for my own comfort, since it's a lot for me to make eye contact) arms behind my back, and "tits presented." 🙂 But this time, he must've sensed how excited I was to wrap myself like a gift to give to him, because he told me to keep the bra on.

Against my tan, and combined with the matching lacy thong, I felt... sexy.

Yeah.

ME.

The girl who was picked on her whole life for being so thin, no curves to speak of, who found it impossible to feel like a "real woman" because "boys like a little more booty to hold at night" and NOT a "stick-figure, silicone Barbie doll." (Thanks for that, Meghan Trainor)

But let me tell you, Zen seems to REALLY like my perfect, full-D silicone fucking tits, so suck my lady dick, Meghan.

And the way he likes me to sit, back arched, my ass resting on my heels, my knees spread... it gives me that feminine curve whether I have any or not. It widens my hips, giving his big, strong hands something to grip after he smooths those masculine palms over my flesh, making me shiver every single time.

I was eager to start his day on a positive note. He's told me numerous times now that his stressful days are so much more tolerable when he takes the time to let me... enjoy his company😊... at the beginning of each one.

I had no expectations for myself today. NONE whatsoever. I'm still sore from begging him to make me forget my bad day a couple days ago, which he did so very impressively and selflessly. At least it seems selfless to me—but he insists he gains pleasure from just giving it to me.

Is he real?

Surely I've died somewhere along one of my disaster-riddled paths and have been sent to some kinky Heaven, where I'm now rewarded for being such a good girl during my life, which never got recognized while I was actually breathing.

Worth it.

Back to this morning—I was there to give him the morning he deserves. Delicious coffee, visual stimulation with my adorable new lingerie, and his addictive cock in my mouth.

And yes, all that happened.

God, did it happen.

But what I wasn't expecting was to be ordered to turn around, finally take my bralette off, and then to bend all the way down, head and shoulders to the floor with my ass up.

I did it without hesitation, but God, for the first time with Zen, I REALLY wanted to question what was happening. He knew how sore I was. The day before, I couldn't even stand tight panties against my wonderfully abused flesh. I couldn't even tolerate the feel of a razor gliding over my sensitive skin. I apologized profusely as I bent over, "I'm sorry I'm not as smooth as I usually am for you, Sir. I was too sore, and when you said we'd give her a rest, I didn't think you'd be—"

My words ABRUPTLY cut off when suddenly... the gentlest touch. So gentle I didn't know if I'd actually felt it.

But there it was again.

Yes, I definitely felt... something. So light, so soft and light I didn't recognize it at first.

A fingertip? One coated in extra wetness so it wouldn't drag against my soreness?

And then I DID recognize it.

And my nervous breaths turned into shocked panting.

Because up until that moment, I had only felt Zen's touch my nipples. I had only felt *his* making me shiver as it teased my ear. I had only felt *his* running along *my own*.

His tongue.

It was his tongue tracing sweet paths along my aching core.

And even though my panic reared up, even though I almost, almost jumped up to tell him he didn't have to do that, his softly growled "That's my good girl. You taste so good" made me melt even more to the ground.

I wanted to cry.

How could he be so sweet to me?

I'm always astonished at how... *nice* he is to me.

I'm supposed to be there to please him. I'm supposed to be the one making HIM feel like he's king of the world.

And yet when I'm self-deprecating, he doesn't just do that usual "friendly" thing people do—"That's not true. Don't say that!". He speaks to me in a way I have never in all my years been spoken to before. He seems to dissect my self-deprecation and turns it around so that I can logically see how wrong I am. Not pretty words or platitudes, no. Not from my Zen.

My anxious fingers will type: "I outdid myself, huh, Sir? I managed to exhaust the inexhaustible? I've disappointed you in some way? Or my pain tolerance isn't high enough? Or I'm too insecure and just add to your stress instead of relieving it? I'm sorry, Sir."

And a while later, his words arrive like his finger beneath my chin, forcing my head up from where it's dipped in shame to look into his sincere, beautiful eyes: "My sweet, good little girl. I'm VERY happy with you. You have been SO obedient and attentive, just as I asked, INCREDIBLY sensual and sexy, and are ALREADY showing that what I'm training you to do, you'll do gladly. You've already shown much more confidence in such a short time, sending pictures I ask for. And I know you'll grow even more into both the pornstar pet and the full service submissive I desperately desire you to become."

My eyes will be teary—this new thing they do, when before I refused to cry over anything that wasn't a dog passing away in a movie—and his words won't just stop there. No, he has to overwhelm my intrusive thoughts. He has to bat them away until they're not just hiding in the shadows until he turns his back, but beat them so severely they never return during that particular subject ever again.

"You're such a good girl. Tell your voices to shut their cake hole because I DO want you, and YOU CAN NEVER, EVER MESSAGE ME TOO MUCH OR SEND TOO MANY PICTURES."

And it continued, but in his deep voice that makes me weak:

"When I open my messages and see you've sent so many, it makes me SO happy. It means you thought about me each and every time and had to let me know I was on your mind."

"I love when you see something that makes you think of me, and then you message to tell me about it. Most people will see something that reminds them of someone and just go about their day. YOU see it, then you rush to your phone to tell me about it so I can enjoy it too. Because obviously if it made you think of me, then it's probably something I'll like, baby."

And then it's like he'll sense a teensy bit more of my doubt holding on, so he delivers the final blow, making me laugh and feel owned and adored all at once:

"I open up my messages and go 'Aw, she's psycho, but she's *my* little psycho."

And that's all it takes.

See? *Nice.*

He gets me better than I get myself.

He acknowledges what I'm saying, what I'm trying to convey, and then he responds to it in a way that doesn't make me feel stupid or silly. He doesn't half-ass reply. He doesn't ignore my concerns. He doesn't automatically tell me my idea is dumb or that my answer is incorrect. He doesn't make it his life's mission to prove me wrong, like it feels everyone else in my life does.

And when he is critical, he does it in a way that doesn't embarrass me, doesn't humiliate or make me feel shamed. He corrects me without man-splaining. He's said over and over he loves my intelligence, and he proves he's not just saying that by the way he talks to me. He knows if he says something I don't quite understand, I won't be able to control the urge to ask him what it meant. THEN he delves deeper into explaining, and God, I could listen to him talk forever.

Shit.

I went off on a tangent. ("What's that? I should kill everyone and escape? Ha! Sorry. The voices...")

Where was I?

Ah, yes. His tongue.

It was his tongue soothing me, tasting me for the first time directly from the source—he'd licked his magical fingers clean after they'd been inside me before. (*whimpers) And there was still this little asshole voice chanting "you're not perfectly shaven smooth" and "you're making him think he needs to do this, and then he's going to *peace out* because it's YOU who's supposed to be doing it to HIM" and "you probably smell and taste like those brand-new panties you were too excited to wear and didn't wash first" followed by "yum, fabric dye and shipping container—exactly what he wants to be breathing in."

But again, he shut them up with his breath against my flesh as he spoke "you're so fucking sexy, sweet girl."

And the next thing I recollect is suddenly being on my back, stretching out long because—again—he could sense without words that my hips were hurting from being locked in position while I sucked his cock and then while I was spun around and he laid beneath me, healing me with his kisses. He ordered me to lie however it made my hips feel better, so I stretched my legs out straight, my feet on either side of his body.

I thought we were just going to talk for a little while—one of my very favorite things to do with him. He's so goddamn smart and funny with all sorts of stories to tell. He's a decade older than me, and God, no one has ever stimulated my mind and body the way he does.

It still makes me laugh and slap my forehead when I remember I told him not long after meeting him "Wow, you're actually smarter than me. That doesn't happen often with men."

Hold that thought.

I just got a message from him...

FML.

I had sent him a meme about how my zodiac tends to hide all their emotions so they're taken more seriously and looked at as a more logical being.

His response: "Hide from the rest of the world if you must.. Suppress nothing with me. I want all of you, all your love, all your hate, all your joys, all your fears, all your obedience, all the crazy... I want YOU and everything that comes with it. I will train you to be more you than you ever thought possible."

One moment please. I need to catch my breath.

Okay, I think I can brain again.

FUCK. Ok, on my back, stretched out, thinking we're just going to talk for a minute until my hips feel better and I can get back up on my knees to please HIM.

Zen had other plans.

Zen has magical fucking fingers.

564 • PLANT DADDY

Zen can suddenly turn flesh that I couldn't stand being touched into pure quivering need.

I was soaked from his mouth and just... me, how completely aroused he makes me, when I had forgotten what that felt like for *years* from being so utterly jaded.

And his fingers were so gentle, so gentle I was shocked he had so much control over himself. Not like... mental control, as in keeping his own desires in check, but that he had such an accurate ability to control such a big, powerful body, such masculine, strong hands. My Rough One could also be my gentle giant?

Is there anything this man *can't* be for me?

Those fingers had me melting into a relaxed puddle of goo at first (after I forced myself to stop worrying about my not-perfectly-shaved-because-she-wasn't-supposed-to-get-any-attention pussy) but then...

Fuck, my eyes just opened after unconsciously closing to vividly remember what it felt like, and I literally just clenched.

Bliss.

Fucking bliss is what it felt like.

A gentle, almost clinical touch, as if he'd slipped into his brilliant mind and occupation to make sure I was really okay, not actually hurt in any way. Slipping one then eventually two fingers inside me, he then pressed his other hand down on my mound and just above it. I'd felt that position many times in my life, always with lubed-up and gloved fingers, my feet in stirrups, shivering cold while staring up at a doctor's office's ceiling.

But this time... the wetness was ours, no glove between our flesh, and my toes were curled on either side of his muscular body. And there was nothing cold about me, but I was most certainly still shivering. Full-body quivering as that familiar position morphed into something so far from clinical it's almost obscene.

And within a matter of what could've been seconds, minutes, or hours—I have no idea—with his sexy voice urging me on, telling me what a good girl I was, thanking ME for making HIS morning so wonderful...

I came so hard I'm pretty sure my soul left my body.

Again.

Because he does that.

Every time.

And I don't know why, but when he had wrung all of my orgasm out of me and he slid his wet fingers up my leg, it felt more like he was marking me with his achievement instead of just cleaning off his hand. Almost like a sexy, confident smirk that said "look what I made you do, little one."

I could go on forever about just this one instance in this one hour of playing, but I do actually have to get back to work now.

But not long after we went our separate ways, I know he was thinking of me, his mind racing with thoughts of his good girl who wants to please him oh so badly. Because after

I sent him a song to listen to while he was working out and told him what it meant to me, this was what I got in return:

"I will listen, love. And you have more than earned every good thing you've gotten, and you're becoming my purrrfect little kitten. I'm very proud of my good girl."

Then:

"I've decided you're like a kitten. I mean cats don't fucking listen… But KITTENs are playful and cuddly, love attention and being touched."

And finally:

"I've been thinking on your official name. You're OFFI-CIALLY Kitten."

My nickname that belongs only to him.

Another link of ownership in the chain he attaches to his collar around my neck.

Thank you for this day, Sir. 🩶

Chapter Sixteen

A GLIMPSE INTO THE FUTURE

Sienna

I shift uncomfortably between Zen's thighs, just a readjustment of my knees on the wide pillow, at the conversation being had right in front of me—or technically over my head. Although my mouth and tight hand never leave his cock, he somehow senses the change in my emotions. Is it possible he knows the teasing about having other submissives made my heart drop into my stomach? Sure, he knows I'm jealous and possessive by nature and from past trauma I'll likely never get over; it's just a part of who I am now, as much as the eye color I was born with or the tattoos permanently inked into my skin. But there's no way he could know the joking conversation being held with the other Dom sets off my deepest insecurity, my biggest fear—being found not good enough and then being replaced.

But like so many times before, Zen reads me as easily as a large-print paperback.

I know this, because as the other Dom turns to start talking to the Domme on his opposite side, their subs servicing them—which I see as I tilt my head to side to lick down then all the way back up Zen's dick and quickly peek over at the other couples—he cups my cheek and stops my downward movement that would place him into my mouth once more.

It's a challenge, but I meet his eyes when he orders me to look at him. When he speaks again, the joking tone from only moments ago is gone, replaced by the voice that could so easily talk me off any ledge.

"Is there anything that would make you feel more secure, Kitten?" he asks, and I swallow nervously, my eyes darting away before locking with his again when I remember his command.

No words come out. Hell, no words even form in my brain, and when I don't answer him, he doesn't punish me. He doesn't even scold me. He knows I'm not purposely disobeying him. I'm not *choosing* to not answer him. He knows me well enough by now that I can't help when my mind and mouth decide to go into freeze mode.

So he words his question a little differently, like an investigator rephrasing to hopefully jog a memory, to draw out more answers. "What's something I could do that would make you believe me when I tell you I'm never getting rid of you?"

Something does pop into my head then.

And while they say the first thing that enters one's mind is how one truly feels, I can't help but be embarrassed by the immature response my brain conjures up. I'm in my thirties. My Dom is in his late forties. Yet my mind screams an answer to his question that would seemingly belong to someone much, much younger. A teenager's desire, or at the very oldest, someone who just became legal to drink. So I clamp my molars together, refusing to let the childish wants escape where I can hide them, keep them to myself so he won't look at me disapprovingly.

But try as I might, I can't think of any other answer. The first one is so strong, so loud—so bright I can't see anything past it. I struggle to come up with something, anything to tell him. I can't very well say "Nothing, Sir." Because one, that would be telling a Dominant there's nothing he could do to help his submissive. I can't imagine any one thing making a Dom feel more out of control— something they crave more than anything else, that control. And two, it would be a lie, and I cannot lie to this man. Lying to him would defeat the very purpose of giving him ownership of me and my submission. It would scuff the trust a couple must have for a D/s relationship to work or mean anything.

"I can see you have an answer for me, little one," he says, leaning forward and speaking against my cheek before placing a kiss there. "Does this position help you confess?"

My eyes close and my head tilts back as if too heavy from the eroticism he just filled it with. How does he do that? How could he possibly know that getting up in my space like this, something that would normally make me flinch away from any other person on the planet, would make me melt instead?

Is it because I no longer feel like I'm in the spotlight, with him staring down at me?

Is it because he's closer, lending me his strength?

Is it because he's lowered himself to more my level instead of making me look up and meet his eyes?

Or is it the feel of his breath and soft beard against my flesh that stupefies me enough that I no longer care about anything, can't even feel my shame or come up with a good enough reason to hold back from him?

"Yes, Sir," I finally reply to at least one of his questions. It comes out as a breathy exhale I can't seem to be embarrassed about.

"That's my good girl," he purrs, and I whimper as my body presses closer to him, my still-tilted head now angling to the side to unconsciously bare my neck to him. "Now, tell me what it is I can do that would make you feel more secure in us, Kitten."

This time, his question is worded as a command, and along with this new position, it makes the answer fall from my lips whether I want it to or not.

"Fetlife, Sir. I know it's stupid. I know it's immature. But… it *would* make me feel more secure if others could see you feel for me even a fraction of what I feel for you, Sir." I swallow, the sound of my own voice instead of his pulling me out of the trance he put me under enough that I gain back some of my nervousness. "I-I know how you feel about social media. I know it's a sore spot for you and that you feel it's a waste of time. But you asked, Sir. And that's what popped into my head first." My voice is quivering now, taking on a defensive, backed-into-a-corner note I try to clear when I continue. "You've said before that it's like someone asking for flowers, that it ruins the gesture and doesn't mean as much as it would as a surprise. And I get that. I totally do. But I'm not trying to dictate anything. I just want you to know it *does* mean a lot to me. It *would* make me feel more secure. And it most definitely would help me believe you truly do want to keep me, that you don't want to find someone better and replace me, if every once in a while you made it known to someone other than me."

My chin wobbles, and I roll my eyes at myself for getting emotional over something so dumb. I push through, wanting him to understand what I'm feeling. "We have to be discreet. I get that. I have no problem with that and would never, ever complain or try to change your mind about that decision. But if that weren't the case, I would be screaming it from the rooftops that I belong to you, that I am owned by the most amazing man I've ever met in my entire life. And I get to do that on my page, because no one knows us. It gives me as close to the feeling of publicly claiming you and being claimed *by* you that I'll ever know. It gives me a sense of pride and confidence when I make posts about my Dom. And God, if I were to go on and see you've posted a photo of me, showing me off, it would feel as if I'm a prize you've won. Something treasured that you want the world to know you own."

My cheeks heat at having spilled all that to him. I hold my breath, dreading his response. Nothing good has ever come from bringing up social media with him. But I hope we've been together long enough, that he knows me well enough now, that he'll understand I'm not like whoever put a bad taste in his mouth about it before. I won't try to tell him what or when to post. I won't complain if he doesn't comment on all my pictures. I just want him to mark me as his on his page like he does my body. When he sees the visible signs of his ownership fading, he wastes no time refreshing the bite mark on my inner thigh, each fingerprint bruise on my hips, and each colorful work of art he makes on my breast with his mouth. So as often as that occurs, it would be nice to open up my page to find a notification from the man I can't get enough of.

Unable to hold my breath any longer, I let it out and fidget on my pillow, until finally his hand still cupping my cheek slides to the back of my head to tilt it until his lips can press to my forehead. I could collapse in relief that I'm not being reprimanded for my honesty, but instead, I follow his order without a moment's hesitation when he says, "Good girl. Thank you for your response, Kitten. I know it's hard for you when you're put on the spot like that, and I'm very proud of you for wording your answer in a way that explains what you'd enjoy and appreciate without it sounding like you're making demands. I love that you remember the lessons I've taught you, little one, and because of that, I'll consider what you've told me. Now, lick me up and down, then climb on top so I can feel that tight little pussy slide around my cock."

Acknowledgments

If it wasn't for my amazing neighbor bestie Tiffany, aka "my wife," aka "Aunt Tits" (Vivi couldn't pronounce Tiff, so now, she will forever be Tits to all of us lol!) I wouldn't know a single thing about plants. If anyone is to blame for this book, it's her. I thought she was hilariously crazy when she literally smuggled cuttings from our Mexican vacation back to the US in her luggage to propogate. But now? I definitely bought a whole extra suitcase while visiting CC in Utah, just so I could bring home a bunch of hoyas.

It's a crazy plant lady thing. I get it now.

Honorable Mentions: my girl Theresa, who encouraged the obsession with her own botanical awesomeness. Check her out on TikTok: @plantpinup <3 And Tonya, with her "Junk and Plants" Group on FB, has been an endless fountain of knowledge and inspiration for not only the plants themselves, but also my love of treasure hunting for gardeny stuff!

Next, Billy Rubino, @BillyRubino22.4 on TikTok, you have no idea how freaking amazing it is to have a cover model who is more excited about the book than even the author is. ESPECIALLY when it's the author's passion project. Your infectious enthusiasm, your literal tears when I asked you to be on my cover, and every single video you've made to get the word out about Plant Daddy are just incredibly heartwarming. It's a level of kindness I've never been on the recieving end of in my career, and I'm so grateful to have you as a teammate, my friend. Thank you!

As always, Barb and Vanessa, you tolerate me like no one else. I couldn't do this without y'all. Thank you, and I love you both so much.

Ashley Brooke. I can't even get my thoughts straight of where to begin with you, woman. The photographer whose stunning work is on my cover. It was your artistry that captured and created my muse. It was your work that jarred something inside my head, which put a crack in my writer's block. And the more I talked with you and saw your photos, the bigger that crack spread, and I could finally see through it just enough that the words started sprinkling in. And then you took my author photo, and I saw myself in a light I hadn't in a very long time, which made the words start coming faster. And THEN we collabed for the covers of Part 2 and the boxed set, and that was all the inspiration I needed to bust out the rest of Part 1 in one fell swoop. You're an amazing woman and artist, and I'm so proud I got to be the one to present to you your "greatest accomplishment in your career." A million times, thank you.

Finally, thank you to my husband, my soul mate, who gives me every damn thing in life I need and want, no matter what insane means it might take. I love you, and thanks for being my real-life plant daddy.

Also by KD Robichaux

All links available at www.kdrobichaux.com

THE BLOGGER DIARIES TRILOGY:

Wished for You

Wish He Was You

Wish Come True

THE CLUB ALIAS SERIES:

Confession Duet (Before the Lie & Truth Revealed)

Seven: A Club Alias Novel

Mission: Accomplished (Knight Novella Boxed Set)

Knight: A Club Alias Novel

Doc: A Club Alias Novel

Astrid: A Club Alias Short Story

CLUB ALIAS MEMBERS SERIES:

Scary Hot: A Club Alias/Until Series Crossover

Moravian Rhapsody: A Club Alias Novella

A Lesson in Blackmail

XOXO

Plant Daddy Part 1

Plant Daddy Part 2

Plant Daddy Part 2

THE SUBMISSIVE DIARIES (a CLUB ALIAS SPINOFF SERIES):

Plant Daddy (Boxed Set of Part 1 and 2)

THE ADVENTURE CHANNEL SERIES

No Trespassing

Dishing Up Love

COWRITTEN WITH CC MONROE

Steal You

Number Neighbor

To Have and to Hold

Bad Medicine

PUBLISHED IN AURORA ROSE REYNOLDS'S

HAPPILY EVER ALPHA WORLD:

Until We Meet Again

Scary Hot

Until Cece

Made in the USA
Middletown, DE
25 February 2023

25600775R00325